Vampire
Darcy's
Desire

Vampire Darcy's Desire

A *Pride and Prejudice* Adaptation

**REGINA
JEFFERS**

Ulysses Press

Published in the United States by
ULYSSES PRESS
P.O. Box 3440
Berkeley, CA 94703
www.ulyssespress.com

ISBN: 978-1-56975-731-4
Library of Congress Catalog Number 2009930127

Acquisitions Editor: Keith Riegert
Managing Editor: Claire Chun
Editor: Kathy Kaiser
Editorial Associates: Lauren Harrison, Kate Kellogg, Elyce Petker
Production: Judith Metzener, Abigail Reser
Cover design: TG Design
Cover illustration: "A Stolen Kiss" by Marcus Stone / The Maas Gallery,
    London, UK / Bridgeman Art Library

Printed in Canada by Transcontinental Printing

10 9 8 7 6 5 4 3 2 1

Distributed by Publishers Group West

AUTHOR'S PREFACE

When the initial concept came to me from the publisher, Ulysses Press, to write a vampire version of *Pride and Prejudice*, my hackles immediately rose. To me, *Pride and Prejudice* is the most perfect novel ever written, and the thought of someone abusing that story line sent me into a state of amusement mixed with pure irritation.

As a member of the Jane Austen Society of North America, I love everything to do with Jane Austen. However, unlike some hard-core Janeites, I read everything related to her works. Some of it I love, and some of it I throw across the room in disgust; but even when I angrily throw the book at the wall, I retrieve it and continue to read, looking for something in it I can enjoy. There are only a few Austen-related alternatives in which I find nothing I can accept to be possible. Most of those I deem ridiculous, however, deal with the story of Fitzwilliam Darcy and Elizabeth Bennet, because like many Austen readers, I hold a preconceived idea of how these two would get on in their lives once they were married. Austen gives us very specific allusions as to how the couple might achieve happiness, so when presented with the concept, I flatly refused to even consider a vampire version. However, after discussing the idea with close friends and with my editor, I conceded. It was my belief the project would go forward with or without me. At least if I was involved, I could possibly maintain some integrity in the story. In a Gothic or vampire-inspired story, undertones of sex, blood, and death are inherently present, although Jane Austen rarely even hinted at any of these elements in her novels.

Originally, the concept was that Darcy would be the vampire who seduces Elizabeth, yet I could not abide such a proposal. If vampirism was to be added to the tale, I wanted Darcy portrayed as a poetic tragic hero rather than as an embodiment of evil. I also wanted to control the representation of sexuality, the combination of horror and lust. Like in *Pride and Prejudice*, Darcy needed to desire Elizabeth and to be willing to put aside his beliefs and lifestyle in order to earn her love. As *Vampire Darcy's Desire* is a horror romance, a more prominent sexual tension than in the Austen version was obviously required, although any astute reader of Austen feels the sophisticated undertones present in her writing.

My story line is based on the traditional Scottish ballad known as "Lord Thomas and Fair Ellender," which I used as the core of the curse upon Darcy's family. The ballad has many versions. Some even call it "The Brown Girl." It is currently listed as one of the ballads brought back into circulation by Francis J. Child, a renowned "songcatcher." The story behind the ballad dates back to the time of Charles II. There are Irish, Scottish, and English versions of the song, as well as similar stories in Norse and European folklore. Popular folk singers, such as Jean Ritchie and Alan Lomax, have recorded versions of the song. Even the Grateful Dead has it in their discography. There is an excellent reading found on YouTube, as well. In keeping with the Scottish ballad, I chose Northumberland as the place for Wickham's home where he is buried because of its proximity to Scotland and because of its numerous border wars. Luckily, Newcastle, where Darcy sends Wickham in the Austen original, is in Northumberland.

In merging the two diverse genres, one must remember that vampire literature springs from early Gothic tales, which ironically peppered the literature of Jane Austen's time. Typically in early vampire stories, a respectable and virtuous woman rejects a man's love. The woman is under the influence of a tyrannical and powerful male from whom the "hero" must save her, and that "hero" possesses a highly developed intelligence and exceptional charisma and charm. A "seduction" of sorts occurs. Are those elements not also present in each of Austen's pieces? After all, Austen herself parodies the Gothic novel in *Northanger Abbey*, even mocking Ann Radcliffe's *The Mysteries of Udolpho*. She uses the stereotypes of the abbey, the mysterious murder, and the evil seducer, yet Austen keeps the theme of the individual's worth that's found in all vampiric literature.

I teach English and have done so for more years than I care to count, and so I am familiar with many of the original literary works dealing with vampires. For example, nearly eighty years before Bram Stoker's *Dracula* became the standard by which vampire stories are judged, Lord Byron's life and legend inspired Polidori's *The Vampyre*, and even Stoker quoted Gottfried August Bürger's narrative poem "Lenore" (1773). Samuel Coleridge's poem "Christabel" also influenced much of the vampire literature that followed.

Yet unlike many modern readers of vampire stories, I realize that some elements of vampire tales come from modern visual media rather than legend or folklore. While doing research for *Vampire Darcy's Desire*, I looked more at the types of vampires, ways to kill a vampire, and general characteristics of vampires. Although I learned tidbits about the Twilight series from my female students, I purposely did not read the book, nor did I see the film. I wanted my characterization of vampires to be as original as possible. Most of my reading of vampire stories came many years ago and fell along the lines of Anne Rice's Vampire Chronicles and Marilyn Ross's Barnabas Collins series. In fact, I once did a stunt for a *Dark Shadows* promotion for a Jonathan Frid live appearance; I was the woman in the crowd he grabs and bites. The hardest part of the staging for me was being put in a coffin. I am too claustrophobic!

A great deal of my research dealt with the Baobhan Síth, Scottish vampires, and with Celtic gods, because I used the traditional Scottish ballad to tie my story line together. Also, I revisited the character of Abraham Van Helsing. In his early notes for *Dracula*, Stoker conceived of three characters that eventually were combined into Van Helsing. Van Helsing represents all the good in the world and is a positive influence in the midst of *Dracula*'s chaos. He uses his intelligence to unwind the mystery of the vampire attacks, he leads the hunt to find Dracula, and he is the one who recognizes the need for God's intervention in ending the demonic possession.

I transferred those characteristics to Elizabeth in my story. She is the impetus for Darcy's ability to change his life. It is also through Elizabeth that the reader learns how Wickham can be defeated. Stoker had Van Helsing similarly instruct his readers. (If you do not believe me, see Chapter 18 of *Dracula*.)

There is also unmistakable social commentary in *Vampire Darcy's Desire*. Elizabeth Bennet is an intelligent woman, and like the original Van Helsing, she uses her "knowledge" as "power." She leads Darcy in his battle to stop the curse on his family. Darcy, on the other hand, is a Renaissance man in accepting help from a woman. The book also speaks to the natural stratification of human society—the exercise of power over others, those who are *weaker*.

Some elements of the Gothic are apparent in *Vampire Darcy's Desire*: an ancient prophecy; dream visions; supernatural powers; characters suffering from impending doom; women threatened by a powerful, domineering male; and the quick shorthand of metonymy to set the scenes. Yet essentials of romance are just as prominent: a powerful love, with elements of uncertainty about the love being returned; the lovers separated by outside forces; and a young woman becoming the target of an evil schemer.

Darcy voluntarily isolates himself because of the family curse; Wickham is the epitome of evil. As in many Gothic tales, supernatural phenomena and prevalent fears (murder, seduction, perversion) are incorporated, but the underlying theme of a fallen hero is central to the story. *Vampire Darcy's Desire* combines terror, horror, and mystery set within the framework of a love story.

A dhampir, the product of the union between a vampire and a human, probably finds its origin in Serbian folklore. Modern fiction holds many examples: *Blade*, a comic brought to life by Wesley Snipes on the screen; the character Connor in the TV series *Angel* (the show's male equivalent of a Slayer); and Renesmee, the daughter of Bella Swan and Edward Cullen from Stephanie Meyer's *Breaking Dawn*. Traditionally, a dhampir possesses the ability to see vampires, even when they are cloaked with the power of invisibility. They generally have similar powers to vampires with only a few complications.

This new dhampir Darcy possesses many of the qualities the reader notes in Austen's character. He is "withdrawn" from society, is generous, is protective of his sister and his estate, and has a sharp wit. He is amused by Elizabeth's verbal battles and is attracted to her physically. Darcy denies this attraction initially and then makes changes in his life to win and to keep Elizabeth's regard. Austen's Darcy says, "I was given good principles, but left to follow them in pride and conceit...I was spoiled by my parents...allowed, encouraged, almost taught to be selfish and overbearing..." This characteristic plays well in the Dhampir Darcy's pursuit of Elizabeth. He more aggressively persists in winning her affection in this book.

PROLOGUE

She was beautiful in all her innocence, much more beautiful than the notorious Mrs. Younge, his latest minion, who arranged this encounter and who waited for him now in the adjoining woods. Long, thick lashes rested on the rise of her high cheekbones, and, although a bit mussed, her golden tresses spread out across her pillow like the rays of the sun. Her deep sigh brought his attention to her lips, and for a moment he thought her awake, but Georgiana Darcy slept soundly, thanks to his spellbinding charm. She was the image—the embodiment—of his beloved Ellender.

One candle lit the room, casting shadows, which danced in the corners. There was nothing mediocre about the room, with its rich tapestries and elegant sculpting. "Only the best for the Darcys," he muttered.

With a unique swagger not found in many of his kind, he glided to the bed's edge. Unable to hide his anger and his contempt, a frown furrowed his brow, and a flash of fire transformed his vision. A torrent of images racked his soul—pictures of blood, of betrayal, and of revenge. "You will do quite well, my dear," he whispered. "I will enjoy spending an eternity with you." He lightly twisted one of her curls around his finger. "This is for the suffering I have endured at the Darcys' hands."

Slowly, he leaned over her, feeling the blood rush through her veins, his hard, dark eyes seeking the indentation of her neck. He relished the feeling of expectancy. The ringing silence of the room was broken only by his breathing.

Fully engulfed in his desire, when the door swung open, it took several seconds before he realized that an intruder had discovered his inexplicable need for her. "Move away from her, Wickham," the tall, dark figure ordered as it stepped carefully into the room. "You will not bring your death and decay into my household."

"You brought it into *mine,* Darcy." Wickham stood, trying to judge his next move. He knew in a fight to the end, the man in front of him stood no chance of survival. But, sensing no fear of the supernatural from the intruder, Wickham questioned what else this confrontation held. Absent of all volition, he hesitated only a moment before moving in a whirlwind to a point of advantage, but the man framed in the light of the doorway did not move.

A dramatic black eyebrow lifted quizzically. "You forget, Wickham, you and I already share certain characteristics. You cannot infect what is already infected. I will not follow you into the darkness, nor will I allow you to convert my sister. This madness ends here. The curse—the wicked allure—will die with us." The deep rumble of his voice filled the room, and a gleam entered his ice blue eyes, intensified by his opponent's muteness.

Wickham glowered. "I have not given up taking my fill of beautiful young women." A squall-like eruption pushed Wickham forward, his arms extended to his sides, sending Darcy rolling along the floor and scrambling to avoid the chasm—an abhorrent shudder of death. "I am coming for you, Darcy," the voice boomed through the room as cold blasts flew from sinewy hands.

Sucking noises filled Fitzwilliam Darcy's ears, and he realized that the tall, pale form loomed over him in an infuriating counterattack. Sliding against the far wall, it was all Darcy could do to bite back a scream, but he ducked first and came up, arm flung overhead, preparing to unload. "*Now,* Wickham," he hissed, and then he released it.

A vial of clear liquid tumbled end over end through the air, splitting the silence surrounding them. Each figure moved in slow motion, playing out its part in a swirling montage.

And then the stopper exploded, and the transparent fluid rained down on the apparition of George Wickham. An agonized scream—full of old blood and dark radiance—filled the room. The shadow hissed in the moonlight, and the odor of burning flesh wafted over both of them.

Fitzwilliam Darcy's smile turned up the corners of his mouth. "Holy water," he whispered in affirmation.

"You will rot in hell!" Wickham threatened. "I will see those you love ruined—see them lick the blood from your body. Sharp fangs jutting from their mouths—smelling of death and decay— ghoulish nightmares!" He started forward again, but Darcy antici- pated the move. Pulling the double crucifix from his pocket, he met Wickham's intent with one of his own. "Iron," he said mock- ingly, unfurling the chain and reaching out to his enemy.

Panic showed in Wickham's fever-filled eyes as he backed away from the symbol of the Trinity, stumbling—recoiling—and sud- denly, he was gone in a grey shadow moving across the lawn, a highly combustible howl billowing upon the breeze in his retreat.

Darcy stood motionless for several long minutes, needing to clear his head. He took a slow breath, trying to control his anger, and then he smelled it—smoke. Against his better judgment, he rushed to the bedchamber's open door. "Wickham!" he cursed. The house he rented in Ramsgate heated with a fiery blaze, which started at three separate points of entry on the bottom floor. Thick black smoke, fueled by heavy draperies and fine upholstered furni- ture, rolled from the doorways of the lower rooms and rose in a blackened drape to cover the stairway. Acrid smoke drifted his way. Immediately, he turned toward the body still reclining on the bed where George Wickham had left her.

"Georgiana!" he called in a panic as he scooped her into his arms and pulled his sister tight to his chest. Darcy grabbed a towel on the washstand and dipped it into the tepid water she had used earlier. He draped the wet towel over her head and face, repeating the procedure for himself. Then he made his way to the top of the stairs. Thick smoke covered the lower half of the rise. He took a deep breath and lunged forward.

Surprisingly, a pocket of air existed once he stumbled his way to the bottom of the steps. He felt Georgiana slipping from his grip as he fought his way past flaming lips, consuming doorways along the corridor. Using the last of his strength to lift her to him again, Darcy braced his shoulders along the wall leading to the servants' entrance, the only door not blocked by flames. Forcibly, he shoved his way into the night—into the shelter of the open air. Heaving from the weight of her—from the fear—from the effort—from the deadly murk filling the night sky, he staggered forward, trying to get away.

When the explosion hit, he was far enough from the house to escape the brunt of the debris, but not far enough to go unscathed. Splintered doorways and shards of glass flew like deadly projectiles, many of them lodging in his arms and legs and back, but Darcy kept moving, trying to get his precious Georgiana to safety. Finally, he collapsed to his knees, laying her gently on the dewy grass before uncovering her face.

"Georgie," he pleaded as he patted her hands and face. For a few long moments he prayed, and then she caught a deep breath and began to cough uncontrollably. A soft moan told him that she was well; only then did Fitzwilliam Darcy allow the exhaustion to overtake him, collapsing—face first—into the dirt.

"Mr. Darcy!" his valet, Henry Sheffield, called as he rushed over to tend to his employer. Covered with ashes and soot, his clothes torn and disheveled, Darcy lay in a defeated heap upon the soft earth.

Georgiana righted herself and crawled to where he lay. "Fitzwilliam," she begged between fits of coughing. "Oh, please… please…talk to me."

"He is hurt, Miss Darcy," Henry told her as he jerked off his coat and wrapped it around her light muslin gown.

"*Help* him," she pressed.

By that time, footmen and neighbors had rushed forward, carrying lamps. Mr. Phelps, the owner of the house to the left, examined Darcy's body. "We should not turn him; he has several lacerations—no telling what might be in the wounds." As the man spoke, Darcy's body arched, seeking air before choking on the same gulping breath. "Georgie," he managed to say between barking gasps.

"I am here," she assured him, draping her soot-covered arm over his shoulder.

Mr. Phelps took charge. "Lift him to his feet, and be careful about it," he ordered. "Jemmy, go for the doctor. You others help Mr. Darcy to my house."

Two footmen shoved themselves under his arms, arranging them about their shoulders and supporting his weight as they nearly dragged him towards Phelps's open door. Townspeople scrambled to the bucket brigades to put out the fire. Darcy's head hung low, and he tried to recover his senses as the servants struggled under his weight. Finally, he forced his gaze towards the gathering crowd across the street. Then, intuitively, his eyes fell on George Wickham, a figure wrapped in a long black cape and sporting a beaver. With a wry smile and a nearly imperceptible salute, he disappeared into the crowd.

Darcy could do nothing more tonight; he stopped Wickham this time; he was lucky. Could he do it again? Could he kill the man who plagued his family? "Come, Georgiana," he urged, demanding that his body relax back into the arms of the rescuers. Then he allowed the men to help him up the steps to Phelps's town house.

CHAPTER 1

It took more than a day to explain it all to Georgiana. At first, she did not believe him, but the truth lay all around them. He explained what he knew of her acquaintance with Wickham—how she met the pretender one day in a village shop—how she saw him several times about the estate—how she thought him to be a friend of her brother's. Slowly, with Darcy's explanation, Georgiana realized Wickham offered her no future.

His seduction held no dignity. Instead, the man provided a ghastly corruption. He had promised marriage, and Darcy's darling Georgiana naively thought his to be an honest proposal. The shame she felt at knowing she had succumbed to Wickham's deception was bad enough, but the truth Darcy later provided of the man's real reason to target her—he feared might complicate Georgiana's recovery.

Darcy secured her safety away from others, and he reinforced his sister's London home with every known amulet to protect her. If others knew to what extreme he went in order to ensure her unassailability, they might think him deranged. Yet the opinions of others never swayed him—call it *lunacy,* but he chose alchemy to fight perfidy. Georgiana promised to wear her half of the iron double crucifix. Darcy inlaid it with jewels and placed it on a finely woven chain. He explained that he would wear the other half, keeping them connected.

Finally, he hired Mrs. Lillian Annesley as his sister's companion. Besides being well educated, the elderly woman possessed one quality that placed her above all other candidates for the position. She was a psychic, a Seer. In fact, she was the reason he went to Ramsgate in the first place. He passed Mrs. Annesley on a street near St. James on ,a cold, windy afternoon. Immediately, this stranger called out to him, and Darcy's good breeding made him stop and listen to her lurid tale. She warned him of the danger to Georgiana. It took him only a few moments to understand that Mrs. Annesley spoke the truth. He ordered a horse and rode at breakneck speed to the seaside resort in Kent. If not for this chance encounter, Georgiana might now be under George Wickham's control. Therefore, Darcy freely trusted his sister to the old woman's matronly care.

He spent the six months following his confrontation with Wickham trying to find his enemy again; and although he had various detective agencies searching for just a sighting of Wickham, his rival disappeared into the bowels of London's underworld. He would resurface eventually; Darcy knew that to be a *fact,* just as it was a *fact* that Darcy would kill Wickham when he found him again.

After his face-off with George Wickham, Darcy reevaluated his own life and his plan to bring this malediction to an end. As a member of the British aristocracy, he had inherited his estate and his position in society from his father. Through a system of primogeniture, he should pass it on to his heir, but Fitzwilliam Darcy planned something else with his position. Besides the land, he had inherited from his ancestors a propensity for evil. Since learning at the age of sixteen of this quirk of nature, he fought against it taking over his life. Because of this struggle, most of his peers saw him as an eccentric; yet the aristocracy easily overlooked eccentricity, and even depravity among its members.

Society expected Darcy to take a wife, but he held no such plans. He pretended to want to marry; he attended social functions, but hung on the perimeter of the group, making it appear that he looked on the season's offerings with a discerning eye. In reality, his search would never come to fruition. Darcy would have no wife—no children—no love in his old age. He would simply never marry, allowing his "eccentric" character to be the excuse. Instead, he would make sure Pemberley thrived and then leave it to Georgiana's heirs. He would not pass on the *unnatural* to a child—to his firstborn son. It would end with him, and if God gave him the strength to do so, he would stop this eternal feud by killing Wickham.

As such, he claimed problems on his estate kept him from London during the spring and early summer season. However, he knew that he had to make some social appearances to keep the tongues from wagging, so in late summer, he joined a friend, Charles Bingley, at a house party given by the Havershams in Sussex. During this time, Bingley repeatedly pressed him to help him acquire a piece of property.

"I need your counsel, Darcy," Bingley pleaded. "Caroline wishes for me to take an estate to establish our family. I found one in Hertfordshire, which I let for the year, but I possess no expertise in this area. Please consider coming with us—help me to determine whether this is a sound investment before I choose to buy it. It will be just Caroline, Louisa, my brother Hurst, and I. We will meet my neighbors and have a quiet time."

Darcy quickly agreed. He could hide away from social obligations for several months because Bingley offered him the perfect excuse. Hertfordshire was close enough to London that he could make the periodic day trip to check on Georgiana and Mrs. Annesley. Luckily, Bingley, one of his closest friends, good-humoredly tolerated Darcy's need for solitude and his other idiosyncrasies. The only downfall to the plan was maneuvering around Caroline Bingley, Charles's sister, who had set her sights on Darcy when her brother became one of Darcy's closest acquaintances several years earlier. Of course, avoiding one woman's attentions was a superior plan to a ballroom full every evening of matrons pushing their daughters into his path.

Michaelmas, therefore, found him with Bingley's family at Netherfield Park. Over the first few weeks, he and Bingley spent their days riding out across the estate, examining the out buildings, visiting with cottagers, planning renovations and repairs, and enjoying each other's company. Darcy cherished these moments of normalcy, although they were often peppered with torment. When

Bingley and his neighbors returned from hunting, he stood with the other men as they butchered a deer. Seeing the blood being drained from the carcass, Darcy held tight to the hitching post—knuckles white from the surge of revulsion shooting through him. The blood spread through the dirt, creating new veins—new paths—still living even though the animal was dead. It crept closer to his boots, and he stepped back in a show of fastidiousness, but his eyes never left the blood—the lifeline. Unconsciously, he licked his lips, although his mouth suddenly felt very dry. Every nerve in his body screamed for action, but Darcy held himself immobile: He must appear a man, and men enjoyed such sport, and he would repeat the required gestures to fit into the group. "It is a fine kill," he muttered to one of the older men close by.

A member of the landed gentry, Mr. Bennet, noticed his paleness. "Are you all right, Mr. Darcy?"

"Something I did *not* eat," he responded with an ironic smile.

Bingley came to his rescue. "My friend eschews meat."

"I never knew a man who did not eat meat," Mr. Bennet remarked in surprise.

Darcy pulled himself up to his full height, knowing it would give him an advantage. "We British seem to think a meal is not complete unless we gorge ourselves, but we are a society plagued by gluttony. How many men do you know who suffer from gout? Many civilizations thrive on a cuisine of grains, vegetables, and beans. Yet I am not a total cretin, Mr. Bennet. I am known to eat fish regularly. Since my twentieth year, I have never known a sick day, Sir. I do not know whether my life choice has anything to do with it or whether God blessed me with a strong constitution, but why should I change what works?"

Mr. Bennet stammered, "I—I would never expect you to change, Mr. Darcy."

To emphasize his point and to escape the rest of the slaughter, Darcy turned on his heel and left the area after saying curtly, "Good afternoon, gentlemen."

"He is an unusual man," Mr. Bennet began his conjecture. "I

would not expect you and Mr. Darcy to have enough in common to be friends, Mr. Bingley."

"Darcy is a true friend. One can never question his loyalty or his sense of responsibility. We all have our peculiarities, and I gladly tolerate Darcy's, as he tolerates mine. It seems you, Mr. Bennet, have the proclivity for taking amusement in your books. Some might take you to be reclusive." Bingley gave his neighbor a level look.

Mr. Bennet looked away in embarrassment. "Point taken, Mr. Bingley."

Elizabeth Bennet put her Aunt Gardiner's letter away. "So the infamous Mr. Darcy is in Hertfordshire and staying with our new Mr. Bingley," she mused. "I wonder what he is really like. I suppose I will soon find out; it should be interesting to see if Aunt Gardiner's opinions hold merit."

The days passed quietly for the most part, but despite Darcy's desire to keep in the background, Bingley's obligations to his neighborhood required they make appearances at some of the local celebrations, the most important of these an assembly where Bingley and his sisters would meet the society in which they would dwell. Although he despised such gatherings, Darcy accompanied his friend. The public nature of village assemblies meant anyone with a ticket could attend. Darcy was sure every available young woman and girl straight from the schoolroom would await Bingley's acquaintance. Bingley's newfound wealth made him a worthy catch, especially for a country miss likely not to experience a season in London's high society. As Bingley's friend, Darcy expected a similar perusal, but he planned to put off any such overtures. He would remain alone tonight and every night.

When they entered the hall, the dancers made their turns and came face-to-face with their newest neighbors. Instantly, everyone froze in place, as if playing a childhood game of freeze tag and they had all been tagged as "it" at once. A stirring and a heightening of expectations spread across the room, and a number of more promi-

11

nent families nudged their daughters forward, the better to catch Mr. Bingley's attention.

Sir William Lucas advanced to welcome them and to make appropriate introductions as the rest of those in attendance turned back to the dance, and the music began again. Darcy held himself stiffly as he followed Bingley, Caroline, Louisa Hurst, and Wayne Hurst into the room. Although the hall teemed with noise, he walked in silence; it echoed in the night; and for the first time in many years, Darcy felt the hair on his neck stand on end, as if Destiny walked beside him—something momentous was about to happen. The feeling moved him to his core. He looked around, half expecting to see George Wickham among the revelers, but only landed gentry and commoners dotted the crowd. A faint trembling shook him, but he forced his steps to follow Bingley to a raised dais at one end of the room.

Having exchanged pleasantries with those deemed by Sir William to be worthy of the introduction, Darcy took up a position along the rear of the dais, keeping his back to the wall so he might guard against any intrusions. For some reason he did not understand, something changed—something he could not pinpoint in the dimly lit hall.

Within a few minutes, a sturdy older woman stepped forward, dragging a half-dozen young women with her. Darcy heard Sir William introduce his daughter Charlotte Lucas, one of the brood, and then the unbelievably pretentious Mrs. Bennet. Darcy smiled at the thought of the easygoing man he knew as Mr. Bennet yoked in life to this woman. As soon as the introductions were uttered, she took over the conversation, imposing herself and her five daughters upon Bingley and his sisters.

"Oh, Mr. Bingley, we are so pleased you came to Netherfield Park. Are we not, girls?" she gushed. "Let me introduce my daughters, if you please," she continued, barely giving Bingley time to nod before she started the presentations. "This is my eldest, Jane. Then Elizabeth, Mary, Catherine, and Lydia." Each girl made a curtsy as her mother announced her name.

"Thank you, Mrs. Bennet." Bingley truly loved all the attention. "These are my sisters Caroline Bingley and Louisa Hurst, with her husband, my brother Mr. Hurst." The women bobbed their curtsies, and then the group directed their attention to him as Bingley gestured to where he stood. "And this is my good friend Mr. Darcy of Pemberley in Derbyshire."

The mother hen responded. "Welcome to Hertfordshire, Mr. Darcy," she cooed. "I *do* hope you enjoy your stay."

All eyes fell on him as he offered the group a proper bow. "Mrs. Bennet, you are most kind," he murmured and resumed his place along the wall.

As the conversation shifted once again to Bingley and his sisters, Darcy, out of half boredom and half curiosity, began a closer observation of the Bennet sisters. The two youngest were insignificant schoolgirls, giggling masses of feminine silliness. He thanked his lucky stars Georgiana never went through such a phase. The middle girl held no true beauty; her strict angular lines took on boyish qualities, and she did nothing to soften the look. The oldest Miss Bennet was a striking beauty; he could easily envision her taking center stage at any of a dozen grand balls as the most beautiful woman in attendance.

Then he let his eyes fall on the second daughter. Although not as arrestingly beautiful as the eldest, Miss Elizabeth was alluring nonetheless—petite, small waist, dark hair with auburn highlights, almond-shaped eyes—a dark green, nearly black—full red lips and a slim, aristocratic nose. She simmered sensuality, and whether he liked it or not, his body reacted to her appearance. As he stared at her, their eyes met, and in amusement, she arched an eyebrow and gifted him with a beguiling smile, almost as if she knew he reacted to her. Her open teasing awakened a dangerous part of him, and he felt an almost visceral desire to possess her. Without wishing to do so, he fought a wildness coursing through his being. Darcy pulled himself upright, crossing his arms across his chest, symbolically sealing off his chance for communication, and then he pointedly looked away to end her hopes of connecting with him.

Bingley, following propriety, asked Miss Bennet for the next dance, and the group moved away en masse to join the assemblage. Darcy stood alone, purposely offering offense—closing himself off from contact with others—keeping himself apart—never allowing for the possibility of being with anyone else. Yet as the evening progressed, his eyes returned repeatedly to Elizabeth Bennet, and each time, with a slight shake of his head, Darcy forced his gaze to withdraw once again.

More frustrating, when her eyes met his, she did not look away, challenging him to do something to make her retreat. A shiver ran down his spine; it seemed as if she almost looked *past* him, scanning his soul instead. For a brief, fleeting second, Darcy wondered if she felt it, too, and then his pride pushed the thought aside.

"Come, Darcy," Bingley called as he approached, "I must have you dance. I hate to see you standing about by yourself in this stupid manner. You had much better dance."

For a moment the image of standing up with Elizabeth Bennet shot through his head, but Darcy forced it away. "I certainly shall not," he declared. "You know how I detest it, unless I am particularly acquainted with my partner. At such an assembly as this, it would be insupportable. Your sisters are engaged, and there is not another woman in the room, with whom it would not be a punishment to me to stand up."

"I would not be so fastidious as you are," cried Bingley, "for a kingdom! Upon my honor, I never met with so many pleasant girls in my life, as I have this evening; and there are several of them you see uncommonly pretty."

Darcy would not betray his interest in Elizabeth Bennet, nor would he succumb to the temptation to touch her hand. "You are dancing with the only handsome girl in the room." As he said the words, his gut clenched in denial.

Bingley sighed audibly. "Oh! She is the most beautiful creature I ever beheld! But there is one of her sisters sitting down just behind you, who is very pretty, and I dare say, very agreeable. Do let me ask my partner to introduce you."

Before he could think clearly, he inquired, "Which do you mean?" Following Bingley's gesture, Darcy turned to look at Elizabeth. His heart jumped, but he withdrew his eyes and coldly said, "She is tolerable, but not handsome enough to tempt *me*; and I am in no humor at present to give consequence to young ladies who are slighted by other men." Although he did not look at Elizabeth, he knew his words, literally, struck her. "You better return to your partner and enjoy her smiles, for you are wasting your time with me." He determinedly walked off in the other direction, leaving Bingley to follow his advice. Darcy knew he left her with no real cordial sentiments towards him, but he could not allow any feelings between them to blossom.

However, later in the evening, he indulged in a perverted torture when he danced with Louisa Hurst, setting her in the same quadrille as Elizabeth Bennet and her partner. He circled Louisa and came face-to-face with Miss Elizabeth. At first, she refused to look at him, but within the dance she placed her hand in his. A jolt of intimacy shot up his arm, and intuitively he tightened his hold, requiring her to finally meet his eyes. As they stepped around each other, their gaze remained locked. Then they parted, but each time they came together, they dueled for supremacy. Without realizing she did so, Elizabeth bit her bottom lip, and Darcy watched the moisture form on the inner lobe, trying to decipher what it would be like to taste her. They spoke no words, but he knew her nerves soared as tautly as his.

As he passed her for the last time, he imagined roughly grabbing Elizabeth and pulling her into his embrace. She would fit nicely under his chin, and her lithe curves would be hard to ignore. He watched her head turn and how her neck elongated with the movement. Darcy smiled with the thought.

Her voice brought him back to reality. "I assume, Mr. Darcy, you find our simple assemblage amusing."

Darcy looked down to see a veil drawn over her expression. "A man may take pleasure in many things, Miss Elizabeth." He did not expect the fathomless darkness of her eyes, and subconsciously his fists tightened by his sides in anger—in confusion. She looked ready to respond, but then she turned away to her partner, and the dance ended on a sour note.

That evening, back at Netherfield, he dreamed of Elizabeth Bennet, and they were not the terrifying dreams he often experienced when he met an attractive woman. Normally, his dreams, when he allowed himself to dream, held images of terror—blood dripping from open wounds and his inner animal overcoming him. Such horror shook his being, and he often smothered his cries of abhorrence with a pillow. But tonight, his dreams took on different overtones. He pushed a strand of hair away from Elizabeth's face while his lips brushed hers fleetingly. She looked deeply into his eyes, and Darcy wanted the security he saw there. Then he kissed her more passionately, his tongue invading her mouth and claiming Elizabeth as his. The scene went no further, but a half-awake Darcy replayed it many times until it felt right—felt the kiss—felt the heat. "Mmm, that is *nice*," he murmured as he rolled to his left side to allow slumber to overtake him again. Surprisingly, he felt alive— felt strong—when he imagined holding Elizabeth Bennet in his arms. It was an exquisite torment; something he could desire, but something he could never do.

Elizabeth Bennet held no such fascinations for Fitzwilliam Darcy, at least, not on the surface. She had observed him all evening, watching his air of superiority—the ultimate master of Pemberley, just as her Aunt Gardiner described him. Mr. Darcy, obviously, thought his actions were above reproof—maybe even above the law.

After that evening, the word of how he snubbed her spread through the neighborhood, and her pride clouded any feelings of attraction she might hold for him.

Her mother lamented her daughter's treatment, much to Elizabeth's embarrassment. "But I can assure you Lizzy does not lose much by not suiting *his* fancy; for he is a most disagreeable, horrid man, not at all worth pleasing. So high and so conceited—he walked here and there, fancying himself so very great!"

Her father shared his surprise at the two men even being friends, in consideration of the great opposition of character. "Bingley is open and easy, and he swears by Darcy's strength of regard and his judgment. In meeting both, I agree; Darcy is the superior. Bingley is by no means deficient, but Darcy is clever. He is also at the same time haughty, reserved, and fastidious, and his manners, although well bred, are not inviting. In that respect Mr. Bingley has greatly the advantage."

Elizabeth agreed: "I could easily forgive *Mr. Darcy's* pride if he had not mortified *mine*."

CHAPTER 2

Over the next fortnight, Bingley's party, including Darcy, found themselves five times in the company of the Bennets. One evening over brandy, Bingley noted how often Darcy spent time with Miss Bennet: danced four times at Meryton, saw her one morning at his own house, and dined in her company four times. However, he did not need to tell Darcy how often they saw the Bennets; Darcy knew exactly. Despite his need to remain alone, he indulged in observing *his Elizabeth,* as he now thought of her. Purposely, he found things to say to her to provoke a response, just to enjoy the natural huskiness of Elizabeth's voice. What he began to notice was how he felt after each of their exchanges. It seemed the more he irritated her, the stronger he grew—each retort increasing his vitality—and he took a twisted delight in annoying her.

So when he walked into Sir William Lucas's home that evening, Darcy anticipated another gathering during which he could watch *his Elizabeth.* He relished the knowledge that she did not suspect his interest. Darcy played it very well: At first, he scarcely allowed her to be pretty; he looked at her without admiration at the dance, and when they met over the subsequent evenings, he looked upon her only to criticize.

But no sooner did Darcy make it clear to himself and his friends that Elizabeth had hardly a good feature in her face, than he began to find it was rendered uncommonly intelligent by the beautiful expression of her dark eyes. This discovery was succeeded by others, equally mortifying. Although on several occasions he tried to convince himself she possessed more than one failure of perfect symmetry in her form, he was forced to acknowledge her figure to be light and pleasing. Plus, as he openly bemoaned the fact that her manners were not those of the fashionable world, their easy playfulness caught him. Of this contrast, Elizabeth was perfectly unaware—to her, Darcy was only the man who made himself agreeable nowhere and who did not consider her handsome enough to dance with.

Tonight, he stood by the window, watching Elizabeth as she conversed with Charlotte Lucas and Colonel Forster, the commanding officer of the local militia. He enjoyed watching her animated movements; *his Elizabeth* exuded pure delight, and Darcy could not help but smile. She made his heart feel lighter; he had never thought that just looking at someone could be so satisfying.

Over the past few weeks, Mr. Darcy appeared in her thoughts more than Elizabeth cared to admit. At first, her interest lay purely in confirming her aunt's suspicions, but now there was something more. Yet she could not let anyone else know. Of late, she would often look up to find him studying her, and just as often, his scrutiny made her senses flare with a smoldering she could not identify. On this particular evening, Elizabeth took note of his constant presence, and, as she was prone to do when she had no other way of dealing with a situation, she began an impertinent confrontation. "Did not you think, Mr. Darcy, I expressed myself uncommonly well just now, when I teased Colonel Forster to give us a ball at Meryton?"

He purposely swallowed the smile that threatened to turn up the corners of his mouth. *His Elizabeth* chose to approach him. "You expressed yourself with great energy—but it is a subject which always makes a lady energetic."

She bristled, not sure of how to take him. "You are severe on us."

"I offer you my apologies. As a gentleman, Miss Elizabeth, I would not wish to offend."

However, Elizabeth had not finished with him; she had determined of late to see if she could ruffle Darcy's usual self-control. "Mr. Darcy, am I to understand your estate in Derbyshire is an extensive one?"

If she hoped to catch him off guard, Elizabeth succeeded. Darcy wondered if she saw him as a potential mate. If so, she would be sadly disappointed, for he held other plans. He forced his face to appear expressionless, although a plethora of emotions rushed through him. "Such is its reputation, Miss Elizabeth," he said warily.

"Large enough to employ several hundred, so I hear." Elizabeth took a small step forward, as if to challenge him, but Darcy did not move.

Darcy kept a steady gaze on her, searching her countenance for information. *To what end is she leading?* There it was again—that look, the one that left him rattled. "If one counts the cottagers, several hundred seems reasonable."

"Do you know everyone who works at Pemberley, Mr. Darcy? I mean, do you know the names of your footmen and stable hands?"

"I do not understand, Miss Elizabeth." His ire grew by the second; he gripped his hands hard behind his back. "Is there a point in this conversation?"

"My aunt is from Lambton, Mr. Darcy. Did I happen to mention that fact?"

Darcy's forehead furrowed in a frown. "I heard as such from Mr. Bingley."

Elizabeth raised her chin in defiance. "My Aunt Gardiner used to tell me of Pemberley when I was younger. In fact, a girl my aunt once knew in Lambton, Vivian Piccadilly, was a washerwoman on your estate. Do you know of Miss Piccadilly, Mr. Darcy?"

Vivian Piccadilly? Yes, I knew her. She lost her life to George Wickham, but how could Darcy explain that? *Does Elizabeth Bennet know more than she pretends?* "I take great pride, Miss Elizabeth, in recalling the names of those who work within my household and who work the land of my estate. Miss Piccadilly was with us for only a few short months. Her father and mother remain as part of our staff, however." His face was completely impassive.

Ah, thought Elizabeth. *Mr. Darcy says more than his words. At least, now he knows that I know,* but…

Before she could retort, Charlotte caught her friend and

coerced her into providing the entertainment by singing for the group. Elizabeth protested good-naturedly. "If my vanity took a musical turn, you would be an invaluable friend." Then, realizing Darcy still remained close by and not wanting to give him more reasons to offer criticism, she quickly added, "I would really rather not sit down before those who must be in the habit of hearing the very best performers."

Over Elizabeth's protest, Charlotte insisted, and for a bit of spite, Elizabeth turned to Darcy and said, "There is a fine old saying, with which everybody here is, of course, familiar—'Keep your breath for porridge,'—and I shall keep mine to swell my song."

Darcy offered her a slight bow as he said, "Excellent advice, Miss Elizabeth; I will heed your words if the situation arises." She scowled, trying to understand how her irreverence amused him. "I look forward to your performance."

Elizabeth walked away briskly and took up a position at the pianoforte. Though by no means capital, she offered a pleasing performance. As usual, Darcy moved to where he could watch her, at least in profile. Tolerably good, she entertained everyone with a couple of light-hearted ditties. Then the group entreated her to sing once more, begging for a love song.

"You desire something sad?" They agreed, so she let her fingers play lightly across the keys at first, trying to find the pitch and to remember the words. Then when she took up the melody, Darcy froze. Of all the songs in the world, she chose this one—his song:

Lord Thomas was an artist
And keeper of the King's leer
Fair Ellender was a lady gay
Lord Thomas, he loved her dear

Lord Thomas and Fair Ellender
Sat all day on a hill;
When night came, and sun was gone,
They'd not yet said their fill.

Lord Thomas spoke a word in jest
And Ellender took it ill:
"Oh, I'll never marry me a wife
Against my family's will."

"If you will never wed thee a wife,
A wife will never wed thee!"
So he rode home to tell his mother
And knelt upon his knee.

"Mother, come Mother, come riddle to me.
Come riddle it all in one,
And tell me whether to marry Fair Ellender
Or bring the Brown Girl home?"

How could she know? he wondered. It made no sense, and he was a
man who prided himself on common sense. But there it lay—Elizabeth Bennet knew his deepest secret; she had set him up. Every
muscle in his body became taut, and Darcy fought to breathe naturally, but he managed to keep his expression constant. Despite his
misery, she continued to sing:

"The Brown Girl gives you houses and land
Fair Ellender, she has none.
And there I charge you, take success
And bring the Brown Girl home."

He dressed himself all in his best
His merry men all in white
And every town he passed through
They took him for a knight.

He went till he came to fair Ellender's court
So loudly twirled at the pin,

There was none so ready as fair Ellender herself
To let Lord Thomas in.

"Bad news, bad news, Lord Thomas," she said,
"Bad news you bring to me.
You've come to ask me to your wedding,
When I thought your bride to be."

She turned around and dressed in white
Her sisters dressed in green,
And every town they rode through
They took her for some queen.

Darcy clenched and unclenched his hands, trying to force the tension away, trying to hide his anguish behind a bland expression. If he could only move; however, her voice mesmerized him as much as it did the others. He had never heard the song done so well and with so much passion.

They rode and they rode till they came to the hall,
So loudly she twirled at the pin
And no one so ready as Lord Thomas himself
To let fair Ellender in.

He took her by her lily-white hand
When leading her through the hall
Saying, "Fifty gay ladies are here today
But here is the flower of them all."

"Is this your bride, Lord Thomas?" she said.
"She looks most wonderful brown
You might have had as a fair a woman
As ever trod Scotland's ground."

"Despise her not, Fair Ellender," he cried.
"Despise her not to me
For I love the end of your little finger
More than her whole body."

The Brown Girl, she was standing by
With knife ground keen and sharp,
Between the long ribs and the short,
She pierced Fair Ellender's heart.

"Oh, what's the matter?" Lord Thomas said.
"You look so pale and wan;
You used to have so fair a color
As ever the sun shone on."

Here it comes, he thought. *The ending!* The story of "Fair Ellender"
he knew well—too well. Ellender D'Arcy began the madness; her
love of Arawn Benning marked them—all the generations to follow—and Fitzwilliam Darcy fought to stop the evil she brought on
his family. Knowingly, or unknowingly, Elizabeth Bennet sang on:

"Oh, you are blind, Lord Thomas!" she said.
"Or can't you very well see?
Oh, can't you see my own heart's blood
As it trickles down on thee?"

He took the Brown Girl by the hand
And led her across the hall.
He took off his sword and cut off her head
And threw it against the wall.

"Oh, Mother, oh, Mother, go dig my grave;
Go dig it both wide and deep,
And place Fair Ellender in my arms
And the Brown Girl at my feet."

He placed his sword against the wall
The point against his breast,
Saying, "This is the end of three poor lovers
God take us all to rest."

They buried Ellender in the old churchyard;
They buried Lord Thomas beside her.
Out of his grave grew a red, red rose,
And out of hers a briar.

They grew and grew up the old church wall
Till they could grow no higher,
And at the top twined a lover's knot
The red rose and the briar.[1]

"Miss Elizabeth," Sir William cried, "you clearly brought me to tears. *Such* a song!"

Elizabeth dropped her eyes, looking away demurely. "I apologize, Sir William. I did not mean to place a cold sheet on your festivities."

"Really, Miss Elizabeth, it was worth the silence to hear one of the traditional ballads done so well; so few people these days remember them."

Darcy stood near, praying for another topic of conversation. Engrossed in his thoughts, he took little note of Mary Bennet succeeding Elizabeth at the pianoforte, nor did he approve of her younger sisters' demand that Mary perform Scottish and Irish airs instead of a concerto. Bingley joined the group of dancers, along with several of the officers; yet Darcy still did not move—he could not—would not.

When Sir William stepped up beside him and engaged in conversation, Darcy wanted no part of the man. He wanted only to retreat to his room and sort out the chaos. He wanted to go home to Pemberley or even to Overton House, but the vast emptiness of

[1] Sir Walter Scott's "Marmion, Canto II: The Convent"

each would drive him to madness. Yet Sir William rambled on about a house in town. *How could the man expect him to maintain such an asinine conversation when he just lost his soul—hexed by the truth of her words?* Moments ticked breathlessly away while Darcy remained silently reserved until Elizabeth came into view again, and despite wanting to throttle her—wanting to run away from her—wanting to question what she knew of him—his body betrayed him, and Darcy hungrily devoured her with his eyes.

Sir William summoned her, and Darcy silently moaned in despair. He needed to be somewhere else, somewhere far away from her. "My dear Miss Eliza, why are you not dancing?—Mr. Darcy, you must allow me to present this young lady to you as a very desirable partner. You cannot refuse to dance, I am sure, when so much beauty is before you."

If Darcy had bothered to look, he would have, obviously, seen that Elizabeth was as miserable as he. She protested immediately, taking a steadying breath. How could she let Darcy know she could not forget the look on his face as she sang? At first, she thought him critical again, but now she was certain she had hurt him somehow. Suddenly, everything she thought about him turned upside down. "Indeed, Sir, I have not the least intention of dancing."

Her voice brought him back to reality, and although he still held the dread of her knowing a secret he swore to take to his grave, Elizabeth's presence—her proximity—forced him to react. Unsettled by his spiraling desire, Darcy forgot his previous trepidation; he wanted to dance with her—like a moth compelled to follow the flame, he felt a need to be near her. "Miss Elizabeth, may I have the honor of this dance?" He offered her a proper bow.

"I appreciate your gallantry, Mr. Darcy, but without meaning offense, I will decline." Instinctively, she knew she could not risk touching him—taking his hand. Elizabeth was not sure if she wanted to know of more Mr. Darcy.

She walked away, but the spell Elizabeth cast on him remained: She was an enigma—one he desperately wanted to solve. The fact that she did not set designs on him went a long way in holding

Darcy's attention. He *must* know more of the woman.

Caroline Bingley suddenly appeared in his path. He had managed to avoid her for several days. Smiling, Miss Bingley placated his every thought. "You are considering how insupportable it would be to pass many evenings in this manner—in such society, and indeed I am quite of your opinion. I was never more annoyed! The insipidity and yet the noise—the nothingness—and yet the self-importance of all these people!—What would I give to hear your strictures on them!"

Darcy knew how to send her away. "Your conjecture is totally wrong, I assure you. My mind was more agreeably engaged. I meditated on the very great pleasure which a pair of fine eyes in the face of a pretty woman can bestow."

"Who might credit such inspiration?" she cried coquettishly.

"Miss Elizabeth Bennet." He smiled as he said her name.

Caroline took immediate offense, but Darcy was unmoved by the wound he had dealt to her vanity. Only *his Elizabeth* brought forth any interest.

When she walked away, Elizabeth felt Darcy's eyes burning her back. She thought she recognized his interest. Where a few hours ago she might have thought him critical, she now believed he watched for another reason, and she took delight in his attention. She could almost smell his desire. She had never expected *this* turn of events. Or was it as she thought? Did she imagine what she hoped she saw or did she truly affect him? She tilted her chin determinedly. If he was besotted, she would use his interest for her own purposes—and soon.

★ ★ ★

A week later, Darcy and Bingley returned home from a pleasant evening with the militia officers to find Jane Bennet unwell and staying at Netherfield. She had joined Bingley's sisters for dinner and taken ill, the result of becoming soaked in a rainstorm. Bingley loved the idea, although his sisters felt put upon.

Darcy found Mrs. Bennet's maneuverings mildly amusing. She, obviously, had set it up for her eldest daughter to be overcome and be at Bingley's mercy. They were, of course, chaperoned by his sisters. *What a perfect way to snare a husband,* he thought. Perhaps the woman should write a manual for young unmarried ladies.

When there was nothing for him to do, Darcy left the Bingleys to tend to their patient and headed to bed. As he undressed, an errant thought occurred to him. If Jane Bennet were to remain at Netherfield for several days, Elizabeth Bennet would join her. He audibly moaned; he and Elizabeth would be in the same house. On the one hand, the thought excited him. And on the other, it threatened his sanity. Darcy had not recovered from their most recent encounter. He had wanted so much to dance with her—to hold her in his arms; and he wanted to stop her singing by kissing her sweet lips—her ears—her neck. Every time he thought of it, he imagined Elizabeth at the pianoforte singing *his* song and then standing slowly and walking into his embrace. They would cling to each other—tongues dueling—silencing his words and even his thoughts. It was one of his favorite dreams of late. Now they could create new dreams, he and Elizabeth. Despite his resolve not to marry, Darcy could not help himself when it came to Elizabeth Bennet. Whether he admitted it aloud or not, she possessed part of his soul. He would battle his demons some other way.

Elizabeth looked at the note from her sister. Jane, lovely and gullible, needed her. Ironically, though, her sister's sudden illness played to her plan. Jane was at Netherfield and so was Fitzwilliam Darcy. *How fortunate an occasion!* She could watch him more closely without bringing undue attention to herself. "I cannot bear to think Jane alone and unwell; I must go to her," she told her parents.

Once again, she replayed Darcy's responses at Sir William's party. Admittedly, Elizabeth liked the way he had looked at her, but she could not be sure whether what she thought she observed was true. At times, Mr. Darcy seemed so haughty, expecting her to grovel at his feet. At other times, she thought he seemed unguarded and sincere.

Before she left for Netherfield, Elizabeth penned a letter to her aunt in London.

24 October

Dear Aunt Gardiner,

This will be short, as I am needed to tend to our dear Jane, who took ill. But it is not serious. When I tell you of Jane's fate, you might find it amusing. Miss Bingley and Mrs. Hurst invited Jane to dinner. As my mother hopes Mr. Bingley prefers Jane to all others, she encouraged my sister to take advantage of the situation. Unfortunately, the gentlemen dined out for the evening. But Mama thought of everything. She denied Jane the use of Papa's coach and sent her on horseback. Because the skies were about to open when Jane left home, Mama's plan worked perfectly. Jane arrived at Netherfield soaked to the bone and became ill enough to remain with the Bingleys while she recovers. I will join her at Netherfield as soon as the skies clear and I can traverse the miles to Mr. Bingley's estate.

While sequestered there, I hope to observe more closely your Mr. Darcy. I know you feel he had some involvement in Vivian's murder, but to date I cannot see it. True, he is withdrawn and sometimes downright rude, but I see that as more from his upbringing than an obsession he wishes to hide. He shows no interest in any of the women who flirted with him ridiculously over the past few weeks. If he is the womanizing master of the estate you suspect him to be, he hides it uncommonly well.

I hope over the next few days to establish some sort of relationship with him. We exchanged pleasantries several times already. I hope to "entice" him into letting down his guard. If he truly uses women as you say, I will see it in the way he treats me. We will have opportunities for private exchanges. Do not concern yourself; I will be most careful. I have heard your warnings. Vivian did not have that advantage.

Much love from your devoted niece,

Lizzy

As planned, Elizabeth walked the three miles to Netherfield—crossing field after field at a quick pace, jumping over stiles and springing over puddles with impatient activity—and finding herself at last within view of the house, with weary ankles, dirty stockings and a face glowing with the warmth of exercise, she was shown into the breakfast parlor, where all but Jane were assembled, and where her appearance created a great deal of surprise. That she should walk so early in the day in such dirty weather, and by herself, was almost incredible to Mrs. Hurst and Miss Bingley; and Elizabeth was convinced they held her in contempt for it. However, they politely received her; and in their brother's manners there was something better than politeness—there was good humor and kindness. Unfortunately for her little experiment in seduction, Darcy said very little, and this disappointed Elizabeth immensely. She would even welcome his disdain just to engender a reaction.

The Bingleys offered unfavorable answers to her inquiries after her sister. "Miss Bennet slept ill, and though up, I fear she is quite feverish, and not well enough to leave her room," Mrs. Hurst informed Elizabeth. Therefore, being taken to Jane immediately pleased her, and her sister, who only was withheld by the fear of giving alarm or inconvenience from expressing in her note how much she longed for such a visit, was delighted at Elizabeth's entrance. Jane was not equal, however to much conversation, and, when Miss Bingley left them together, could attempt little besides expressions of gratitude for the extraordinary kindness with which she was treated. Elizabeth silently attended her.

When breakfast was over, the Bingley sisters joined them in Jane's room, and Elizabeth tried to reconcile her earlier feelings of how haughty she found them. They showed Jane affection and solicitude, and that went a long way in winning over Elizabeth's regard. The apothecary came, and having examined his patient, said, as might be supposed, that Jane caught a violent cold, and they must endeavor to get the better of it. He advised an immediate return to bed and promised to bring restoring draughts later in the day. As Jane's fever returned, Elizabeth did not quit her sister's room for a moment, and because the gentlemen were out of the house, the Bingley sisters stayed as well.

When the clock struck three, Elizabeth felt she must return to Longbourn, and very unwillingly said so. Miss Bingley graciously offered her carriage, and Elizabeth just as graciously accepted. Yet Jane's fever raged on, causing Elizabeth to linger longer and longer. Finally, Miss Bingley obligingly converted the offer of the chaise to an invitation to remain at Netherfield for the present. Elizabeth most thankfully consented and the Bingleys dispatched a servant to Longbourn to acquaint the family with Elizabeth's stay and to bring back a supply of clothes.

Back in Jane's room, Elizabeth lovingly sponged her sister's weary brow, but her thoughts remained on the mysterious Mr. Darcy. By stalling and manipulating, she managed to wheedle out an invitation to stay. *I am as bad as my mother,* she thought, but the smile turned up the corner of her lips when she saw how easily it happened. She could take care of Jane, and she could more closely watch Mr. Darcy. It was the perfect arrangement.

At five o'clock the two ladies retired to dress, and at half past six, they summoned Elizabeth to dinner. To the civil inquiries which then poured in, and among which she had the pleasure of the much superior solicitude of Mr. Bingley, she could not make a very favorable answer. Jane was by no means better. The sisters, on hearing this, repeated three or four times how much they were grieved, how shocking it was to have a bad cold, and how excessively they disliked being ill themselves, and then thought no more of the matter and their indifference toward Jane, when not immediately before them, restored Elizabeth to the enjoyment of all her original dislike. *They are as awful as I suspected.*

Their brother indeed, was the only one of the party whom she regarded with any complacency. His anxiety for Jane was evident, and his attentions to herself most pleasing, and they prevented her feeling herself so much an intruder as she believed the rest of his family considered her to be. As for how Mr. Darcy felt, Elizabeth could not be sure. He barely spoke to her, and used to having him watch her every move, today he made a point of never meeting her eyes. Instead, throughout the dinner he entertained Miss Bingley and Mrs. Hurst, leaving Elizabeth to converse with Mr. Hurst, an indolent man, who lived only to eat, drink, and play at cards.

When dinner was over she returned directly to Jane. When summoned to coffee some time later, Elizabeth refused the invitation as Jane was still very poorly. Only when her sister finally found sleep did she make an appearance in the drawing room. Finding the whole party at loo, she made her sister the excuse for not joining them and, in a few minutes, excused herself again. Late in the evening, she made a final appearance, joining them only to say her sister was worse, and she could not leave her. Bingley urged Mr. Jones being sent for immediately; while his sisters, convinced no country advice could be of any service, recommended an express to town for one of the most eminent physicians. This she would not hear of; but she was not so unwilling to comply with their brother's proposal; and it was settled that Mr. Jones should be sent for early in the morning, if Miss Bennet were not decidedly better. Bingley was quite uncomfortable; his sisters declared they were miserable. They solaced their wretchedness, however, by duets after supper, while Mr. Bingley could find no better relief than by giving his housekeeper directions that every possible attention might be paid to the sick lady and her sister.

Much to Darcy's dismay and to his delight, he saw very little of Elizabeth that first day: She spent much of her time with her sister Jane. Out of Elizabeth's earshot, Bingley's sisters criticized her for walking the three miles to Netherfield, but Darcy saw no reason to do so. Her windswept appearance made *his Elizabeth* look more natural—and, if possible, more beautiful. Later, goaded by Caroline's trying to demonstrate her intimate relationship with him in front of Elizabeth by inquiring about Georgiana's studies, he bested Miss Bingley with a remark on how Georgiana and Elizabeth were of the same height. Even more daring, Darcy challenged Caroline's opinions on what constituted the requirements of an accomplished woman, a point on which she prided herself.

"Your list of the common extent of accomplishments has too much truth. The word is applied to many a woman who deserves it not otherwise than by netting a purse or covering a screen; but I am very far from agreeing with you in your estimation of ladies in general. I cannot boast of knowing more than half a dozen, in the whole range of my acquaintance, who are really accomplished," he told Bingley.

"Nor I, I am sure," said Miss Bingley.

"Then," observed Elizabeth, "you must comprehend a great deal in your idea of an accomplished woman." God love her, she rose to the challenge, and for a moment, Darcy was alive again.

"Yes; I do comprehend a great deal in it." *Take that Elizabeth—respond again so I might hear your voice and experience the sparkle of your eyes.*

"Oh, certainly," Caroline interrupted. "A woman must have a thorough knowledge of music, singing, drawing, dancing, and the modern languages, to deserve the word; and besides all this, she must possess a certain something in her air and manner of walking, the tone of her voice, her address and expressions, or the word will be but half-deserved."

Darcy watched as Elizabeth fought the urge to roll her eyes. He agreed: Caroline was insufferable, but *his Elizabeth* was a different story. "All this she must possess," he taunted, "and to all this she must yet add something more substantial in the improvement of her mind by extensive reading." Darcy knew Caroline never read a book unless forced to do so; however, Elizabeth sat on the sofa with one in her hand. He suspected that with Mr. Bennet's reputation for extensive reading his daughter would follow suit. Besides, as well as Elizabeth battled verbally with him, he knew instinctively that she devoured books.

"I am no longer surprised at your knowing only six accomplished women. I rather wonder now at your knowing any," she dared to question his opinion.

"Are you so seve.. upon your own sex as to doubt the possibility of all this?" By now, he saw only her—only Elizabeth made him feel this way.

"I never saw such a woman. I never saw such capacity and taste and application and elegance as you describe, united."

You! He wanted to scream. You are that woman! But before they could continue, Mr. Hurst and Mr. Bingley cried out against the injustice of her implied doubt, and the conversation died a slow death under their protests. Darcy, energized by the exchange, wanted more, but he realized the grave danger being in Elizabeth's presence created. Luckily, or unluckily, Elizabeth soon afterward left the room.

For Darcy, the knowledge that she was in the same house and only a few doors away tormented him throughout the day, so at bedtime, unable to put that last exchange from his mind, he made his way to Netherfield's library. "Possibly," he muttered to himself, "something decent to read will distract me." He chose a book on military history and took up residence in one of the wing chairs before the hearth. Having read a couple of chapters, he had nearly nodded off when he heard a noise on the stairs. Put on alert, he sat perfectly still, praying it was not Caroline Bingley.

Midnight—and still unable to sleep after her nearly heated conversation with Mr. Darcy—Elizabeth paced the room. She checked on Jane, but her sister rested soundly. All day long she had thought of him, even though she saw him only during dinner. Images of where he might be in the house kept her awake. She would give anything for a way to unwind. "Why not?" she said aloud.

Reaching for her wrapper, Elizabeth pulled it over her muslin gown. "At this time of night, who else could be awake?" She lit a candle and eased her way out the door. The carpeting muffled the sound of her footsteps, but she heard the squish of each step on the marble stairs.

A dim light came from the library as she approached the door. Assuming it to be only the fire burning down slowly, she entered without thinking; but seeing a movement near the hearth, Elizabeth froze, poised for action. Then she recognized the figure, slowly coming to its feet in the shadows.

"Mr. Darcy!" she gasped.

Turning towards the sound of her voice, he felt a pull in his groin, a strange sense of lust and longing. Maybe it was because his heart thudded to a complete stop when his eyes beheld her. Elizabeth stood in the middle of the room, barefoot and in her night shift and dressing gown. His dreams of her did not come close to her exquisite beauty. His heart clenched with the recognition of how much he wanted her. She was everything—pure intelligence—pure control—pure loveliness. "Miss—Miss Elizabeth," he stammered, "I did not expect company at such an hour."

Elizabeth let her gaze wander over him. He wore tight breeches and a loosely fitted shirt open at the neck. Standing so tall and erect, she thought him one of the most handsome men she ever met. "I beg your pardon, Sir. I could not sleep. Netherfield has a reputation for possessing an exceptional library. I came in search of a book." Then with a touch of mischief she added, "Improve my accomplishments and all."

Darcy muffled a chuckle and gestured towards the shelves. "I am sure you may find something of interest here." He knew he should excuse himself, but he could not leave her. His gaze slid over her once again. "May I help you find a book to your liking? It seems that since I came to Netherfield, I have spent an inordinate number of hours in here."

Elizabeth smiled uneasily; she should not be found in her nightclothes in the middle of the evening spending time with a man. Yet if she really wanted to learn more of Mr. Darcy, what better way than a private conversation? "I am a voracious reader: politics, military history, science—"

"What? No romance?" his voice held a playful quality she was beginning to recognize.

"Mrs. Ratcliffe is entertaining, but my favorite is Fanny Burney's *Cecilia*. In poetry, William Cowper reigns supreme." She walked towards the shelves, pretending to peruse the offerings, although her body remained attuned to the man sharing the room with her.

He thoroughly enjoyed watching her walk away—the slight sway of her hips. A wave of lust washed over him as Darcy laughed quietly. "No Lord Byron, Miss Elizabeth?"

She turned with a blush, a redness rising across her chest and neck. "I suppose that *men,*" she charged, "prefer such decadent reading, Mr. Darcy, but I assure you, *I* do not!"

"Then you *have* read Lord Byron?" he countered.

For a moment, she started to deny his assertion, but then Elizabeth laughed at herself. "I am my father's child. I read when and what I should not."

Darcy walked to where she stood. "Mr. Bennet has the reputation for being quite the bookworm. With your quick wit and love of twisting the King's English, I should have known. You played me fair in our verbal duels." He reached for a book on one of the upper shelves and handed it down to her. "You might enjoy this one, Miss Elizabeth."

She stood looking up into a face with which she was beginning to become more comfortable. In silence, he held her laughing green eyes with his. Her eyes sparked with passion and some indecipherable emotion. "You deserve my reproofs, Mr. Darcy," she asserted.

Darcy's smile spread across his face. "I have been taken to task before, Miss Elizabeth, but I cannot say I ever enjoyed it quite as much." Unconsciously, nearly trancelike, as in his dream, he reached out to tuck an errant strand of hair behind her ear. Elizabeth did not flinch, just continued to stare deeply, seemingly into his soul. She tilted her face towards his palm. Darcy was on the brink—a precipice—a stepping-off point, and he was helpless to stop it. "It is a scandalous proposition, but would you consider keeping me company for awhile? I will freshen the fire to make the room more comfortable."

"I would enjoy that very much, Mr. Darcy." She swallowed hard, trying to force the desire, as well as the nervousness, away.

He took her hand and led her back to a wing chair. Then he added additional logs to the flames and stirred the embers. "May I get you a drink, Miss Elizabeth? I am afraid that it is too late—or maybe too early—for tea."

"Some wine would be nice, Mr. Darcy." As he turned to tend to the drinks, Elizabeth consciously inhaled deeply to regain her composure. The touch of his hand—so tempting—so strong—so warm—had shattered her senses.

In a few brief moments, he returned, carrying two glasses—a brandy for him and a glass of wine for her. He noted she sat with her feet tucked up underneath her to fend off the chill, so Darcy reached for a knitted shawl lying across the back of a nearby chair. "Let us lay this across your lap for warmth." He boldly placed it over her legs, delighting in the intimacy of the moment and experiencing a rush of desire. "Might I get you another for your shoulders?"

"No, Sir, I am very comfortable. Please have a seat." She gestured towards his chair.

He returned to his chair, picking up the book he had left lying upon her entrance. "How is Miss Bennet?" he asked as he laid the book on the table.

"My Jane is tougher than her beauty might lead a person to believe. She will suffer for a few more days, but the illness will run its course. It is very kind of Mr. Bingley to open his home to us."

"Charles is delighted to be of service." Darcy knew his friend to be "delighted" for other reasons, but he kept that information to himself. "I took note, Miss Elizabeth, you chose to walk to Netherfield this morning."

Politely ignoring his implied criticism, Elizabeth offered one of her amused smiles. "I did, Mr. Darcy. I am assuming Miss Bingley also *took note* of my ramblings."

Darcy returned her smile with one of his own. "Miss Bingley prides herself on being observant. I simply meant that, unlike your sister, you chose to walk rather than to ride or to come in your father's coach."

"My father's coach was unavailable, Mr. Darcy, and I am no horsewoman."

"Really? That surprises me. I would guess you to be a daredevil on a horse." He took a sip of his brandy, letting it trickle down his throat. "You have an adventurous spirit."

She turned crimson again, a bit surprised by his forwardness, but Elizabeth nodded her head in acceptance of his veiled compliment. "I do not fear riding. Unfortunately, the opportunity to learn never presented itself. My father's stable is limited."

"I could give you lessons while you are at Netherfield. Mr. Bingley has several fine choices, and I would take great pleasure in offering you my expertise." He looked at her in all sincerity, hoping she might accept, as it would give him an excuse to spend more time with Elizabeth.

For a moment, Darcy could tell she seriously considered his offer, but she flashed a regretful smile, and then declared, "I cannot, Sir, impinge on your kindness." He would not embarrass her with his insistence; he let it pass, realizing intuitively that her decision was for the sake of economy. "Would you tell me about your estate, Mr. Darcy? I understand it to be quite grand."

"Pemberley House sits at the top of a considerable eminence and is situated on the opposite side of a valley through which the entrance road lies. It is a large, handsome, stone building, standing well on rising ground and backed by a ridge of high woody hills. In front, there is a stream of natural importance. Its banks are neither formal, nor falsely adorned." For some ten minutes, he expounded on the property he loved. "I—I apologize, Miss Elizabeth," he stammered when he realized how long he spoke. "I am afraid you touched on a favorite subject of mine."

She nodded. "It sounds heavenly, Mr. Darcy. I was far from bored. To think you take on such obligations! It is a great responsibility for a young man."

He swallowed hard; Elizabeth seemed to understand his obsession with the land, a fact for which he was not prepared. "My father passed six years ago—my mother shortly after the birth of my sister. In retrospect, I know my father groomed me for the position of Pemberley's master and Georgiana's guardian from an early age. It is all I ever knew."

"Georgiana? Your sister? Is she much younger than you, then?" Elizabeth finished off the last of her wine and placed the empty glass on the table.

"She is twelve years my junior. Often I feel I am her parent more than her brother," he confessed.

"Then she is of the age of Lydia and Kitty," Elizabeth observed, unobtrusively examining his reaction.

"Georgiana is not as outgoing as your sisters. She is very shy and reserved." He did not want to seem to criticize Elizabeth's family. The thought of family made him remember how Elizabeth sang about his ancestor Ellender D'Arcy; he had debated for days whether to tell her of his connection to the song. "I never complimented you on your performance at Sir William's, Miss Elizabeth. You have a mesmerizing voice. I do not believe I ever heard 'Lord Thomas and Fair Ellender' done so well."

Elizabeth looked off, as if remembering some lost detail. "It is one of my favorites."

"Such a song—a favorite?" His voice rose with anticipation. He nearly leaned forward to be closer to her.

"May I share a family secret with you, Mr. Darcy?"

He heard the mischief in her voice. "Sharing secrets?" he teased her. "Our relationship moves to another level."

"Mr. Darcy, you love to lampoon my words, but I take no offense." She gazed at him steadily. "I love the song because Lord Thomas, upon whom the tale is based, is a distant relative. My father's family came here many generations ago from Scotland. The story of Lord Thomas Benning and his love for Fair Ellender haunts many a child in my bloodline. Is that silly? A woman's fancy?"

Darcy felt his breath rush from his lungs. His ancestor Ellender D'Arcy loved Elizabeth's ancestor Lord Thomas Benning. How could that be? Did Elizabeth know of the curse Ellender created with that love? *Was it design or Fate that brought us together?* The thought rang clearly in his head. "It is not silly, nor is it simply a female fancy," he began. "Traditions—family traditions—are cherished, even if they take a tragic twist." He stood quickly, not sure he wanted to continue the conversation. Thoughts of curses and darkness and black magic filled him. "I intend to retire on that note. Might I escort you to your room, Miss Elizabeth?"

She stood also, folding the shawl to replace it on the chair. "Thank you, Mr. Darcy."

He picked up the candle to light their way, and Elizabeth fell in step beside him. At the top of the stairs, they turned to their right. When they paused outside her room, Darcy waited until she reached for the door handle. "Miss Elizabeth, this was a pleasant way to end an evening. Thank you for the company."

"It was…it was…eye-opening," she whispered as she impulsively leaned towards him. She allowed herself to steal a glance at him and was amazed at how handsome he was.

Darcy never used the powers he possessed on a woman—powers to make her not remember what happened between them—but he was sorely tempted to do so now. It would be so simple; Elizabeth would never know, and he could indulge his desire to kiss her and to touch her.

For long moments, they remained—neither of them moving—only inches apart, so close he could see the fringes of her thick lashes resting on her cheekbones. "Scandalous propositions are always eye-opening," he murmured as he edged even closer. A pull—something greater than himself—bade him to move.

"I believe I need to partake of scandalous propositions more often." She rested a hand on his chest, feeling his heart pound beneath it. Lightly, she added, "Can you think of anything more scandalous than standing here in the middle of the night, dressed as we are?"

"*Elizabeth,*" he whispered, before lowering his mouth to hers. Drinking of her lips, he pressed closer, but did not take her into his embrace. Instead, he angled his mouth to deepen the kiss, allowing his tongue to slip between her lips. He knew he moaned, but could not stop himself. His world tilted suddenly, and he felt himself slip into dark, uncertain depths. Never was he so impetuous! If she wanted, Elizabeth Bennet could claim seduction and demand he marry her; all of his plans to end the curse would be for naught; but Darcy did not care. He kissed Elizabeth Bennet, and she returned his intrusion of her mouth with one of her own. She clutched the collar of his shirt in her hand, and Darcy felt his pleasure mount. If she demanded marriage, he would agree wholeheartedly.

Reluctantly, he ended the kiss, drawing his tongue across her sharp teeth, one at a time, wondering what they might do to his body. Their mouths lingered inches from each other, and their breathing came in short, chest-heaving gasps. He felt her presence in his blood. "I believe that is as much *scandal* as I can bear for one night," he murmured.

Elizabeth dropped her eyes and quickly began to straighten the wrinkles she had created in his shirt. "You are right, Mr. Darcy. I am more adventurous than I first imagined."

She started to step away, but Darcy caught her wrist. "Please…do not regret this moment. It was exquisite." He let loose of her wrist and stroked Elizabeth's chin line with the back of his hand. "Nearly as exquisite as you." He paused, wondering if he should kiss her again. "Good night, Miss Elizabeth," he said finally, breathing the words into her hair before turning and striding away.

"Good night, Mr. Darcy," she whispered to his retreating form.

CHAPTER 3

Elizabeth floated into the room. She—Elizabeth Bennet—had kissed Fitzwilliam Darcy! Little over a fortnight earlier, he had snubbed her at the assembly. Now, they were up in the middle of the night—talking—enjoying a drink—and kissing. When she meant to observe him for her aunt, Elizabeth had never expected to be the one upon whom he would shower his attentions. His kiss had melted her heart. At that moment, she would have done anything he asked, including going to his room. She could see how women became entangled with rich men like Mr. Darcy. She could see how a washerwoman on his estate might lose her heart to him—and how a man of his build—his strength—could kill a woman with just a twist of his hands about her neck. But when he stroked her chin line with the back of his hand, he did not feel like a murderer; and when he kissed her, his lips said hunger but not a cold lust. How was she to know what to believe? She wanted desperately to prove her Aunt Gardiner correct; yet she certainly did not want to believe Fitzwilliam Darcy's attentions to her to be part of a game of seduction he played with many women. Especially a fatal game of seduction.

Darcy did not breathe until he had closed the door to his room behind him. What had he been thinking? She tasted of wine and of woman, and immediately Darcy imagined possessing her completely, drinking of her essence. Kissing Elizabeth Bennet was excruciating torture. Excruciating in the fact that he wanted more—much more of her. Torture in the fact that he knew he could never marry, and that was exactly what he wanted to do. After one kiss, Darcy now wanted to make Elizabeth his wife—take her to Pemberley and live happily ever after. However, there could be no "happily ever after" for him. Ellender D'Arcy saw to that fact centuries earlier. What could he do? He knew Elizabeth held him in a spell as easily as Wickham held his victims.

★ ★ ★

When he stepped into the morning room, her exotic, catlike eyes met his and held his gaze for several long seconds before looking away. In some ways, Elizabeth's presence in the room surprised Darcy. Most women he knew would still be abed, especially after a long night, but there she was, looking freshly scrubbed and ready for the day. "Miss Elizabeth," he said and bowed to her. "I hope the morning brings your sister better health."

"Thank you, Mr. Darcy," she said as she laid her fork on her plate. "I believe it does."

He moved to the side bar to pour himself some tea. He carried the cup back to the table and took up the place across from her. Darcy tried to ignore the jolt of desire in his groin and his preoccupation with the point on her neck where Elizabeth's pulse throbbed visibly beneath the skin. To compensate, he addressed his friend. "What say you, Charles? What are your plans for the day?"

Bingley fidgeted in his seat, but his voice did not waver. "Darcy, if you do not mind, I would like to stay close to the house. Mr. Jones is to call to administer to Miss Bennet. I wish to assure myself of her recovery."

"Of course, Bingley." Then, with an unanticipated pleasure, Darcy turned his eyes back to Elizabeth. "It seems, Miss Elizabeth, my friend releases me from my obligation. If you are of the persuasion, I could give you that riding lesson after all."

She went very still, and Darcy watched as shock played across her face, but Elizabeth recovered quickly. "Mr. Darcy, I could not intrude on your time," she began to protest.

"Miss Elizabeth," Bingley jumped into the conversation, "if you want to learn from the best, Mr. Darcy is your man. I watched him teach Miss Darcy, and she is a superb horsewoman. It is an excellent idea, Darcy. Which horse do you suppose best fits Miss Elizabeth? Ceres, perhaps?"

"Out of your current choices, Ceres is a good one—gentle but a spark of *adventurousness*." He looked at Elizabeth to see if she picked up on his words. "If I were at Pemberley, I would choose a gelding—maybe Apollo—but we will make do with what we have."

"Mr. Darcy," her protest returned, "I have no riding habit."

Darcy smiled as he moved to the sideboard to fill a plate. His eyes told her to follow him. "We will send to Longbourn for it," he said matter-of-factly.

Bingley turned his attention to the entrance of his brother-in-law Wayne Hurst. Elizabeth stepped next to Darcy, standing closer than propriety allowed. "Mr. Darcy, I have no riding habit," she hissed under her breath.

Her breast touched his upper arm, and Darcy shrugged his shoulders to rub against her. His flirtation was out of control, but Darcy never experienced such freedom—never allowed himself to be reminded of what his life could be. He turned his head and spoke to her hair: "You do now, Miss Elizabeth. It will be here by two."

"Mr. Darcy," she avowed, "I *cannot* accept gifts from you."

"Another scandalous proposition," he whispered as he placed a bun on her plate. "Would you like chocolate, Miss Elizabeth?" he said, loud enough for the others to hear.

Elizabeth glared at him. "I do not think so, Mr. Darcy," she said meaningfully.

Darcy leaned across her to choose a hard-boiled egg because it put him even closer to her. "What would Bingley say if he knew what happened last night?"

"Mr. Darcy, I do not like being blackmailed," she said huskily.

"I will not blackmail you, Miss Elizabeth. I just want to spend time with you." His voice pleaded for acquiescence. She stared at him—held his gaze with the most luminous eyes he ever beheld—before nodding her assent. "Thank you," he mouthed as he turned back to the table. When he left her the previous evening, he sent one of his footmen to London with specific instructions for

Madame Lucinda, a renowned modiste, for a plainly cut riding habit in a dark green or gray. Darcy did not want anything ostentatious because it would not be *his Elizabeth*. He could not imagine how he reached this point, but surprisingly, he enjoyed it. He felt more alive than he ever had. For some reason, Elizabeth Bennet made him stronger.

He sent a note he would meet her at the stable at three. Elizabeth did not join them for the midday meal, tending to her sister instead, so Darcy was unsure whether she would show. Relief rushed through him when he watched her approach. The green riding habit needed to be adjusted some in the hem and the waist, but, overall, no one would know it did not belong to her.

A groom hurried forward to meet her; he took Elizabeth to where Darcy stood, holding the horse's bridle. "Miss Elizabeth," he acknowledged her with a tilt of his head. She curtsied. "May I introduce you to Ceres?" He held the horse's head still. "You should become familiar with the animal before you take your seat."

Elizabeth stepped up to the horse and patted her head. "Easy, girl," she said softly.

"She likes you," Darcy noted.

"And you, Mr. Darcy?" she asked boldly, giving him a sideward glance.

He chuckled. "I like you, too, Miss Elizabeth." Lord! She could charm him with just a look.

She finally whispered, "Thank you for the riding habit. I do not know how you arranged it so quickly or how you knew what to buy. The experience has *quite* gone to my head; I never owned anything so fine."

"The green brings out the brightness of your eyes," he murmured. She looked away with a blush. "Let us get you into the saddle," he said loudly for the ears of the grooms standing around. "We will use the mounting block."

Courageously, Elizabeth allowed him to lead her up the steps of the block while the groom held the horse steady. With pleasure he placed her feet in the stirrups, lifting her skirt tail to adjust the straps. "We will take it slow and easy, Miss Elizabeth. The groom will lead Ceres, and I will walk beside you to assure you do not slip. Do you trust me?"

Staring at his lips, Elizabeth said nothing for a few moments, which Darcy found to be very discomposing. "I trust you, Mr. Darcy," she said in a low voice. He placed the reins in her hands and showed her how to hold them.

They took a couple of turns around the enclosure. He noted how she bit her lower lip, probably with anxiety, but she said nothing, concentrating on the animal. He was attuned to Elizabeth's slightest move. "Relax your arms a bit," he coached her. "The animal can feel your tension. Despite the size of the horse, it will respond with the least flick of your wrist. The bit in its mouth tells it what to do. Ah, that is better," he assured her. A few more turns, and he could see she was a natural. "Straighten your back, Miss Elizabeth. It will stop you from bouncing so much." Darcy moved closer to her. "You look fine, Miss Elizabeth," he said.

"This is exciting, Mr. Darcy," she said with a slight smile. "I cannot believe I am actually sitting on a horse." Darcy nodded to the groom, and the man stopped by the block. "Is the lesson over?" she asked with some disappointment.

"Not if you do not want it to be," he said while reaching up for her. "I want the groom to adjust the lead. I thought we might take a short ride together. I will lead your horse behind mine." She slid down into his arms as he helped her to the ground. Darcy resisted the urge to pull her into his embrace—to let his grasp tighten about her. Instead, he inquired, for the benefit of all within earshot, "Are you adventurous enough for such a trip, Miss Elizabeth?"

"Of course, Mr. Darcy," she declared politely.

The grooms scrambled to bring out his horse and to fix the straps. Darcy moved her out of the way as they worked. "It will be fine, Miss Elizabeth. If you tire or become frightened, you must let me know at once. Do you understand me? I will not have you injured or afraid simply to prove something to me."

"I understand."

At last, he led her back to the block and helped her up to Ceres's back. The straps were adjusted again, and he handed up the reins. "We will go slowly and stay to the lower path." She nodded, and Darcy strode to his horse and swung easily up into the saddle. He turned to her and said, "I am proud of you, Miss Elizabeth. Normally, it would take a person a week or more of lessons to be able to follow along with another rider."

"*Truly,* Mr. Darcy?"

"*Truly,* Miss Elizabeth." He nodded, and they started out of the stables. They rode in silence for nearly ten minutes. Darcy pulled his horse up near a copse of trees overlooking the estate house. Letting the reins loop around a nearby bush, he slid out of the saddle and then came around to help Elizabeth down. This time, he let her body slide down the length of his, and he did not move away. Instead, he trapped her between him and the horse and gazed at her. Something important existed between them. Of that, he was certain.

The corners of Darcy's mouth turned up in a smile. "How long have I known you?"

She blinked, trying to explain the pleasure seeping into her veins. "Less than a month, Sir," she said teasingly.

"Not long enough for you to call me Fitzwilliam?"

"Not in public."

His hands drifted to her waist, and he pulled her closer to him. "In private, then." He lowered his mouth to hers. The kiss started innocently enough, tender actually, but within seconds passion swept over them. Elizabeth slid in even closer to him, and Darcy's arms instinctively tightened around her. "*Elizabeth,*" he moaned. Finally, he forced his mouth from hers. "Only a month?" he asked hoarsely. He kissed her temple. "Let us talk. Over here." Taking her hand, he led her to some felled trees and helped her to sit. He took a place beside her and then took her hand in his. "Miss Elizabeth, I assure you, I do not normally respond as I have with you, and I cannot explain why I behave as such now. Please understand; I am a man of honor. If you wish to marry, I will bring you home as my wife." *Will she accept?* He choked back the fear she would refuse.

Elizabeth was shocked. What started as a favor to her aunt took a most *unexpected* turn. Her heart fluttered. And then she considered what Mr. Darcy—Fitzwilliam—said; or rather, what he left unsaid. "But you do not love me?" she blurted out.

"I never considered love," he murmured uneasily and stopped short. He could not admit to her his desire to possess her, to fulfill his uncontrollable need for her.

"Do you *want* to marry, Fitz—Mr. Darcy? If you want a wife you do not love, any woman would suit you. You would not need *me.*" Elizabeth removed her hand from his. "I do not normally act so recklessly. I enjoy our verbal battles more than I should. Most of the men I meet lack the acuity to understand what wit I may possess. I never set my sights on a man; I do not need to marry. In fact, I decided long ago only love—a passionate attachment—would persuade me to do so. Otherwise, I should be just as happy being Aunt Lizzy to my sisters' broods." She blushed profusely. "It is, I know, an eccentric stance. Nonetheless, it is mine." Darcy stared at her, astonished by such a declaration, one no fashionable society woman—no lady of the *ton*—would make.

"It is—it has been my plan not to marry." He could not look at her. How could he explain the turmoil she created in him?

"And your estate? Do you not need an heir?"

Elizabeth's words rang in his ears. *An heir? A child with her?* He could not do it. He fought every day to control the evil in himself. He could not pass that wretched—that cruelly unfortunate trait down to another. "Pemberley will be left to Georgiana's children. What I do, I do for her."

"I see." But Elizabeth did *not* see how a virile man such as Fitzwilliam Darcy could not consider marriage and a family. It made no sense! His reaction to her guaranteed—did it not?—that he possessed no perverted ideas of sexual relationships. After a long pause, where neither of them breathed, Elizabeth said with finality, "If neither of us wishes to marry, why must we end what we started? I will be at Netherfield for only a few more days. You will be at Netherfield for only a few more weeks. As long as we keep it to a few stolen moments such as these—innocent moments—why must it end? Perhaps I will recall this flirtation when I am old and tending Jane's children," she said playfully.

"You never having children of your own, Miss Elizabeth, seems an aberration of nature," he whispered huskily, but he could not look at her because, to him, she was everything good in the world. "I would like the memory of you to brighten my dreams." *Dreams of what might have been, if not for a curse.* Darcy stood and offered her his hand. "We will let this run its course, then."

Elizabeth stood and, without thought, stepped into him, sliding her arms about his waist and resting her head on his chest. Darcy kissed the top of her head and sighed. Being with her felt so utterly right—no hesitation. She tilted her head back as she looked up at him. She repeated his gesture from the night before, stroking his chin line with her fingertips. "Do we meet again this evening?"

Darcy's eyes sparkled with anticipation. "In the ballroom—not the library."

"The ballroom? Finally, we will dance?" Elizabeth's breath caught in her chest. "Am I now tolerable enough to tempt you, or is it because I will no longer be slighted by other men?"

"You, my Minx, knew even that evening at the assembly that you tempted me, and I was a fool to deny it. If I offended you, I apologize. I fought, but not so gallantly, what I saw from the first time my eyes rested on you."

"Even without music, we dance at last?" she repeated.

Darcy smiled mischievously. "I thought I might teach you to waltz. We can hum if you require music, my lady."

"*Waltz?*" she gasped. "It is so…so scandalous!"

"Exactly," he said, as he pulled her into his arms and lowered his head to kiss her. Their lips met. Elizabeth felt his body harden and her hungry response. "*Fitzwilliam,*" she moaned—a moan not of rejection, but of want—when they separated.

The need in her voice sent his senses spinning, and he rained kisses all about her face and behind her ear. He laid kisses down the length of her neck and across her shoulders, igniting a fire in both of them. At the indentation of her neck and shoulder, he paused. Darcy felt the blood rushing through her—knew the feeling it invoked in him—could nearly taste it. She was under his power, and he could take her; she could belong to him for an eternity. Automatically, his lips sucked lightly on the spot, but Darcy fought the ravening hunger pulsing through him—fought it with an intensity he never knew he had. He let his teeth graze the spot, raking over it several times—and then his tongue lapped it before he kissed the indentation tenderly and continued along her shoulder and the nape of her neck. A white-hot heat coursed through his body. He groaned. "How do you have such power over me?"

"I put a spell on you," she said mischievously.

Darcy pulled back to look at her questioningly. "I am a man who believes in spells, Miss Elizabeth."

"Really, Mr. Darcy? I would think you much too sensible." Her tone remained playful.

His thumb traced the outline of her lips. "My judgments are often based on more than the facts; gut feelings come into play as well. I accept what others cannot see."

"What do you see when you look at me, Fitzwilliam?"

"A conundrum." He brushed his lips across hers. "A beautiful woman. An adventurous spirit." He wanted to add *soul mate,* but did not. "A beautiful, adventurous woman who looks thoroughly kissed," he added slyly.

Elizabeth arched one eyebrow. "Shall we return to the house? Jane should be awake by now, and I am sure Miss Bingley is in need of your company."

"Do not remind me, Vixen. You will pay sorely for my attention to you," he warned.

"I can handle Miss Bingley." Elizabeth stepped away and began to straighten her clothing. "Better yet I can claim Jane's illness as an excuse to avoid her. *You* must be the one to endure her rebuke." She looked up and smiled sweetly.

Darcy smiled back as he reached out to tuck a stray curl under the edge of her bonnet. "You have no idea how often I pretend interest with Miss Bingley. Sometimes I imagine that is what marriage is—an endless meal with Caroline Bingley." He saw her flinch. "Elizabeth, you misapprehend me. Caroline may have her hopes, but it will *never* be. I will not marry."

"Let us go, Mr. Darcy." She walked in a huff towards the horse.

Darcy followed close behind her. She turned so he could lift her to the saddle, but Elizabeth took no pleasure in his touch. He placed his strong hands at her waist. "Elizabeth Bennet, I give no attention to anyone but you, and you know it. Now, are we going to fight over someone as insignificant to me as Caroline Bingley? Surely you know the charms of my estate are such that if I wanted Miss Bingley, she would be mine." He raised her chin with his hand. A single tear ran down her cheek. "No tears," he chastised her as he wiped it away with his thumb. "Only memories."

Elizabeth nodded and swallowed hard—her fit of jealousy so *inappropriate*. "Only memories."

Darcy lifted her to her horse and helped her to adjust her seat before leading her back to the stables. They spoke no more of desire or of marriage or of anything besides how to sit on a horse properly. In the evening, she dined with her sister in their rooms while Darcy tolerated Caroline's dismay at his teaching Elizabeth Bennet how to ride. He bit back many of his retorts, knowing they would only increase Miss Bingley's vexation and her denunciation of the Bennet sisters. He did it more for Charles Bingley than for himself. While Caroline's voice droned on, Darcy imagined holding Elizabeth in his arms and kissing her soft lips. The image sustained him and aroused him. The point on her neck where the blood coursed through her veins throbbed in him also. He nearly groaned in remembrance. "Tonight," he mumbled as he forked up a piece of carrot.

"Did you say something, Mr. Darcy?" Caroline called out from her end of the table.

Darcy's head snapped up. "Nothing of significance, Miss Bingley." He started to return to his second course when he added impulsively, "Do you not want Charles to take his place as the leader in the local society?"

"Of—of course, Mr. Darcy," she stammered.

Darcy smiled, realizing he had her. He knew Elizabeth would not be so easily bested and would not agree with his every statement. "Then how is my giving attention to one of Charles's nearest neighbors a detriment? A benevolent act builds goodwill, whether it is tending to Miss Jane Bennet or giving her younger sister a chance to learn to ride properly. The skill will only help Miss Elizabeth find a proper husband when she must marry. A landed gentleman would expect as much."

"But *I* do not ride, Mr. Darcy. Are you implying an accomplished woman should take to horse?" Her voice held disbelief and a bit of suspicion.

"Couples often ride together in Hyde Park during the season. Why do you think I taught Georgiana?" His level gaze dared Caroline Bingley to deny what he said.

"If you wish to learn, Caroline, I will arrange a riding master," Charles offered.

Caroline puffed up in her self-importance. "I will consider it, Charles." She returned to her meal, slicing away at her full plate of meat. "If I choose to ride, I will ask Mr. Darcy to teach me, as he does Miss Elizabeth."

"That cannot be, Miss Bingley. In our social circle, it is not done unless the lady and the gentleman are engaged, and we are *not* so attached. Country society allows more latitude. No one locally would reproach Miss Elizabeth, but the *ton* is not so kind to those of our standing."

"Darcy is right," Wayne Hurst added. "An unmarried woman in London must maintain certain standards."

Louisa Hurst confirmed what her husband said. "Maybe you should let Charles find you a suitable teacher."

"As I said, I will consider it!" Miss Bingley said, flushing with irritation. The conversation was closed.

★ ★ ★

At midnight, the ballroom door opened, and Elizabeth Bennet slipped into the room. Darcy was dressed much as he had been the previous evening, except he kept his loose-fitting shirt tucked into his breeches; he wore neither waistcoat, nor jacket, nor cravat. He stood to one side of the floor, having just lit all the candles in a candelabrum. The room was a bit chilly, although fires burned at both ends. Elizabeth smiled when she saw him waiting there for her.

Hearing the click of the door, he turned in anticipation. Elizabeth wore a simple day dress, but she had let her hair down, tying it back loosely from her face with a ribbon that matched the reddish brown of her dress. His heart jumped when he saw her. "*Finally,* you are here." Although he spoke softly, his voice carried in the empty room.

"You missed me?" she asked lightly.

"You know bloody well I did, Vixen." Darcy strode to her and scooped her into his arms and twirled her around as she giggled and shrieked. Finally, he set her on her feet in front of him. "Are you ready to dance with me?"

Elizabeth entwined her arms about him. "Why I must learn to waltz is beyond me. It is not as if I will ever have the chance to dance the waltz after tonight."

"Who knows? Someday you may travel abroad. You will be the belle of the ball—an Englishwoman who knows how to waltz." Darcy placed their hands into position. "We are to keep at least two inches between us," he whispered as he placed one hand on her lower back.

"Too bad." She went on her tiptoes to kiss his cheek.

"Ah, Vixen, you would drive a sane man crazy with your flirtations." He brushed her lips with his. "Let us dance." He positioned her and slowly began the steps, showing her where to place her feet. Then he picked up the pace. She bit her lower lip as she concentrated on repeating the steps. "Elizabeth, look at me," he coaxed. "Relax into my hands. Feel the pressure; as subtle as it is, you will feel my lead."

She raised her thickly lashed eyes to his and let out a deep sigh as she straightened her shoulders. Then she became his—gave herself up to the man. They were one being, moving rhythmically about the floor, twirling around the corners. "I feel like I am flying." Her voice held pure exhilaration, and Darcy smiled. He alone could give her this.

"Purely scandalous." He actually laughed out loud.

The sound of his laughter pleased her. The more Elizabeth knew of him, the less likely she thought him to be involved in Vivian's murder. The man had too many layers of kindness and decency to be part of a crime. "Positively disreputable!" she exclaimed.

After half an hour, he brought them to a standstill. "It grows late. But will you sit with me for awhile before returning to your room?"

"Of course," she said, still swaying in place from the music in her head. "Oh, I do hope England will accept such a dance soon. It was *glorious!*" She remained a bit breathless.

"I never danced it with such an enthusiastic partner." Darcy traced the line of her jaw with his fingers.

"Do not provoke me, Mr. Darcy," she warned. "My day was one beyond belief—riding—waltzing—being with you—kissing under a copse of trees. I am packing a lifetime into a few short hours. What woman would not succumb to the joy of it all?"

He took her face in both his hands and looked into her eyes. "You make me feel alive as no woman has ever done." His words stung her heart. She had started a flirtation because she wanted to prove him a murderer; now, all she thought of was being in his arms. He led her to nearby chairs, but instead of seating her in her own chair, Darcy pulled Elizabeth down on his lap. "You enjoyed your day?"

"Did I not just say so?" She kissed his face, placing small pecks on his forehead, cheeks, and chin.

"You did, Vixen, but I am *vain* enough to want to hear it again." He kissed her deeply before withdrawing. "What scandalous events may I next add to your repertoire?"

Without missing a heartbeat, she declared boldly, "Teach me to use a sword."

Darcy broke out in laughter once more. "With your spirit, your father should have had a son!"

Thinking he might refuse, she returned to kissing along his chin line. "So will you teach me some of the basics?"

For a fleeting moment, Darcy imagined slicing away the strings that tied up the bodice of her dress and then the strings of her corset with a flick of his sword. "I will arrange it." His voice betrayed his need for her. "It must be out in the open. We cannot meet here at night; it would be too noisy."

"There is an empty manor house in need of repairs on the other side of the estate. We could ride over, use the manor for a fencing lesson, and ride back. We could meet there even after I leave Netherfield." Elizabeth snuggled into his chest.

Desire burned through him, but Darcy kept his tone undisturbed. "So you do not want this to end either?" He kissed the top of her head, and then released the ribbon holding back her auburn curls. He ran his fingers down the length of her tresses.

"No, Fitzwilliam, I do not want it to end. The day will come when you return to Pemberley, and my life will go back to the mundane, but until that time I choose to be near you." She fell into his embrace, and their bodies reacted to the intimacy. Her fingers pulled at the opening of his shirt, and Elizabeth arched towards him. "There is something unfinished between us."

Darcy's hands slid up and down her arms and back. Then he let his fingers drift down her neck. At the point where he could see her pulse, a red mark surprised him. "Elizabeth?" he questioned, while touching the spot very gently.

"It is nothing—really nothing," she said casually. "Just a bit of whisker burn, I suspect."

In a tenuous, terrible moment, he saw the truth. "Lord, I am sorry. I never wished to hurt you or mar you." His voice trembled with fear, imagining what he could do to her if he let himself go.

"I *know,* Fitzwilliam. It is all right. Perfectly all right." She tried to soothe away what she did not understand.

Repulsed by himself, he started to set her away from him. "Let us retire for the evening."

She resisted by pushing him down into the chair. "Fitzwilliam, what did I do to upset you?"

"If I tell you, you will think I am a candidate for Bedlam, and you will turn from me. I do not believe I could tolerate the reproach in your eyes, Elizabeth." Darcy's fingers circled the mark on her neck—a mark *he* left there.

"Tell me, Fitzwilliam. If it is a part of you, I need to know." She would brook no dissent. If he wished to keep her in his life, he must tell Elizabeth the truth.

Darcy smiled ironically, his lips twitching with a grim acceptance. "Actually, it is a part of both of us, but I did not know that until last night." His eyes returned to the mark. "You said the story of Lord Thomas and Fair Ellender was a favorite tale in your family, but in mine, it is a tale of horror—a plague on us all." He heard her breath catch, but Elizabeth did not interrupt. She stroked the hair away from his face and kissed his forehead, wordlessly encouraging him to continue.

"It is a tale of nightmares," he began cautiously. "Two centuries ago, Leána, a beautiful muse of a vampire, fell in love with Arawn Benning, a young artist. She offered him inspiration and success. If he succumbed to her charms, he would belong to her for an eternity. Those who previously weakened went on to fame and glory—but in exchange for eventual madness, followed by a premature death.

"However, Arawn Benning refused the attentions of the *muse* because of his passionate love for Ellender D'Arcy. Because of his refusal, Leána was to become his slave for a decade, helping him but never knowing where his true affection lay." Terror and uncertainty flashed briefly in Elizabeth's eyes.

"Infuriated by the slight, Leána sought the help of her Baobhan Síth sisters. The coven placed a curse on the couple: Arawn's descendants would forever envy the D'Arcy family, and they would never achieve the greatness they sought. In addition, the Baobhan Síth planned to take Arawn's life. Desperate, Ellender offered another of her suitors in Arawn's stead. She gave them Seorais Winchcombe, a young man who depended purely on his looks to manipulate his way into people's lives."

He paused. "Shall I continue?" he inquired softly. Elizabeth, overwhelmed by what he said, simply nodded. "Seorais, a true vampire, lives on the blood of his victims. Besides his preoccupation with death, Seorais has one other overpowering goal: revenge on the D'Arcy family. Each generation, he converts a D'Arcy—or someone a D'Arcy loves—to eternal damnation. Ellender D'Arcy became one of his victims, and she passed along those tendencies through—and to—the firstborn sons of her descendants. Her descendants, who are known as dhampirs because they are part human, have the right to choose their destiny. Depending on the choices they make every day of their lives, they could escape the curse. However, no one has yet to do so. The lure of eternal life and the seduction of fame and glory proved too much for them." By degrees, Darcy drew her gaze.

"Elizabeth, Arawn is the Scottish name for Thomas. Your ancestor and mine loved each other. We are bound in a twisted fate." His voice held such sadness; Elizabeth fought back her own tears.

She closed her eyes as the real terror crept over her. "Are you telling me that you suffer under this curse as a vampire?" Her words were barely audible in the empty ballroom.

Darcy looked directly into her eyes, trusting her with his awful secret. "I am telling you that I am the firstborn son of my family."

CHAPTER 4

"I did not think you would come." Darcy met her at the gate, Ceres in tow.

"I changed my mind several times before deciding that whatever this is between us, I will see it through."

"Your thoughts are my own. May I?" He reached to lift her to the horse. They were both very aware of the servants watching them. "A little farther today, Miss Elizabeth?"

"You may choose, Mr. Darcy."

As they rode off, Darcy pulled on Ceres's lead line to bring Elizabeth beside him. "I am sorry for last night," he offered. "I never told anyone, not even Georgiana, about the whole bloody mess in which I find myself." He did not turn to look at her, and Elizabeth found herself fascinated by how the haughty Mr. Darcy had returned. "I plead for your discretion—not for myself, but for Georgiana, and for the people who call Pemberley home."

"You do not need to ask. Even if what we had these few days ended this very moment, I would not disclose your secret. Besides, I am involved, too. Fitzwilliam, you have to know that." Her voice demanded his agreement.

"Of course, I know." He turned finally to look at her. "I would not have told you if I thought otherwise." His eyes rested on her, as if he tried to memorize her features. "How many more days do you expect to be at Netherfield?"

"More than likely two—possibly three—but Jane seems determined to return to Longbourn by Sunday."

"What have you told her about us?"

Elizabeth pulled gently on the horse's reins to maneuver around a fallen tree. Darcy thought it nearly impossible that only yesterday she had first sat on a saddle. She would make him a perfect partner;

they could ride out over Pemberley's grounds daily and inspect the farms. *No.* He must be stern with himself.

"I said nothing; she thinks you accompanied me on my morning walks about the estate."

They fell silent until the house came into sight. "I rode over earlier with the swords. I assume you still wish to learn something about the weapons. I started to light a fire, but I feared someone might see the smoke and come to investigate."

"We will be moving around; that should keep us warm," she said, trying to brighten their spirits.

Darcy pulled up the horses. He dismounted and came to help her down. "Go on in. I will put the horses out of sight in the lean-to." Elizabeth headed to the door. "Do not touch the swords until I get there," he called out in an attempt at playfulness.

"What will happen to me if I do, Mr. Darcy?" she retorted.

"Do not toy with me, Miss Elizabeth." He did not look her way, but Elizabeth was sure he smiled—the first sign of affection from him that day.

When he entered the house, she was in the game room. At one time, a billiard table probably filled the space, but now it was quite empty. "This room seemed the best suited for our purpose," she said as he walked briskly into the room.

"So what will it be? A lesson in self-defense?"

She corrected him, "A lesson in self-esteem, Mr. Darcy."

He raised a quizzical eyebrow. "Self-esteem, Miss Elizabeth? That is not something that you lack." He strode to her side.

"Ah, you are mistaken, Mr. Darcy. In my household, Jane is the beautiful one. Mary is the talented one. Kitty is the creative one. And Lydia? She is my mother's darling. I am simply Elizabeth, superior in no way to any of them. Quite the contrary. What I have to recommend me—if indeed it could be called a recommendation—is a quick wit and a biting tongue. At least, now I will have a skill no one else in my family possesses; I will truly be the eccentric, but it will be something."

"What rot, Elizabeth! I wish you could see yourself through *my* eyes!" He took her into his embrace. "You are an astonishing and enchanting woman. The man who wins your heart will have a rare jewel." He kissed her completely, trying to ward off the bad spirits of the past twelve hours.

Elizabeth broke the kiss, burying her face into his chest. "Fitzwilliam, this all frightens me."

"May I assume you do not mean the swords?"

She clung to him more tightly and made a peculiar noise—half laugh, half sob. "The swords are what I fear the least."

"Fate brought us to the same place at the same time. We will figure it out together, Elizabeth. Somehow or other, we will—we must." They remained locked in their embrace for several minutes. "Maybe we should start the lesson," he said gently. "It will distract us—possibly even dissipate the gloom we brought with us today."

Elizabeth nodded and moved away from him, picking up one of the rapiers lying on a small end table. "My goodness! I never expected them to weigh so much!" She playfully swished it through the air. "What am I supposed to say? *En garde*?"

Darcy chuckled. "Most swords weigh between 2 and 3 stone." He picked up the matching rapier. "Let us try some basic thrusts and parries. Then I will show you a few different attacks and defenses."

He set her in the proper position, moving behind her to adjust her feet and shoulders. Each adjustment led to a kiss on the back of her neck or behind her ear. On the fifth such adjustment, she turned her head quickly and caught him full on the mouth. Then she said softly, "Thank you, Fitzwilliam," her lips lingering below his.

"Kissing you, Vixen, is payment in full for anything I gave you." His raspy voice betrayed his rising hunger for her.

"You see me when others do not. They see only the outside—the façade I give the world; you look beyond that." Elizabeth brushed her lips across his again. "I never *lived* until the past few days."

"And you, Vixen, see me as no other can. You looked beyond your first impression. You allow me to laugh, and you have allowed me freedom from my deepest secret. It is good to be Fitzwilliam, not Mr. Darcy of Pemberley."

"You avoid the lesson, Fitzwilliam." Elizabeth spun out of his embrace. "*En garde!*"

"You win, Minx." He smiled at her as he lifted his sword in a salute. "Let us try a *prise de fer.* Do not forget to keep your right foot at a quarter angle....Watch my shoulder; does it tilt or drop? That will signal what I plan as part of my attack...Keep your eyes on my face, but see my body's position as part of your preparation...Now, observe what I do and see if you can mimic it." Darcy made the same move several times before she made a reasonable reproduction of the intricate form. Then he showed her how to counter the move. Starting in slow motion, he executed the form, giving her time to adjust to the weight of his sword striking hers. Each thrust became more powerful, allowing Elizabeth to feel the strike reverberate through her body.

"Let us try a combination—three basic thrusts and then the *prise de fer.* I want you to parry each of the thrusts and then fully block my attack. I will come at you quickly and with some force. I want you to think, but—more importantly—I want you to respond. Take your position, Elizabeth." He paused for a moment, and then he circled her. "*En garde!*"

Elizabeth was stunned by Darcy's lightning speed and accuracy. She could barely think, but she got her sword in position to have it slide off his before it flew from her hand. "Again," he demanded as she picked up her rapier. She had barely taken up her position before he thrust again. This time she held onto her handle, although Darcy's sword pulled up before he would have cut her. Breathless, she started to protest, but he simply walked back to his position and barked out the dreaded word, "Again." With an anger she did not know she possessed, Elizabeth dared him in her mind this time, and she responded with an expertise Darcy expected. When the crossed swords pushed against her, she fought back, shoving with all her might.

"Perfect," he whispered as she still struggled against his weight.

Realizing the fight had ended, Elizabeth released the tension in her shoulders and smiled up at him. "*Truly,* Fitzwilliam?"

"*Truly,* Elizabeth!" He smiled in response. "With a bit more practice, you could best some of the men at my club."

"This was exhilarating. I never felt such freedom. Please teach me one more before we leave today," she begged.

"I could never deny you, Miss Elizabeth, but we have not much time. We will not be able to practice it."

"I will practice it in my room. I will find a stick or broom handle or some such article. Oh, thank you, Fitzwilliam." She bubbled with excitement, her eyes dancing with delight.

Darcy enjoyed her enthusiasm; it made him feel alive. "You will like the sweeping motion of this one; it is called a *demi-volte.*" He showed her the move several times, again allowing her to imitate his movement. "I will show you the counterattack tomorrow," he said once she had the basics. "And now, we must leave. Hide the swords, my temptress. I will get the horses."

She did as he asked, wiping the swords with a polishing cloth before stowing them behind a chest in the corner. When she left the house by the back door, Darcy held the horses behind the garden. "Miss Elizabeth, you are flushed from the exercise."

"Maybe I am flushed for some other reason," she retorted, her chin lifted and her eyes sparkling.

Darcy stepped over to help her up to the horse. Before he lifted her, he restored two curls, which had come undone as they fought. "When you say something provocative, Vixen, I cannot guarantee I will continue to act in an honorable way." He hefted her with ease up to the horse's saddle.

"Fitzwilliam?" she said hoarsely.

He tightened the straps on the saddle, refusing to look at her. "Yes?"

"Do you enjoy flirting with me as much as I do with you?"

Darcy held back a burst of laughter. "Vixen, I do not know how I ever lived without it."

★ ★ ★

For the next two days, they continued with their secret meetings. Fencing lessons proceeded as before; Elizabeth's enthusiasm fascinated Darcy. They laughed; they played; they kissed. Meeting in the conservatory, they found an out-of-the-way bench, which observers could not see without entering the room. There, Darcy and Elizabeth spent time simply talking, enjoying the company and the exchange of ideas. He never found anyone as interesting as she was; Elizabeth never felt such acceptance from a man—never criticizing her beliefs, although he obviously did not always agree with her.

Darcy explained his plans for his estate; he shared his frustrations in raising Georgiana. Elizabeth spoke of her dreams of traveling, and she vented about the "silliness" of her mother and siblings, especially when it came to finding mates for all the Bennet sisters. They were friends; Darcy and Elizabeth had built a trust.

Their time alone became more noticeable to the others, although no one knew the true extent of their blossoming relationship. By silent agreement, around others, they still sniped at each other. Caroline Bingley, vexed by what she could not identify, undermined Elizabeth every chance she got; Elizabeth found Miss Bingley's jealousy amusing and amplified each situation by feigning an ignorance of rank and consequence. Darcy fought to keep a neutral countenance during each exchange.

One particular evening, Caroline's plan backfired. She hoped to demonstrate her superiority over Elizabeth Bennet by walking elegantly about the parlor. When Darcy took no notice, Caroline, in desperation, turned to Elizabeth and said, "Miss Eliza Bennet, let me persuade you to follow my example and take a turn about the room."

Caroline's declaration surprised Elizabeth, but seeing the chance to befuddle her hostess, she agreed to it. Miss Bingley succeeded no less in the real object of her civility; Mr. Darcy looked up. He was as much aware to the novelty of attention in that quarter as Elizabeth herself could be, and unconsciously closed his book. Watching Elizabeth Bennet side-by-side with Caroline Bingley would give him a chance to judge how he truly felt about *his Elizabeth*. Plus, how they reacted towards each other could allay gossip.

Having his attention at last, Caroline asked, "Will you not join us, Mr. Darcy?" He considered how Caroline might feel if he stood and took Elizabeth's hand and placed it on his arm to walk with her alone. Elizabeth must have understood his thoughts because she stifled a laugh.

He fought the urge to ridicule Miss Bingley's play. "You could but have two motives in choosing to walk about the room, and I would interfere with both."

Elizabeth saw his eyes flash with anticipation. *Poor Caroline Bingley,* she thought. *She would never understand this man!*

"Whatever could he mean, Miss Eliza?"

Elizabeth took pity on the woman. "He means to be severe on us." She looked at Darcy and pursed her lips. "The surest way of disappointing him will be to ask nothing about it." But Elizabeth knew that Caroline could not let it go.

"Oh, please tell us, Mr. Darcy," Caroline pleaded.

Darcy leaned back in his chair. "I have not the smallest objection of explaining. You either choose this method of passing the evening because you are in each other's confidence and have secret affairs to discuss or because you are conscious that your figures appear to the greatest advantage in walking." Darcy's lips turned up in a smile. He paused for a dramatic effect. "If the first, I should be completely in your way; if the second, I can admire you better from here."

Caroline pretended shock, but Elizabeth expected as much. He loved to twist the spoken word. "How shall we punish him?" she called to Elizabeth.

"Nothing so easy," Elizabeth taunted. "We can all plague and punish one another. Tease him—laugh at him. Intimate as you are, you must know how it is to be done."

"Mr. Darcy is not to be laughed at," protested Caroline.

Elizabeth inquired lightly, "Then you think him to have no imperfections?" Darcy flinched. Had he made a mistake in trusting Elizabeth? She circled where he sat before she spoke again. He felt the intensity of her eyes on his body, and despite his current angst, he reacted to her scrutiny with an unexpected surge of desire. Elizabeth analyzed him from head to toe. "Can a man be so perfect?" she mused. "I wonder what secrets he keeps!"

"I made no such pretension. I have faults enough, but they are not, I hope, of understanding." Darcy commented dryly, attempting to distract himself from his lust. He wondered if she comprehended his double meaning. *Did Elizabeth truly understand him?* "My temper I dare not vouch for.—It is, I believe, too little yielding—certainly too little for the convenience of the world. I cannot forget the follies and vices of others so soon as I ought, nor their offenses against me. My temper would perhaps be called resentful. My good opinion once lost is lost for ever."

"I would not wish to be a recipient of your wrath, Mr. Darcy." Elizabeth thought she might like to be the recipient of something else, but not his temper. "There is, I believe, in every disposition a tendency to some particular evil, a natural defect, which not even the best education can overcome." She started away from him. "Do you not agree, Mr. Darcy?" She gazed at him intently over her shoulder.

"Agree, Miss Elizabeth?" He smiled seductively. "We rarely agree."

"Do you have a need to hate everyone?" she challenged, his superior attitude causing irritation.

Darcy shifted uncomfortably. *Hate?* All he wanted now was to touch her. "You, Miss Elizabeth, willfully misunderstand me."

"I will provide you the opportunity, Sir, to convince me otherwise," she taunted.

Before he could respond again, Caroline cut them off with a call to her sister for some music. Darcy, reluctantly, returned to his book.

Elizabeth took up her embroidery again. His words shook her sense of well-being. *Does Mr. Darcy really think that I misunderstand him?* Elizabeth felt she truly knew the man. There was a time when she thought he might be the man who had killed three young women in and about Derbyshire, but no more. He could be haughty; he could be infuriating; he could be aloof. But she knew the heart that beat in his chest was a loving one.

★ ★ ★

Elizabeth and Jane Bennet would return to Longbourn on the morrow. Darcy was loath to see his and Elizabeth's time together end.

For their last evening, they took up residence on a settee in the alcove of Charles's study. The household had been asleep for hours, but they chatted on. "Do you not see, Elizabeth, Wellesley must make a stand, or Napoleon will march right to King George's door."

"But the number of lives!" she protested. "So many men killed."

"The numbers would be great," he conceded.

They sat on either end of the furniture. Darcy stretched out his legs in front of him. Elizabeth, on the other hand, draped her legs over his lap, and he lightly massaged the arch of her foot. An outsider might think them to be an example of perfect marital harmony. After a long silence, he spoke the words that neither of them wanted to say: "You return to Longbourn tomorrow?"

"Jane is well, and we cannot intrude on Mr. Bingley's kindness any longer." Impulsively, she drew up her legs, tucking them under her and sitting up straighter, symbolically withdrawing from his touch. "We leave after services tomorrow."

Darcy sat up also, straightening his waistcoat and jacket. "I see," he mumbled.

"We knew it had to end." The silence roared in her ears.

Darcy removed imaginary lint from his sleeve. "Of course. It was expected."

Before they could say anything else, they heard someone in the hall. Elizabeth scrambled to her feet and plastered herself to the wall so no one would see her. Darcy stepped forward into the room and into the light. "Miss—Miss Bingley!" he stammered.

"Mr. Darcy!" she gasped. "I did not expect to find you here. I came down for a book, but saw the reflection of the candle and came to investigate."

Darcy knew that she lied. First, Caroline Bingley never read unless someone made her; and, second, she could not see the reflected single candle under the closed door. However, he would not let her find Elizabeth here. "I hoped Charles had some of that excellent brandy we shared earlier." He held up the glass he had left on the table to indicate the truth of his words. "As you can see, I found it; but now it is late. Why do you not let me show you back to your room, Miss Bingley?"

"We could sit and talk for awhile." Caroline started for a chair. Out of the corner of his eye, Darcy saw Elizabeth cling closer to the wall, trying to become invisible.

He sprang forward and caught her arm, forcibly turning Caroline as he spoke. "Miss Bingley, you know that is not possible. It is too forward even for intimate friends, such as you and me, to spend time alone, and my breeding will not allow a lady to remain unescorted. I have the candle"—he reached for the one in her hand—"and I insist you let me see you upstairs." He hustled her towards the door. Caroline nearly tripped, but he supported her.

"Thank you, Mr. Darcy, you are most kind," she said, simpering.

"Think nothing of it, Miss Bingley."

Darcy hated to leave Elizabeth to find her own way to her room; he took great pleasure in kissing her good night. Her soft lips left a trail of fire over his; such thoughts brought a moan to his lips, but he stifled it. Leading Miss Bingley to her door, he bid her a pleasant night before heading for his own room. He could not turn around. Caroline Bingley would smudge Elizabeth's reputation if she saw them together.

Elizabeth waited a quarter hour before she made her way to the servants' staircase. She and Darcy normally returned to their rooms via the servants' narrow stairway. He took Miss Bingley up the main staircase, some distance away from the stairs Elizabeth now climbed. She admired his sense of honor—the way he protected her. Elizabeth hoped they might continue to meet at the manor house as they planned, but they would have to be careful. It would not be as easy as the past few days. Slipping quietly into her room, she prepared for sleep. Finally, after brushing her hair and donning her gown, she got into bed. "I will miss these times together," she whispered, just to hear the words said out loud. Then she blew out the candle and slid down under the covers.

Darcy paced his room. Despising the way he left Elizabeth, he could think of nothing but *her.* "I wonder," he said, running his fingers through his hair as if to clear his mind. He knew he could do it, but Darcy never tapped into his "powers," those he inherited along with the curse. He could suspend time. No one would know he was there; he could transport himself to Elizabeth's room without physically leaving the one he was in. Yet should he dare? *Would she welcome me?* Without dwelling any longer on the possibilities, Darcy cleared his mind and forced all his energies into moving through the hallways unseen. Like a vortex sucking in time and space, his mind projected a conjuration, beguiling those who slept in each of the rooms he mentally touched.

Silently, he entered where Elizabeth slept. He crept slowly to the bed's edge—moving without sound. She was so innocently beautiful; his heart ached with a hunger he could never expect to fill. Lightly, Darcy traced the outline of her jaw—the chin, which she loved to raise in defiance. Enchanted by the moonlight streaming across her countenance, he bent to kiss her cheek.

His breath tickled Elizabeth's skin, and she brushed at the touch of his lips, as if they were a butterfly's wings flitting across her flesh. Darcy fought back a chuckle; she slept so soundly. Instead of touching her again, he pulled up a chair next to the bed and sat, watching her. He took great pleasure in watching Elizabeth sleep—the evenness of her breathing eased the anxiety he felt since leaving her in the study.

Her subconscious knew he was there; Elizabeth dreamed of him—dreamed of Darcy's eyes on her. The image made her smile. What she would not give to open her eyes and find him in the room! Slits of fractured light brought her forward to meet wakefulness, although she fought to remain asleep and glory in his gaze. Yet something unknown called to her, and Elizabeth's eyes fluttered open. Pale blue eyes, so clear they were nearly transparent, met her gaze. "Fitzwilliam," she muttered and stretched out a hand to the apparition.

When Darcy clasped her hand in his, the realization of what he did—where he was—shot through Elizabeth, and she bolted upright. "Mr. Darcy!" she gasped, "What are you doing here—in my room?"

Darcy smiled—she had not screamed out—not that it would matter after his enchantment. "Watching you sleep, Vixen."

She clasped the sheet to her chest in an attempt at modesty, not remembering he had seen her in her nightgown previously, but Darcy did not protest. Elizabeth pushed her hair from her eyes. "How did you get in here? I locked the door!"

"Can you comprehend I possess powers we have not discussed?" He dropped to his knees beside the bed and eased her back onto the pillow. "I did not come to seduce you, my temptress. But I did not want our night to end with my escorting Caroline Bingley to her room."

Elizabeth's shoulders relaxed, but her eyes never left his. His icy blue ones searched hers as if he could read her innermost thoughts. "I dreamed you watched over me, and when I woke, there you were. Is that possible?"

"Is what possible, Vixen?" His fingertips circled the outline of her palm.

She whispered, "Such a connection?"

Darcy shook his head. "I cannot say—I do not know. I never used my powers before. But I could not leave you tonight of all nights."

"How do the powers work?" She slid to one side so he might sit on the edge of the bed.

"I know not how to speak of them. They remain latent—resting beneath the surface. Focusing my energies allows me to move through time, bending it to my will. No one will know I am here; they sleep in another time. I came through a split—a narrow opening—it is like falling into quicksand—the grains of time swirling about—moving, but standing still at the same time. If someone were to open your door right now, they would observe you asleep, because that is how you were when I entered your world. I have no other way to explain it. Think of it as a tear in time, one I slipped through."

Quickly putting together the facts, Elizabeth noted, "I suppose that is how Evil finds its victims."

"You have nothing to fear from me, Elizabeth. These powers might be how others trick their human sacrifices, but I never used them before tonight."

"I do not *fear* you, Fitzwilliam," she assured him. "I simply thought out loud. This is all so new to me; I did things in the past week I never considered doing before."

"I understand." Darcy touched her lips with his fingertips. Then he lowered his head to kiss her lightly. The darkness held a light—a brightness shining from each of them.

"Fitzwilliam, I do not want this to end." The words rushed from her like water breaking through a dam. "I want to continue to ride—to practice with the swords—to waltz—to spend time just talking."

He brushed his lips across hers. "Do not forget the kissing."

Elizabeth slid her arms around Darcy's neck, pulling him close. "No, let us not forget the kissing." Her words shot through him. He kissed her again, searching her mouth with his tongue.

When they broke apart, he started to pull away. "I must leave."

"*Must* you?" Her words hung in the air between them. They were together because they needed to be. It was as if they lived in another world—one parallel to this one, where only they existed.

"Would you allow me to hold you? To lie next to you? I will not take advantage; on my honor, I will not." He had taught himself not to hope for any true happiness; now, he feared Elizabeth might be his one disappointment.

They did not light a candle; the moonlight told the story. After a few uncomfortable moments, Elizabeth nodded her assent and threw back the covers on one side of the bed. Without conversation, he removed his boots before slipping in beside her. Darcy lay next to Elizabeth, one arm embracing her; Elizabeth's arm was on his chest, and her head nestled against his shoulder. He rested his chin on top of her head as he stroked the hair on the nape of her neck. "I will leave you with the light. Sleep; I will be here to protect you." He breathed in her fragrance and held his breath to keep it there. Happiness had claimed him.

Breathing in the smell of maleness and sandalwood, Elizabeth kissed his chest. Then she closed her eyes and let the feeling of rightness overcome her.

Darcy waited until he was sure that she slept, and then his own eyes drifted closed. How natural all this felt! She was like a beacon for his tortured soul. He wanted more of this—this sense of contentment. Walking away from Elizabeth Bennet might take more strength and more courage than he possessed. He knew himself to be obsessed with her, but an addiction was hard to fight, and Darcy was unsure he wanted to go to battle. Losing would have its benefits. Such thoughts carried him into the realm of sleep.

CHAPTER 5

When dawn broke, he no longer slept beside her. Several times during the night, Elizabeth woke to assure herself Darcy laid next to her in her narrow bed. Even though the warmth of him lingered on her body, she did not trust that she had slept in his arms throughout the night. *It was a dream—an exquisite dream, but a dream nonetheless.* She touched her lips; she could still feel the pressure of his mouth on hers. He hypnotized her with his charms—his desire to please her. Elizabeth Bennet was bewitched.

She saw him only briefly during the morning services; Darcy sat with the Bingleys on a pew in the front of the church, while she and Jane joined their family on the other side of the aisle. By leaning forward, she could see his profile. He sat with his eyes downcast throughout the sermon on Samson killing the honey-filled lion and then vanquishing the Philistines.

Elizabeth wondered how Darcy could sit in a church—could walk about during the day. Every tale she knew of werewolves and vampires and zombies rushed through her head. Were not vampires supposed to sleep in a coffin during the day? Were they not supposed to shun the daylight? Were they not supposed to subsist only on blood, eschewing food and water? Did the sight of the cross not make them flee? Yet Fitzwilliam Darcy, an avowed vampire, did none of these. He slept in a bed, walked in the sunlight, ate food—although it was true that he did avoid meat—and he sat before the cross in a church. Elizabeth could not justify these discrepancies.

When he took her hand to help her into the carriage, Elizabeth felt Darcy slip something into her palm. She clasped his note tightly, and without notice from anyone but Darcy, she slipped it into her reticule. He nodded silently to bid her farewell as she and Jane rode away from Netherfield. Elizabeth felt a sinking in the pit of her stomach; she had left a part of her behind.

Darcy fought the urge to chase after the carriage that transported her away from him. Last night was the best night of his life. He closed his eyes and felt her stretched out along the length of his body, their legs entangled, her hair mussed and falling across his arms. Desire shot straight to his groin, while frustration swam in his veins. *Why can I not have her? Why has Fate shown me such great unkindness?* Reluctantly, he followed the Bingleys into the house. Charles seemed to feel almost as destitute as he did, but Darcy could not share his misery, for no one could understand what he possessed with Elizabeth.

Finally, at home and alone in her room, Elizabeth reached for the reticule. The note rested on the bottom, and she withdrew it slowly from its recesses, savoring the moment. He had touched it; she brought it to her face and smelled it—traces of sandalwood—traces of *him*. A smile flitted across her lips. She unfolded the paper and gave it her full attention.

Vixen,
Will you come to the house tomorrow? I will be waiting, counting the moments.

D.

Elizabeth's heart jumped in her chest. *Yes.*

★ ★ ★

Elizabeth hurried up the pathway to the back of the manor house. Darcy watched her from the kitchen window, delighting in the sight of her. When she burst through the door, he caught her in his arms and pulled her full to him, burying his face against her hair, kissing her with all the hunger of a starving man—starving for her.

When he broke the embrace, she giggled. "You missed me, Sir?"

"I greet all my lady friends this way," he countered.

"I beg to differ, Mr. Darcy. I do not believe you kissed Miss Bingley in such a fashion." She pulled away and crossed the room.

Darcy chuckled behind her. "I will grant you that, Vixen. I never kiss Miss Bingley."

"And your other lady friends?" she said tauntingly.

He confessed, "Any there might have been are long ago forgotten. There is only you."

Elizabeth smiled. "The perfect answer, Mr. Darcy." Then she took his hand and led him towards the hall. "I need more practice."

"I never saw a woman who loved to fight as much as you." He laughingly followed her from the room. The practice rapiers lay on a nearby table. She picked up the nearest one and bent the steel, testing it. He picked up the other one and made a few practice forays. "Are you ready, my Lady?" He made an exaggerated bow in her direction.

"I am a willing vessel in your hands, Mr. Darcy. Teach me what I need to know," she nearly purred.

"Oh, Vixen," he moaned. "You should never say such words to a man who looks on a woman as I do you."

She walked towards him, sashaying her hips, and cupped his cheek in her palm. Darcy turned his head to kiss the inside of her hand. Then she rose on her tiptoes to kiss him briefly. "You, Fitzwilliam, see a woman no one else does. Now, Sir, teach me my next move."

He sighed deeply with resignation. "First, we will practice the *demi-volte*. Have you tried it on your own?" Elizabeth nodded and he led her to the center of the room, where Elizabeth practiced what she had seen him do. They stood side by side, almost as if in a dance—stepping and sweeping the sword through the air while turning. "Now, let us try opposite each other. I will come at you; I want you to block what I bring. Keep your sword horizontal, not vertical." He executed the move in slow motion, giving her time to adjust, but she needed no pampering. *Elizabeth Bennet, were she a man, could take her toll on a dueling field.* "Excellent," he declared after the fourth attempt.

"A new move, please," she begged excitedly. "I love this; it is such freedom!"

"Whatever you wish, Vixen." Darcy stepped to the side again. Raising his right hand above his head, he arched the sword in a sweeping loop, turning it under and lunging forward. "This is called an *envelopment*. Follow me." He stayed next to her and repeated the move several times before she copied it exactly; then he took a place in front of her, switching the sword to his left hand, so he could mirror her movement."

"You can use both hands equally well," she mused in surprise. "That *is* unusual."

"Yet one more thing about me that makes me different from other men," he grumbled.

Elizabeth laughed. "It is a mark of distinction, Sir."

Darcy laughed along with her. "Let me see you complete the fence." He took up a position along the wall to allow her room to execute the form. Elizabeth moved with perfect symmetry, using her free arm for balance, looking as if she partnered the sword in some intricate dance step.

"What do you find so amusing, Mr. Darcy?" Her words brought him out of his trance.

He shook his head. "Nothing, Vixen." He turned to lay his sword on the table. "You learn quickly. Soon, my services will be unneeded."

"Your services—not yourself."

Darcy touched her cheek with his fingertips. "I brought a light meal. Will you join me?" He reached for the basket along the wall.

Elizabeth nodded, took the blanket he offered, and spread it on the floor. She laid the rapier to the side before helping him remove the food from the basket. "Cheese, hard bread, fruit, wine, and apple tarts. It is a picnic in November. How adventurous!"

"You mean *scandalous*." He sat on the blanket and pulled her in front of him, spooning her body with his, allowing his arm to drape over her shoulder. Elizabeth broke off some of the bread and cheese, putting it on a plate they could share. Then she turned and fed him some of it, enticingly kissing his cheek. He licked her fingertips, sucking them into his mouth. The rest of the world seemed to drop away when they were together. "Would your sister, Georgiana, like me?" she asked as she snuggled into his chest.

"Georgiana would like anyone with whom I choose to spend my time; she trusts my judgment. But I believe she would like you independent of my feelings. I wish she had a bit more of your spirit; she is an intelligent girl, yet she lacks sensibility—too naïve—too trusting."

"Then you think I am jaded?" she asked mockingly.

He kissed the nape of Elizabeth's neck and behind her ear, feeling the beat of her heart at the base of her neck. "Do not put words in my mouth, my Lady."

Since they had discovered their need for each other, Darcy had gave given her a world she would never know again. She turned to face him. "Another memorable day."

"It is not over, Elizabeth." He leaned her back onto the blanket, looming over her. "I cannot send you home without kissing your lips properly." He held himself tantalizingly above her, his words a whisper on her cheek. Then he lowered his whole body over hers, pressing his mouth to her own. His tongue parted her lips, and Darcy was lost to the moment. His hands caressed her shoulders, and he rolled with her, positioning her to lie on top of him. Her heat burned his very soul. His hands moved up and down her back. The blood coursed through him—pounding into his senses. Finally, she broke the kiss, burying her head into the side of his neck. Breathing heavily, Darcy rasped her name, "*Elizabeth!*"

"We cannot let this happen, Fitzwilliam." She spoke the words while remaining wrapped in his embrace.

Darcy could feel his heart thunder in his chest. He turned to tuck a loose curl behind her ear. "It will not. You must forgive me, Elizabeth. For a moment, I allowed myself to believe this to be real." He spoke to the ceiling, unable to turn his head and see the disapproval on her face.

Although she knew they must stop, part of her wanted Darcy to take her. Elizabeth remained with him, not moving, and then, reluctantly, she rolled away from him.

Ahh! She screamed out in pain, cupping the palm of one hand in the other. Blood flowed from a cut across her palm, the result of her hand coming down on the edge of the rapier she had foolishly laid on the floor.

Although not bleeding profusely, the wound lay open and fresh. Darcy scrambled to his knees, and without thinking, he pulled her hand to his mouth and sucked the blood away. It was an innocent action. Yet the moment the blood touched his lips, something inside him changed. He shuddered visibly, and his eyes closed, as if savoring a fine wine. He sucked again, and his eyes glazed over, an icy coldness, the color of snow crystals floating through the air.

Elizabeth watched in horror. "Fitzwilliam!" she cried out in fear, trying to dislodge her hand from his mouth, but he held her fast, his tongue washing over the gap in her skin. "Fitzwilliam!" she demanded, pulling harder, but he kept hold of her. Finally, in desperation, she grabbed the sword and swung the butt of the handle against his face, cutting a gash into his cheek.

Darcy fell back, his fingers releasing her. Elizabeth sprang to her feet, the sword grasped tightly in her hand. Anger filled her, but the remorse she saw spreading across his face made her want to comfort him all the same.

Darcy covered his eyes and face with his forearm. A moan of disgust burst from his lips. He never looked at her, afraid to witness the disdain in her eyes. "Now," he said, his lips trembling, "now, you see the animal I am." The hollowness in his voice was nearly as frightening as his actions. "I can never live a normal life." He lowered his arm to his side. He still lay flat on his back while she remained poised with the sword above him. "Put the sword away, Elizabeth, and tend to your wound. I will injure you no more." He licked his lips, bringing moisture back to them, but still tasting her lifeline there, making her a part of him. "Leave, Elizabeth. We must not meet again; it is too dangerous."

Tears ran down her cheeks. "I will *not* leave you, Fitzwilliam," she whispered as she knelt beside him.

Unable to trust himself any longer, Darcy grabbed her wrist, pulling them both to their feet. "Bloody hell, Elizabeth! I cannot do this! I will kill myself rather than hurt you!" He grabbed her cloak and violently shoved it around her shoulders. "Do not return." He placed his handkerchief into the palm of her hand to stop the bleeding. Then he carried her to the back door. "It ends today; I cannot have the life we created here! Fate dealt me a different hand, and I must play *those* cards." Bitterness laced his words.

Elizabeth fought him every step of the way, beating her hands forcefully against his chest. "No!" she screamed repeatedly, but when he tugged the door open with one hand and pushed her out the entrance with the other, she quit fighting. Her sudden stillness forced him to react, and Darcy froze. No trace of his temptress remained. Instead, she stood there miserably, with tears dangling from her thick lashes. They stood in a terrible tableau, muscles flexed for action. Her words were barely audible, but he heard them nonetheless. "I do not want to leave you, Fitzwilliam. You need me—whether you like it or not—you need me."

"I *need* no one!" his voice boomed in defiance.

Elizabeth shook her head. "That is where you are wrong, Mr. Darcy. You *never* needed anyone, and this moment—this *very moment*—is where it has gotten you. You may deceive yourself; but you cannot deceive me." With that, she stormed off down the path.

"Damn!" She heard the curse as she strode away from him, followed closely by the dramatic slamming of the manor house door. Despite the histrionics of the last few minutes, she smiled with the knowledge that Fitzwilliam Darcy had no idea what he just *started*—with a fatalistic certainty, she knew this was not the end.

★ ★ ★

"Elizabeth, where have you been?" Jane called out as Elizabeth came through the door. Elizabeth hid Darcy's handkerchief in her pocket before she entered the house.

"Nowhere in particular," she assured her family. "I went for a walk. I slipped and fell on a sharp stone and cut my hand. It took me a few minutes to stop the bleeding."

Mr. Bennet looked up in concern. "You staunched the wound, Child?"

Elizabeth nodded to reassure him. "I cleaned it as best I could, but if you will excuse me, I will go to my room and wash it thoroughly."

She had started away when her mother added, "You have a letter from your Aunt Gardiner on the table by the door."

"Thank you, Mama. I will return shortly." She grabbed the letter and bounded up the stairs.

Tossing both her cloak and the letter on the bed, Elizabeth poured water into a nearby bowl. Taking the soap from the tray, she began to wash the wound completely. Although the blood had stopped long ago, the feel of his mouth remained. Her eyes inspected the opening, looking for evidence of his perversion, but she saw none—only the cut. She took the handkerchief from her pocket and placed it in the soapy water to soak.

Returning to the bed, Elizabeth picked up the letter, breaking the wax seal with her finger. A page of close handwriting greeted her. The beginning traditionally shared the latest on the antics of her cousins. Elizabeth adored the children; secretly, she wanted a large brood of her own. She had lied to Darcy on that matter. But her aunt did not discuss her children in this letter. The crux of the letter became immediately apparent:

> *Lizzy, exercise the* utmost care *regarding Mr. Darcy. He is a powerful man and used to having his own way. There are things I never told you about Vivian's murder; now that you have thrown yourself into Mr. Darcy's path, I must share it all with you.*
>
> *As you are well aware, Vivian was not his only victim. Two others died before her; all three of them worked on the estate. I begged Vivian to give up her position, but her family needed the money, and the Darcys pay well. I suppose it is to keep their secrets. Vivian claimed she could make twice as much at Pemberley as she could anyplace else in Lambton.*

I was with her father when he and the others found Vivian's body. It was a sight I will never forget. She lay in a ditch close to a stream on the estate. A gash the size of my hand opened her neck; the muscles and the tendons holding up her head were ripped to shreds, and her head lolled to the side. The magistrate ruled that a wild dog or a wolf had torn away the neck, but all of us who found her knew otherwise. Her skin was dry and withered. Every ounce of blood in her body was drained. No animal has this power.

Oh, Lizzy, the other girls were reportedly the same way. I spoke to Margaret O'Donnell's sister. She told me poor Maggie was so mutilated they could not find enough of her to bury her properly. It drove her poor mother to madness. The woman roams the countryside, searching for the missing pieces of her daughter.

Two years ago, I saw Mr. Darcy in the warehouse district. I was there to meet your uncle for supper. The next morning, the papers were filled with the report of a mysterious murder of a female factory worker in that area. Three days later, the report of another murder appeared; a third one came within the week.

Do you not see, Elizabeth, this is no coincidence? Wherever Mr. Darcy is, women turn up dead—*their bodies torn and mangled and drained of blood, like something—or someone—sucked it from them.*

There is an evil in the Darcy family. I beg you, avoid the man. I could *not bear to lose you.*

M. G.

Elizabeth reread the letter twice before setting it aside. Hands shaking, she returned to the task of cleaning the handkerchief. It was real, and it belonged to Darcy, the Darcy she spent the past week talking to, riding with, and kissing. It did not belong to the Mr. Darcy her Aunt Meredith described. *That man does not exist.*

Yet as she scrubbed the blood from the cloth, she felt his mouth on her wound—felt his teeth touching her neck. A shiver ran down her spine. Could he have told her the truth? Could he be a vampire?

What if he did kill those women? Yet it did not make sense. She took the cloth from the water and hung it close to the fire to dry. She traced the embroidered *FD* with her fingertip. "Fitzwilliam," she whispered. His name brought her comfort, not repulsion. Now, she would have to see him again, whether he wanted her as part of his life or not; she could not walk away from the mystery.

★ ★ ★

For two days, Elizabeth heard nothing of and nothing from Mr. Darcy. She fretted and fussed and fumed about Longbourn, much to the annoyance of her family, although none of them knew why she felt out of sorts.

"I know just what you need," Lydia asserted, barging into her bedroom. "Mr. Denny is on his way, and he is bringing a friend—a *handsome* friend."

"Oh, Lydia, tell me you did not do this," Elizabeth protested.

"Too late." Lydia twirled around the room. "They just came into the garden. Arrange your hair, Lizzy, and come downstairs. Jane, Kitty, and Mary are already in the drawing room."

Elizabeth went to the mirror to check her looks. "What makes you think a man can solve what ails me, Lyddie?" However, as she observed her reflection, she could think of one man in particular who could remove her anxiety with just a sideways glance.

"Meeting new gentlemen *always* cheers me up," her youngest sister declared, as if it were a given fact for everyone.

"You are our mother's child," Elizabeth remarked. "You go on down, dear, with the others, and I will follow momentarily."

Left alone, Elizabeth fished out Darcy's handkerchief from a dresser drawer; she placed it in her pocket, where she might touch it. When Elizabeth entered the room, Mr. Denny addressed her directly and entreated permission to introduce his friend, Mr. Wickham, who returned with him the day before from town, and he was happy to say accepted a commission in the corps. This was exactly as it should be; for the young man wanted only regimentals to make him completely charming. His appearance was greatly in his favor; he had all the best part of beauty, a fine countenance, a good figure, and very pleasing address. His best characteristic, Elizabeth quickly noted, was his steel grey eyes. She thought that she had never saw seen any like them.

"From where do you hail, Mr. Wickham?" she asked out of politeness.

Wickham sat beside her on one of the drawing room settees. "Originally, I am from Scotland, Miss Elizabeth, but more recently I lived in Bakewell, as well as in London. I returned eight months ago from a short stay in Kent."

"Bakewell? In Derbyshire?" she demanded, latching onto the words.

Wickham shifted his weight, as if he would like to change the topic or quit the room. "You know Derbyshire, Miss Elizabeth?"

"Our aunt, Sir, comes from Lambton." Taking real note of the man at last, somehow she felt she sat next to evil. His smile was too perfect—his manners were too perfect—*he* was too perfect.

Wickham's voice changed tenor; suspicion appeared at once. "Outside Pemberley? Do you know the estate?"

"Only by reputation."

Before the conversation could go further, Lydia and Kitty interrupted. "We wish to walk to Meryton; Aunt Philips invited us all to tea. You will come, too, will you not, Mr. Wickham?" Lydia asked flirtatiously.

"I will happily see you to town, Miss Lydia." He stood and made a quick bow to her. "I am most anxious to hear of your luck with lottery tickets. I understand from Mr. Denny that you win quite often. Do you have a method you employ?" He took her hand and placed it on his arm as he led Lydia to the entrance hallway.

Needing the exercise and Jane's company, Elizabeth trailed along—despite her misgivings about the fine-looking stranger. Of late, Jane shared secrets about Mr. Bingley with her; Jane told her everything he had said to her while she recuperated at his house. Elizabeth would like to reciprocate and tell Jane of Mr. Darcy, but she could not. It was a secret not even Jane would understand.

Upon reaching the village, they turned towards their aunt's house. Luckily, Aunt Philips met them coming from the shops. Introductions were made once again. The introduction was followed upon Mr. Wickham's side by a happy readiness of conversation—a readiness at the same time perfectly correct and unassuming; and the whole party were still standing and talking together very agreeably, when the sound of horses drew their notice, and Darcy and Bingley were seen riding down the street. Elizabeth's heart leaped.

On distinguishing the ladies of the group, the two gentlemen came directly forward then and began the usual civilities. Bingley was the principal spokesman, and Miss Bennet the principal object.

"Miss Bennet," Bingley said as he tipped his hat to Jane, "I was just now on my way to Longbourn to inquire after your health."

"I am well, as you can see, Mr. Bingley." Jane blushed from his attention.

As the two openly flirted, Darcy and Elizabeth both fought the urge to fix their eyes on each other, and then Elizabeth noted his distress at the sight of finding Mr. Wickham a member of the Bennet party. Elizabeth, happening to see the countenance of both as they looked at each other, was all astonishment at the effect of the meeting. Both changed color: One looked white, the other red. Darcy's ice-blue eyes hardened in apparent hatred. Mr. Wickham, after a few moments, touched his hat—a salutation, which Darcy just deigned to return. What could be the meaning of it? Elizabeth's curiosity was piqued. It was impossible to imagine; it was impossible not to long to know.

In another minute Mr. Bingley, without seeming to notice what passed, took his leave and rode on with his friend. Mr. Denny and Mr. Wickham walked with the young ladies to the door of Mr. Philips's house and then made their bows, in spite of Lydia's pressing entreaties that they should come in.

Before the gentlemen could escape, Aunt Philips invited them all to dinner for the next evening. The younger girls readily agreed for the whole family, while the gentlemen agreed on their own behalf.

Elizabeth followed her sisters into the house, where she tried to enjoy their company and the tea, but her mind rode with a stranger across the rolling hills of Hertfordshire. Why had Darcy snubbed Mr. Wickham? Even in distress, his good breeding took over and Darcy would act the gentleman. It had something to do with Derbyshire, she surmised. Obviously, Darcy would not tell her; she would just have to ask Mr. Wickham for his story.

As he rode away, Darcy's anger boiled over. Trying to respond to Bingley's happiness at seeing Jane Bennet only complicated his feelings. Wickham was in town. Even worse, he was in *Elizabeth's* company. Had Wickham followed him here to Hertfordshire? Did he know how Darcy felt about Elizabeth—how lonely the past two days without her had been? He, Darcy, had to stay away from her, for if Wickham knew, he would target Elizabeth as revenge against himself. Wickham had tried with Georgiana, and now *his Elizabeth* was in danger from the same evil. Darcy had to figure out a way to protect her. Staying away from her completely seemed the only logical course of action, but he knew her. His absence would increase her inquisitiveness; she had observed his reaction to Wickham today, and she would not let it rest.

CHAPTER 6

The woman flirted with him brazenly, and Wickham allowed her to sit upon his lap. Her dark skin indicated that she was of Mediterranean descent. "You are beautiful, my pet." He bit down on her earlobe, harder than most men might, but the lady did not complain. Instead, she pulled his face to her breasts, allowing him to rub his lips, his nose, and his tongue along her cleavage. Wickham caressed her breast and then he whispered eagerly, "Where can we be alone?"

She giggled and wanted to be kissed, but he hated kissing any woman other than Ellender. Only Ellender fulfilled those needs he tried to bury deep within.

"Let me get my shawl."

"I will keep you warm," Wickham insisted.

The woman said playfully, "I expect you will, Love."

Within a few minutes they walked along a quiet country road. "Me house be just down here." She gestured to a small cottage.

Wickham pulled her to him. "I do not believe I can wait that long." He slipped the bodice down, exposing one of her breasts.

"You be an anxious one, Love," she reprimanded him, but she did not withdraw from his aggressive touch.

Wickham shoved her chin up, so that she might look into his eyes. He held her there with his grasp and with his stare. "Let me show you how anxious," he growled. He lowered his head and sank his teeth into the tender flesh of her neck. Tasting the blood, he closed his jaw, and with the strength of a wolf, he bit harder and ripped away the flesh. The woman did not scream as he took her; instead, she lolled back into arms. He licked and sucked and tore away more of her. The fear in her eyes remained as her body went rigid. Now, he felt the erection, and he laid her on the ground to ravish her completely.

Determined to have her answer, Elizabeth set out for Meryton as early as propriety would allow. If necessary, she would find Mr. Wickham with the rest of the militia. Luckily, the man lazily sauntered down the main street of the village. She crossed the street at an angle, with the purpose of seeming to accidentally meet with him. She positioned herself as if interested in a fine bonnet displayed in the window of a mercantile. Waiting, her heartbeats anxious, Elizabeth counted to ten before he stepped up beside her.

"The color would do nothing for your beautiful hair, Miss Elizabeth." He spoke close to her ear—intimately close.

Elizabeth did not turn; they could behold each other's reflection in the store's window, and although hers was crystal clear, even showing the wrinkles in her sleeves, Mr. Wickham's was a blur of color. A shiver ran down her spine, but her words hid her fear. "I thought it to be a gift." With deliberate innocence, she turned to face him. "Good day to you, Mr. Wickham. I see you have your lieutenancy." His regimentals added to his perfection. Her mouth went dry as his rapier-sharp gaze narrowed on her.

"I am a lowly foot soldier, Miss Elizabeth." He made an exaggerated bow.

Forcing herself not to look directly into his eyes, Elizabeth feigned delight. Cool and calm came her words: "I am pleased to know Meryton is safer than it was this time yesterday." Setting her mind to her task, she reached for Wickham's arm. "And now, Mr. Wickham, I might implore you to escort me safely to my Aunt Philips's house."

"My true pleasure, Miss Elizabeth."

He reached for her hand to place it on his proffered arm when Elizabeth took note of a birthmark or tattoo on the back of his hand. When Wickham saw her staring at it, he withdrew his free hand and turned her towards her aunt's house, but Elizabeth was aware of how he stiffened with the action. "It is a burn," he offered before she could ask. "My father was a strict disciplinarian." Wickham lowered his voice. "I made a poor choice on that particular occasion, and my father thought it best that I had something by which to remember my folly."

It was all the explanation he presented, and no other avenues of conversation could be had with pursuing it, so Elizabeth let it drop with simply a nod of her head. Instead, they walked slowly, pausing often to peer into the nearest window. At last she asked, "Do you suppose the militia will be long in Meryton, Mr. Wickham?"

"I hope not." He let his smile fade. "My hopes are to see action on a battlefield." His expression was unreadable.

"I do not know many men who wish for battles."

Eyes—hard and bleak—traced the outline of her face. "Some may call it irrational, but I *live* for the action—the smoke—even the *deaths*."

Elizabeth hated the war—the useless loss of life. She did not answer. How could she? Marshaling any arguments against the determined curve of his lips seemed fruitless. "May I change the topic, Mr. Wickham?"

"Of course, Miss Elizabeth. Forgive me for speaking so passionately on such an indelicate subject."

"Speak to me of your time in Bakewell. I wish to know more of the area in which my Aunt Gardiner resides. She is so dear to me; anything you could tell me would bring me pleasure."

"I suppose you realize, Miss Elizabeth, that the terrain in Derbyshire is more rugged—more intense—the winters are colder and the summers milder; therefore, the vegetation is thicker. I am not one to look at things for their natural beauty, but I do enjoy the wildness of the Peak District. It reminds me of Scotland. Next to Northumberland, it is the most pleasing of areas, although the population is growing steadily and taking away the privacy we all cherish."

"Ah, yes," she said with deep regret in her tone, "my aunt speaks as such. She is in London now, but one hears the wistfulness in her voice when she speaks of *home*."

"Indeed."

Elizabeth paused, as if considering her next question. "I could not help but notice, Mr. Wickham, you and Mr. Darcy seemed acquainted, although you did not speak. I thought it quite unusual."

His face paled slightly, and he tapped the fingers of his free hand impatiently against his thigh. "I am vaguely familiar with the younger Mr. Darcy, Miss Elizabeth. My father served as his father's steward for several years. Old Mr. Darcy looked upon me as a second son at one time. Of course, that was before the current Master of Pemberley took over. Fitzwilliam Darcy is a cruel man, I am sorry to say, Miss Elizabeth."

Elizabeth knew that she would have to lie convincingly to keep Wickham talking, but Darcy ruled her heart, and she worried she would betray her true feelings. "He was very cold and haughty to everyone upon his arrival in Hertfordshire. Many tolerate him only because of his wealth and because Mr. Bingley is his associate." She did not lie; many did indeed see Darcy as such.

Wickham considered what she said for a moment, watching her, before he added, "I once saw him whip a man simply for dropping a tea service. He is a man of wealth and above the law, and Darcy lets nothing stand in his way. If he wants land, he takes it. If he wants a woman, she is his. However, again, I speak too explicitly, and I beg your forgiveness, Miss Elizabeth; but I have no respect for Pemberley's Mr. Darcy."

"My!" she pretended to quail at his anger. "I certainly did not mean to upset you, Mr. Wickham!" Wickham's seductive insolence and intense passion were wildly arousing. A woman could easily feel empathy and feel as incensed as he at hearing his words, but Elizabeth Bennet knew Fitzwilliam Darcy. "Yet I agree." She had set her trap. If he lied to her, she would return the favor. "Mr. Darcy can be most presumptuous."

"We will speak no more of the man, Miss Elizabeth." Wickham took her hand and brought it to his lips. "I am not a reasonable being when I think of his offenses. Let us finish our walk."

"Of course, Mr. Wickham."

★ ★ ★

Elizabeth hurried along the road to Longbourn. She had stayed at her Aunt Philips's only as long as required without raising questions. Now she strode along the familiar path. *How many times have I walked these lanes in my twenty years? Surely, at least three times per week for the past six years, and how many times before that as part of family excursions?* The sun shone brightly, and it made her feel lighter, even after her emotionally charged discussion with Mr. Wickham. She nearly skipped at times, glad to have long since learned to follow the road of least resistance. She marveled at her own cleverness.

And then she saw it—a dark shadow lingering in a copse of trees. *Is it a wild dog? A wolf? A man?* Elizabeth could not tell, and she did not want to know. Something told her to beware—primitive impulses of survival set the hairs on the back of her neck on end. The shadow disappeared, but to be sure, Elizabeth cautiously moved to the side of the road, straddled the stile, and came down on the other side of the hedgerow, where she might hide if necessary.

She moved slowly and as silently as possible, given the ground cover. She gulped for air, suddenly realizing that she had held her breath for many long moments. Elizabeth never let her eyes leave the cluster of trees. *Is something there?* A cloud covered the early winter sun, and suddenly the air chilled with the unknown. Then, pure chaos broke out. A flock of birds exploded from the woods, sending screams of distress into the shadowy day. A figure burst from the trees, headed straight towards her. Although she did not wait to see it clearly, Elizabeth knew that whatever it was, it did not run, but rather glided across the field in a swirling, twisting motion that made her nauseous to observe.

Elizabeth bolted—raced—hair falling from her bonnet—cloak flying like wings behind her. She fought to loosen it, finally pulling the clasp from her neck and letting it fall behind her. She hiked up her skirts and ran as if her life depended on it. She did not look back—whatever it was, was still there; she felt it. A wind whispered, *I am coming for you*. A vicious growl seemed to reverberate in her ears.

She ran with all her strength, jumping over stumps and branches, racing against the cruel wind—and then her foot caught on a tree stump and she flew through the air. Elizabeth hit the ground with full force. The air was knocked from her lungs, and her face was shoved into the hard soil. She struggled to get up, ready to run again; yet her foot remained trapped in muck. She pulled frantically, trying not to lose her slipper, when suddenly what she thought to be tangled weeds and clumps of fur from a dead animal rolled away from her, and the shriveled face of a brown-skinned girl stared blankly up at her. Elizabeth heard someone scream hysterically as she pushed herself away from the figure, scrambling backwards on her hands, trying to put distance between her and the brown-skinned woman. The blood-curdling scream continued, and then she realized that it came from her.

Darcy and Bingley rode across the outskirts of Bingley's property. The scattering of the birds attracted their notice, but it was the sound of the whirlwind Darcy insisted they chase. He knew the sound intimately—it was George Wickham's calling card—but to hear it in the daylight shook him. Then, in the distance, he saw her—Elizabeth running over the crest of the hill.

Darcy could barely breathe, but he dug his heels into the flanks of the horse and rode after her with all his might. Elizabeth was no longer in sight, but he knew the direction she ran. Just as he hit the swell of the hill, her scream brought him to a complete halt; he reined in the horse and bounded towards the sound.

She screamed hysterically, and each note of the lament pierced his heart. *Could Wickham have harmed her?* Anger coursed through him. He should never have left her yesterday. *Some way, somehow, he must kill Wickham!*

Then he saw her crawling—crawling away—with horror on her face. Before the horse stopped, Darcy was on the ground, running to where she was. When he reached her, Elizabeth fought him at first, but Darcy caught her in his embrace, holding her to him and cooing endearments into her ear. He heard Bingley ride up, but he did not turn around, although he stood and scooped Elizabeth into his arms, cradling her to him.

"Darcy, is she well?" Bingley implored him.

All he did was shake his head as he turned towards his friend. Her arms clung to Darcy's neck. "Elizabeth? I have you; it is all right," he whispered next to her ear. He wanted to kiss her, but Bingley stood too close.

"The—the *woman,*" she whimpered.

Darcy adjusted her in his hold. "What, Sweetling?" he murmured.

"The woman." Her voice held more strength, but she still did not look at anything but him. Elizabeth flung her arm out in the direction of the body.

Darcy followed her motion with his eyes, and then he realized her fear. Lying in a crevice where two hills met, lay what appeared to be the mangled body of a woman. Her face and neck showed the telltale signs of mutilation. "Elizabeth," he whispered, "may I put you down so I can see to the woman?"

"I am *afraid.*"

"I will not leave you," he assured her, "but I must see to the lady."

Elizabeth nodded, and he put her down gently under a tree. He cupped her chin with his palm. "I will be right back." Tears formed in her eyes, and her bottom lip trembled, but she sat quietly and waited for him.

Darcy and Bingley moved quickly to where the woman lay. "Do you know her?" he asked Bingley as they checked for a sign of life.

"I have never seen her." Bingley was pale with terror. "My God, Darcy, what kind of animal creates such wounds?"

"None you have ever seen." A thud reverberated in his chest. "Bingley, I need to take Miss Elizabeth home. You must ride to Meryton and inform the constable and maybe even Colonel Forster. Please be careful."

"Certainly, Darcy. Tell Miss Elizabeth I will call once everything is settled." Bingley stood and headed to his horse, but Darcy stopped him with just a clearing of his throat.

Darcy looked back at Elizabeth. "Get Miss Elizabeth's cloak; it is at the top of the hill. Cover the body with that."

Bingley mounted and rode off in the direction of the black cloak.

Darcy hurried back to where Elizabeth sat. "Come, Sweetling." He pulled off his greatcoat and wrapped it around her as he helped her to her feet. He hid her in the security of his shoulder as he led her to where his horse nibbled on grass. "I will take you up with me."

He mounted the horse and then reached down for her hand, pulling her up into his lap. Settling her comfortably in his arms, he touched the horse's flanks with his heels and the animal set off at a brisk pace.

Once they crested the hill and headed towards Longbourn, Darcy leaned into her and kissed the side of Elizabeth's neck. "Can you tell me, my dear, what happened?"

Again, Elizabeth's eyes misted over and her lips trembled. "Do I have to?"

"The constable will ask, Elizabeth. What will we tell him?" Darcy knew her fear.

"I became frightened and I ran. There was nothing there, but all the same, *something* was there. Oh, Fitzwilliam, that woman's face!" She buried her head into his chest, covering her eyes with her hands.

Darcy kissed the side of her head and promised to protect her. "Bingley went for the authorities."

"You will stay when we get to Longbourn?" She seemed so vulnerable.

"If you wish." Darcy wanted to protect her—to keep Elizabeth safe forever. "My darling, I must ask, did you speak to George Wickham about me?"

Elizabeth looked up in surprise. "I knew you would not tell me, Fitzwilliam. I did not mean to go behind your back. I am so sorry. He told such lies about you; I could not understand why or how you two were connected. I saw the way you snubbed him yesterday." Her words rushed out in one long breath.

"It is all right, Sweetling. Later, you will tell me exactly what was said, so we can determine what to do next, but none of that is what really matters." Darcy kissed her upturned nose and tried to give her a smile of assurance. He tightened his grip about her. "What I need for you to understand, Elizabeth, is that Seorais is the Scottish name for George. Seorais Winchcombe of the story of Lord Thomas and Lady Ellender is George Wickham."

He heard her gasp and felt her shudder as the truth washed over her. "Fitzwilliam, *Fitzwilliam,* the woman…the woman was the *brown girl!*" Her arms searched his body, trying to find security.

"It was a warning, Elizabeth, to me, and now to you. The brown girl of the song simply had brown hair. Wickham chose this woman for symbolic purposes. I will explain it all in detail later—when we are alone—but I need for you to know, I managed to get to Georgiana in time to save her, although Wickham tried to seduce her at Ramsgate. He nearly killed us both in a house fire."

"He said he was in Kent of late." The truth of what Darcy said now made perfect sense.

He did not look at her as he spoke. It was impossible for him to break the aura of implied danger. "Elizabeth, Wickham tried to seduce Georgiana to take revenge on me—on the Darcy name. He has done so with each generation. I fear if he knows of us, you will become his target. It is best I stay away, best for you."

"No!" she demanded. "I cannot face this without you!"

"If I withdraw," he insisted, "you will not have to face any of this. I will take my evil with me."

Anger flared in her and, without thinking, Elizabeth struck his chest with her fist. "You are *not* evil and I will not hear you speak as such! Fitzwilliam, I will not *permit* it!"

By now, Longbourn loomed on the horizon. "We will talk it out later. For now, we will tell everyone a wild dog chased you. We cannot hide the death, but it will all be coincidental." Elizabeth nodded in agreement. "I will stay and help you until everything calms down, and I will return to you tonight; you will sleep in my arms for another night."

"Thank you, Fitzwilliam."

He stopped the horse far enough away that those in the house could not make out their forms. "I missed you," he said quietly.

"Of course, you did," came her retort. Elizabeth snaked her arms around his neck and tried to pretend nothing had changed. "Now, kiss me before I must face my family."

He considered shoving her away, but a heartbeat later, he groaned and pulled her to him. The kiss made time stand still; it was what he needed—what she needed. Otherwise, there was no sense left in the world.

Darcy had other concerns, which he did not want to deal with, but he would do so. As he rode into the entranceway to Longbourn, the other issues consumed his thoughts. He must get back to the woman's body and destroy it without anyone's knowledge.

"*Elizabeth!*" Mary called from the open doorway. Alerted by the housekeeper, Mrs. Hill, her family, all chattering at once, poured from the house.

"Mr. Darcy, what means this?" Mr. Bennet demanded.

"Miss Elizabeth met with an unfortunate accident of some consequence." Darcy's voice boomed over the clatter, and they all fell silent. "We will explain once we get her into the house."

Mr. Bennet reached for Elizabeth to help her down as Darcy lifted her from him. "Come, Lizzy," her father insisted as Jane and Kitty rushed forward to help her.

A few steps towards the door, Elizabeth stopped suddenly. "Papa," she called over her shoulder. "Have Mr. Darcy come in; he *saved* me today and we owe him our gratitude."

At her insistence, Mr. Bennet reached for the reins of his horse. "Come in, Mr. Darcy. Pray, come in."

Darcy dismounted and followed the others into the parlor. Bingley had called there before, but Darcy had not. Although comfortable, the furniture seemed worn and a bit frayed. But that was to be expected with five daughters. Elizabeth took up residence on a settee covered in a floral design. Before anyone could object, she looked up at him standing in the doorway and ordered, "Mr. Darcy, please join me; I will need your support in making my family understand what happened."

Again, silence and inquiry filled the air. "Of course, Miss Elizabeth, if it allays your fears."

"Lizzy, may I get you some tea?" Jane fussed with Elizabeth's hair. "My!" she gasped. "You have leaves entangled in your curls. Would you not wish to freshen up before we discuss why you are so disheveled?"

Elizabeth laughed and accepted the tea. "Possibly, Mr. Darcy would like some port, Papa."

Mr. Bennet did her bidding. The rest of the family huddled together; miraculously, no one spoke. They allowed Elizabeth to orchestrate the situation. Darcy wondered if she was always in charge; he could imagine her in the role. When Darcy held his drink, Elizabeth cleared her throat. After the earlier fright, she was thoroughly enjoying the situation.

"First of all, I want to assure you I am well, physically—despite how I might look. I went to town this morning to see if Aunt Philips needed any help for this evening's gathering. On my way back, I heard something unusual. I do not know what it was, although Mr. Darcy here seems to think it might have been a wild dog or even a *wolf*." She actually reached out and patted the back of his hand as it lay on the seat between them. Darcy thought about catching it and holding her hand close to him, but propriety overruled the impulse.

"Anyway, I thought whatever it was came in *chase,* and I took off running. In hindsight, it was a *silly* thing to do, but I was afraid."

"Of course, you were, my dear," her mother consoled.

Prolonging the drama, Elizabeth took a sip of her tea before continuing. "I ran towards Thompson's barn; I thought I might seek shelter there." Suddenly, Elizabeth lost her nerve. She glanced at Darcy, and her lips began to tremble. "Would you…Mr. Darcy?"

She buried her face in her hands. Her tears made him want to shelter her, but instead, he leaned over and whispered softly, "I will tell it, Miss Elizabeth."

Darcy knew of what they agreed, and he began the tale from there. "Mr. Bingley and I were out riding."

"Mr. Bingley?" Jane looked around, wondering where he was.

"Charles will be here shortly," he assured them. "Anyway, we rode along the outskirts of his property. Suddenly birds took flight in fear, and almost immediately Charles and I heard a sound of something running. When I looked in the direction of the sound, I saw Miss Elizabeth, in obvious distress, running with all her might over the crest of a hill. Instantly, Charles and I took off after her. However, before we could reach your daughter, Mr. Bennet, we heard Miss Elizabeth's screams. When I finally found her, Miss Elizabeth was on the ground, crawling away in terror."

"I do not understand, Mr. Darcy." Mr. Bennet leaned forward in his chair.

Elizabeth now sobbed audibly, her eyes downcast. "Should I go on, Miss Elizabeth?" Darcy asked softly. "Would you rather retire to your room and let me speak of this incident?"

She looked up suddenly and caught his eye. "Would you mind? I will return when Mr. Bingley arrives."

"You go," he said. The tenderness in his voice was not lost on Elizabeth.

Mr. Bennet motioned for Mrs. Hill to help Elizabeth. No one else in the family wanted to miss Darcy's story. When Elizabeth was safely on her way up the stairs, Darcy added, "Your daughter tries to be brave, Mr. Bennet, but she was traumatized today. As Miss Elizabeth tried to escape from the dog or wolf or whatever she thought was there, she fell as she ran. Neither Mr. Bingley nor I saw her fall, but Miss Elizabeth was on the ground when we reached her. And the fear was very real! The cause of her fall was the body of a woman lying in a crevice where the slopes of two hills meet." He heard a collective gasp from those in attendance. Mrs. Bennet began to fan her face, as if to swoon. "Mr. Bingley rode into Meryton for the authorities. I brought Miss Elizabeth back here to the safety of her home."

"Oh, my goodness!" Jane whispered. "Poor Lizzy."

"Did she see the woman's body?" Mr. Bennet wanted to know.

Darcy took a drink of the port, taking time to weigh his words. "Unfortunately, I believe she did; it was a gruesome sight, especially for a gentlewoman such as Miss Elizabeth. If you ask if your daughter knew the woman, I doubt it. Mr. Bingley did not recognize the woman's face, and her clothes and appearance would indicate she was of the *working class*, not likely to be of Miss Elizabeth's acquaintance."

Mr. Bennet mused, "I see."

Mrs. Bennet began to cry audibly, and her younger daughters saw to her immediately, patting her hand and offering supportive hugs.

Darcy had planned what to say next. "The constable and possibly Colonel Forster will be here soon to ask Miss Elizabeth some questions. She will need all of your support," he said with authority.

"Naturally," Mr. Bennet said as he stood. "Jane and Mary, I believe Elizabeth could use your help."

"Of course, Papa." And they were gone.

Mrs. Bennet's lament became so agitated Mr. Bennet sent his wife to her room, along with his other two daughters. "Give your mother a dose of her nerve draught," he ordered as they led the weeping woman from the room.

When they were all finally removed, Mr. Bennet asked, "Was the woman murdered?"

"The body was badly mutilated. She did not die naturally, but I cannot say whether she died at the hands of a man or was attacked by a wild animal. She was in the middle of a field where two hills intersect." Darcy kept his voice soft, trying to portray the seriousness of the situation.

"Was Elizabeth chased by an animal or a man?"

Darcy did not know how to answer that one. "I saw no pursuer, Mr. Bennet, but from the reaction of the birds, I would suspect an animal. Yet for Miss Elizabeth, the pursuit was very real and very harrowing."

"Do you know where Elizabeth's cloak might be, Mr. Darcy? She did not have it on when you brought her home; she wore your greatcoat." Mr. Bennet made it easy for him. Darcy would use the cloak as his excuse to return to the body. He originally thought he would tell Mr. Bennet that he planned to meet the constable before the man came to question Elizabeth; now, he had a ready excuse. "Did she throw it at the pursuer?" Mr. Bennet continued.

"I cannot say, Mr. Bennet. Your daughter did not wear a cloak when I found her, but it is logical she would wear one because of the weather. It was the least of my thoughts at the time."

"I am thankful, Mr. Darcy, that you and Mr. Bingley were there when Lizzy needed you." Tears misted the man's eyes.

"Mr. Bennet, I believe I will ride out and see if Miss Elizabeth's cloak is there; I am sure the constable went to the scene first. Possibly, I can intercept him and ease the pain of the questions he will be asking your daughter. I would not want Miss Elizabeth to suffer any more distress today than necessary."

"Thank you, Mr. Darcy. We are in your debt." Mr. Bennet stood and Darcy followed.

"Miss Elizabeth seemed most insistent that I stay with her today, but I shall not be gone long. Simply tell her, if she asks, that I went to find Mr. Bingley." Darcy picked up his gloves from the entrance table, needing to hurry now that he had *permission* to do so. "I will be back within the hour, more than likely sooner." And with that, he was gone.

Back in the saddle, Darcy circled Longbourn House, hoping to find what he needed in the barn or stables. If not, he would have to ride to the manor house on Netherfield's land and retrieve one of the swords. Then he saw it, resting beside a stack of firewood. Leaning down from the horse's back, he caught up the short-handled ax with one hand and rode on.

He rode with a purpose, praying he could reach the woman's body before Bingley brought the authorities. Seeing Elizabeth's cloak draped over the corpse made him realize how lucky he was with both Georgiana and with Elizabeth.

Reaching the site, he slid from his mount, surveying the area before taking the ax from the saddle. No one could see him unless they came the way he had from Longbourn. He still had time to right one of Wickham's wrongs; he would not let this victim become one of the walking dead.

He bent by the body and forced himself to withdraw the cloak. From his neck, he removed the cross on a chain. First, he touched it to the woman's forehead. "In the name of the Father," he began. Then her chin. "And of the Son," he continued. Finally, he laid it between her breasts. "And of the Holy Ghost," he whispered. "Dear God in heaven, take this woman's soul and guard it from the evil it knew recently. Ask her to forgive me for what I must now do to her body."

He rose to his knees, where he might have more leverage. It took three sharp whacks of the ax to sever the head from the body, but he did so without remorse. Otherwise, the woman—whoever she was—would become like Wickham, searching the land for innocent victims. With no blood circulating through her veins, it was a matter of bone and tendons. Afterwards, he adjusted the head to make it look as it had when he and Bingley last saw it, retrieved his cross, covered the woman again with Elizabeth's cloak, and mounted his horse to leave.

When he reached the cover of the tree line, Darcy looked back to see Bingley and Colonel Forster riding towards the site. Overweight and out of shape, the constable lagged behind, but Darcy watched as he joined the others. Bingley pulled back the cloak he placed there less than an hour earlier. All three held handkerchiefs to their noses as they examined the body. Eventually, the colonel touched the head, and Darcy watched their reactions of shocked alarm.

After a few moments, during which he uttered another prayer, Darcy turned his horse towards the main road leading to Longbourn. He would meet Bingley's party there once he hid the ax among some bushes along the road. He would return it that night to the woodpile when he came to Elizabeth.

"Darcy," Bingley called when they saw him approach, "how is Miss Elizabeth?"

"The lady puts up a good front, but she suffers greatly." Darcy said. "Please be kind to her, Sir."

The local magistrate puffed with self-importance. "Of course, Mr. Darcy. We will treat Miss Elizabeth with all decorum."

"That is all I can ask, Sir."

CHAPTER 7

True to his word, the magistrate asked only a few tactfully phrased questions of Elizabeth. Her story echoed what Darcy and Bingley said earlier. During her interrogation, Darcy stood close behind her, filling in details where she seemed unsure. With Darcy's impeccable reputation, Bingley's new status in the country, and the presumed innocence of Elizabeth Bennet, their retelling satisfied the law. Colonel Forster asked a few probing questions, but nothing Darcy did had not anticipated. When both gentlemen left, Mr. Bennet issued an invitation to dinner for Bingley and Darcy.

"We cannot impose, Mr. Bennet," Bingley said quickly.

As she motioned Bingley to the side, so that Elizabeth could not hear, Jane Bennet pleaded, "Please, Mr. Bingley. Elizabeth is still distraught; Mr. Darcy's presence seems to bring her peace. Please remain for a few more hours."

Bingley looked at Darcy, seeking his approval. With a nod from his friend, Bingley readily agreed. "Thank you, Mr. Bennet. We accept your hospitality."

As her mother still suffered from a case of nerves, Jane Bennet took care of details. "I will go tell Mrs. Hill."

Elizabeth stood upon hearing the news. "I am in need of some fresh air. Mr. Darcy, would you accompany me to the garden? I do not believe I care to be outside alone."

"Wait, Miss Elizabeth, and Miss Bennet and I will join you." Bingley wanted to ensure they were properly chaperoned.

"That is not necessary, Mr. Bingley. Mr. Darcy and I will go no farther than the nearest bench. We will be seen by any eyes that wish to observe us." She continued, "Please do not judge me as impertinent. I want to feel the fresh breeze on my face—feel clean air in my lungs. The house seems so confining right now. If I felt entirely safe in doing so, I would shun Mr. Darcy's company as well."

Mr. Bennet watched her closely, trying to judge what was best for his daughter. "Stay close to the house, Lizzy."

"Yes, Papa."

Elizabeth headed for the entrance hall, and Darcy dutifully followed her. She reached for her wrap on its usual peg. "Where is my cloak?"

Darcy stepped up behind her and spoke softly into her hair. "You left it in the field, Miss Elizabeth."

She spun around, her eyes filled with remembrance. "It was slowing me down as I ran." She paused, totally consumed by the mental image of herself in flight. "I have no cloak. What will I wear?"

"The cloak was ruined, Elizabeth. Mr. Bingley and I finally used it to protect the woman's body from the elements." He kept his voice even to allay her fears. "When I brought you home, I wrapped you in my coat."

"I remember now." Elizabeth's glazed-over eyes told Darcy she was replaying in her mind the whole scene of his finding her in the field.

"You will use one of your sister's cloaks this afternoon." He reached for a plain brown wrap and placed it over her shoulders.

Elizabeth's hand tightened around his wrist. She looked up at him, her fathomless green eyes luminous with need. "What will I wear tomorrow?"

He swallowed hard. "I will buy you a new one, the most beautiful cloak you can imagine." He would give her anything if she would continue to look at him with those mesmerizing eyes. He whispered, "I will buy you a hundred cloaks if you wish."

Elizabeth giggled nervously with the absurdity of what he said and the absurdity of the situation in which they found themselves. "I cannot accept even one from you, Mr. Darcy."

"That is where you are wrong, Miss Elizabeth." He continued to fasten the brown cloak's clasp at her neck. "I will insist. It is my and Mr. Bingley's fault we could not salvage your other one." He hooked the button under her chin. "I will claim extreme shame at having failed you." Darcy smiled at her, enthralled by Elizabeth's closeness.

"After the riding habit, Mr. Darcy, I put nothing past you." She sighed. "Come, Mr. Darcy, we will finish this conversation in the garden." She led him out the front door; they proceeded in silence along the gravel walk that led to the copse.

Once seated among the trees, Darcy slipped her hand into his. They sat with their backs to the house; no one would notice them from the window views. "Do you wish to speak of today, my dear?"

"We should." Beneath it all, Elizabeth felt fearful, but she was unsure of the source of her apprehension. Part of it was the terror of the afternoon, but some of it also lay in her growing feelings for the man who sat next to her.

His apologetic manner spoke of his true feelings. "Elizabeth, I am deeply sorry I inadvertently placed you in danger." His slightly husky voice was serious and passionate. "It will be on my conscience until the day I die. I hope someday you forgive me; you deserve so much better than the horror I brought into your life." He caressed her hand, stroking her palm with his fingertips.

"Fitzwilliam, you did *nothing*. Nothing at all to *harm* me."

His icy blue eyes remained fixed on hers. "Tell me what George Wickham said to you," he said in a quiet, dangerous voice.

Through tear-filled eyes, she related her complete conversation with Wickham. "I was wrong to speak to him without your knowledge." Darcy did not push further; he simply waited for her to continue. "Wickham spoke of your cruelty to your cottagers and to the villagers. I am ashamed to say there was a time when I would have believed him. The man has a way of playing on a person's sensibilities. We need to do something, Fitzwilliam."

Darcy knew she would reach this point eventually. He had the argument with himself often enough that he expected it from her. "And what would you suggest, my dear?"

"We tell the authorities."

For years, Darcy had avoided emotional involvement with any woman. It was all in the past now, however; this woman looked into his heart. It was difficult for him to fathom how much she meant to him in such a short time. "It is not that simple, Elizabeth. You tell the authorities that George Wickham is a vampire. And they ask you how you know this to be true, and you tell them I assured you of that fact. Then they say, *How does Mr. Darcy come by this information?* And you disclose that my family is cursed, thanks to our ancestors' love affair, and I could be as evil as Wickham if I chose. We would be ruined. My reputation—Georgiana's future—your future and your sisters' futures—your entire family's status in the neighborhood—some will believe the tale and believe I am also evil. Others will consider your words madness."

She glanced at him, her thoughts scattered. "You are right," she finally acknowledged, "but we cannot let him get away with killing that woman."

"From what I know of Wickham's pattern, he will not strike again for a week or more, other than the occasional animal—a dog or a sheep."

"I cannot believe you speak so lightheartedly about this wickedness," she said challengingly.

Darcy's face reddened with anger. "You are mistaken if you think I find no contempt in this situation. I have lived with it longer than you. It has been my existence, and what I relay are the absolute facts. Forgive me if I am aware that evil corrupts absolutely."

Elizabeth wondered momentarily what she would be doing right then if Darcy had not entered her life—certainly not considering how to kill a vampire before he struck again. "So we cannot go to the authorities. What do we do, then?"

"First, I need to lure Wickham from the area—get him away from you. His normal mode of operation means he comes looking for easy victims. He chooses very vulnerable targets; rarely does Wickham select a woman of circumstance. If he did, he might draw more notice from the local law officers. In most small villages and towns, the law is incompetent, at best. By the time someone makes a connection, he is gone."

"That does not make these women not worth saving!" she

protested. Her eyes widened and then shimmered with tears.

He spoke coldly and curtly. "I never meant to imply otherwise, Miss Elizabeth." He belatedly realized his rudeness.

"Did Wickham kill Vivian Piccadilly?" she blurted out in frustration.

Darcy spoke unguardedly. "I always assumed he was the perpetrator. Miss Piccadilly's body was found close to a stream. Her father was devastated by the condition in which he found her. I always felt the shame in my part of his pain."

"*Your* part?" Elizabeth seized upon the words. "What part did you play in Vivian's death?"

Darcy seemed reconciled to his role in the murder. "Does it matter?"

"It matters to *me*, Fitzwilliam." Elizabeth stood suddenly, staring at Darcy as if seeing him for the first time.

"If I tell you, you will turn away from me."

Suddenly, she saw things in a sharper focus; she remembered her aunt's description of Vivian's body. In a voice of resigned contempt, she said, "You prevent them—Wickham's victims—from following him, do you not?" She was acknowledging as much to herself.

"The only way I know to stop them from becoming one of the walking dead is to break the connection between the body and the soul…letting the soul out, so to speak, to make its way to heaven, rather than dwell in hell." His words pierced the air, increasing the cold, which invaded their bodies.

"How can you *do* such a thing?" she insisted.

"It is the most responsible thing I do. I offer prayers of redemption for the victim's soul and forgiveness for mine, and then I do what must be done." His eyes were dark with anger at the injustice.

A frown creased across her forehead. "Did you do the responsible thing today?" she whispered.

"It is done."

"Oh, Fitzwilliam!" She collapsed onto the seat beside him and took his hand in hers; he needed the comfort now. "You have been placed in the most tragic scenario. It is no wonder you try to withdraw from society—giving us a skewed picture of you." Her slim, strong fingers intertwined with his.

"I did not succeed where you are concerned, Vixen."

"You simply like a challenge, Mr. Darcy."

"I suppose you could be right. I want what I cannot have."

Taking to heart her role in this mad situation, Elizabeth demanded, "Explain to me what you plan to do."

Darcy summarized his plans for the next few days. "I will come to you tonight. Tomorrow, we put in place some tried-and-true deterrents to vampires—to Wickham—at Longbourn. We will decorate the sashes of all the windows with garlands containing cloves of garlic, work iron crosses or bars at each door, and a few other such ornamentations. I will ask you to do so without raising the attention of your family members. Tell them these are gifts from Netherfield; I am sure your mother would wish to please Mr. Bingley. We must be careful. Wickham cannot cross the threshold of any house unless invited to do so. As he already was in attendance at Longbourn, we need stronger deterrents than usual. The garlands and iron will keep him from entering the individual rooms. Wickham may cross the main entrance, but his evil will not be able to seep into your lives."

"I will see to it," Elizabeth said in a businesslike tone.

"I suspect," Darcy continued, "that Mr. Wickham will call upon you in the next couple of days."

Elizabeth's eyes grew wide with surprise. "He would not!"

"He will, Elizabeth, and you will respond graciously to his concern for your well-being. It will soon be common knowledge that Mr. Bingley and I found you, and the three of us discovered the body. Mr. Wickham will want to know how you feel about me after this incident. With your words and your actions you *must* convince him that although you appreciate my gentlemanly behavior towards you, your feelings have not altered. I am still the man who cut you at the assembly."

"I doubt I can feign those feelings," she asserted.

"You will do the responsible thing, Elizabeth, because what you do will affect your family and many others."

The truth of his words settled over Elizabeth like a cold fog.

Darcy continued, "Bingley plans a ball at Netherfield in less than a week; I cannot leave before that time without disappointing him severely. Without Wickham's knowledge from where the suggestion comes, I will convince Colonel Forster to send Wickham to London for several days. After the ball, I return to Pemberley. With luck on my side, Wickham will follow; he is not likely to stay in the military, for it has too many regulations. I cannot imagine why he places himself in a situation where he is constantly watched and supervised."

Elizabeth speculated, "Maybe he thought they would send him to the front. He has no fear of dying, and he would have access to plenty of bodies."

Darcy considered her words. "As bizarre as it is, I do not think your theory is an unlikely one."

Her jaw clenched as she studied him carefully; she could see the worry in his eyes. "*Must* you leave, Mr. Darcy?"

The emotion in Elizabeth's words soothed his aching heart. She would miss him for himself—not his estate—not his wealth. Even with all the chaos, Elizabeth would feel the deprivation of his departure. It was a heady feeling; yet Darcy knew he could not stay. His preference for her put Elizabeth in danger. His primal need to protect her overruled his primal need to possess her. "We said our—our *flirtation*—would be for the memories. My staying would only make the situation awkward."

"For the memories," she repeated softly.

★ ★ ★

Darcy leaned over her, lightly kissing her eyelids, which fluttered open like the wings of a hummingbird. "Ah, there you are," she mumbled. "I tried to stay awake until you came."

"I am happy to just watch you sleep." He kissed her temple before brushing a curl from her face.

Elizabeth rolled on her side and turned the coverlet back. "Come join me," she invited him.

Darcy slipped off his boots and crawled under the bed linens. He settled her into his arms. "Rest," he said. "I am with you."

Elizabeth wrapped her arms around him. "Someday you will tell me how you do this," she mumbled, drifting back to sleep. "How you keep us in our own cocoon while the rest of the world is suspended in sleep."

"It is not worth knowing, Sweetling." Darcy kissed the top of her head. As she drifted back to sleep, he prayed to have this night last forever.

When the first rays of daylight broke through the draped window, Darcy gently rolled Elizabeth to her back. "Wake, my Vixen," he whispered close to her ear. "It is nearly light, and I must leave you."

Elizabeth wrapped her arms around his neck, but she did not open her eyes. "It is so warm here under the blankets." She kissed his cheek as she pulled him down to her. Darcy nuzzled her neckline playfully, and Elizabeth giggled.

Then those icy blue eyes slid over her in deepest approval before he began to kiss her in all seriousness. Elizabeth's eyes drifted shut as Darcy rolled her to her back. His lips traveled from her face to her jawline and down her neck. Her pulse hammered there at its base, and he was drawn to the spot by an ancient hunger. His tongue circled the point, teasing her with its rough texture. Elizabeth's skin was pale in the light of the dawn, and Darcy audibly groaned in an acknowledgement of what he most desired. He could barely tear his gaze from the spot. He burned to possess her, but he fought the urges coursing through him. At last, he snarled, "Sweetling, you are tempting, but I can maintain the spell for only so long." Brushing his lips across hers, he whispered, "Before someone finds us together, we must part." Then he rolled away from her, sitting on the edge of the bed to put on his boots.

Elizabeth crawled up on her knees behind him and slid her arms over his shoulders, her breath warm upon the side of his neck.

"When will I see you again?"

"You will not—unless danger is evident." It hurt to say the words, but Darcy knew she was in peril. "A servant from Nether-field will bring the ornaments we spoke of as a gift from the Bing-ley household later today. Among them will be something special for you—a crucifix. It will be like the one I gave Georgiana; it is made of iron, something to which Wickham's sect is most suscepti-ble. Promise me you will wear it always."

"I promise." She withdrew to sit cross-legged behind him on the bed, but Darcy did not turn around. Even without touching, he felt her.

"You gave me a taste of the life I could never know otherwise," he blurted out.

"I did nothing."

He continued, as if checking off items from a list. "Do what you must do to protect yourself from Wickham. You must convince everyone that you hate me."

Elizabeth fought back tears. "Everyone but me," she whispered softly to his back.

★ ★ ★

As Darcy had anticipated, George Wickham, along with Mr. Denny, made a late afternoon call on the Bennet household. Step-ping into the room with her eldest sister, Elizabeth felt nauseated by Wickham's presence, but she hid her contempt for Darcy's sake. Receiving the creature who had forced Darcy to leave made her want to scream in frustration, but she schooled her countenance into the semblance of a smile.

"Mr. Wickham." She offered her hand, and he kissed the back of it. Elizabeth fought the urge to scrub away his touch.

"Miss Elizabeth, we came at once to assure ourselves of your well-being," Wickham began. "I chastised myself for not having seen you home. The horror of such a discovery!"

Elizabeth gritted her teeth in disgust. "It was incomprehensible at the time, but I am recovering."

Mr. Denny took the seat to which Jane gestured. "Colonel Forster, Ma'am, is conducting a thorough investigation."

"I hope the woman finds peace in that." Elizabeth and Jane settled together on a settee.

"You were missed at Mrs. Philips's gathering," Denny continued.

"It was not appropriate," Jane declared, "under the circumstances."

Wickham wasted no time in getting to the reason for his visit. "I understand, Miss Elizabeth, that Mr. Darcy served as your rescuer."

"Mr. Darcy was a gentleman in the way he aided my sister," Jane asserted.

Mr. Denny concurred, "I would expect nothing less from a man of Mr. Darcy's lineage."

"Mr. Darcy and Mr. Bingley found me when I was most distraught; they both stepped in to protect me. Mr. Darcy was the first to reach me, so he became my initial source of comfort. I clung to him unreasonably, I am ashamed to say. He allowed me time to recuperate."

Jane took Elizabeth's hand in hers. "Lizzy, you were so overwrought; it was natural, and Mr. Darcy is a responsible young man."

Elizabeth noted how Wickham's eyes searched for the truth in their faces. With distaste for her task, she spoke again, giving Wickham the opinion he sought. "I am thankful for both Mr. Bingley and Mr. Darcy; and although my gratitude to both men is of the highest order, I openly admit I would give anything not to be indebted to Mr. Darcy."

"Elizabeth!" Jane protested.

Having watched Wickham take the bait, Elizabeth continued, "The man leaves Hertfordshire soon, and I will not be among those counted as wishing he stays. He repeatedly showed himself as superior to the rest of the country, and I shall be happy to see him go."

"You know how I feel about Mr. Darcy," Wickham interjected. "He does not belong in civilized company."

Jane started to object, but Elizabeth cut off her words by ordering tea for the group. When it arrived, she changed the subject to their aunt's social the previous evening. Darcy warned her about "protesting too much." Wickham would see through her plan if she *harped* on Darcy's faults.

The visit lasted less than an hour, but for Elizabeth it was a lifetime. When the gentlemen stood to leave, relief set in. "The colonel asked me to see to paperwork for the unit in London; I absent myself with regret, Miss Elizabeth," said Wickham.

"Will you not be at Mr. Bingley's ball?" Jane inquired with interest, thinking Elizabeth might find Mr. Wickham appealing.

"I cannot say, Miss Bennet. The colonel knows I am well familiar with London; he has several tasks for me to complete there."

Elizabeth could not make herself say the words she knew she should offer him to maintain the ruse. All she could say was, "Your absence will be felt, Mr. Wickham." It was the truth, and that was better than a lie. Wickham's absence meant she might spend a few minutes with Darcy before he left Hertfordshire and her forever.

★ ★ ★

As he promised, Darcy refused to call on Elizabeth, even when Bingley encouraged him to do otherwise. "I will not see Miss Elizabeth; it would seem as if I courted the woman."

He made sure the garlands arrived in the afternoon. Darcy knew Elizabeth would anxiously open the packages, and she would know disappointment when she found no necklace. He promised to send it, but when the time came, he withdrew, afraid someone else might see it. He could not put Elizabeth in such a position.

Instead, he took it to her himself. Darcy sent the same trusted footman to the nearest township to find a competent jeweler and mercantile. He removed the crucifix he wore and gave it to the man with orders for the jeweler to duplicate it, creating a replacement for Darcy. Then he ordered an array of loose diamonds and emeralds set into the metal of the one he already owned. He would risk being without one for a few days to protect Elizabeth. The footman paid the merchant well to complete the work on the one for Elizabeth in a few precious hours. In addition, Darcy's orders included a new fur-lined cloak for her.

In the middle of the night, he paid her a visit. He did not wake Elizabeth, although his desire to kiss her ruled his body. He stood in the center of the room, staring down at her. When she rolled over and snuggled into a pillow, he smiled with remembrances of her wrapping her arms and legs around his. "You are beautiful, Vixen," he murmured. "Now, let us see if this works." He set the package holding the cloak and the necklace on the end of her bed, and then Darcy turned slowly in place three times, extending his arms level to his shoulders. "Forget...remember...forget...remember...forget...remember," he chanted as an aura of blue light spread through the room, like fingers caressing every corner. "Forget the old." The light continued to surge through the walls, filling each of the rooms in succession. "Remember the new." The light turned in on itself and rolled back towards him, having touched all in the sleeping Bennet household. "Forget the old. Remember the new," he repeated once more, turning counterclockwise to pull in his power. Like the swooshing crack of a whip, the energy balled itself into the pit of his stomach and disappeared within him. Darcy sank to his knees in exhaustion.

He remained slumped over for several minutes, devoid of feeling. Then he pushed himself to a standing position, although he held onto the bedpost for support. At last, he moved beside the bed to take in her image before he left. She had captured his eye—his *imagination*—from the beginning. Despite her tenacious spirit, her innocence moved him; oh, to be the man who won her heart! Elizabeth created in him a need to protect and shelter her, but also a desire to possess her completely. Under other circumstances, she would be his destiny—his *wife*. "Wear the gifts with pleasure, Vixen," he murmured and then touched her auburn tresses before leaving her to the end of a dream.

Returning to Netherfield, he sat in his room for hours, staring into the fire, finishing off more than one glass of brandy. Since he had met Elizabeth Bennet, he had engaged in unseemly behavior, insinuating himself into her life and tempting her modesty. They had slept in the same bed, more than once; they had shared kisses, some quite intimate; they had flirted with each other shamelessly. And he had used his powers; first, creating a privacy of which no one knew, and now, giving Elizabeth gifts others would think of as having always been hers. She could wear both the cloak and the necklace openly.

His use of his supernatural abilities surprised even himself. Wickham had used such powers against Georgiana—enchanting her—making her know nothing but what the cad desired. Until recently, Darcy had considered his powers part of the evil he fought in himself every day. Then he had reconsidered that position. But the truth was that he had used the same powers Wickham had to control his victims. With a twisted grin, Darcy now wondered, *How different am I from George Wickham?*

Elizabeth woke to find the package at the end of her bed. *He was here!* In her sleep, she felt him in the room, watching over her. Fascinated, she sat up in bed and took the box upon her lap. She let her fingers caress the ribbon, imagining his tying it off, knowing no other hands had touched it but his. She brought her fingertips to her lips and sensed his kiss lightly on her mouth.

Then, very slowly, savoring each moment, Elizabeth untied the knot and peeled the ribbon back from the package. She would keep it in the drawer next to his handkerchief. Unfolding the paper, she gasped upon seeing the cloak. It was a deep forest green; she had never saw seen anything so fine. She stood up on the mattress, bouncing a bit in happiness as she swept it from the wrapping and draped it around her. For warmth, white rabbit fur trimmed the hood and cuffs. Elizabeth ran her fingers over it, enjoying the softness.

Immediately, she dropped to her knees on the bed, still wrapped in the cloak. She fished into the bottom of the layers of paper and found a jeweler's box, along with a note. She unwrapped the small box slowly; she knew what it contained. The jeweler's box cracked with a faint squeak of unoiled hinges. She gasped audibly when she saw it: a jeweled crucifix, covered in perfectly matched diamonds and emeralds.

She undid the chain and hooked it around her neck. The cool metal burned against her skin. She kissed the back of it and let it drop; it nestled between the rise of her breasts. The jewels disguised the base iron of the design, but Elizabeth knew Darcy sent it as protection from Wickham. The night she and Darcy discussed the curse, he told her the legend behind the Baobhan Síth—how they killed a group of men but one man escaped because he hid between the horses—the iron horseshoes protected him from their vampire attack. Elizabeth felt safer just putting it on—an amulet to protect her.

Finally, she unfolded the note and read—her fingertips followed along as if the letters rose up and touched her:

Vixen,

You would tempt a sane man with your beauty, and considering what I am doing is far from sane, I admit to being enthralled by the mere thought of you. If you knew what great joy I felt in being with you, you would blush.

I used a special power to protect you from censure upon accepting these gifts. No one will remember what you owned before. You may wear the cloak and the necklace without fear. As far as your family knows, they were in your possession for years. The riding habit will be seen the same way.

How I wish I could see your face right now—see the luminousness of your eyes and be lost in the depths of them. How I wish I could kiss your lips and give myself up to the world we create when we are together!

The memory of you will stay with me forever.

F. D.

Elizabeth refolded the note. Without thinking, she brought it to her face and inhaled. It smelled of him—of sandalwood and maleness.

She breathed deeply, bringing images of Darcy to mind. Clutching the necklace in the palm of her hand, she swept the cloak from around her and draped it over her body as she slipped back down into the bed linens to sleep again—to dream of Fitzwilliam Darcy.

CHAPTER 8

"Lizzy, I *cannot* wait for the ball this evening. Just three short hours away, Sister! It will be so *glorious* to dance at Netherfield. Do you not think so?" Kitty twirled around the room, holding her dress to her as she did.

Elizabeth looked forward to the evening, for she would see Darcy again, but she dreaded it also, for after tonight, he would be gone from Hertfordshire—and from her life. How would she bear it? "It is to be hoped that Mr. Bingley continues his preference for our dear Jane, and that you and Lydia have numerous partners to satisfy your tastes," Elizabeth said sadly.

"And what of you, Lizzy? Do you want a special dance partner to sweep you off your feet?" Elizabeth immediately thought of Darcy, but she forced images of waltzing with him away. "Maybe Mr. Wickham has returned from London. Do you wish him as a partner?" Kitty collapsed in a heap of silken material at Elizabeth's feet.

"I assure you, Kitty, I have no desire to dance with Mr. Wickham," Elizabeth asserted while busying herself with cleaning her shoes.

Kitty looked about nervously, as if fearing someone might overhear. "I am pleased to hear it, Lizzy. Aunt Philips says he paid his attentions to Miss King on the evening of your attack and then again two days later, right before he left for London, at Colonel Forster's evening of cards. I suppose it has to do with her recent inheritance."

"Let us trust Miss King's dowry is safe from Mr. Wickham." Elizabeth hoped Miss King was safe—period; she would tell Darcy this evening of Wickham's interest in the girl. He would know what to do about it.

Standing in the receiving line, Elizabeth made eye contact with Darcy, who stood next to Wayne Hurst. Darcy's eyes lit up, becoming piercing blue ice crystals, when he saw her. She waited patiently for her turn to pay her respects to Mr. Bingley and his sisters. "The splendor of Netherfield is enthralling, Mr. Bingley," she offered as she and Jane made their way through the line. At last, she was in front of *him*. Without preamble, she dropped to a deep curtsy, allowing him a peek at the swell of her breasts and his gift resting between them. "*Mr. Darcy,*" she purred.

"Miss Elizabeth." He bowed over her hand and brought it to his lips. Her eyes flashed with a need he recognized. "I am sure Mr. Bingley is pleased your family is here. May I inquire as to your continued recovery?"

"It is steady, Mr. Darcy. *Of late, I feel safer.* Thank you once again for your gallantry." She could say no more because the line formed behind her, so Elizabeth made a quick curtsy and followed Jane into the main parlor.

Darcy, unwillingly, followed her with his eyes. Elizabeth Bennet set his heart pounding in his chest. Her tempting way of displaying the jeweled crucifix he had given her shot straight to his groin. If she held any idea of his desire—his dreams of her—she would never speak to him again. Drawing a steadying breath to release the tension, Darcy stopped the images that were creeping into his mind. If he were normal, he would apply to her immediately and satisfy himself in her body. But he would never know such pleasure; and to continue their entanglement would not be fair to Elizabeth. He had already involved her enough in this quagmire. Tomorrow, he would return to Pemberley, leaving Elizabeth behind to find a husband and to have children of her own—children not cursed by a Scottish vampire two hundred years old.

As the number of party-goers in the receiving line dwindled to a trickle, Darcy excused himself. "I will check the service, Charles. Mr. Hurst is headed towards the game room." Charles Bingley nodded his agreement.

Caroline Bingley reminded him of her earlier request: "You will keep your promise and stand up with me for the first set, Mr. Darcy?"

"Of course, Miss Bingley. I shall not be long." He made a polite bow before heading towards the service entrance. Darcy intended to stay out of sight as much as possible this evening. He would stay on the periphery and watch for Wickham's appearance. Although unsure Wickham would come, Darcy intended to take no chances. If luck were on Darcy's side, his enemy would remain in London.

It took only moments to check on the serving staff and the food presentations, but the task was a good excuse to be away from the crowd, where he could think. However, only one thought consumed him: *his Elizabeth* was in the house once again. He caught a glimpse of her talking to Charlotte Lucas in the drawing room; he stayed behind her as she made her way to the refreshment table for lemonade; he delighted in watching her provoke some of the military officers and then spin away from them. She captivated everyone with whom she came in touch—including him. Darcy swallowed hard, forcing the increasing hunger away.

Strains of a melody played by musicians tuning their instruments brought him out of his reverie. Dutifully, he found Caroline Bingley and escorted her onto the dance floor. Out of the corner of his eye, he saw Elizabeth accept Mr. Denny as a partner, and irrational jealousy coursed through him. She was *his;* her attentions belonged to *him.* When the music finally started, he counted the steps and the changes in partners until he came to her. He would have only two chances to speak to her during this form, and he would make the most of each. As he took Elizabeth's hand in his for the first time, he gave a little tug to pull her closer, and then he murmured, "Vixen, I am happy to see you hold me close to your heart."

She reddened with his boldness, but recovered quickly enough to challenge him. "Your eyes take liberties, Mr. Darcy." Elizabeth heard his laughter as he moved on to the next woman in line. That woman and Caroline Bingley both probably thought he enjoyed their company. But he called no one *Vixen* except her.

As they wove their way towards each other for the second time, she prepared for his teasing, but this time all he did was lick his lips slowly, as if tasting her. Impulsively, she pursed hers in a pretend kiss. He smiled, leaned in, and growled into her ear before moving on. Despite the fact that he partnered with Miss Caroline Bingley, Darcy could not remember a dance he had enjoyed more.

Afterwards, he returned Caroline to her place of honor while keeping track of Elizabeth's presence. Seeing her head towards the ladies' retiring room, Darcy slipped out a side servant entrance, making his way to the upper floors.

When Elizabeth came through the dimly lit hallway, she thought of nothing but Darcy. Consumed with thoughts of him, when a hand clamped over her mouth to stifle her scream and another wrapped around her waist to pull her backwards, a heart-beat passed before she began to fight. Kicking his legs and biting the hand that smothered her, it took a few more heartbeats before she heard his voice next to her ear: "It is I, Vixen."

Immediately, she relaxed into him and allowed Darcy to pull her into the nearest empty room. Inspecting his hand for punc-ture wounds, he growled, "I should have known you would put up a fight."

"Oh, Fitzwilliam," she said as she caressed his face. "I am sorry. Did I hurt you?"

She leaned against the door, and Darcy pinned her between his arms, fencing her in. Wolflike, he leaned down to speak to her lips: "I might forgive you if you kissed me," he taunted her.

Elizabeth slid her arms about his waist and intuitively massaged the firm muscles of his back. "I might forgive *you* for frightening me if you kissed me."

Darcy grinned, the corners of his mouth turning up in a smirk. "You missed me, Vixen?" His warm breath caressed the side of her neck, lingering over the spot he most desired.

"No more than you missed me," she said and giggled as she stroked his chin line.

"Then you have had a powerful void in your soul." The depth of his admission made her shiver, and Elizabeth moved in closer to feel his warmth. His head lowered, and Darcy dissolved into her. Nothing else mattered at this moment except holding Elizabeth to him and kissing her lips.

When they parted, Elizabeth rested her head on his chest, breathing as heavily as he did. "Fitzwilliam, I do not want you to leave," she whispered.

"I must, Sweetling. It is the only way to protect you. I can offer you nothing, Elizabeth—nothing but darkness. If things were different...."

Elizabeth balled her hands into fists as she stepped away in an act of defiance. "If things were different, you would be married to some lady of the *ton* by now, but you and I both know she would be your wife in name only. You would take her to your bed to produce the required heir. Yet you cannot tell me you want that kind of life, Fitzwilliam, any more than you want the kind of life you have now. I do not believe you dream of nothing more than that."

"I dream of *you,* Elizabeth. Are you satisfied? I dream of you every night. I will always dream of you." He turned away from her in defeat.

"Fitzwilliam," her voice came softly behind him. He heard the tears in her words. "I will not mention it again. I know you must go; you must do the responsible thing. I will stay here. You can fight better without me."

"*Nothing* is right without you, Elizabeth." His words soothed the hurt she felt knowing he would do what he said—he would leave her behind.

"Do you know that when I first accepted your *scandalous* proposition of a midnight conversation in the library, I wanted only to prove you to be a womanizing rich man who used women for his own pleasure—and sent them to their death? My aunt was so sure you were at fault in Vivian's death that I had to find out." She circled around to stand in front of him. "I thought to flirt with you to see what type of person you really were, but the more I was with you, the more I knew how wrong Aunt Gardiner was. You are a fine man, Fitzwilliam Darcy, and an honorable one." Tears streamed freely down her face.

Darcy opened his arms and welcomed her into his embrace. He

used his thumbs to wipe away the tears. "Vixen, you own my heart." His words spread through her like a soothing balm. "You see all my weaknesses and make them strengths." He held her to him. At last, he spoke: "I must return you to the ball before you are missed."

"Are we to dance tonight, Mr. Darcy?" She cupped his face in the palms of her hands. "We have never danced in public; it would be fitting after your earlier snub. A change in your opinion of Elizabeth Bennet!"

"I was a complete fool," he admitted before turning his head and kissing her palm.

"Yes, you were, Sir." She became serious. "Please, Fitzwilliam, I want to be acknowledged by you just once before you leave, and without Wickham's attendance tonight, no real danger exists."

"Have you promised the third set to anyone?"

"No."

"Then arrange your hair, Miss Elizabeth, and I will claim your hand in front of everyone." He brushed his lips across hers. Darcy slid his finger along the neckline of her dress, retrieving the jeweled crucifix. "Oh, Sweetling, to be a piece of metal would be ecstasy."

She laughed lightly. "You *do* have a singular mind, Mr. Darcy." With that, she slipped away.

Twenty minutes later, she stood with several of her sisters and other young women from the village, waiting for the next set to begin.

"Should I have Mr. Jameson partner you, Lizzy?" Lydia asked as a gentleman came forward to claim his dance.

"That will not be necessary, Lydia. I have a partner for this set."

Kitty looked around and saw the rest of the officers lead the ladies to the dance floor. "Really, Lizzy? It is not Papa, is it?"

"No, it is neither Papa nor any of the officers."

The first strains of the music sounded to call everyone to the dance, and her sisters scrambled to their places. And then Darcy stepped to the edge of the floor. Everyone's eyes turned to him. In all his time in Hertfordshire, other than the three or four times he had dutifully escorted one of Bingley's sisters to the floor, he had never danced. Now, he strode purposefully across the floor towards Elizabeth. The couples parted like the Red Sea until he stood in front of her. Darcy made a proper bow before claiming her hand. "I believe that this is my dance, Miss Elizabeth." His resonant voice rang out through the room.

In the background, Elizabeth heard her sisters and Caroline Bingley gasp. She made a quick curtsy before taking his arm. "Thank you, Mr. Darcy, I believe it is."

He led her to the head of the line. As the highest-ranking and most affluent man at the ball, it was his accepted place of honor, and although he had never claimed it for previous dances, for this one—the one with Elizabeth—he would. Once he released Elizabeth to her place across from him, the music began. They circled and twirled about each other, but never once did Darcy take his eyes from hers. "Vixen," he whispered as they passed each other, "you possess an allure I cannot resist. You are exquisite."

"I am only sorry we will not get the chance to waltz," she whispered back.

"Would you like to waltz?" he asked as they stepped around each other.

"Would I like to be in your arms?" she asked sotto voce. "What do *you* think, Mr. Darcy?"

"I can make it happen, Vixen. I can use my powers. Just say the word."

The temptation was too much. "Ye—Yes," she stammered. "Yes, Fitzwilliam."

They finished the set in silence, both engrossed in what was to come. When the second song ended, Darcy led her to the back of the ballroom. "Meet me on the balcony in five minutes, Sweetling."

Elizabeth waited a few minutes until no one paid attention to her any longer, and then she slipped through the unlocked patio door. Although it was November, the evening was warm. Darcy waited for her in the shadows. He watched as she made her way to the baluster, and then he came up behind her and encircled her in his arms. "I never tire of watching you," he whispered in her ear as she leaned back into him.

She tilted her head up and kissed him along his chin line. "The dance was lovely, Fitzwilliam."

"It was. Stay here, Sweetling, and let me work my magic." Darcy released her and turned back towards the house. Then he spread his arms wide and concentrated his power on the household. Streaks of blue light snaked across the marble balcony, bathing the windows and doors in a sealed energy. Everyone inside remained as they were before, repeating the same motions over and over in a continuous loop. Men bowed over ladies' hands, cards were shuffled constantly, and drinks were poured and then emptied. And then, uncannily, the strains of a waltz began.

Darcy heard her giggle behind him. Before he turned around he asked, "Do I amuse you, Miss Elizabeth?" He dropped his arms to his side, but the blue light continued to zigzag about the house, encasing it in a snowstorm of energy.

She came up behind him and slid under his arm and into his embrace, and, for him, the threat of the curse lessened. "That is something to see," she murmured. "I am impressed, Sir."

He could learn to love this magic, especially if it made Elizabeth happy. Darcy turned her to him and then stepped away before making an elegant bow. "May I have this dance, Miss Elizabeth?"

Exhilarated by his show of power on her behalf, Elizabeth nearly collapsed into his arms. Steadying herself, she replied, "You may, Mr. Darcy." And, placing her hand in his, she allowed Darcy to pull her to him. The night suddenly turned very warm as Darcy stepped into the dance.

Elizabeth felt the expanse of his chest against her bosom and the warmth of his breath against the side of her face. His hand rested on the small of her back, and she felt Darcy move her in closer with just an adjustment of his fingers. It all felt perfectly scandalous—perfectly sinful. They glided in long, rhythmic steps and turns so tight that their feet worked in unison. Elizabeth's gown swirled about her legs in harmony with the music.

The song continued as they spun in a breathless circle, their bodies pressed tightly together. Elizabeth would live on the memory of his attentions for a long time.

Darcy, caught in the moment, at first did not sense the danger, but then he knew—knew with a sickening certainty—that they were no longer alone. He protectively spun her behind him and whispered softly to her before he turned around, "Follow my lead."

"What *do* we have here?" George Wickham stepped from the shadow of a statue, a manifestation of the unreal. "Darcy, I am thunderstruck. I was unaware your powers developed so quickly. In my limited experience, you showed no interest in your innate abilities previously." He came forward with a defiant swagger. "Whatever you are doing differently, Sir, continue it. You might prove a worthy opponent, after all."

"What are you doing here, Wickham?" Darcy reached behind him to feel Elizabeth. Her fingers trembled when he touched them.

"I followed the blue lights." Wickham nodded in the direction of the dancing rays. "I was stunned to find the whole household under your spell." He took a few steps to the side to get a better look at Darcy's partner. "And who is with you? Ah, Miss Elizabeth Bennet. I should have recognized your preferences, Darcy."

"I have no preferences, Wickham." Darcy countermoved to block Elizabeth from Wickham's view again.

Wickham laughed sardonically. "Then what do you call this private party?"

"Boredom." Darcy sneered. "This supercilious collection of know-it-alls bores me. I thought to enliven my last night here."

"Last night here? And why Miss Elizabeth Bennet?" Wickham asked warily. Although he knew he could beat Darcy in a battle to the end, seeing the increase in Darcy's powers made him more cautious than usual.

"Why *not* Elizabeth Bennet?" Darcy feigned indifference. "Why not take my revenge on my most vocal adversary? I am sure you heard her; Miss Elizabeth does not hide her disdain for me."

"The lady does not seem to disdain you tonight, Darcy."

Darcy thought quickly. "Miss Elizabeth is under my spell. I

thought I might enjoy *touching* her as part of my revenge." Darcy spun Elizabeth into his embrace; she moved in a zombielike manner. "Kiss me as though you desired me," he ordered. He pulled her to him and kissed Elizabeth in the way he had always wanted to do. His mouth invaded hers, and his hands cupped her buttocks and lifted her to him. Elizabeth's fingers ran through his hair, and she arched into him. Finally, he broke the kiss and set her from him. "Would Elizabeth Bennet kiss me in such a fashion of her own free will? Even you are not foolish enough to believe so, Wickham. She was brought up as a lady."

"Maybe so, Darcy." Wickham seemed amused. "When will you make her yours forever? It is so easy to do when they are under your spell."

Darcy stepped to where he might shield Elizabeth once again. "I was bored, Wickham; I have not sunk to your level of depravity."

"A pity," he returned mockingly. He spun in a whirlwind to the roof of the overhang. "If I were not satisfied already, I might take the lovely Miss Elizabeth off your hands." Then his tone changed and he issued a threat. "Beware, my friend, for I am coming for you." His warning hung like icicles in the air. "By the way, Darcy, I left you a present by the servants' entrance." Again, a gush of air wrapped them in a maelstrom of debris and swirling energy, and, in an instant, Wickham vanished.

Elizabeth sank to her knees in a release of smeddum. Darcy scooped her up in his arms. "Elizabeth, please, are you all right?" he asked urgently as he brushed the hair from her face.

"Ye—Yes," she stammered. "That was *so* close."

"Elizabeth, we have to find out what he meant by a present by the servants' entrance."

She nodded, and he placed her on her feet. Darcy led her down the steps to the garden below. They wove their way through the maze of plants until they reached the back gate. "Stay close," he whispered in her ear, wrapping his hand completely around hers. Then they followed the outline of the house until they came to the steps leading down to the kitchen. The horror of the night stared out at them: eyes full of terror in a waxy, pale countenance.

Elizabeth buried her face against his shoulder to stifle her scream. "Elizabeth," he said, "I must examine her. Stay here." He caressed her face before he approached the body. As with the others, the woman's neck was ripped open..

Moments later, Darcy returned to her side. "Come, Love. You must quit this place."

He hurried her back along the path they had just followed. He held her next to him, and they moved as one. Back on the balcony, he asked, "Who is she?"

"Emily King," Elizabeth mumbled in shock. "I wanted to tell you about her this evening, but I forgot. Lydia told me Wickham paid her attention before he went to London. I *should* have told you. We could have stopped this!" Self-recriminating, Elizabeth's voice rose in anger and remorse.

"It would not have mattered, Elizabeth." He took her by the shoulders to force her attention. "Listen to me; it would have made no difference. Miss King has been dead for many hours, probably since early this morning. You did nothing wrong."

"Oh, Fitzwilliam, this is awful!"

"Yes, my love, it is, but we must work fast or Miss King will join Wickham as one of the undead."

Elizabeth began to tremble with his words. "Oh, Fitzwilliam, we cannot—I cannot!"

"*I* can, Love. I know what to do. My fear is for you. I cannot release the spell on the house until I take care of Miss King. I cannot, therefore, send you back inside. Either you must stay here until I return or go with me. Do you understand, Elizabeth?"

"I cannot watch you—"

"Then you will stay here." Darcy stood her against the wall. "Use your crucifix. I doubt if Wickham will come back tonight, but if he does, the sign of the cross will protect you. Believe in the Trinity, and you will be safe. His kind cannot come past the iron in the necklace."

"Are you sure?"

"Absolutely, my love." Darcy kissed her forehead. "I have only moments to rescue Miss King's soul. I will be back as soon as the deed is done."

Darcy disappeared into the darkness. Elizabeth heard his steps amplified along the gravel walkway of the garden. The crunch of his boots reverberated off the house's masonry. She stood wide-eyed, the jeweled crucifix held tightly in her fist, watching for any movement, ready to defend herself from Wickham's attack.

Darcy made his way to the tool shed by the barn before heading back to the house. *Twice in one week,* he thought. Twice in one week he was obliged to do the unthinkable—mutilate a corpse. At last, he knelt beside the body once again. Darcy took his new crucifix from his pocket and said the required prayers for Emily King's soul and forgiveness for his. Then he used the ax to remove her head—four carefully placed strikes loosened it from the body. Then he positioned it in place, so as not to create a scene of even greater horror when her body was found. Returning the ax to the shed, he made his way across the lawn to the back of the garden.

Elizabeth heard his return and said the last of her prayers. As soon as he stepped upon the balcony, she was in his arms, raining kisses upon his face and lips, grateful he was safe. Darcy held her to him and tried to breathe again. With Elizabeth by his side, he knew the hope of eventually winning this battle.

"Sweetling, you must return inside and I must release the spell." He set her away from him. "We will let the others discover the body."

"Did you…?" She could not say the words.

"It is taken care of. She will be Emily King for eternity." Darcy took her hand and led Elizabeth to the door. "You and I cannot be a part of finding Miss King's body. It will throw suspicion on us, which is what Wickham wants to happen." He stopped by the door and took her into his arms. "I hate that the memory of our dance has been ruined. It was *perfection.*"

"I will remember the kiss always." She went on her tiptoes to brush her lips across his. "It was *perfection.*"

Darcy kissed her tenderly, as if she were the most fragile thing he owned. "Anytime you need me, Elizabeth, send word, and I will be with you." Then, before she could say anything else, he pulled open the door. "Go straight to the retiring room. Be sure someone sees you going in or out of there. I will wait one minute and release the spell." He stepped back and spread his arms to withdraw the energy. She slipped through the portal he created. As instructed, Elizabeth wove her way through the crowd, each person repeating the moment in which he had placed them there. It would have been comical under different circumstances, but not tonight; she ran up the stairs past the room in which she had kissed Darcy earlier. She reached the doorway just as the light receded—back to its source—back to the man she had left standing on the balcony—to the man who controlled her heart as surely as he controlled the rays of light.

The strains of music and the roar of voices continued. Elizabeth entered the retiring room and freshened her hands and face—making a point of speaking to one of Charlotte's younger sisters while she was there—and then returned to the ballroom. Darcy was at the other end, talking to Bingley and Colonel Forster. When the footman rushed forward to whisper in Bingley's ear, Elizabeth knew the content of the message.

She watched Bingley and the colonel follow the footman out. Darcy remained behind to see to the guests and the party. Elizabeth tried to stay calm, but she found herself gasping for air. Darcy appeared before her, a glass of champagne in his hand. "Sip this," he whispered as he handed it to her. "I am here, Elizabeth. We will find a way to end this madness."

She took a sip of the restorative liquid. "We will find a way," she repeated automatically.

Darcy walked slowly away from her—not wanting to call any more attention to their relationship than he had by singling her out for a dance earlier—but he watched her every gesture.

A half hour later, Bingley and the colonel returned. Reluctantly, Bingley made his way to the portable stage set up for the musicians. He motioned for the music to stop, and after clearing his throat twice, he spoke to the crowd. "My friends and neighbors, I have grievous news." A rippling hush ran through the room as all eyes fell on Bingley. "The colonel and I discovered the body of a second woman. It was deposited on the back steps of Netherfield." A collective gasp filled the air. "The woman is Miss King. We found her relatives at the party and took them to quarters upstairs, where they might have some privacy. The colonel sent one of his men for the authorities. It is our belief the lady was killed elsewhere and then left here for some twisted reason." Elizabeth saw Darcy edge towards her. "However, we are sure some of you might have noticed something, as insignificant as it *might* seem. The colonel requested that everyone stay until he speaks to each person in attendance. Then your carriages will be brought around. Food and drink will continue to be available to everyone until this is re-solved. The colonel will set up headquarters in my study."

Elizabeth glanced quickly at Darcy, and he moved even closer to her. His eyes told her what to do. As others began to whisper their concerns, Elizabeth swooned and collapsed onto the floor. Darcy was by her side instantly. "Miss Elizabeth," he said as he patted her hand, and her eyes fluttered open and closed. "Miss Elizabeth!" he demanded with a bit more force. Mrs. Bennet knelt by her daughter. "Oh, my dear girl. Lizzy, are you all right?"

"Let me carry her to Mr. Bingley's library." Darcy scooped Elizabeth into his arms and pulled her close to him. She lay limply against his chest as he carried her away from the crowd. Her mother followed close on his heels. Impatiently, he spun around to face the woman. "Mrs. Bennet, perhaps you might get Miss Elizabeth something to drink and have your husband come to her. I am sure your daughter would feel safer with her father in the room, and I will need to assist Mr. Bingley."

"Of course, you are right, Mr. Darcy. I will return." She hurried away to do his bidding.

Darcy pushed the door of the library open and placed Elizabeth on the nearest settee. "Here you are, Sweetling." He knelt beside her on the floor. "Elizabeth, listen to me; we have only a moment before your family comes. After we danced, you went to the retiring room and then returned to the ballroom. I danced with you and then spoke to Bingley and the colonel. You must tell them that story, which they will believe. They—everyone else—were frozen in time until I released the spell—no one saw you enter the house. Do you trust me, Elizabeth?"

"With my life."

"Then do as I ask, Love. It is the only way."

"Yes, Fitzwilliam." Yet she knew half-truths could not save the world they created.

CHAPTER 9

Elizabeth saw Darcy no more for the rest of the evening. She spent her time with the Lucases and her own family, holed up in Mr. Bingley's library, where Darcy had left her. Her current relationship with Fitzwilliam Darcy began in that very room. *Was it less than a fortnight ago?* Darcy and Bingley evidently were assisting the colonel in organizing the party-goers for questioning. Elizabeth heard Darcy's voice in the hallway twice, but she could think of no reason to excuse herself and go to him. So she remained with her family and friends, who hovered together in whispered conversations.

"Who do you suppose is next?" A pale Maria Lucas joined Elizabeth on a settee.

"Maria, this business does not seem to be planned. These are acts of opportunity. If we do not allow the attacker the opening to commit a crime, he cannot hurt us."

"I know you are right, but it frightens me, Lizzy."

"It should," Elizabeth took the girl's hand in comfort, "but it cannot control your life. Colonel Forster and the magistrate will get to the truth soon." Actually, Elizabeth hoped neither man succeeded in discovering the truth.

Later, after she told *her* version of where she was during the ball to the colonel, the Bennets departed Netherfield. Everyone accepted that Elizabeth had fainted due to the stress of the discovery of another body, which irritated the lady in question. Dawn broke on the horizon. Darcy and Bingley saw them off, and Elizabeth seized the opening. "This is farewell *forever*, Mr. Darcy?"

Darcy traced her countenance with his eyes, trying to memorize her image. "It is, Miss Elizabeth." The thoughts of leaving her had plagued him for days. Now, the reality of it sucked the life from him. "It is for the best."

"You would think so."

Darcy offered her a formal bow. "I enjoyed our time together, Miss Elizabeth. It is rare to find a woman who converses on a variety of topics."

"I think you would find, Mr. Darcy, that women are capable of many things; the lack lies in men, who, at present, do not accept accomplishment in a woman," she said haughtily.

Darcy smiled, recognizing the source of her displeasure; it pleased him that Elizabeth would miss him. "I know barely a half dozen accomplished women, Miss Elizabeth, because I believe a truly accomplished woman needs to add something more substantial, in the improvement of her mind by extensive reading. Although you do not meet some of Miss Bingley's criteria of accomplishments, you more than surpass mine."

Elizabeth's cheeks flushed with the heat his words created in her heart. "I wish you a safe journey, Mr. Darcy." She could say no more; her family waited in the carriage.

Darcy took her hand and brought the back of it to his lips before handing her into the carriage. "Au revoir, Miss Elizabeth."

As the carriage pulled away, Darcy stepped to the road to watch her departure. At the curve, Elizabeth intuitively turned around for one last look. Hearts touched in the early dawn, and then she was out of sight. Dejectedly, he returned to the house to prepare for his own departure.

Elizabeth settled under the blankets of her bed, although light streaked through the slits in the draperies. She decided on a brief nap rather than sleep all day. Her mind remained on Fitzwilliam Darcy. Earlier that night she told a lie for him. How many lies had she told recently? More than she could remember ever telling, and they all revolved around Darcy—their clandestine meetings, his belief in a curse, their knowledge of the murders, his battle with Wickham, their intimacy, and his powers. How had she become so entrenched in his life? How had she become so *needful* of his attentions?

On second thought, most of her lies were not lies at all. They were simply half-truths—like telling someone her new dress created an "interesting silhouette" when one really meant it made her look as plump as a melon. Elizabeth laughed at her own ability to justify anything she said. She did what she did in order to protect Fitzwilliam Darcy. She needed no further justification than that.

A vicious wind chased her. Debris swirled around her feet, churned by the force following her. Elizabeth ran through the trees; shadows, kept in place by the drapery of overhanging branches, stretched across the path. Vaguely aware of the sound of footsteps behind her, Elizabeth hurdled over fallen trees and gnarled roots, trying to escape. A black adumbration flitted by the corner of her eye, but she did not break stride. Sweat streamed down her face, and she wanted desperately to wipe it away, but that would break her concentration.

The foliage thickened, reaching out for her, tearing at the sleeves of her dress, pulling the strands of her hair free from its chignon. Suddenly, dark eyes penetrated her consciousness as she skidded to a halt in front of a copse of trees.

Wickham stood among the shrubbery, wrapped in a cape of blackest ebony, so dark that it gleamed blue, even in the impenetrable murkiness. "Miss Elizabeth," his words slithered through the air, "I am happy you joined me."

Elizabeth wanted to flee, but his eyes held her in place. The sweat continued to flow down her sides and between her breasts; yet nothing else moved. She stood there, transfixed by the sight of him.

When the rain started, Elizabeth wondered irrationally how it could penetrate the thick foliage, which even light could not reach. Soaked immediately to the bone, her vigil continued—Wickham's eyes—his smile—only on her. "Come to me," he whispered, his words caressing her cheek.

Elizabeth's footsteps made a sucking sound—pulling free from the mud in which she now stood—the sound reminiscent of a person inhaling quickly. She moved towards him, and Wickham's sinister smile grew broader with each step she took. The rain and the wind did not touch him; only she felt the torment of the elements.

Then, miraculously, a deer stepped from the shadows. Its eyes were the color of ice. Intuitively, she knew what to do. The deer bowed its head, and Elizabeth reached out to its antlers. Her hands encircled the base, and she lifted the antlers above her head. Without ceremony, she charged at Wickham, who now stood as transfixed as she once was.

A sound of terror filled the air, along with the crack of bone as each of the antler points pierced his body—blood oozing from each puncture—the blood, a rainbow of colors, as if it came from many sources. She heard herself say, "Not so happy to see me now, are you, Mr. Wickham?" Then he disappeared, vanishing in a puff of grey ashes.

She bolted upright, her heart pounding so loudly that it drowned out the noise of the busy household. The image of Wickham's blood seeping out onto her hands still clung to her mind. On impulse, she studied her hands, expecting to find a rainbow of blood across each palm. Elizabeth shook her head to clear her thoughts and to make sense of the nightmare—Wickham was obvious, and the deer with Darcy's eyes made some sense. But why would a deer's antlers kill Wickham? *Heavens!* Falling to sleep with thoughts of Darcy and the lies she created to protect him left her sensibilities in the dust.

Forcing herself from the bed, Elizabeth drifted to the window, wondering how the day would greet the chaos of her mind and the void she felt without Darcy. *You will just have to go on without him,* she told herself as she opened the drapes wide. The early winter sunlight danced across the floor, revealing flecks of dust floating in the air.

At first, she squinted into the brilliance of the light—so bright it half blinded her. She had always loved the view from her bedroom—the rolling meadow behind the garden, so green during the summer and dazzling with the colors of wildflowers in the spring. Now, the frost clung to the remaining blades of grass and dusted the ground with shimmering fairy dust. She touched the damp sill while idly taking in the beauty of the winter scene—and then she realized that a horse grazed in the meadow. A magnificent animal—she knew it well. *Ceres!*

Grabbing her dressing gown, Elizabeth snuck down the back stairs, making her way to her father's study.

"Papa?" She tapped lightly on the door to draw his attention. "What is Ceres doing in the meadow?" she asked as she approached her father's desk.

"Ceres?"

"Mr. Bingley's horse, Papa."

"Ah! Of course. Ceres," he said absent-mindedly. "Mr. Bingley is leaving Netherfield for awhile; he asked if I would house the animal until he returned. He left me a generous allowance to tend to her. Another horse on the farm will be useful."

"Mr. Bingley is gone? Jane will be devastated!" Elizabeth realized that Darcy really was gone if Bingley no longer was in residence at Netherfield. He certainly could not be there without his friend.

"The man should return in the spring, I would suspect. Mr. Bingley's sisters left Jane a note. It is on the table in the foyer. They left one for you also, Lizzy." Her father shifted his attention back to the book he read. "You take Jane's to her, Child. She might need you when she reads it."

Elizabeth's heart jumped to her throat when he mentioned the note from the Bingley sisters. She knew it was from Darcy; Caroline Bingley would never bid her farewell. "Yes, Papa." Elizabeth started towards the door. "Do you suppose I might ride Ceres occasionally?"

"Hmm? Oh, yes. You mentioned Mr. Darcy gave you lessons. I imagine that could be arranged."

"Thank you, Papa." Elizabeth slipped from the room. Darcy had brought *her* the horse; she was sure of it. Somehow he had manipulated his friend into sending Ceres there. Elizabeth hurried to the entranceway to retrieve the notes before someone else found them.

Grabbing the sealed missives, Elizabeth felt a sense of anticipation, recognizing his distinctive script. Once she read the directions, she slid hers into the pocket of her dressing gown before bounding up the steps to her room. She would not give Jane's to her immediately; she doubted her sister was even awake. She would read hers first. Slipping in the door and locking it behind her, she scrambled to her bed and tore at the seal, anxious to read Darcy's farewell:

My dearest Elizabeth,

As I write this, I believe myself perfectly calm and cool, but I am convinced it is written in a dreadful bitterness of spirit. By the time you read this, I will be miles from Longbourn, but my thoughts will be with you, today and forever. You brought me a joy I never knew existed and gave me acceptance even though you knew the worst of me. How might a man explain how unique that is?

Ceres is yours; Bingley sold him to me, and I give the beauty to you. Continue your lessons, and learn to ride with the wind. In my old age, I will imagine you riding breakneck across the rolling hills of Hertfordshire, shocking the neighborhood with your "scandalous" behavior. A saddle is in the barn; it is well worn, but you will find it serviceable. The swords are still hidden in the manor house; they are yours also. Horrify your nieces and nephews with your sleight of hand. No one handles a rapier as you do, Vixen.

Someday I hope you will think fondly of the time we spent together. I will cherish each of the moments as the best of my life.

F. D.

Tears streamed down her cheeks. Elizabeth wanted to be with him more than she had ever wanted anything, but even being with Darcy would not be enough. She wanted all the things every woman wants: a husband who loved her and children they shared. Elizabeth could never have that with Darcy, and—as much as she desired him—she knew he could offer her no future. He was right; their separation was for the best.

Wiping her tears away, she picked up the note for Jane. Her sister would feel the loneliness of departure as much as she did. Elizabeth wished she could share her feelings with Jane, but Jane and Bingley courted openly. Darcy had acknowledged her only with a dance—and that was because he was leaving and because she begged it of him. No one would ever know how she would compare every other man with him.

Caroline Bingley's letter to Jane said she and her sister, Louisa, demanded their brother return to London. It was too dangerous in Hertfordshire; they were terribly frightened. Elizabeth suspected otherwise. "Although some truth obviously exists as to their fear, I am more inclined to believe Miss Bingley sees her brother is in love with you," she asserted as Jane tried to hide her disappointment.

"Listen to this." Jane Bennet took up the letter and read. "Unable to feel safe in Hertfordshire at this time, we believe this provides us an opportunity to renew relationships with friends and family in town. Besides, Mr. Darcy is impatient to see his sister, and to confess the truth, we are scarcely less eager to meet her again. I really do not think Georgiana Darcy has her equal for beauty, elegance, and accomplishments; and the affection she inspires in Louisa and me, is heightened into something still more interesting, from the hope we dare to entertain of her being here after our sister. I do not know whether I ever before mentioned to you my feelings on this subject, but I will not leave the country without confiding them, and I trust you will not esteem them unreasonable. My brother admires her greatly already; and by leaving for London, he will have frequent opportunity now of seeing her on the most intimate footing; her relations all wish the connection as much as his own, and a sister's partiality is not misleading me, I think, when I call Charles most capable of engaging any woman's heart. With all these circumstances to favor an attachment and nothing to prevent it, am I wrong, my dearest Jane, in indulging the hope of an event which will secure the happiness of so many?" Jane handed the letter to Elizabeth. "Is that not clear? Mr. Bingley is intended for Mr. Darcy's sister."

"Indeed, Jane, you ought to believe me." Elizabeth knew Darcy, and she could not imagine he had such aspirations for his sister. As much as he esteemed Charles Bingley, it was likely Mr. Darcy planned a more auspicious match for his sister, especially if her heirs would inherit Pemberley. They were, after all, the children of Lady Anne Darcy, the sister of the Earl of Matlock, and the Bingleys were rich only through trade. However, Elizabeth spoke not her thoughts; instead, she tossed the letter into the nearest drawer and slammed it closed. "No one who ever saw you together can doubt his affection. Miss Bingley, I am sure, cannot. She is not such a simpleton. Could she have seen half as much love in Mr. Darcy for herself, she would have ordered her wedding clothes." Elizabeth smiled with the knowledge that Caroline Bingley would never know Darcy in that way. "We are not rich enough, or grand enough, for them; and she is the more anxious to get Miss Darcy for her brother, from the notion that when there has been *one* intermarriage, she may have less trouble in achieving a second. But my dearest Jane, you cannot seriously imagine because Miss Bingley tells you her brother greatly admires Miss Darcy, he is in the smallest degree less sensible of *your* merit than when he took leave of you last evening, or it will be in her power to persuade him that instead of being in love with you, he is very much in love with her friend."

Jane Bennet continued to believe Caroline Bingley to be honest in her words; Elizabeth knew better, but she did not trust herself to discuss it at length without confessing how distraught she was about Darcy's departure. Little could be done, however, either way. Mr. Bingley had left the country, and Jane had no recourse except to pray he would return soon. Elizabeth realized Mrs. Bennet would lament the bad luck of losing such a prime catch as Mr. Bingley. She would not soon let her daughter forget her loss. For that reason, Elizabeth was happy her mother knew nothing of Darcy's attentions.

The morning slipped by as the household began to stir after the long evening. Elizabeth roamed from room to room, driven by an unbearable restlessness and unsettled by the feeling of loneliness and the question of whether Wickham would actually follow Darcy. What if he did not and chose another victim? What could she do then? Could she tell the colonel what she knew? How could she keep Darcy out of it? Elizabeth knew she could not stand idly by and allow Wickham to leisurely choose victim after victim. And what of the victims? Unless someone helped to free their souls, they were damned for all time. Elizabeth did not believe she could do what Darcy did.

In the early afternoon, she stole away to her room to read each of Darcy's notes again, overwhelmed by the void he had left in her life. Once more, she drifted to the window, thinking to watch the horse he had left her, a way of keeping him in her heart. She stood watching the animal toss its head with an unknown anxiousness, mimicking the feelings she experienced. Elizabeth thought it the most magnificent animal, full of fire and brimstone—like Darcy. It pawed the earth with its hoof before flicking its tail and skittering away towards the barn. Then she saw him. Darcy stood along the hedgerow on the far side of the meadow, among the trees. He watched the house, obviously looking for her. *He has not left me, after all.* Grabbing her shawl, she quickly headed out to meet him.

"Where are you going, Lizzy?" her father called from the front parlor.

Elizabeth anxiously retraced her steps and entered the parlor. "I thought to take a walk, Papa."

"Do not go out alone, Child, after what happened last night. It is too dangerous, Lizzy."

Elizabeth tried to think of a plausible excuse to leave the house. She worried Darcy might leave if she did not hurry. She had no idea how long he had waited in the woods, but how could she go against her father's wishes? "Yes, Papa." She returned to the upper floors, searching each window to see if he still remained nearby.

Finally, her eyes found him. He stepped back into the shadows, but Darcy lingered, his countenance turned towards Longbourn. She knew intuitively that he wanted her to go to him. Elizabeth could imagine the smile on his face when she approached. Despite her father's warning, she recognized her need; she must fly to him.

Impulsively moving towards the kitchen, she found her mother overseeing the day's menu. "Good afternoon, Mama." She bestowed a peck on her mother's cheek.

"Good afternoon, Lizzy." Her mother looked up quickly, distracted by the hustle and bustle of a busy household. "Where are you headed?"

"I believe I will go out to the barn and feed the new horse an apple or two." Elizabeth pulled her shawl tightly around her shoulders.

Her mother's expression changed, and her voice rose in contempt. "Our dear Jane was played poorly by Mr. Bingley. Have you spoken to her? She took breakfast in her room."

"Give her time, Mama; Jane will come around," Elizabeth murmured.

"Well, I wish the man a dreadful stay in London. He treated your sister ill, and I may never forgive him."

Elizabeth could not help but agree with her mother's sentiments; Mr. Bingley should not be so easily persuaded! Mr. Hill opened the door to bring in some wood for the fire, and Elizabeth took the opportunity to leave. To avoid telling another lie, she did go to the barn, and, finding Ceres in one of the open stalls, she fed the animal an apple from the barrel. "Afternoon, my lovely," she whispered softly into the horse's ear as she petted its nose gently. "I plan to find Mr. Darcy," she confided in the animal, wanting to be able to say the words out loud. Then she rushed to the open door and clung to the side of the barn, making her way to the back of the structure. Knowing no one would see her if she walked a straight line from the barn to the far-off hedgerow until she was more than halfway across the now-barren field, Elizabeth did not break into a run until she reached the midpoint, hoping to evade any eyes watching from the upper floors of Longbourn.

Assured that Darcy saw had seen her coming before he dropped back into the tree line, Elizabeth skirted the stile on the far-off hedgerow and plunged into the woods. She saw him turn towards Netherfield, leading away from the house. Impetuously, she called to him, but he did not answer, simply moving ahead.

Elizabeth quickened her pace, but he remained a focal point, not a reality. No matter how fast she moved, he seemed to continue on at an equal distance from her. She called out again, but he did not hear. So Elizabeth simply followed, doing the only thing she could do—keep him in sight. When he turned suddenly towards the manor house, she smiled, knowing he led her to their secret place. Darcy, she thought, probably relished the idea that she would foolishly follow him just because he appeared on the outskirts of her father's property. She knew she played to his vanity with her actions, but his teasing always intrigued her.

At the door, he turned to look back at her. Elizabeth saw the corners of his mouth turn up in a smile, and then he slipped inside. Moments later, Elizabeth crossed the threshold. Calling out his name, she rushed forward into the room, and then—then time stopped—her heartbeat ceased when she saw what stood before her.

A whimper escaped her lips, but no other sound was heard in the empty house. Leaning casually against the mantle of the cold hearth, George Wickham nodded his head in acknowledgment. "I fear your precious Fitzwilliam is not here, Miss Elizabeth." His voice sounded to her ears like that of the snake in the Garden of Eden.

She swallowed hard and wondered whether, if she broke into a run, she could clear the deserted path before he caught her. Wickham noted the twitch in her eye. "Do not consider it, my dear; you will never make it," he warned. Neither of them moved as he continued his taunt. "Obviously, your Mr. Darcy never told you I possess unique abilities. How easily you were deceived into thinking I was your lover!"

"Mr. Darcy and I are not lovers!" she protested, while she tried to formulate a plan for escape.

"What do you call this rendezvous, Miss Elizabeth? There are remnants of a picnic lunch and a blanket in the other room. You call the man by his given name, my dear. What does that sound like to you?" He dropped his arms to his sides and edged forward as he spoke.

Feeling the sudden stillness of the room, Elizabeth gingerly stepped back, but she never took her eyes from his face. "Mr. Darcy gave me riding lessons; that was all there was between us."

"If you say so, Miss Elizabeth." He eyed her mockingly. "Yet you provide me with a unique opportunity, and I exist for such prospects. Whether you return his feelings or not, your Mr. Darcy never showed a partiality to any woman until you. I make it my business to know Darcy's weaknesses. Other than his sister, Darcy cares for no one; he has never allowed himself such a pleasure. Then, all at once, he—by your own admission—is giving you riding lessons, waltzing with you on a private balcony, kissing your tempting lips, and rescuing you from unknown terrors. You did like how I staged that one, did you not?" he taunted. "I am sure he was the one who placed the wreaths and the iron ornaments about your home. They only served to confirm my earlier suspicions."

Elizabeth furtively reached for the jeweled crucifix she wore at her neck. Wickham took note of the slight shift in her stance.

"Did your lover give you the Christian symbol to protect you from me?" Again, he inched closer to her, while Elizabeth countered his movement with a retreat of her own.

"*I* purchased this crucifix," she asserted.

"Do not try to mislead me, Miss Elizabeth. I am not so easily deceived. I saw Miss Darcy wear a similar one after my special evening with her, so I am aware of the source of your enchantment. Mr. Darcy hopes to protect you." By now, Wickham was near enough to reach her if he so wished; yet his hands remained at his sides; she stayed alert for his attack. "It will be a pleasure to take you from Darcy. It will be a revenge like no other; he is the first of his family to dare to challenge me, and *I do not like to lose,* Miss Elizabeth."

She shivered. "Mr. Darcy is gone." She hoped her words might stop his plan or, at least, give her a chance to convince Wickham to release her. "In fact, everyone at Netherfield has fled your carnage."

"My carnage?" Wickham sounded amused. "Two females hardly rates as carnage, Miss Elizabeth." He finally reached out to her, lightly tracing a line along her jaw to her mouth. Elizabeth wanted to bite his hand, but she was sure that Wickham would enjoy it too much. "I must congratulate you, Miss Elizabeth; Darcy grew stronger with you by his side. That display last evening at Netherfield would never have been possible six months ago. So, you see, my dear, I must stop your power over Darcy. It will kill him to know that he left you to me. The fact will eat away at him. Plus, eliminating you will keep his powers in check. Whether he is here to see your demise or not will make little difference. I will make sure he learns of your tragic end."

Elizabeth knew that she must do something or die at his hands. A flash of humor crossed his expression as she broke away from him, shoving furniture into his path as she attempted an escape. Just as she reached the door, grabbing it to pull it open, Wickham appeared behind her. An iron grip took hold of her arm as his left hand shoved the door closed. He pulled her back into him, breathing into Elizabeth's hair. "Good," he hissed, "I was afraid you might not *fight* me. I prefer my followers to be *spirited*."

Elizabeth struggled and flailed, trying to dislodge his hold on her, but Wickham's grip simply tightened around her waist. "My, you are a spit-fire," he said and laughed. "It is no wonder Darcy prefers you."

She screamed as he half lifted, half dragged her towards the stairs. Elizabeth scratched at him and fought him, but her efforts were futile. Wickham overpowered her. Halfway up the stairs, he halted suddenly and violently pulled her face within inches of his. "I would give anything to see Darcy's face when he discovers I took you in the bedroom of the manor house at Netherfield. It will be a *delightful* revenge." Wickham pulled her mouth to his and kissed her with such force that he bruised her lips.

Elizabeth's stomach turned. She strained against him, releasing her mouth from his unwelcome assault. Disgusted by his closeness, Elizabeth spit in Wickham's face. For a brief moment, Elizabeth's countenance displayed a gratified smile as Wickham wiped the moisture from his cheek, but then a backhand slap forced her head to the side and split her lip. Blood seeped from the opening.

"The first course?" His hand turned her chin roughly, and he licked the blood from her mouth. "Thank you, my dear." Wickham started forward again, dragging her behind him.

CHAPTER 10

Darcy sat with the Bingleys at the posting inn. Caroline Bingley *needed* her refreshment, although they had traveled only a few miles from her brother's estate. At this rate, they might never reach London. The woman who wanted to be as far from Netherfield as humanly possible only a few hours earlier now seemed content to drink her tea and command the servants to indulge her every whim. All Darcy heard from the time they left Meryton was how Charles and Georgiana would make an eminently suitable match. Louisa Hurst had traveled with her husband to his Hampshire estate, so it was just the three of them.

Bingley miserably shifted his weight with each of his sister's remarks. As much as Darcy admired Bingley, he would hope to find a different sort of match for Georgiana. He had considered a match between the genial Charles Bingley and his very shy sister when he first met the man, but within the hour of meeting, Darcy had abandoned those hopes. Although real affection existed between his best friend and his sister, Darcy knew they could never be happy together—and he wanted both of them to be happy. Charles had glowed with love when he met Jane Bennet; Darcy hoped the man would resist his sister's manipulations and find true love.

Thoughts of Charles and Jane Bennet brought Darcy's thoughts back to Elizabeth. He wondered how she had reacted when she saw Ceres on her lawn. Elizabeth's eyes had danced with excitement; of that he was sure. A secret smile formed with the thought of her riding the horse he had given her and wearing the habit he had purchased for her.

At first, when the family livery passed by him, Darcy did not see it because Elizabeth's countenance consumed his consciousness, but as the man took the food the innkeeper gave him and neared the table again, the traditional colors of Steventon House registered in his brain.

"Lucas!" Darcy called as the man strode past.

Lucas Stamson skidded to a halt upon hearing his employer's voice. "Mr. Darcy," he said as he turned towards the sound. "I was on my way to find you, Sir. I stopped to change horses because the other one took on a stone."

Darcy approached him. "What is wrong, Lucas? Is something the matter with Miss Darcy?"

"No…no, Sir. Miss Darcy was well when I left her, Sir."

Darcy allowed himself to breathe again. "Then what is it, Lucas? Why are you here?"

The groomsman searched in the pouch he carried around his neck and drew out a note. "Miss Darcy bid me bring this to you with the utmost speed, Sir."

Darcy snatched the letter from the man's outstretched hand. "Thank you, Lucas. I will be with you in a moment."

"Yes, Mr. Darcy." The man retreated into the shadows of the public room, while Darcy made his way to a window to use the natural light to read.

> *Fitzwilliam,*
>
> *Mrs. Annesley woke this morning in a dreadful agitation, and she begged me to convey what she knows to you. As she was able to see George Wickham's attack on me, my faithful companion's Sight has shown a new attack. I do not know of whom she speaks or the place, but Mrs. Annesley is sure you will comprehend what eludes me.*
>
> *Mrs. Annesley describes an abandoned house, although it was once a fine home. Within the house, she sees a forsaken picnic basket, of all things. Yet more important, Mr. Wickham is there with a petite, auburn-haired woman.*
>
> *Save her, Fitzwilliam. Mrs. Annesley believes the woman is the answer to our family's problems; she is your future. I hope that this*

makes sense and that you know what to do.

God be with you, Brother,
Georgiana

Darcy's throat tightened and he gasped for air. *Elizabeth!* Could Wickham have Elizabeth? *I abandoned her!* he chastised himself. "Lucas!" he shouted.

"Yes, Mr. Darcy." The servant appeared immediately.

"Did you order a fresh horse?"

"Yes, Sir."

"*Get it,* man. I need to leave at once." The servant scrambled to do his bidding. Darcy's thoughts raced as he tried to make sense of what he needed to do. Mrs. Annesley had saved Georgiana; with her warning and with luck, he would reach Elizabeth in time. Impatient for action, he returned to the table. "Bingley, a situation has arisen that I must attend to. Lucas will ride back to London with you."

"Of course, Darcy." Bingley hastened to his feet. "May I help somehow?"

Darcy headed towards the door, consumed by his need to reach Elizabeth. "It is a family matter," he told Bingley. "I must go." Then he bounded from the room to find the waiting groomsman. "Ride back to London with Mr. Bingley," he ordered as he mounted, and then Darcy rode off towards Hertfordshire. He did not care that both Bingley and Caroline noted the direction he took. Neither of them spoke of it, however, as they boarded Bingley's chaise and four.

Darcy rode low in the saddle, trying to speed his way back to her. His senses told him Elizabeth was indeed in dire straits. He reproached himself for leaving, but he never broke stride. He prayed for God to protect her, but he never broke stride. He cursed the Fate that placed her in danger, but he never broke stride. When he rode onto the graveled pathway leading to the manor house, the horse was lathered in foam. Darcy slid from the saddle, hurriedly tied his horse to a post, and ran to the house.

He burst through the front door, begging not to be too late.

"Elizabeth!" he bellowed repeatedly as he dashed from room to room. In the billiards room, the blanket upon which they had lain was draped across the small table. Automatically, Darcy grabbed the rapier, removing the tip as he continued his search.

A thump—a muffled sound from above—told him where she was. Leaping over the lower banister, he bolted up the stairs. Breathlessly, he swung the door open. As it banged against the wall, a terrible drama opened up in front of him. Elizabeth's limbs—her arms and her legs—were tied to the four posts of the bed. She was stripped down to her chemise—her face rigid with terror from what she experienced at Wickham's hands. Her shining eyes, misted with tears, flooded his heart with anguish. Wickham himself sat in a wing chair next to the bed. He caressed Elizabeth's arm lightly with his fingertips.

"Darcy? You came back." Wickham's smile increased by the moment; the changing scenario pleased him. "It is as I said, Miss Elizabeth; he cares for you."

Tears streamed from Elizabeth's eyes. "I am sorry, Fitzwilliam." A slight shake of his head told her he did not blame her; Darcy blamed only himself.

"Leave her be, Wickham; you seek me." Darcy's eyes searched the room, trying to find a way to save Elizabeth.

Wickham stood casually; to taunt Darcy, he ran a fingertip along Elizabeth's breasts. "Of course, I want you, Darcy, but not enough to give up Miss Elizabeth. You would gladly die in her stead, but that is just it; you would *gladly* die. In fact, you want to die to end this. However, when I kill the woman you love, *that* will hurt you."

Wickham spoke the truth. Darcy would happily sacrifice himself to save Elizabeth. With no other choice and without preamble, Darcy grasped the sword tightly and charged the apparition lurking beside the bed. Barely two steps into the room, a jolt of gale force winds hit his chest, sending his body flying through the air like a rag doll—and like a rag doll, Darcy slithered down the wall in apparent defeat. The rapier skidded away towards the bed.

"Close your eyes, Elizabeth," he ordered as he staggered to his feet. Darcy brought his arms out to his sides and pivoted to bring forth the power within him; Wickham was strong, but Darcy would not die until Elizabeth was free. It was suicide to attack Wickham; however, he vowed to end this, and end it he would. His death would mean life for Elizabeth. She depended on him; and her determination—her passion—made him strong. Like Wickham's wind, Darcy's light held an energy of its own—potent and formidable. It bent Wickham backwards, knocking him from his feet and momentarily blinding him with its power.

Shielding his eyes, Wickham teetered for a moment before regaining control. Mockingly, he challenged, "Excellent, Darcy, but you are still no match for me." Again, a whirlwind skittered across the hardwood floor towards Darcy, followed by a biting, sucking sound intended to rip the skin from his body.

Intuitively, Darcy tucked and rolled away, trying to draw the power away from where Elizabeth lay. Attempting to free herself, she wriggled, but for naught. The knots held her captive to whatever would come.

As he escaped the evil sent at him by Wickham, Darcy grabbed the rapier, which was resting by the foot of the bed. Excitement swirled around them—shadows prowled the corners of the room as he and Wickham evaluated the situation. Their bodies tensed—their muscles flexed for response—their hearts pounded in their ears. Steel grey eyes met ice blue ones, and pure energy crackled between them. The minutest movement took on great importance. The only noise in the room was Elizabeth's shuddered breathing. And as quickly as the battle had stopped, it began again. Wickham lunged to reach him first, and, mechanically, from his place on the floor, Darcy plunged the sword into Wickham's chest, pushing up on it to open the wound more.

Wickham's face contorted in obvious surprise, knowing the folly of his attack on Darcy. "Die!" Darcy roared as he clamored to his feet, pushing the rapier deeper into Wickham's heart.

Wickham snarled a smile—a mixture of pain and defiance.

"After *you*, Darcy." With a mocking salute and a blast of absolute power, the whole room swirled—rotated. Darcy grabbed for the four-poster, diving onto the bed to protect Elizabeth at all costs.

"I have you," he growled as he draped himself over her.

Within seconds, it was over. Silence ruled where chaos had been. The room stood still, and the roar of the wind miraculously vanished. Only the echoing sound of the broken sword hitting the floor remained in the room. For Darcy, the darkness of a moment ago disappeared with the sunlight of knowing Elizabeth to be alive.

Her muffled cough brought him back to reality. Darcy rolled from her, straining to right himself and his world. "Elizabeth?" He pushed the hair from her face. "*Elizabeth!*" He kissed the side of her face, needing to feel her closeness. "Tell me you are well." He caressed her jaw line in the palm of his hand, searching for the woman he cherished.

Sounding frightened and a bit childlike, she managed to whisper, "You came. I thought you were gone."

"Oh, Vixen," he moaned as he drank of her lips tenderly. "I will explain it later." His mouth rested only inches above hers. "We must leave now."

Elizabeth nodded, unsure what it all meant, but glad to be back in his arms again. Darcy reached for the knots that held her. "Please tell me the blackguard did not—harm you."

"Just frightened me, Fitzwilliam."

She watched his face contort with self-blame as he loosened each of the bindings. Gently, Darcy massaged the welts. "How can you ever forgive me?" he whispered before kissing the inside of each wrist. "How may I make this up to you?"

Sitting up in bed to survey the damage strewn about the room, Elizabeth did not answer. Instead, she helped him loosen the rags that bound her legs.

Afraid of what he saw in her face as she worked the last knot, Darcy backed away from her, thinking she wanted only freedom from him forever. He could not blame her, but it stabbed his soul nonetheless. "I am sorry, Elizabeth," he murmured before dropping his gaze from hers.

But as soon as she was free, Elizabeth bolted from the bed into his arms. Darcy staggered backwards, absorbing the impact of her impetuous move. The surprise of her bold attack radiated through them both, and he laughed before pulling her to him and lowering his head to kiss her. He trembled against her and muttered something incoherent before sinking his tongue into her mouth. "I missed you, Vixen."

They touched heaven as they pressed against each other. After they took their fill, Elizabeth whispered, "We did this last night."

"Not enough." Groaning, he pulled her closer still and stroked her hair. "I must get you to safety," he said gently, and she nodded.

Darcy helped to find her discarded clothing and quietly aided her in restoring her appearance. "Turn," he ordered as Elizabeth worked to secure the bodice of her dress. As he laced up the last of the eyelets, Darcy kissed the nape of Elizabeth's neck. "I nearly lost you today."

"I was so happy to see you." Impulsively, she turned in his arms, and the passion began anew.

Lost in the kiss, neither of them heard the intruders surreptitiously making their way up the stairs until a voice came from behind Darcy. "Mr. Darcy, kindly remove your hands from my daughter."

Elizabeth froze, but she did not release the hold she had on Darcy's jacket. "Papa, let me explain." Her voice held a resolve that startled both Darcy and Elizabeth's father.

Mr. Bennet turned to hustle his servants from the room before he answered her. "There is little to explain." He closed the door after their departure. "It appears you and Mr. Darcy are more intimate than any of us suspected. How long has this clandestine affair been going on?" His voice was unaccustomedly grave.

Darcy did not turn around; he let Elizabeth take the lead. When he had ridden back to save her, he had committed himself to this moment.

Elizabeth took a half step to the side, but she left her right hand resting on Darcy's chest. "Papa, this is not what it looks like," she began. "I went out to give Ceres an apple in the barn. When I left, I spotted someone along the far hedgerow. I should *not* have—I know that now—but I followed him. At first, I simply wanted to know why he watched the house, but the closer I got, the farther away he moved. My curiosity and my anger got the best of me, and I followed the man deeper into the woods."

"Who was it, Child?"

Elizabeth shot Darcy a warning glance. "I do not know, Papa. He was dressed as a gentleman. Before I could turn around, he grabbed me from behind and hit me in the face." She touched her bruised lip for effect. "He brought me here and tied me up."

"Tied you to the bed?"

"Yes, Papa." She raised her arm for him to see her wrist.

Mr. Bennet's gaze focused on the obvious abrasion. "How did Mr. Darcy come to be here with you?"

"I rode back to Netherfield because I forgot something important." Darcy's voice held a calmness he did not feel. Elizabeth's hand rested over his heart, and she knew it raced as violently as hers.

Elizabeth spoke again. It would be *her* lie, not his. "Mr. Darcy saw the strange horse tied up in the front of the manor house and came to investigate. That is when he found me. He and the man fought, but my attacker escaped."

"Could you recognize the man?" Mr. Bennet asked as he surveyed the damage to the room.

Darcy's did his best to follow Elizabeth's lead. "I do not think so, Sir. It all happened so quickly, and the man wore a mask. My only concern at the time was your daughter."

"Mr. Darcy saved me, Papa."

"It seems Mr. Darcy does a great deal of *saving* where you are involved, Elizabeth." Mr. Bennet did not want to reproach Darcy's behavior, but he would not allow Elizabeth's reputation to be sullied. He cleared his throat, trying to find the right words with which to approach a man of Darcy's standing. As her father moved away towards the window, he casually inquired, "May I ask, Mr.

Darcy, why you returned to Netherfield? What did you forget, Sir?"

"*Me,*" she blurted out before Darcy could respond. "Mr. Darcy came back for me, Papa. He has just asked me to marry him."

"Elizabeth?" Darcy's words were barely audible to Elizabeth. "How can we?"

"Fitzwilliam," she whispered, "we have no choice. Wickham knows who I am. Even if you leave again, I am in danger. He will not rest until I am dead—he will do anything to hurt you—hurt you through me. I am safe only in your arms."

"I never meant to bring you into this," he said sotto voce.

"I am in it, nonetheless. Will you protect me with your name, as well as your body? I told you before you need me if you are to defeat Wickham."

Darcy caressed her chin with the palm of his hand. "I would give you anything, Elizabeth."

"Then we will find a way."

"How will this work?"

Elizabeth glanced over her shoulder at her father, who appeared to be no less astonished than Mr. Darcy. "I do not know, but only when we are together does this madness seem under control."

Darcy nodded his agreement. "Mr. Bennet, may I speak with you?" he said, more loudly.

"Lizzy, please repair your appearance. I would not wish for your mother to see you right now." Elizabeth blushed at her father's reprimand.

Darcy and her father stepped out into the hallway as Elizabeth tried to right her clothing and hair. Mr. Bennet kept his voice low, but his anger was evident. "Mr. Darcy, you have placed Elizabeth in a most awkward position. Although I am eternally grateful for your interference today, I am also appalled by your behavior. I am not eager to have Lizzy paraded around Hertfordshire as your betrothed while my servants gossip about what they saw here."

"Mr. Bennet, I assure you I do not want that for Miss Elizabeth either. Your daughter and I judged poorly and allowed our emotions to control our response, but please know I hold genuine regard for Elizabeth. In light of that fact, I suggest we dispense with the usual reading of the banns. I will procure a special license, and Elizabeth and I can marry immediately in London. We will leave for there tomorrow. Does not Miss Elizabeth have an aunt and uncle in London?"

"In Cheapside."

"Cheapside?" Darcy refused to let his initial contempt show. "I am sure they will be happy to aid your daughter. She may be married from their home. We will explain to all that ours is a love match. With my withdrawal from Netherfield, I did not want to leave Miss Elizabeth behind."

"That sounds like the most logical solution, Mr. Darcy. Thank you for your discretion. Let us take Elizabeth with us and return to Longbourn to tell Mrs. Bennet the happy news."

The reappearance of Mr. Darcy sent the residents of Longbourn into a tizzy. When Darcy and Elizabeth repeated their parts of the story to the rest of her family, there were gasps of disbelief—first at Elizabeth's foolishness for following the stranger and then at Darcy's proposal.

When Mrs. Bennet protested the plan for an immediate marriage, Darcy interceded. "I must return to Derbyshire, Mrs. Bennet," Darcy explained, "and I will not be returning to Hertfordshire for a year or more. I came back today to plead with your daughter to accept me now. I would not want to wait a year in hopes she might retain any feelings for me at that time. Last night, I dreamed of Elizabeth at Pemberley for the upcoming festive season; today I felt compelled to make it so."

"Of—of course, Mr. Darcy," Mrs. Bennet stammered. "But do you not wish a large wedding?"

"No, Mrs. Bennet, I am a very private man. I understand your reluctance to part with your daughter. However, you may take comfort in knowing that despite the urgency with which I make Miss Elizabeth my wife, your daughter will be the mistress of one of the largest estates in England. In addition, she will have a house in town, as well as having access to several other properties."

Mrs. Bennet drew in a deep breath, recognizing the advantage of Elizabeth's marriage to Darcy. "The festive season is a problem; we have multiple commitments from which we may not be excused." She thought of her other daughters and hoped Elizabeth's engagement to Darcy might encourage matches for them. "Jane must travel with Elizabeth to London, Mr. Darcy." Mrs. Bennet began to plan how she might advance the chances of her three younger daughters at the local celebrations. "We cannot have our dear Lizzy spoken poorly of."

Darcy nodded his head in agreement. "Miss Bennet's presence is most welcome."

"Come, Lizzy." Mrs. Bennet stood suddenly. "Let us see to your packing."

Darcy reached for Elizabeth's hand. "If you would have no objections, Mrs. Bennet, I would like for Elizabeth to join me in the garden. Everything has been so hurried, I would appreciate a few moments to speak to my betrothed in private."

"Certainly, Mr. Darcy."

Darcy stood and offered Elizabeth his hand. "Would you care to join me in the garden, Elizabeth?"

"Very much, Fitzwilliam." She smiled at his formality. She slid her hand into the crook of his arm as he led her away.

Once outside, the formality went by the wayside. "Elizabeth, do you realize what you have done?"

"I have committed myself to *you,* Fitzwilliam. Would you wish me to do otherwise?" Suddenly, his hesitation angered her. "Do you wish me to end this now?"

"It might be for the best—you might be safer from Wickham."

"If this is such a poor *idea*—if I am such a poor *choice*—let us end it this moment, Mr. Darcy!" She tried to jerk her hand away from his, but Darcy caught it with a firmer hold.

"Elizabeth, please listen. You are a beautiful—exquisite— woman, and any man would thank his luckiest of stars to have you. You have looked into my soul and accepted a part of me that I have showed no one else. I question *your* choice—not *mine*. We could never consummate our marriage. I will not chance bringing a son into this world under these circumstances. My opinion in that matter has not altered. Are you willing to accept never knowing a child of your own?"

"We could adopt, Fitzwilliam," she suggested innocently. "Truthfully, I do not know what I am willing to accept, but one thing I cannot accept is your walking out of my life. The only way any of this makes sense is if we are together. Do you really want to spend the rest of your life alone?"

"I do not wish to be without you," he conceded. "I suppose adoption is a possibility, if it is what you wish." Darcy wiped her tears away with his thumb. "Could you live such a life, Elizabeth, never knowing the passion of the wedding bed? I cannot share you with someone else; I care too much for you. I will not spread my seed elsewhere, nor can I tolerate your giving yourself to another."

Elizabeth mentally sorted through these limited options. "I will be satisfied with what we have, Fitzwilliam. Having only part of you would be superior to knowing anyone else fully."

Darcy stared at her; his lovely Elizabeth was so young—so sheltered. "You will want for nothing, Elizabeth. I promise you that. We can travel—see all the places you have only dreamed of. Anything you want, my love."

"To be with you, Fitzwilliam—then I will be happy."

He brought the back of her hand to his lips. "Then you will be my Vixen forever and ever."

Impulsively, Elizabeth took his hand in both of hers. "Keep this kiss"—she planted one on the inside of his palm—"to hold until we can share our lips again freely."

"You are a tease!" He traced her mouth with his fingertips.

"Which you more than appreciate, Sir."

He laughed—that deep rolling laugh he shared only with her. "You make me feel alive, Vixen."

"Wickham said something similar." She spoke the creature's name with distaste.

Darcy's attention was suddenly on alert; surely he had not heard her correctly! "Of what do you speak?" he demanded.

Elizabeth directed him towards the nearest bench. "Mr. Wickham claimed your powers have grown in intensity since we met. He said that was one of the reasons he needed to eliminate me."

As was his habit, Darcy spoke bluntly. "I have not dwelt on such thoughts. I noted the exhilaration I felt in the beginning, when I taunted you into a response, and, it is true I now understand the depths of some of my powers, but, of late, I have thought of nothing but you." His fingers massaged the back of her wrist.

"It is a factor we must consider in our quest to rid ourselves of Wickham."

Darcy looked about for anyone lurking nearby before he said dryly, "I thought I killed him today."

"I saw," Elizabeth said solemnly.

Darcy began to whisper again, almost as if saying the words out loud violated what they most cherished. "I thought... I know this sounds impossible... I thought the silver of the sword would kill him."

Elizabeth challenged him. "Who says that it did not?"

"He disappeared as he always does, so I likely did not kill Wickham. I tried to pierce his heart with the sword." Darcy could not understand how he failed.

"Wickham has no heart; no wonder you missed it."

Darcy snorted. "Maybe the sword was not real silver."

"No heart or no silver—either way, Wickham still is a problem we will face together. First, we go to London and marry. My Aunt Gardiner will be quite *surprised* with this turn of events."

"You understand you cannot tell her our secret, Elizabeth."

"Do not worry. I will convince her we are marrying only for love. You will show me proper attentions in front of her?" Elizabeth asked coaxingly.

Darcy smiled. "It will be my pleasure, Sweetling." He stood to help her to her feet. "Georgiana will be surprised when I bring you to London."

"She knows nothing of us?" Elizabeth said uncertainly.

Darcy smiled down at her. "That is not totally true, Love. Georgiana knows there is *someone*. Mrs. Annesley, my sister's companion, had a vision of Wickham's deceit. Georgiana sent one of my men to find me at Netherfield. Luckily, we connected on the road. Her note described you and the manor house; that was when I rode to find you. Mrs. Annesley says you are my future. It seems the fine lady's vision was accurate once again. First, she saved Georgiana and now you. She has been an invaluable asset to my household."

Elizabeth shivered involuntarily, but she spoke cheerfully. "I am most eager to greet both your sister and her companion."

"We will leave early tomorrow." They started back to the house, settled in their understanding. Darcy damned the feeling of inadequacy he felt as a potential bridegroom. Elizabeth deserved better. Although he could never give her a "real" marriage, he vowed she would want for nothing else. He would cater to her least whim.

"Fitzwilliam," she caught his arm before they entered her home, "once we are married, we must reconsider everything we think we know about Wickham—and about vampires. Some of your knowledge appears to be nothing more than folklore, inaccurate folklore. The jeweled crucifix affected him, but it did not stop him from taking me prisoner. The silver sword *hurt* him, but did not *kill* him. What we are doing provides some protection; yet it does not end the curse. We must pool our understanding and discover Wickham's secret if we are ever to be free of this."

Her large green—nearly black—eyes met his, and his breath caught in his throat. "I have always taken great pride in holding myself aloof and never requiring another's assistance; now I find I am in your debt, Sweetling. Your suggestion makes sense. I met Wickham's attacks, but I never launched my own assault. It seems I must act, rather than react." He cupped his hand over hers. "I do not deserve you, but I will make you happy, Elizabeth. That is my vow to you on this day."

CHAPTER 11

Mr. Bennet's carriage pulled up in front of a serviceable town house in Cheapside. Darcy recognized Elizabeth's trepidation. There had been no time to prepare her aunt and uncle for the announcement of their marriage, and with her sister's company, they had experienced no privacy to discuss what they would tell her Aunt Gardiner.

As Darcy helped both ladies from the carriage, their aunt and several children scrambled out the door to meet them. Both Elizabeth and Jane affectionately hugged each of the children and showered their aunt with love. Then the woman saw that the gentleman with them was Mr. Darcy, and she stiffened immediately.

"Aunt Gardiner," Jane began, "I am sure you recognize Mr. Darcy." The woman presented a quick curtsy before allowing her gaze to settle on Elizabeth. "Mr. Darcy, this is our aunt, Meredith Gardiner."

Darcy bowed. "Mrs. Gardiner, I am pleased to have your acquaintance. Elizabeth speaks so fondly of you."

"Elizabeth?" Mrs. Gardiner's voice was tight.

Elizabeth caught her aunt's arm to steer her towards the door, not wishing a scene on the street. "Yes, Aunt, I am Elizabeth to my dear Fitzwilliam. Mr. Darcy has seen me to London, for we are to marry the day after tomorrow."

Mrs. Gardiner stopped dead in her steps. "You jest, Lizzy!"

Elizabeth turned to the woman again. "I do not, Aunt. Mr. Darcy and I will marry, and I would like for you to be happy for me."

Mr. Gardiner joined them in the front foyer. "Who is getting married, dearest Elizabeth?" He offered Jane a quick kiss on the cheek.

Elizabeth left her aunt and walked to where Darcy stood, waiting for the next round of questioning. Possessively, she took his hand. "*I* am getting married, Uncle. This is my betrothed, Fitzwilliam Darcy."

Mr. Gardiner stammered at first, but he quickly recovered. "Mr. Darcy, welcome, Sir. Please, let us all go into the parlor and hear this surprising story."

Jane took her aunt's hand, while Darcy led Elizabeth into the room. The young couple sat together on a settee. Mrs. Gardiner ordered tea, and when civilities were finished, an explanation seemed needed.

"Papa sent a letter explaining everything." Jane produced the note for their uncle.

Mr. Gardiner put it into his pocket. "I will read my brother Bennet's words later. What I would like right now is a few words from Lizzy and Mr. Darcy."

"As Aunt Gardiner knows, Mr. Darcy came to Netherfield Park with Mr. Bingley, and our relationship began. We were cool to each other at first, but upon further acquaintance, grew exceedingly fond of one another."

Mrs. Gardiner interrupted her. "Lizzy, are you in love with Mr. Darcy?"

Elizabeth blushed. Neither she nor Darcy spoke of love. "Yes, Aunt." Elizabeth's voice was barely audible. "I have fallen in love with Mr. Darcy."

Darcy's hand cupped hers where it lay between them. He lifted the back of it to his lips for a kiss.

"And you, Mr. Darcy?" her aunt inquired, astounded. "Do you love our Lizzy?"

"I would give my life for Elizabeth." Elizabeth knew he desired her, but part of her hoped he would acknowledge some feelings for her beside the need to protect her.

Jane interceded, "Mr. Darcy actually saved Elizabeth's life twice, Aunt."

"*Twice?*" Mr. Gardiner demanded.

"I will explain more later. We have so much to do before the wedding, but suffice it to say, without Fitzwilliam, I would not be alive now."

"It was romantic," Jane volunteered. "Mr. Darcy left Netherfield, but he realized he did not want to lose Lizzy, so he returned for her. Luckily, he came just as an intruder tied her up and planned to hurt her. Mr. Darcy fought him off."

Mr. Gardiner's eyebrows shot up; Mrs. Gardiner fanned herself.

"That is the reason for our hurried marriage," Elizabeth confided. "I was so happy to see Fitzwilliam that I foolishly threw myself into his arms. Unfortunately, Papa and some of our servants burst into the room and found us in a compromising position. Mr. Darcy felt it best that we marry quickly to protect my reputation."

"But do you *wish* to marry Mr. Darcy?" her uncle asked.

"Yes, Uncle, I do. We would wait for a proper calling of the banns except for my impulsive behavior; but either way, Mr. Darcy is my chosen mate."

"Then that is all that matters, Lizzy. Neither your aunt nor I wish to see you *forced* into marriage. How might we help you two with the upcoming wedding?" Mr. Gardiner said.

"Unfortunately, I must leave to make arrangements." said Mr. Darcy. "When I returned for Elizabeth yesterday, my baggage continued on with a traveling companion, Mr. Bingley. So I must return home to make myself presentable. Then I must make a trip to the ecclesiastical courts to procure a special license."

"Would you like to use my carriage, Mr. Darcy?" Darcy prepared to take his leave. "As we promised Mr. Bennet to send his carriage back to Longbourn as soon as possible, I would appreciate your kindness, Mr. Gardiner. Might I also ask for your assistance in securing the church? It would allow me to call upon my sister with the good news."

"It would be my pleasure, Mr. Darcy. Let me have my man bring around the carriage."

As he stood, Darcy reached out his hand to Elizabeth. "Would you see me out, my dear?"

"May I meet Georgiana this evening?" Elizabeth took his arm in preparation for his departure.

"I would relish that very thing if your aunt and uncle could see fit to spare you for supper. Plus, it would give you an opportunity to see your new London home."

"Would you and your sister care to join us for the evening meal, Mr. Darcy?" Mrs. Gardiner asked reluctantly. Her expression was troubled.

"Aunt Gardiner, that is too much on such short notice. I would not intrude on your household staff for such an important occasion. If you are willing, I will meet Miss Darcy this evening. From all of Fitzwilliam's reports, his sister is quite shy. Meeting her brother's future wife *and* all the family might be too much for her at one time. Shall we dine together tomorrow instead?"

"Excellent solution, Lizzy." Mr. Gardiner took up her cause. "And Jane must accompany you as your chaperone."

"Then it is settled," said Elizabeth. "Now, off with you," she said to Darcy as she maneuvered him towards the door. Alone in the entrance hall, she went up on her tiptoes to kiss his cheek.

Darcy caressed her face. "I will call on you at four, if that is acceptable. That will give you time to tour the house before Georgiana arrives. She will delight in having an opportunity to speak privately with you before we all sit down together."

Elizabeth took his hand in both of hers. "Fitzwilliam, I vow to make you proud of me. I will do my best for Georgiana, and although I will be out of my element in your world at first, I will learn quickly."

"Listen to your intuition, and we will live well together. Now, I must leave. Your uncle's coach awaits." He kissed her knuckles tenderly. "It will be good to acknowledge you to my staff and family."

With that, Darcy was gone. Elizabeth sighed, feeling bereft of his presence already. She straightened her posture and returned to the parlor; before Darcy returned, she would make her aunt understand that their initial opinion of Darcy had been erroneous.

★ ★ ★

Surprisingly, Elizabeth convinced her aunt and uncle to allow her to dine with Darcy without the company of her sister, although they did insist that a maid accompany her. Darcy called promptly at four, arriving in a curricle. Even though there was a crispness in the air, Elizabeth loved the idea of an open-air carriage. "I thought you might enjoy the opportunity to see a bit of London's architecture." Darcy placed Elizabeth's hand on his arm as he escorted her to his vehicle.

"I have never ridden in a curricle," Elizabeth confided as he lifted her to the seat.

Darcy flashed her a wicked grin. "Our adventure continues! You will enjoy the wind in your face." After the Gardiner maid climbed on the back with Darcy's footman, he mounted the carriage beside Elizabeth, offering her a lap blanket for warmth.

Darcy maneuvered the carriage out into the late afternoon traffic of the warehouse district. Once they were on their way, he leaned close to her ear and whispered, "You look lovely, Vixen."

"Do you like my new cloak?" she asked coyly.

The corners of Darcy's mouth turned up. "It flatters your eyes, Miss Elizabeth, making them a deeper green; I find it quite enchanting."

"It was a gift," she said banteringly. "From a wealthy gentleman."

"I seem to recall that *I* am that wealthy gentleman." He caught her hand up in his lap.

They sat in silence for several moments. "I assume, Sir, that you procured the license," Elizabeth ventured.

"I did." Darcy lowered his voice, making sure the servants could not hear. "Your uncle sent word that the church is reserved for ten for our nuptials."

Elizabeth shifted closer to him. "Yes…he said so. Uncle Gardiner read Papa's letter. Papa explained everything…the two incidents…" She glanced around to make sure the servants still maintained a detachment. "Our discovery…the reason for our coming here."

"They are agreeable—your aunt and uncle?"

"Aunt Gardiner is withholding her approval, but she will not object. Jane will remain with them for several weeks, which should assuage my aunt's need to nurture."

"I am sorry if…" A dreadful, guilt-ridden remorse laced his words. "If…your…my proposal…placed you in a poor light with your family."

Elizabeth giggled. "Believe me, Mr. Darcy, I am often *in a poor light with my family*. Remember, I am the unremarkable one. I suppose my father might argue the point, as well as Jane"

Darcy chuckled. "I can imagine, Miss Elizabeth. I have observed you are spirited. Yet you just admitted your opinion could be skewed."

Darcy drove on and Elizabeth pointed to different buildings. Darcy dutifully identified them, amused by her awe and her curiosity.

"You rarely come to London?" he observed.

"My mother would have had no objection, but my father hates London."

Engrossed in recounting her most recent trip to town, Elizabeth did not notice he had stopped the carriage in front of a stately town home in an upscale district of Mayfair. Darcy jumped down, tossed the reins to a waiting groomsman, and came around to lift Elizabeth from the vehicle. He whispered close to her ear, "Welcome to your new home, Elizabeth."

"Fitzwilliam, this is where you live?" Her voice was barely audible.

"No, my love, this is where *we* will live; at least, when we are in London." He led her up the steps and into the front entrance. A butler awaited Darcy's orders. "Mr. Frasser, this is my bethrothed, Miss Bennet." He handed her cloak and bonnet to the man. "Is my sister in?"

"Welcome to Overton House, Miss Bennet." The butler bowed. "Miss Darcy has not arrived, Sir."

"Then I will show Miss Bennet the house. Tell Miss Darcy we will join her in the front parlor."

"Yes, Mr. Darcy."

For the next twenty minutes, Darcy showed Elizabeth through many of the rooms. Her amazement delighted him. "Fitzwilliam, the house is magnificent," she said, gawking at some of the furnishings before turning her attention to the family portraits in the gallery.

"I am happy you approve, Elizabeth." He cupped her hand with his own, pulling her closer to his side, where he might lightly kiss her cheek. "I want you to make this your true home. You may decorate rooms or arrange them as you see fit."

"I would never be so presumptuous!"

"You will, at least, make changes in your chambers and sitting room. Please make them comfortable for yourself. They were my mother's rooms before her passing."

Elizabeth leaned into him, resting her head on his shoulder. "Thank you, Fitzwilliam, for making this transition easier. I am honored at having Lady Anne's rooms."

"You will be happy here, Elizabeth. That is, I will do my best to make it so."

She gazed up at him. "I will be happy as long as I am with you, Fitzwilliam."

Upon entering the front parlor, Darcy rushed to embrace the delicately beautiful girl who rose to her feet to greet them. "Have you been waiting long, my dear?" he said and bent to kiss her cheek.

"No, Fitzwilliam, we have just arrived."

Darcy took the girl's hand and led her to where Elizabeth stood. "My dear, this is Miss Elizabeth Bennet," he began. "Elizabeth, this is my sister, Georgiana Darcy."

Both women dropped a curtsy. "Oh, Miss Darcy," Elizabeth said, "you are as lovely as your brother declared. I am so pleased to meet you at last." And she took Georgiana's hand in hers.

"Miss Bennet," Georgiana said in a whispery voice as she shot a quick glance at Darcy, "it is my pleasure to make your acquaintance."

"Come sit with me, Miss Darcy," Elizabeth said as she led Darcy's sister to a nearby settee. "I am delighted to be given another sister. I do not know whether my dear Fitzwilliam told you, I am one of five girls, and as much as I look forward to becoming your brother's wife, I must secretly confess that I dread losing the company of my sisters. It pleases me to have you as part of my new life."

Georgiana appeared shocked by how quickly Elizabeth assumed familiarity, but as the evening progressed, Elizabeth charmed Darcy's sister with her witty repartee and natural good humor. Before long, Georgiana's nervousness went by the wayside.

When Darcy left them alone so he could sign the papers needed for the settlement and the wedding, Georgiana finally mustered enough courage to say so. "Miss Elizabeth, I have never seen my dear brother so happy!"

"Really?" Elizabeth seemed amused with the observation. "Maybe it is because your brother realizes he does not have to face the world alone—he has someone who knows his deepest secrets and stands by him."

"Then you believe there is hope for my family, Miss Elizabeth?" Georgiana lowered her voice. "I do not wish to see Fitzwilliam sacrifice himself in order to put a stop to the family madness."

Elizabeth touched the girl's hand. "I wish the same, Miss Darcy. I am determined to change what your brother accepts as his fate."

"Mrs. Annesley believes you are Fitzwilliam's future."

"And he is mine," Elizabeth asserted.

★ ★ ★

The next morning Darcy escorted Elizabeth, Jane, and Georgiana to Bond Street. "Fitzwilliam, this is ridiculous," Elizabeth protested for the third time that day. "I do *not* need a new wardrobe."

He helped her from the carriage. Impulsively, he used his finger to tilt her chin up to where he could see her eyes. "Elizabeth, as my wife, you will be expected to attend certain functions. London society is judgmental, and clothing acceptable in the country is frowned upon here."

Elizabeth bit her bottom lip, a habit Darcy now recognized as a mixture of fear and determination. "Are you sure about this arrangement? Would not a more fashionable lady be to your liking? Despite everything else, you have an obligation to your name."

Darcy leaned close so that only she could hear. "I would never force you to become part of my life, but you know very well, Elizabeth, if I do not marry you, I will not marry." Elizabeth nodded her understanding. "Then allow me to share my wealth with the woman who devotes her life to me." He placed her hand on his sleeve and led her into the modiste's shop.

"Mr. Darcy," said a heavy-set woman with silver-grey hair who left the counter to greet them. "We are pleased to serve you again, Sir."

"Madame Lucinda, this is my betrothed, Miss Bennet. She will need several new items. I assured her you are the finest modiste in London."

"Of course, Mr. Darcy. Your patronage is appreciated." She motioned for two waiting seamstresses to come forward. "Miss Bennet, if you will go with these young ladies, they will take your measurements." Elizabeth, Georgiana, and Jane followed the two employees into the back room.

Darcy moved towards the seat the matron offered. "What do you have in mind for the young lady, Mr. Darcy?" She offered him a cup of tea.

"Miss Bennet will protest, but we will ignore her sensibilities," he said as he sipped the hot brew. "The lady will need at least three gowns, four day dresses, a traveling ensemble, and appropriate accessories," he began. "Cost is not an issue. Whatever my sister suggests should be considered as one of my own suggestions."

"Certainly, Mr. Darcy."

"If you have something appropriate that would need but a few alterations to fit Miss Bennet, she will take those items immediately. The rest you may send to my home by the end of the week. We marry tomorrow and leave London soon for my estate."

"To—Tomorrow?" the woman stammered.

Darcy enjoyed the surprised look on the dressmaker's face. He knew she would pass the story of his engagement on to others, and so he told her the story he had prepared. "You know I am not a patient man, Madame Lucinda. I have courted Miss Bennet since Michaelmas, almost from the first moment I laid eyes on her. Once she agreed to be my wife, I moved heaven and earth to make her mine. She stays with her aunt and uncle in London; that is the reason I have returned so suddenly from the country. In fact, her aunt is from my home county of Derby—from Derbyshire, the community surrounding my estate."

"Ah, then this is a love match?" Madame Lucinda knew many ladies pursued Fitzwilliam Darcy, to no avail.

"Yes." Darcy took another sip of his tea. "Would you care to show me some of your newest items? My sister speaks of your excellent taste."

While Elizabeth endured the fittings in the privacy of the dressing rooms, Darcy chose some items, which he knew she would consider frivolous, but which gave him pleasure to choose especially for her. Among them were a new nightgown and wrapper, a painted fan, leather kid gloves to match her riding habit, and several pairs of silk stockings. He imagined Elizabeth's blush when she saw what he had chosen. Madame Lucinda would see these intimate items as proof he and Elizabeth were indeed a love match.

"Be sure to include a new bonnet for Miss Bennet's sister, the lady who accompanies her. Send the bill to my home."

"Certainly, Mr. Darcy." Mentally calculating what the bill might total, she hurried away to fulfill his needs.

After an hour, Darcy became restless. Georgiana's appearance relieved his boredom. "Fitzwilliam," she confided, "Miss Bennet is so amusing. You would not believe how she entertains Madame Lucinda's staff!"

Darcy chuckled. "Miss Elizabeth's expertise in word play is one of her many charms."

"She is so petite," Georgiana continued. "Madame Lucinda says Elizabeth is the perfect size. Those of the *ton* will be jealous when they see our Miss Elizabeth."

"Georgiana, I need to see my solicitor today. May I return for you and the Misses Bennet in an hour?"

"Be on your way," Georgiana assured him. "We will be ready for your return."

Over Elizabeth's repeated reproofs, the footmen stored multiple packages in Darcy's carriage. Georgiana directed the staff. Jane reluctantly chose a new bonnet, at Madame Lucinda's insistence. Two complete ensembles, plus the items Darcy had chosen earlier, would go home with Elizabeth that day. Another dress would be delivered to her aunt's house by the end of the day.

"Fitzwilliam will return soon," Georgiana assured Elizabeth and Jane. "He had business with his solicitor."

"Might we see some of the other shops on the street?" Jane asked as they waited.

Elizabeth caught her sister's arm. "Let us walk."

They strolled the length of the street before stopping to look at items in an upscale storefront. "May we go in?" Jane pointed to one of the displays. "I would like to find a birthday gift for Mama."

Georgiana led the way, but just as they reached the door of the shop, Elizabeth spotted a more intriguing store. She caught Georgiana by the arm. "Miss Darcy, I would like very much to explore the bookstore next door. Would you object to accompanying my sister?"

Georgiana looked around, unsure what to do. Darcy would expect her to stay with Elizabeth. "I—I suppose," she stammered, "but you should not go alone." She motioned for one of the footmen. "Take Belton with you."

The ringing of the bell on the door echoed throughout the store, but no one seemed to be in attendance when she entered. Elizabeth waited patiently for several minutes before asking Belton, "Would you see if someone is available in the back, please?"

"Yes, miss." The footman made his way towards the rear of the store while Elizabeth began to leisurely browse the floor-to-ceiling shelves to her right. Most bookstores organized their offerings by genre, and she searched for the poetry section.

She drifted into one of the center aisles and began to read the titles; most dealt with historic battlefields, a sign of the public's continued interest in the Duke of Wellington's efforts to stop Napoleon. Then a row of old bindings caught her eye. *Perhaps they are first editions,* she thought. Carefully, she tilted a book forward to look at it more closely. *Slavic Spiritualism,* written in gold, enticed her to thumb through the pages. She slid it back into place and selected another, titled *Kathasaritsagara.* The hairs on the back of her neck stood at attention when she found a picture of a demon with blood dripping from his lips illustrating a story dubbed "Baital Pachisi."

Engrossed in the pictures, Elizabeth did not hear the man's approach. "May I be of service, my Lady?" his voice slithered past her as she jumped. "Do the black arts interest you?"

Elizabeth laughed nervously. "Heavens, no!" She shut the book quickly and shelved it. "I...I was looking for the poetry section. I was not sure anyone was around."

"Yes, your man found me in the alley, unloading some boxes. I apologize for not hearing the bell." He touched the books she handled, straightening them into an even row. "Poetry is this way, Miss."

Elizabeth noted the man's appearance—a bit disheveled—his clothing hanging on his frame—a florid face with beady eyes squinting behind spectacles. *He would make the perfect schoolmaster,* she thought. "Do you have a preference, Miss?" He stopped suddenly to look down at her.

"William Cowper." She had nearly forgotten what she sought. "Something by William Cowper."

The man's gnarled fingers delicately selected one of the volumes and handed it to her. Elizabeth flipped through the pages and nodded. "This is excellent. Might I have it wrapped?"

"Yes, Miss." The man took back the tome and led the way to the front of the store. "Is there anything else, Miss?"

Elizabeth looked around anxiously, making sure Darcy was nowhere around. "Might I write a note in the book before you wrap it? It is to be a gift."

The man reached under the counter, bringing forth a pen and

ink. Elizabeth handed him the money to complete the transaction, and then she took up the pen.

Fitzwilliam,
   To give you pleasure in your late-night library visits.

Yours always,
Elizabeth

When the package was wrapped, Elizabeth slipped it under her cloak, not wishing the others to note her sentimentality or her intimacy with the man she would marry. She would give it to Darcy as a wedding gift.

"Lizzy!" Jane called as Elizabeth stepped into the street, followed closely by the footman. "Mr. Darcy is coming this way."

Elizabeth watched him approach. She appreciated his fine physique—his tight-fitting jacket and stylish greatcoat only made him look more debonair. More than one lady's head turned, but his eyes stayed on her.

As he neared, Elizabeth rushed forward to meet him. Taking his proffered arm, she bestowed a smile on Darcy. He took her hand, lacing it through his and pulling her closer to his side as he turned back to the carriage. "Am I conceited to think you missed me?" he whispered close to her ear.

Elizabeth laughed lightly. "I did, as foolish as that may seem. You were absent for barely an hour."

"Long enough to feel bereft of your touch on my arm," he said flirtatiously.

She countered, "Long enough to wish the day to end and a new one to begin."

At the carriage, he brought Elizabeth's hand to his lips before helping her climb into the luxurious seats of his coach. "Tomorrow," he said seductively.

CHAPTER 12

George Wickham gasped for breath. Somehow he had made it to London—to Edward Street—to the home of Mrs. Younge. She let rooms, although very few people stayed there; Mrs. Younge, since she had given herself up to George Wickham, "selected" her renters carefully after interviewing them. Edward Street offered her a plethora of individuals from whom to choose, and the lady picked only those who would not be missed when they disappeared. At one time, she served as Georgiana Darcy's companion, a respectable way for a lady to earn a living, but that was before Wickham seduced her and showed her the dark side. Currently, Mrs. Younge lived in the bowels of a teeming city, taking the lives of some of its least upstanding citizens.

Wickham rapped sharply with the knocker. Barely able to stand, his patience wore thin when no one responded, so he pounded on the door with his fist.

"Enough!" A sharp voice demanded on the other side. Someone unbolted the locks and cracked the opening. "What may I do for you?" A syrupy sweet voice spoke from the darkness.

"I need help," Wickham hissed.

The door swung open immediately. "Wickham? My lord? What happened?" Mrs. Younge slid his arm around her shoulder to brace his weight against her.

"A little run-in with your former employer, Mr. Darcy." He reached for the doorframe to steady himself.

"I am here for you, my lord." She helped him to the nearest chaise. "What can I do?" Mrs. Younge lifted his legs, so Wickham might lay flat.

"I have a silver shaft festering in my abdomen. You must remove it so that I may heal." His skin was grey.

"A silver…?" she asked, shocked. But then Mrs. Younge

retrieved a knife and a razor along with bandages. "I thought," she began again, "that a silver stake would eliminate you."

"The idiot missed my heart," he gasped, "although Fitzwilliam Darcy came close last evening to achieving his goal of destroying me." He ripped open his shirt to give her easier access to him. "I will heal quickly once the implement is removed. Now be about it."

★ ★ ★

Darcy sent word to the Gardiners that his cousin Colonel Damon Fitzwilliam would join the party for dinner. Colonel Fitzwilliam, who would stand up with Darcy the next morning at the church, had arrived unexpectedly while they were out. Elizabeth and the Gardiners found the colonel quite amiable and enjoyed his tales of his and Darcy's childhoods. His stories went a long way in confirming Elizabeth's opinion of her betrothed. They also seemed to allay some of Aunt Gardiner's suspicions.

Besides the colonel, Darcy's aunt and uncle—Lady Anne Darcy's older brother—arrived at the church in time for the service.

"Uncle," Darcy said as he bowed to his only family. "I am so pleased you arrived here in time. I feared you would not."

"You gave your aunt and me very little notice," the Earl of Matlock declared, "but Her Ladyship would have no peace until we were on the road."

The Earl pulled Darcy to the side, assuring some privacy. He motioned for his son to join them. "Why the haste? The lady is not compromised, is she?"

"Miss Elizabeth is the woman I wish to marry, Your Lordship," Darcy replied testily. "We shared no more than a few kisses. Unfortunately, on one of those occasions, her father and some of his servants spied us in an embrace. Although her father would be discreet and allow for a proper calling of the banns, Mr. Bennet and I feared the servants would show less discretion."

"Then it is a match based on love?"

Calmer now, he replied, "It is."

"Excellent. Her Ladyship will be pleased to hear as such. Your parents knew a deep devotion for each other. I hope you and Miss Elizabeth will be equally suited to each other."

The colonel touched Darcy's arm. "Darcy, the cleric indicates it is time to take our places. Miss Elizabeth is in the alcove with Mr. Gardiner."

"Then let us commence!" The earl headed back to his seat, beside his wife and Georgiana.

Darcy took a deep breath. For a brief moment, he considered telling Elizabeth he had made a mistake; he could not do this. Then she stepped around the corner, holding onto her uncle's arm, and Darcy's world shifted. Elizabeth's eyes locked with his. In that moment, nothing else mattered except that Elizabeth Bennet would be his wife. She would spend the rest of her days with him. He would protect her from George Wickham and the rest of the world, and Darcy would provide for her. She would never want for anything, and—in his own way—he would love Elizabeth above all others.

Mr. Gardiner indicated to the vicar that he gave Elizabeth's hand in marriage, and then Darcy felt her fingertips entwine with his. He breathed deeply to steady his nerves and squeezed her hand to tell her he understood if she, too, felt nervous, but Elizabeth's eyes held a calmness he did not expect. She chose to pledge her life to his, and she would not waver in her decision. Darcy could not either: Elizabeth was his present and his future.

At the end, Darcy escorted Elizabeth up the aisle to sign the registry. It was official; she was now Elizabeth Darcy.

No one suspected that Elizabeth seriously considered finding the nearest church door and running for her life. She reasoned she could hail a hack and have it take her to the closest posting inn. A coach could take her back to Longbourn and her own room. Then she saw Darcy waiting for her, and nothing mattered other than being with him. Fate had thrown them into a relationship, and she would see it through.

As she repeated her vows, Elizabeth heard the thinness of her own voice, but she knew she was making the right decision. She had no doubts.

★ ★ ★

Amelia Younge checked on Wickham's progress. He staggered to a second-floor bedroom once she removed the broken shaft of a sword lodged deep within his lower abdomen. He made no sound as she cut around the metal, dislodging a three-inch pointed piece before he finally allowed himself an audible sigh.

"Thank you, Amelia," he whispered. Theirs was an odd connection. He had chosen her solely because she served as a companion to Georgiana Darcy. The sexual intimacy he often felt with his victims did not exist between them. Unlike Elizabeth Bennet, Amelia Younge believed his every story about Fitzwilliam Darcy and gladly participated in what she thought would be Darcy's downfall. Wickham used her completely and she succumbed to his scheme. Now, she existed as one of his minions—his followers. At one time, he had wanted only one woman in his life—Ellender D'Arcy. Now, many followed him into hell. For Mrs. Younge, he served as her dark lord; she did his bidding without question.

When he recalled Elizabeth Bennet, a blasphemous oath escaped his lips. His pursuit of her had nearly caused his demise. Obviously, Darcy cared about the woman; except for the time Wickham tried to seduce Georgiana, he had never seen Darcy so incensed by his actions. It was personal at last. Wickham enjoyed stripping Elizabeth Bennet down to her chemise and binding her to the bed. Having Darcy find her in such a state was even more pleasing. Sadly, Wickham had not managed to place Miss Elizabeth fully under his spell. It was more than the insipid iron crucifix that Darcy had given her. If that were all, he would have simply ripped it from her neck and taken his chances.

No, it was something more than that old wives' tale about iron being his bane. Wickham knew intuitively that she did not totally believe in the power of the necklace, even though she had clutched it in her hand for several minutes. Elizabeth Bennet believed in the power of the man who had presented her with the piece of jewelry. Its magic lay in their connection, and Wickham found that this force held him back, kept him from making the woman his. He toyed with her, but he could not control her. Elizabeth Bennet fascinated him because of her steely determination to prevent him from fulfilling his promise to Darcy. She presented an extraordinary challenge. He did not know if he could win against Miss Elizabeth Bennet—but he felt compelled to try.

"What else, my lord?" Mrs. Younge stood by the bed, gazing down at him.

"Two things." His voice already was stronger. "Take this pouch." He unstrapped a folded leather bag from his leg and handed it to her.

"What is it?" she muttered as she began to open it.

Wickham offered a wicked grin. "It is home. At least, it is the earth I call home. Sprinkle some of it over the blanket so I might rest. Without it, my soul roams the underworld at night." She did as he instructed, leaving a thin line of dark soil tracing his form. Then she handed the container back to him.

"The second thing?" she prompted.

He reached inside his jacket pocket. "These are the ashes of my father. The village hunted my parents as if they were animals once the Baobhan Síth turned me into what you see before you. My parents were burned alive in the bedroom of our home; they sought shelter in the only place they knew. Spread a paste of these ashes over my wound. It will heal me by the morrow. My father's life will seal the wounds in my body."

Again, Mrs. Younge followed his instructions to the letter. She had no reason to doubt what he said.

"Now leave me to my rest. I will sleep until tomorrow night. Close the door and lock it, my dear. I will trust you to guard me as I regain my abilities."

"I will do as you ask." She headed towards the open door.

"Sleep well, my lord." Mrs. Younge extinguished the candle flame with her fingertips and left him to find his own serenity.

★ ★ ★

The wedding breakfast took place at the Gardiners' home. Although Gracechurch Street was not the most fashionable of addresses, no one who ever met the Gardiners would judge them to be anything less than the finest and most respectable people. After spending some time with Elizabeth's family, Darcy realized Mr. Gardiner was a sensible, gentlemanlike man, greatly superior to his sister Mrs. Bennet, by nature as well as education. He suspected Bingley's sisters would have difficulty in believing a man who lived by trade, and within view of his own warehouses, could be so well bred and agreeable. Mrs. Gardiner, who was several years younger than Mrs. Bennet and Mrs. Philips, was an amiable, intelligent, elegant woman. Because there subsisted a very particular regard between Elizabeth and her aunt, Darcy spent more than an hour cultivating a relationship with the older lady. To think the woman once considered him a murderer created an awkwardness between them. Even now, he could not be certain she entirely believed he was *not*. But he would alter Meredith Gardiner's opinions for Elizabeth's sake.

"Thank you, Fitzwilliam," Elizabeth whispered close to his ear.

Darcy smiled at her, happy in his own right. "I will take your gratitude freely, but for what do you offer it?"

"For inviting my aunt and uncle to Pemberley this summer," Elizabeth explained. "Aunt Merry can speak of nothing else. She will renew old acquaintances; you gave her the perfect excuse to return home."

"If it makes you happy, Elizabeth, I will entertain all of Hertfordshire at Pemberley." He traced circles on the back of her hand as they shared a settee in the Gardiners' main drawing room.

Elizabeth laughed. "It is lucky for you, my Husband, that I hold no desire to share you with others."

"Share me or share my secrets?" Darcy lowered his voice and moved closer, so that no one else could hear.

"*Never* your secrets!" she protested. "I hold only your highest good in my heart and my mind."

He smiled. "I do not deserve you, Elizabeth Darcy."

As no one paid them much attention, Elizabeth slid her hand into his. "Whether you deserve me or not, Fitzwilliam Darcy, you must suffer my heartfelt attentions."

"Willingly, Sweetling." He took her hand in his grasp. Turning it over, he kissed the inside of her wrist. After a few moments of silent contemplation, he suggested, "We should make our farewells."

Elizabeth blushed. "I suppose you are correct."

Darcy helped her to her feet. They bid their families a good day and thanked the Gardiners for their generosity. While Elizabeth hugged Jane for the third time, Darcy turned to his cousin. "You will see Georgiana home, Damon?"

"With pleasure, Darcy." He shot a furtive glance at Elizabeth, who stood talking to the colonel's mother and father. "I am happy for you, Cousin. Mrs. Darcy appears to be a sensible sort."

Darcy's eyes rested on his bride. "Mrs. Darcy suits me."

The colonel maneuvered Darcy to the privacy of a secluded corner. "Then she knows?"

"My wife knows everything." Even though it was his cousin, Darcy preferred not to be reminded of his situation. "You, of all people, should realize I would not involve an innocent in this."

The colonel nodded. "If you are satisfied, Cousin, I will speak no more of the matter."

"If you will excuse me, then." Darcy moved to where Elizabeth waited for him. "Are you ready, Mrs. Darcy?"

"Yes, Mr. Darcy," she said self-assuredly. "I am ready."

In the carriage headed towards the new couple's London town house, Elizabeth inquired, "Fitzwilliam, why, pray tell, did Mr. Bingley not attend our wedding? I thought him to be your closest friend."

"Bingley is not in the city."

"Then he knows not of our joining?" Elizabeth gazed out the window at the sunny early afternoon scene. Passersby—shopping, greeting one another, or shepherding children—seemed unaware this day was a momentous one.

"Bingley planned to spend Christmas with his sisters at Mr. Hurst's estate in Hampshire," Darcy said matter-of-factly. "Bingley does not have a town house. When we left Hertfordshire, they were to spend the night at my home and then proceed on to Hurst's property."

"I understand your choosing the good colonel to represent your family during the ceremony, but Mr. Bingley's absence was felt." Elizabeth paused before adding quickly, "I hope Mr. Bingley's removal had nothing to do with his sister's aspirations to be Mrs. Darcy. It would grieve me to know that our marriage separated you from your friend."

Incredulously, he retorted, "After all I have shared with you, you cannot still believe I would have chosen Caroline Bingley!"

Elizabeth looked away in embarrassment. "I did not mean to vex you, my Husband."

Darcy caught her hand up in his. "Sweetling, you must know I have only two regrets in our union, and neither involves your being my choice. My regrets have to do with your deserving more than I will be able to give you." He turned her hand where he could lightly kiss the inside of Elizabeth's wrist. "I suppose I could have sent word to Hampshire. Actually, I considered it, but I did not want to subject you or the Gardiners to Miss Bingley's censure. I would not want her disdain to ruin our day. Plus, I was unsure how Jane might feel about seeing Mr. Bingley. His leaving so unexpectedly must have played on your sister's sensibilities."

"Do you suppose Mr. Bingley affects Jane?"

"I cannot say how deep Charles's interest might be. I protected my own feelings by avoiding speaking to him regarding your family."

Elizabeth purposefully put aside her earlier concerns. "I do like the colonel, and Her Ladyship was most kind. She pleaded with me to have us visit with them often. It seems your uncle feels a need to keep his connection with his late sister through you and Georgiana."

Darcy chuckled. "I expect you promised we would attend to my uncle's wishes."

Elizabeth giggled. "I did try to allay Her Ladyship's qualms, my Husband."

"I will do my best by you, Elizabeth," Darcy suddenly blurted out. "If it is possible, you will be happy; I will see to it."

"Fitzwilliam," she chastised him, "I know what you can give me. I am happy, very *happy.*"

Darcy reached for her, pulling Elizabeth to sit nearer him on the coach seat. "I thought we would spend another week in London, and then we would travel to Pemberley before the roads become too bad," he said pensively. "I sent word to Mrs. Reynolds, my housekeeper, to expect us and to prepare the house for the holidays." He looked wistfully out the window. "It will be the first festive season in nearly eight years that I have been at home."

"Would you prefer to remain in town?"

Darcy paused before answering. "I believe it is time to claim my life—or, at least, as much of my life as I can. Plus, it can only be good for Georgiana to have more of a family. I hope you can accept her as a sister."

"I have a great admiration for Miss Darcy," she interjected.

He stroked her chin line with the back of his hand. "You, my dear, have a tender heart."

Elizabeth blushed. "If we travel to Pemberley soon, may I send some gifts to my family with Jane? I would want them to remember me in their celebrations."

"Shall we return to Longbourn for Christmas?" he offered.

"As much as I will miss my family in Hertfordshire, I think it best if we keep danger away from them. Besides, you are also my family now." Elizabeth's eyes scanned his profile in the light of the afternoon. "I am excited to see your home—to see Pemberley."

"*Our* home," he corrected her. "Apropos of which, when I left you and our sisters in order to speak to my solicitor yesterday, I placed a jointure in your name. If something occurs where I cannot be with you, you will have a home at Pemberley. If it comes to pass that Georgiana's heirs assume control, you will be given the dowager house, as is your due. The paperwork will be delivered tomorrow."

Elizabeth gasped, "Fitzwilliam!" Her eyes grew luminous. "Why?"

"Because you are my wife…because it is the least I can do to protect you…because I need to do this. It is important, Elizabeth."

She recognized his need to be a provider—to assure her safety. "Thank you, my Husband," she whispered. Elizabeth allowed her fingers to seek his strong grasp, and his large hand encircled hers.

When they arrived at their London home, Mr. Frasser met them at the door. "Mrs. Darcy, the staff of Overton House welcomes you."

"Thank you, Mr. Frasser." She tried not to appear nervous, but Darcy felt Elizabeth's fingers tighten on his sleeve.

"Mrs. Darcy and I will have a light supper, Mr. Frasser. Let us say at six." Darcy pulled her closer to offer his support. "My wife will meet the individual staff members tomorrow."

"Certainly, Mr. Darcy." The butler bowed and began to exit. Then, remembering the rest of his charge, he turned to his master once again. "Mrs. Darcy's trunk from Gracechurch Street arrived, as well as one from Hertfordshire. Joseph placed both in Mrs. Darcy's room. I asked Sally to serve as the Mistress's maid while you are in residence at Overton House. I hope that meets with your approval, Mr. Darcy."

"It seems a fitting choice, Mr. Frasser." Darcy smiled with the knowledge that today was one for which his staff had long hoped. "I think that a more leisurely tour of the house will be in store today. We will dress for supper at half past five."

"Yes, Sir."

"The staff conveys you and Mrs. Darcy all best wishes, Sir. We await your pleasure, Mrs. Darcy." He bowed out this time.

Elizabeth leaned into Darcy's shoulder, grasping his forearm tightly with her free hand. "All of this is so *new* to me. Will I meet this challenge?" Elizabeth bit her bottom lip as her eyes darted about the entranceway, taking in the changes in her life. It was overwhelming in many ways, and her green eyes grew large with anxiety.

"Yes, my darling, you will," he reassured her. "My staff will respond to your natural good humor and your kindness. Most of the staff members have served the Darcy family for years—generations, even. They are loyal and will open their hearts to you as my wife." They entered his study. Darcy leaned down to whisper. "I am sure they are thankful I did not choose *Miss Bingley*."

"I, too, am grateful you did not choose *Miss Bingley*," she responded mischievously. Elizabeth left his arm and closed the door to the room. Returning, she wrapped her arms around Darcy's waist. "At last—alone," she said. "I am ready for our first kiss as a married couple in our home. Pray do not trouble yourself, Mr. Darcy. There is no pressure for it to be a momentous occasion."

Darcy chuckled at her taunt. "You will not leave me if I do not make your world tilt out of control?"

Elizabeth edged closer still. Her breast rose and fell. "It will need to be spectacular to surpass the one on the balcony at Netherfield, but I am willing to give you the chance."

"I may need much practice," he countered.

Elizabeth angled her head. "Then let us *begin*," she whispered.

Darcy's lowered his mouth to hers. His stomach tightened with the ecstasy of the moment. She tasted of chocolate and of cinnamon and a bit of nutmeg. Her perfume wafted over him, and nothing else mattered besides having her in his arms. His senses were awash with Elizabeth. She was everything to him—beauty and love and life—all wrapped in the gloriousness of *his Elizabeth*.

After several delightful moments, Darcy groaned and he forced himself to withdraw, although self-control came slowly. Fury and hunger mingled. Elizabeth was flushed with heat and utterly mesmerizing.

Elizabeth blinked. "I believe th-that my world tilted after all, my Husband," she stammered.

"I believe mine did also," he confirmed before setting her from him. "How can one, Mrs. Darcy, be both a married lady and a temptress?" He caressed her cheek with the back of his hand. "It is probably best that we open the door and let the rest of the world in. With it closed, we could easily believe that only the two of us existed."

"I will let the world in for now, Mr. Darcy," Elizabeth retorted, "but not forever."

At supper, Darcy placed Elizabeth next to him, rather than allowing one of the footmen to set her a place at the head of the table. The servants at the meal gossiped about how often the young master and his new wife reached out to touch each other, how Mr. Darcy was seen holding her hand, how Mrs. Darcy blushed when he whispered in her ear, and how Mr. Darcy *laughed out loud*. Those who had served Fitzwilliam Darcy for many years knew something extraordinary had happened when he married Elizabeth Bennet. And hope began to return to Overton House—hope for a future for the Master of Pemberley.

Darcy excused his valet. It was his wedding night, and he knew not what to do. Darcy recognized what he wanted to do; he wanted to go to Elizabeth—to his wife—and take her, as a husband should. She was sultry and flirtatious and seductive and innocent all at once, and Darcy was so very aware of her physically that sometimes he could barely breathe. When she had been Elizabeth Bennet, and he had lain beside her at night, he controlled his desire by telling himself he could not compromise her and destroy her reputation—but *those* compelling reasons no longer existed. She was his; he had the right to take her as a man takes a woman. Yet he must resist; he could not love Elizabeth as a man because he was not a man; he was a dhampir—a wretched being, half vampire and half human—and Darcy would not create another of his kind. Elizabeth deserved better.

Darcy knew not how he could tolerate her presence in the next room. She would spend the rest of her days and nights in their home, and he could reach her simply by crossing through their adjoining dressing rooms. He must remain strong—but as he shored up his resolve, images of the nightgown-clad Elizabeth flooded his mind. His eyes drifted closed, and a sigh escaped his lips.

He could see her arch against him—see her lips part as he deepened the kiss—see her head fall back, exposing her lovely, pulsing neck. His muscles tightened, and his breath became shallow just thinking of her softness pressed next to him. Passion filled him.

When Elizabeth burst through the door to Darcy's bedchamber, she was filled with enthusiasm. Her thoughts were of the newness and luxury of her quarters. Yet when she saw him, Elizabeth froze.

Fitzwilliam Darcy was a magnificent man to look at when he was dressed in waistcoat and cravat and tailored jacket. But Elizabeth found him especially appealing when his hair was a bit disheveled, and he wore a loose-fitting shirt and breeches. Tonight, however, he was perfect.

The muscular line of his back caught her attention—the expanse of his broad shoulders and slim tapering of his waist. Elizabeth gasped and Darcy spun around to find her there.

"Fitz—Fitzwilliam," she stammered, trying now to force her eyes from his muscular chest. *Do you not realize you are an aristocrat—a soft and pampered person, not hard and sculpted?* she thought with amusement.

His voice came out clipped. "Yes, Elizabeth?" *She is radiant. She is exquisite.*

"I apologize." She began to back out of the room, embarrassed at having intruded on his privacy.

"No," he called out, moving quickly to stop her retreat. Darcy forced himself to sound calm. "Please do not leave." He caught her wrist and held Elizabeth in place.

"I should not have come," she said and flushed.

Darcy could not take his eyes from her. "You are my wife, Elizabeth. You need never apologize for entering this room." He loosened his grip, but did not release her hand. "Come sit with me."

He led her towards a small chaise, sitting back before settling her between his legs. Elizabeth leaned against his bare chest, sighing as his arms encircled her. "This is comfortable, Sir," she murmured, snuggling into him.

Darcy kissed the top of her head.

"I came to thank you." She kissed the expanse of his chest and heard Darcy's breath catch in his throat.

"I do not believe I deserve thanks." Darcy's voice sounded strained, as if he fought to control his emotions. His thumb stroked the side of her arm.

Elizabeth leaned back so she could see his face. "Oh, but you do. My wardrobe is filled with new gowns and finery such as I could never imagine. I do not merit such extravagance, but it is wonderful, just the same."

"Then Madame Lucinda finished her work? I hoped as such." Darcy kissed the tip of her nose.

"It is not just gowns; it is these!" Elizabeth reached into a pocket of her dressing gown and pulled out a pair of silk stockings. "Feel how fine these are." She handed them to Darcy.

Darcy chuckled lightly; he thoroughly enjoyed making Elizabeth happy. "I think I would prefer them on your legs when I touch them. When I purchased them, it was with such a thought."

"Mr. Darcy, you are a *cad!*" Elizabeth swatted at his chest.

Darcy leaned down to kiss her tenderly. "Am I not to appreciate the beauty of my wife?" He pulled her closer into his embrace. "You should know, my Love, that when a man desires something as I do you, he will do whatever he must to possess it."

Elizabeth closed her eyes and inhaled deeply, overcome by the scent of him—of his maleness. "I will wear them especially for you, my Husband." Darcy's arms tightened around her, needing the pleasure of opening his life to Elizabeth. They remained as such for several moments before she sat up with a start. "Oh, I forgot." Elizabeth's green eyes caught the reflection of the light and glowed with excitement. "Wait here. I have something for you."

She scrambled from the chaise before Darcy could stop her. Elizabeth disappeared into his dressing room, and he heard her move into her own adjoining one. "Elizabeth," he called out, "this is not necessary."

Just as he got the words out, she reappeared in the doorway. Her hands were clasped behind her as she approached where he sat. "This is not as sensual as a pair of silk stockings—" she began.

"*Three* pairs," Darcy corrected her.

"Yes, three pairs," she said and laughed. "But I hope my small present will please you nonetheless. It is a token of my regard." Elizabeth extended her hand towards where he sat.

Darcy sat up straight and accepted the package. He unwrapped the string and brown paper. Elizabeth watched as he lightly touched the raised letters on the front of the book. "You remembered our first conversation in the Netherfield library," he said.

"There is little about you, my Husband, that I forget."

When he opened the book to read the inscription, Elizabeth looked away, suddenly shy. When he said her name aloud, Elizabeth turned and Darcy clasped her to him. "Oh, my love," he moaned, and he lowered his head to kiss her lips in earnest.

Elizabeth had no idea what she d had done with her inexpensive, yet heartfelt, present. If Darcy had any qualms about whether he needed her in his life, the book buried them. Since his parents' passing, other than Georgiana, no one ever searched out a present especially for him. His uncles and aunts all had people on their staff who took care of such things. For Elizabeth to find time in the chaos of the past few days to choose something personal for him— it meant more than he could explain. Unwilling to control his ardor, Darcy deepened the kiss and clasped her harder into his embrace. Their mouths angled to press closer. For a few minutes, they were both lost one in one another until Darcy's reason invaded the passion of the moment. "Elizabeth," he moaned as he broke from the kiss, trying to get control of his traitorous body.

"I will have to buy you a library full of books if this is my reward."

Darcy released her and strode away. He raked his fingers through his hair in disappointment. "I cannot do this, Elizabeth."

She stood there, stunned.

"I cannot allow myself to succumb to your charms! I cannot ruin your life by touching you the way I wish to touch you!"

"Fitzwilliam," she whispered softly.

"I did not make you my wife to wreck your chance at happiness. I married you to *protect* you from Wickham; I will not allow my passion to *rule* me."

"I am sorry, Fitzwilliam. When I am with you, I am happier than I have ever been. It is natural I should wish to express that."

"Yes. I feel the same, my darling." His words soothed her aching heart. "But I must control my urges," he continued—causing her fresh pain. "As husband and wife, we will spend time together during the day, but at night, I will sleep in my chambers, and you will sleep in yours. Lock your door, Elizabeth. My resolve is strong now, but it could weaken."

He made it sound like a business deal, and Elizabeth cringed with the reality of their lives. "We will *not* do that, Mr. Darcy," she countered. "Ours is supposed to be a love match, and your staff will gossip. They will say you married me because you compromised me, and they will criticize you for bringing your sister into the house with a woman of loose morals." Elizabeth raised her chin, daring him to challenge her.

Darcy blew out a long breath. "Elizabeth, when I lay with you at Netherfield, I did so at great risk to you, for I desire you. I am consumed by my need to take you. More abhorrent is my need to possess you in every way possible, as Wickham might."

Elizabeth flushed with anger. "Then you must find a way to control your desires, Mr. Darcy. Neither your sister nor I will suffer shame because of your actions. Our arrangement was that I would be treated as your wife in every way except one. My reputation as a genteel woman and as the mistress of your estate depends upon the façade we show the world. People will accept my eccentricity, but they will not accept my being treated as an *afterthought* by you."

Darcy rose and came towards her. "I would never put you in a bad light, Elizabeth. You must know that."

"Then you will join me in my chamber." She glared at him and left his room.

Darcy gazed at her retreating form. What she said made sense, but Darcy did not know how he would control himself. Whenever he was in her presence, he wanted her in so many ways. He wanted to drink in her naked body with his eyes. He wished to kiss her passionately and feel her quiver beneath him. He desired to lose himself in her body until his passion was satiated. And then there was the one point on her neck, where Elizabeth's lifeline pulsed below the surface. Darcy could not forget the sweet taste of her blood on his lips. Never had he felt such a compelling need for anyone; never had his blood lust run so wild. Darcy did not know which expression of desire would satisfy him more. He closed his eyes to visualize Elizabeth standing before him, her luminous eyes only on him. A groan escaped his lips.

With resigned self-contempt, Darcy opened the door to the adjoining dressing rooms, leading to his wife's bedchamber. Entering the open door to Elizabeth's room, he noted the presence of only a single lit candle on the bed stand. The only other light came from the fireplace. He walked to the far side of her bed and, turning back the covers, Darcy slid his long frame into the bed. He blew out the candle and moved to spoon her body with his, draping an arm over her waist and pulling Elizabeth's back to his chest. The smell of lavender drifted over him as he tried to clear his mind and to welcome sleep.

"Thank you, Fitzwilliam." Her voice was barely audible in the darkened room.

"It is for the best, Elizabeth," he said quietly.

She smiled with triumph. Lately, she contemplated the great pleasure of surrendering her maidenhood to the man she now called her husband. She shivered with anticipation. Her dreams of their joining increased after her Aunt Gardiner explained what the wedding bed might hold. Even more appalling, Elizabeth knew she would surrender to his seductive mastication as well.

CHAPTER 13

Wickham had expected that the morrow would bring him strength, but Mrs. Younge tended to his needs for three days before he stirred for more than a few minutes at a time.

Each time he woke in the shadow-filled room, George Wickham forced terror-filled dreams from his mind. Fitzwilliam Darcy had nearly found the key to killing him—ridding Darcy's life of Lady Ellender's curse. Wickham would need to do something about Darcy before long. Darcy's having discovered Elizabeth Bennet gave the man an advantage Wickham needed to eliminate before his enemy realized how valuable the woman was to his cause. It was not that she possessed powers of her own; it was the faith she held in Darcy's powers that made the man such a formidable force. Plus, Wickham suspected that Elizabeth Bennet held the key to Darcy's fate. In today's dream, she led Darcy to Wickham's lair, and he and the man fought to the death. When, in the nightmare, Darcy drove a stake through Wickham's heart, Wickham awakened with a terrible scream. An abrupt jerk of his limbs told him it was just a dream, but the feeling of dread stayed with him long after he rolled from the bed.

"My lord?" Mrs. Younge tapped lightly on the door.

"Come in, Amelia." Wickham had dressed for the day. He motioned the woman inside. "I appreciate your efforts on my behalf, my dear." Wickham took the woman's hand and brought the back of it to his lips. He was now completely healed, and so he dropped automatically into his seductive mode.

Amelia Younge watched his movements carefully. She had fallen for his temptation months earlier, and she knew there was no true reason for him to shower her with attentions now. But she enjoyed them, false though they were. "I am pleased you are well, my lord."

"You served me faithfully." Wickham finished tying his cravat. He stood in front of the mirror, as if to use it in his efforts, although only a wavy reflection—a blur of colors—appeared. It was a reflex action—a muscle memory—that even after all these years he had never abandoned. It made him feel human.

"My lord," Mrs. Younge said tentatively, "I have news."

Wickham folded the cravat so that it might be pinned. "Yes, Amelia? Speak." The length of material frustrated him.

Mrs. Younge walked to the door and picked up a newspaper she had left lying on a table. "This is the *Times*—today's edition. I believe you should see it."

Wickham snatched it. "What is it you deem so important?"

Mrs. Younge pointed to the third column. "There."

Wickham's sight adjusted quickly to the dim light. He read the first paragraph of an announcement:

Monday, December 2, 1811, St. Blaise Church, London, celebrated the union of Fitzwilliam James Darcy of Overton House and of Pemberley in Derbyshire, son of the late Mr. James Darcy and Lady Anne Darcy, to Elizabeth Victoria Bennet of Hertfordshire, daughter of Mr. and Mrs. Henry Bennet of Longbourn.

The news visibly shook him, and Wickham shoved the paper back into Mrs. Younge's hands. "Bloody hell! The woman will be my death!" He grabbed the paper again and began to search for his answer before he asked the question. "Does it say whether they left for the country?"

"It does not say."

"Well, I know where to find him; Darcy retreats to his ancestral home, the same house where I stalked every other generation. I will stop this before it gets started." He threw the paper on the bed. "Join me for the day."

"I will be happy to serve you, my lord."

"We leave in a quarter hour."

★ ★ ★

Sally tapped lightly on Elizabeth's door before entering the room. She waited, and hearing the Master bid her enter, the maid rushed into the room, only to find her mistress curled up in Mr. Darcy's arms in the bed.

"Beg—begging your pardon, Sir," she stammered, stunned to find her employer in his wife's bed.

When Darcy heard the light tap, he knew what to expect. Immediately, he brought the blanket up to cover Elizabeth and rolled her towards him. The maid discovered "the reality" they created.

"Nonsense, Sally. It is commendable that you are so attentive to your new mistress."

"I will come back later, Sir." She started backing towards the door.

"Tell her to return in half an hour." Their voices had awakened Elizabeth, and she snuggled into his chest.

"I believe you heard Mrs. Darcy."

"I did, Sir. Yes, Sir." The woman blushed with embarrassment at her intrusion upon their domestic scene.

However, before she could exit the room, Darcy called to her: "Sally, please lay out Mrs. Darcy's riding habit, and tell Morris I will need similar attire. And have the staff saddle my horse and also Ceres."

"Ceres?" Elizabeth was suddenly fully awake. "Ceres is here?"

"I sent for her yesterday. I paid your father fifty pounds for his trouble. I meant to surprise you." Darcy's smile told of the pleasure he took in taking her unawares.

"Thank you, my Husband," she said and spontaneously hugged him tighter.

"Will that be all, Mr. Darcy?" The maid waited to be excused.

"Certainly, Sally. We will ring when we are ready to dress for breakfast."

"Yes, Sir." She curtsied and was gone.

Elizabeth kissed him immediately. Surprise and happiness filled her. "You did this for me?" she whispered. Her green eyes darkened in disbelief.

"You are my wife, Elizabeth. I would do anything for you." Pure joy at seeing her excitement showed in his tone.

"Where may we ride in the city?"

"Hyde Park holds several riding trails, and as the season is over, we should have the park pretty much to ourselves. Once we travel to Pemberley, we can ride regularly. It will give me a chance to show you the entire estate."

Elizabeth now kissed along his chin line. "You are the most charitable man; I cannot believe I ever once thought *ill* of you."

Darcy rolled her to her back and loomed over her. "And when was that, Sweetling?"

"You know perfectly well when that was, Mr. Darcy." Elizabeth laced her arms around his neck and urged his mouth towards her. "When you thought me only 'tolerable.'"

"I believe I tolerate you very well," he said teasingly as he rained light, feathery kisses across her face.

Elizabeth instinctively wriggled her body against his, creating heat and energy between them. Darcy lowered himself across her and drank of her mouth. Her lips parted, and Darcy's mouth pressed harder. Elizabeth's hands searched the muscles of his back before he caught her hands in his grip and raised them above her head. Darcy's lips trailed a line down her neck; he loosened the strings tying her nightgown and pulled it from her, exposing the swell of her breasts. His mouth followed his fingers along the curve of her neck and down the crevice between her breasts.

Elizabeth's moan only encouraged his efforts, and Darcy cupped her breast in his palm before returning to plunder her mouth. Elizabeth arched into his palm, lost to the pleasures of his hand and mouth.

Darcy's lips and tongue slid down the length of her neck, coming to rest on the spot he most desired. He kissed it and licked the point, feeling her blood under the surface and knowing it could easily mix with the moisture of his mouth. Gently, he sucked on the indentation and felt his arousal increase. She made an inarticulate sound as he circled the spot, nipping the flesh. Every sweep and thrust of his tongue brought her a new awareness—a primitive hunger for more. Elizabeth tilted her head to the side and wrapped her arms around him, tightening her hold, keeping him with her.

Without realizing she did so, Elizabeth's body responded by grinding her hips into him, flooding Darcy with nearly uncontrollable desire as he continued to kiss along her shoulder and returning to tongue and suck at the pulse point. When she begged, "Please," Darcy's reason fought for control, and he forced himself to withdraw, although the effort was painful to them both.

"Oh, God, Elizabeth," he moaned into her hair as he buried his face in shame.

Elizabeth tried to control her breathing, needing to calm her racing heart. "You did nothing wrong," she assured him. "You did nothing more than what I wanted; it is as much my fault as it is yours," Elizabeth reassured him. She wanted desperately to keep him locked in her arms.

"As the man, it is still my responsibility," he asserted.

Elizabeth tried to defend their actions. "We are *attracted* to each other. Is that terrible? Some marriages are purely *business*."

"If ours were a normal joining, our attraction would have miraculous appeal." Darcy rolled away from her and prepared to stand.

Elizabeth turned back the blankets and followed him to her feet. "I will not, Mr. Darcy, regret the fact that I desire my husband's touch, and I will not be portrayed as a wanton because I want to lie in his arms and feel the pleasure of knowing him intimately." Elizabeth realized she argued for something totally out of their control. "Fitzwilliam, do you not realize how truly exceptional our connection is?"

Darcy wheeled around to face her. "I told you before; you have lived with this evil for a few months; I have known it all my life. Our perspectives are different."

Tears misted her eyes, but Elizabeth fought to keep her emotions under control. "Well, it is time your perspective changed, because you are no longer alone in this. *You* might have known this curse for eight and twenty years, but *we* will deal with it for many more than that. So the decisions are no longer yours alone to make."

Darcy stared at her in disbelief; his authority was rarely questioned. It struck him as amusing, and he started to laugh his rolling laugh—softly, at first, and then loudly. Elizabeth was struck with the absurdity. *Were we not just arguing?* Darcy came forward, scooped her into his arms, and twirled her around as he let his head fall back in a deep, room-filling laugh. "You, my lovely, are magnificent!"

His laughter was contagious; Elizabeth could not remain angry with him. Automatically, she locked her hands behind his neck and pulled herself closer to him. "And you, my Husband, are a conundrum."

"Now that *that* is settled," he said, still chuckling, "let us begin our day."

"Did we *settle* something?"

"We decided we would disagree," he stated matter-of-factly.

"Well, as long as we are clear on that." Reluctantly, she allowed him his ambiguous logic. Offering him a full smile, Elizabeth added, "I am happy you see it my way."

Darcy laughed again as he set her on her feet. "I did no such thing, and you well know it, Sweetling."

"But I will use all my arts and allurements to win you over," she warned.

"I will enjoy the battle." Darcy reached for the bell cord to summon the servants. "I will meet you downstairs for breakfast." He left her standing in the middle of her room as he crossed to the adjoining dressing rooms. Reaching his suite, he waited patiently for Morris to attend his needs. He replayed the past few minutes, as well as their confrontation the previous evening—his wedding night. Elizabeth was right about one thing—he would protect her reputation as his wife. The Darcy staff would soon know that Sally had found him in Elizabeth's bed; by midafternoon, neighboring household staffs would know.

Then a horrible thought struck him, and Darcy quickly returned to Elizabeth's room. She had just removed her nightgown, and under other circumstances he would have appreciated her sensual beauty. His wife's waist was small, and her legs were elegantly curvaceous.

Elizabeth clasped the garment to her and gasped, "Fitzwilliam!"

"My apologies, but we have only a moment." He stood immobile, his thoughts distracted by his nearly naked wife's proximity. "The servants believe we spent our wedding night in that bed." He gestured towards the rumpled bed linens.

"Yes?"

"They will assume you were no maiden." He stumbled through his thoughts, which were divided by his need to hurry—his need to act—and his need to touch her.

Elizabeth smiled, realizing perfectly where his thoughts lay. "I took care of it. Actually, I did so last night before you joined me." She indicated a reddish brown stain on the linens—only a few droplets, but, obviously, proof of their night together.

"How?" Darcy's thoughts returned to her semiclad body, and his groin swelled. He wondered—almost idly—whether he would spend the rest of his life in a *perpetual* state of arousal.

"A simple prick of the finger, Mr. Darcy." She held up her left index finger. "Aunt Gardiner kindly regaled me with details of what to expect on the wedding night. She thought to protect my sensibilities, but I found her tale quite enticing. She cautioned me about the pain and the blood." She, too, gestured towards the linens. "It creates a nice effect, does it not?" She sat on the bed, still holding the gown to her breasts.

Darcy took in the perfect curvature of her hips and how Elizabeth's hair streamed down her back and draped over her shoulders. He prayed for her to drop the gown so that he might see all of her. It seemed for a moment that she might do just that, but a light tap on the door told them Sally had returned.

He motioned for her to wait before claiming her maid's services. Then he bowed and disappeared quickly into her dressing room. Elizabeth smiled at his retreating form. Then she called out, "Come."

★ ★ ★

Wickham followed Darcy and Elizabeth to Hyde Park, watching them ride side by side while he hid in a copse of trees near the Serpentine. He noted Darcy's attentiveness to the woman and Elizabeth's devotion to the man. Even he, although he was loath to admit it, saw they made a charming couple.

Wickham's finely honed intuition told him Darcy loved Elizabeth. The rules of the game were now altered. Elizabeth would become another source for revenge against the Darcy dynasty, but his opponent's love for the woman—the first true affection Wickham had noted between a descendant of Ellender D'Arcy and another human being—the first in nearly two hundred years—created dangerous complications. If Darcy were alone in the world, he might gladly die, but Elizabeth Darcy provided him with reasons to live and to fight.

Wickham had questioned a new footman of the Darcy household earlier in the day, learning exactly the nature of Darcy's plans and where each of the players would be later and at what time. Wickham had paid the servant handsomely for the intelligence, and then journeyed away from the Darcys' scene of domesticity. At the entrance to Rotten Row he met up with Mrs. Younge, who waited patiently on one of the park benches. "We have some time before we make an appearance. Let us return to Edward Street and set our plans for the day." He took her hand on his arm and led Amelia Younge away, as if they were a real couple. Wickham enjoyed playing the role; it gave him a sense of what he missed in life, which reinforced his resolve to deny Darcy the same pleasures.

★ ★ ★

Darcy and Elizabeth called for Georgiana at her residence. He escorted both ladies on a shopping excursion—last-minute details before they left for Pemberley. The changes in the family dynamics demanded they search for special gifts to commemorate Christmas.

Darcy dutifully led the ladies from shop to shop. Elizabeth, who at twenty was not much older than Darcy's sixteen-year-old sister, understood what Georgiana experienced as a girl, giving them a natural, easy, and lighthearted connection. Darcy complimented himself for choosing a younger wife. *Or did she choose me? No matter.* Many men chose a younger wife because childbirth was long, difficult, and sometimes fatal, and the choice of a younger bride meant the woman stood a better chance of producing the required heir. For intensely personal reasons, that factor had in no way affected his decision to marry Elizabeth Bennet. He had chosen Elizabeth because he cared deeply for her, plus, she needed his protection. The fact that she could serve as counsel for his sister had not occurred to him at the time. Instead, it was a wonderful revelation.

"You look smug, Mr. Darcy," his wife whispered as he held the door of the next shop they entered.

"Just thinking how lucky I am, Sweetling." His smile showed his sense of contentment.

Elizabeth laughed. "Why should you not feel lucky?" she taunted him. "Two women idolize you—your dear sister and Caroline Bingley." She swatted his arm with her fan before following Georgiana into the well-lit store.

She paused at the counter and waited for his approach. When Darcy stepped up behind her, Elizabeth's body reacted to him as it always did. Her breath came more quickly and her cheeks flushed. Darcy spoke close to her ear. "Does my wife not idolize me?"

Elizabeth answered softly, delivering the lines without turning around. "Your wife, Mr. Darcy, is of a practical nature. Idols are for schoolgirls and desperate women. I prefer the flesh-and-blood man, someone who strives for perfection and often falls short, but someone who stirs my very soul."

"Then I am not just lucky, but blessed."

Elizabeth stayed at the counter, counting to ten before she, too, moved. She walked around the displays, but her eyes never left her husband's back. As she strolled leisurely among the tables bearing gloves and scarves and fans, he half turned and his profile revealed itself. The strong chin line, the aristocratic nose, the thick brows, and the lips held tightly as he fought back a grin—all these were almost as familiar to her now as her own reflection. The flesh-and-blood man was indeed something to behold.

Feeling flirtatious, Elizabeth glided up to him and placed her hand on his arm. "My Husband, may your sister and I leave your company for a few minutes? We wish to choose some intimate garments for ourselves, and we both need to purchase a special gift for the idolized man in our lives, and as you are that man, it might be easier if you were not part of our company."

"Now I am your idol, Mrs. Darcy?"

Elizabeth laughed at her own words. "I bow to the higher intelligence of such an accomplished lady as Miss Bingley. After all, the woman cannot be wrong about everything."

He chuckled. "How long?" He resigned himself to doing as she asked.

"An hour should suffice. I know what I seek."

"Very well, my love, but I will leave Belton to tend to your purchases. I shall meet you at the carriage in an hour."

Darcy started for the door, stopping only long enough to give the footman orders. Elizabeth turned immediately to Georgiana. "We have an hour to purchase a gift for your brother. I know what I wish to purchase, but I know not where to look. If I tell you, will you lead me in the right direction?"

"Certainly, Elizabeth. What did you have in mind?"

"New riding boots." Elizabeth sparkled with excitement. "Do you not think it an excellent idea, Georgiana?"

The girl glowed with delight. "Yes, I do. And I could get him a new riding crop. It is a perfect idea, and Fitzwilliam's boot maker has a shop the next street over. Let us hurry before my brother returns." With that, they headed out, arm in arm, to see Darcy's cobbler.

The boot maker assured them he would have the new boots and riding crop ready before the holidays. He would deliver them to Pemberley well before Christmas. Next, they found gifts for the

Gardiners' children and Elizabeth's younger sisters. Georgiana helped find the newest piano music for Mary and a stylish bonnet for Kitty. For Lydia, white lace gloves seemed appropriate. Elizabeth had purchased a locket for Jane at one of the stores they visited earlier in the day, along with a new fan for her mother. Only her father remained on Elizabeth's list. "Could we return to the bookstore we found the other day? If I am correct, it is just down this street and to the left."

"I could buy a book for Lord Matlock," Georgiana reasoned.

They hurried along the street, knowing not much time remained of the hour. When they entered, the bell tinkled, and the same man Elizabeth had seen before hustled in from the back room.

"Yes, ladies," the man said automatically, "may I be of service?" As he approached, he took note of Elizabeth. "Ah, my lady, did you return for another book of poetry?"

"You remembered, Sir?"

The old man had a playful nature. "I have an eye for a fine book or a fine lady." His eyes twinkled with humor.

Elizabeth blushed. "I am Elizabeth Darcy of Overton House." It was the first time she had said those words. "My husband's sister and I would like to make several purchases. You will send the bill to Mr. Darcy afterwards."

It was a statement rather than a question, and the man nodded. "I knew you to be a fine lady from the first moment I saw you. I am never wrong about a book or a woman."

"I assume that means you will honor my request," Elizabeth responded good-humoredly.

"Naturally, Mrs. Darcy. I am Mr. Henley. May I show you something, or would you prefer to browse?"

"I would like a piece on the British navy," Georgiana piped up.

"Certainly, Miss Darcy. Follow me."

The man led the way through the narrow aisles. Georgiana whispered to Elizabeth, "My uncle loves to harass my cousin, the colonel, with the victories of the navy. It makes for good dinner banter."

"Oh, this is the section where I found all those books on spiritualism," Elizabeth observed aloud as they came to an abrupt halt. The man pulled out three books for Georgiana's perusal, ignoring Elizabeth's comment.

Georgiana rejected two right away as being ones His Lordship might already own. She retained the last one in her hand as a possibility, but she asked to see others. Dutifully, the bookseller replaced his original choices and stepped farther down the row to offer up more.

As if they held a great power all their own, Elizabeth turned to the books directly over her right shoulder. One title seemed most compelling—*Vampire Burials* called to her. She pulled it from the shelf and began to page through it. She read, "A corpse swells with gas, making the body appear to be full of blood. Believers in vampires, although the Church is sore to accept these pagan rituals, often stake the decomposing body, releasing the blood left in the corpse. The escaping air makes a sound often associated with a groan, causing believers to assume that the vampire is still alive."

"Obviously, the author of this book never met a real vampire," she mumbled.

Unimpressed, she carefully returned the book to its place. Next, she selected *Tales of the Vampire*, containing the poem "Der Vampir" by Heinrich August Ossenfelder, Gottried August Bürger's "Lenore," and Goethe's ballad "Die Braut von Korinth." Elizabeth slipped that book under her arm.

Now on a mission, she began to select others. She pulled out one on pagan worship of the *upyri*, adding it to her growing stack. *Vampires: Folklore and Myth* became her next choice because it included a chapter on how to prevent the corpse from turning into an undead revenant. *Maybe something other than removing the head,* she thought.

Suddenly, Georgiana rejoined her, having made her selection. "Elizabeth, what are you doing?" Georgiana hissed, seeing the subject of her choices.

Elizabeth eyeballed the seller, who was close by. "If you would choose a book of poems by Sir Walter Scott, I will bring our other choices to the counter."

"Certainly, Mrs. Darcy." The man disappeared into the depths of the store.

When he was out of earshot, Elizabeth took Georgiana by the arm. "I saw all these books, and I needed to read them, to know more. This may sound bizarre, but I believe that we need to *confront* Wickham, not wait for him to come to us. The thing is....we know little about vampires. For example, how does this iron crucifix work? When Wickham kidnapped me, I wore this cross. It prevented him from making me one of his own, but it did not stop him. Why? These books are filled perhaps with facts, perhaps with myths and legends—things we do not know. When we arrive at Pemberley, I plan to start compiling all the specifics we know about Mr. Wickham. Maybe from the compilation and from these books we might have a better idea of how to rid ourselves of the curse."

Georgiana wanted to believe in what her new sister proposed. "Do you actually think it possible?"

Elizabeth reasoned, "What have we to lose? The cost of a few books?"

Georgiana looked about, making sure that no one was near. "We cannot simply buy books on vampires. The man knows our name; he may talk."

"We will choose a variety, suggesting that we are looking for information on local well-dressing ceremonies. Let us choose some Celtic folklore to make the ruse more believable. We will say that with your brother's marriage, he feels a new responsibility to the village traditions and beliefs."

"You are so clever," Georgiana remarked. "No wonder my dear brother loves you."

"Let us hurry, Georgiana. You choose some on Celtic religion and maybe one on Scottish beliefs and culture. I will pick out a few more of these."

Georgiana moved along the aisle to the religious tomes. Quickly, she made three choices.

Elizabeth, meanwhile, selected two more volumes. To balance out her search, she chose a history of Scotland and a similar one on the British Empire. Impulsively, she even selected a novel by Mrs. Ratcliffe, trying to create an eclectic look to her choices.

Just as she reached the end of the aisle to turn towards the front, she spotted a book lying on the floor. The old man treated each book he touched with reverence, so she wondered if Georgiana had unknowingly dropped it. Jostling the stack she carried, Elizabeth bent down gingerly to retrieve the volume from the floor. Bringing it up with her, she laughed when she saw the title: *Apotropaics*. "How appropriate," she murmured, and added it to her choices. Perhaps the book would fulfill the promise of its title and turn away evil from their lives.

Arms loaded, Elizabeth made her way through the twists and turns of the shelving. Arriving at the front, she found Georgiana pacing back and forth. "Elizabeth, Fitzwilliam must be waiting by now. He will be frantic."

"Go, then," she urged her. "Take Belton and hurry to meet your brother. I will wait here for the two of you."

Georgiana was already moving towards the door. "Are you sure?"

"Of course. I will be fine. I will take care of the transaction. With your permission, I shall have your choice for His Lordship and mine for Papa sent to Overton House; the others I will forward on to Pemberley."

"Fitzwilliam and I will return momentarily." Then her sister was gone, hurrying towards the waiting carriage.

CHAPTER 14

When a distracted Georgiana stepped off the walkway to cross the street, she took no note of the broken slat of its wooden frame. She stepped fully on it, and a protruding nail easily penetrated her day slippers. "Ow!" she screeched, before limping out of the way of the street traffic.

She fought back tears as Belton rushed to her side. "Miss Darcy," he inquired urgently, "are you hurt?"

"I do not think I can walk," she whispered.

"Shall I carry you, Miss?"

"My brother would be furious," Georgiana responded. "Help me to the bench behind me, and then go find my brother. Have the carriage come here."

Belton straightened before protesting, "Mr. Darcy will not like my leaving both you and Mrs. Darcy behind."

"Belton, my foot is bleeding into my slipper. Now, hurry, please."

Belton helped her take a few steps to the bench outside the storefront. "I will return with the carriage and your brother, Miss." The man took off at a near run.

Elizabeth thumbed through the book she had found on the floor as the clerk totaled her purchases and prepared them for shipping to Derbyshire. She noted references to the crucifix, the rosary, and holy water, as well as beliefs about mirrors. She remembered Wickham's blurry reflection in the window in Meryton, and suddenly things made sense. Darcy had told her about using the vial of holy water when Wickham approached Georgiana at Ramsgate. On another page, she discovered the Germans believed the head should be buried between the feet to release the soul. *It seems as though Darcy was right on that point,* she thought.

Flipping the page again, her eyes fell on a picture of a woman holding a crucifix and a vampire backing away. She thought how foolish the drawing appeared until she read the caption: "Say the vampire's name backwards as you bring forth the crucifix." *Well,* she thought, *I wonder if that would do the trick?*

Elizabeth closed the book and slid it towards the clerk. "This is quite an agglomerate," the old man said with amusement.

"My father reads everything having to do with Scottish beliefs, folklore, and customs," she lied. "I thought to share these with him after I learn more about the beginnings of the well-dressing cere-monies. I understand them to be based on ancient pagan customs. Mr. Darcy and I only recently married, and I have yet to see his estate; I do not want the villagers to judge my ignorance on such traditions as being a poor reflection on my husband."

"That is admirable, Mrs. Darcy," the man observed as he stacked the items. The shopkeeper picked up the last two books. "And these are to be delivered to Overton House?"

"Yes, that is exactly what I need."

Georgiana's attention was focused on her injury. She expected her brother or her new sister to appear at any moment, so when George Wickham slid in beside her on the bench, she was too startled to react at first—and then it was too late to respond.

Wickham waited until the street was momentarily deserted before he made his appearance, and then he was suddenly next to her, with a knife aimed right above her kidneys. He whispered softly to her before she turned her head, "I missed you, Georgiana." She turned immediately, and Wickham took great pleasure in watching the terror spread across her face. "We have unfinished business, my dear." He brushed his lips across her cheek. "Have I ever told you how you remind me of someone I once loved? Now, be a good girl and stand slowly. We are going to step into the alley." He watched her face as possible ways to escape ran through her mind. Wickham was used to this scenario and expected it. "Do not consider it, my dear," he warned. "I have a knife poised at your side. I can either kill you right here before I disappear, or you may come with me and join me in eternal life. The choice is yours."

Georgiana did not move, so Wickham took her arm and pulled her to her feet. "You will join in the pleasure," he taunted her, while directing her to the shadowy alley. "I look forward to this, Georgiana. I have waited a long time." Trancelike, she walked beside him, never looking back.

As Elizabeth stepped from the bookstore, she found neither husband nor carriage. "Where can they be?" she mused out loud. "Surely Georgiana and Belton are at the coach by now. Maybe Mr. Darcy was late." Impatient, as usual, Elizabeth began to pace along the walkway. It was not like Darcy to be late; never had she known him to be late for anything. Agitated, she took off at a steady pace, searching both sides of the street for her husband, Georgiana, or even one of the servants in the Darcy livery.

Reaching the alley, a flash of color along a row of boxes caught her eye, and, intuitively, Elizabeth turned towards the bright object. *It is Georgiana's slipper! How did it get there? And where is she?* Impulsively, she rushed forward to retrieve it.

The overhang of the buildings blocked out the little winter sun the day offered, and the alley itself, although not totally black, was heavily draped in shadows. "Georgiana?" she called, and then listened before stepping farther into the opening. Nothing moved in the empty alleyway, and Elizabeth turned to leave, but then a muffled whimper froze her in place.

"Georgiana!" she yelled louder, before charging into the dusky obscurity.

As if a theatrical light were thrown on the scene, Elizabeth stared in horror at the tableau playing out before her. Georgiana, wide-eyed, stood in the narrow, gloom-filled passageway. Wickham held one hand over her mouth and the other wrapped around her waist, and although her efforts were in vain because her hands were tied behind her back, Georgiana struggled to free herself. Wickham's mouth was poised above the indentation of her sister's neck and shoulder.

"Step away from her, Wickham!" Elizabeth's voice rebounded off the brick walls.

"Mrs. Darcy," Wickham raised his head but did not release his captive. "You can be next, but you must wait your turn, my dear. Your lovely sister is ahead of you."

Elizabeth squared her shoulders. She must protect Darcy's sister at all cost. If she could delay the wretched creature who was hovering over Georgiana, maybe Darcy would arrive in time to help her. She spoke slowly and loudly: "I *said* to let her *go!*"

"If you insist," Wickham said and he laughed, but he did not slacken his hold on Georgiana. "You may go first, Elizabeth."

"I am not *Elizabeth* to you," she insisted. Taking a smaller step forward and lifting the chain from around her neck, exposing the jeweled cross, Elizabeth continued, "You will remove your hands from Mr. Darcy's sister."

He challenged, "Do you really think that pitiful little crucifix has any effect on me?"

"Actually, I do believe it does," she asserted. "If not, you would have had *me*, back at the Netherfield Manor House." She extended the cross in front of her for protection. "I think, Mr. Wickham, the reason Georgiana is still alive is because she wears a similar crucifix."

"*This* thing?" Wickham used his hand to flick at the chain, but Elizabeth noted he did not touch the cross.

Realizing she needed to give Georgiana hope if they stood a chance of getting out of the situation alive, Elizabeth addressed Darcy's sister directly: "Georgiana, you must believe in your brother. And the crucifix protects you as long as you wear it." She watched with satisfaction as the terror on the girl's face diminished. "Your brother would do anything to protect you; continue to believe in him."

Wickham jerked Georgiana closer. As he feared, Elizabeth Bennet was a calming force for the Darcys, making them stronger opponents.

"Why do you care if I take her?" Wickham countercharged. "I swore to take *one* of each generation. If Miss Darcy is my choice, that leaves you and your beloved Fitzwilliam to your happiness. Why not take the freedom you will earn with her death?" He wrenched Georgiana's head to the side to expose her neck once again.

"Because we all swore to end the curse our ancestors began," Elizabeth said coolly.

"*Our* ancestors?" Wickham repeated sneeringly.

Elizabeth smiled. "Do you really not know that Arawn Benning was my ancestor, just as Ellender D'Arcy was Fitzwilliam's? How ignorant you are! It is Fate that brings my dear husband and me together. You cannot defeat us, Wickham," she insisted.

"Yet I can still exact my revenge."

Elizabeth tried to stall, tried to think of something to frighten Wickham away. She still clutched the crucifix before her. Then she thought of the diagram from the book. "Wickham George!" she called out as she took a step forward.

Wickham did not turn a hair. "My followers call me *My lord.* You may do so when you join me."

"Pigs will sprout wings first." Elizabeth's mind raced. *If Darcy were coming, he would be here by now. Reverse the letters. Visualize Wickham's name and reverse the letters.* It was a silly thought, but why not try it? "Mahkicw Egroeg!" she tried.

"Gibberish, Mrs. Darcy?" Wickham inquired mockingly. "You are grasping at straws, my dear." He lowered his voice and spoke in an intimate tone: "Taking *you* will double my pleasure—revenge on both the D'Arcys and the Bennings in one fell swoop."

Darcy bounded from the coach almost before it could stop. Belton jumped from the rear perch. Both men looked to the bench where the footman had left Georgiana. "Where is she?" Darcy demanded.

"I do not know, Mr. Darcy," the servant stammered, afraid for both his position and for the girl he left sitting on the sidewalk bench. "Perhaps Mrs. Darcy took your sister into the bookstore to tend to her wound where no one could see."

Darcy did not respond; he simply strode towards the storefront and burst through the door, fully expecting to find both Elizabeth and Georgiana waiting for him; but no one was to be seen, not even the clerk. "Hello, in the store!" he called at the top of his lungs.

A stirring from the back of the building could be heard, and within a few seconds, the old man appeared. "Yes, Sir. May I be of service, Sir?"

"I am Fitzwilliam Darcy. I believe my wife and sister were both in here minutes ago," Darcy said impatiently.

"Your sister, Mr. Darcy, left first with your footman there. Your wife followed five minutes later. Mrs. Darcy took her leave at least ten minutes ago, Sir."

Darcy tapped his cane to his hat in a salute of gratitude, but his mind was not on the conversation. Immediately, he was back on the street, searching the storefronts for the faces he most loved. "Belton, go down the other side as far down as where you found me, and work your way back here."

"Yes, Sir." The man took off at a trot, searching every nook and cranny. Darcy would do the same after ordering the carriage driver to wait, in case Elizabeth and Georgiana were close by.

Darcy had taken no more than ten steps along the walkway when he heard her voice. Elizabeth stood in the darkened alleyway, talking loudly to someone even farther back in the shadows. Georgiana must be there also; otherwise, Elizabeth would back away. Of course, someone could be holding a gun on both of them. A silent click of the switch and a twist of the handle, and he slid the sword, a narrow blade edged on both sides, from the cane; and he reached for the small gun he carried in his boot. Easing his body along the wall and line of boxes, Darcy tried to maneuver to where he could see his wife and better assess the situation. From his current angle, all he could view was her skirt tail and the back of her bonnet. He fought to control his breathing and to curb his urge to burst upon the scene. If her assailant had a gun, she would be dead before

Darcy could clear the obstacles in his line of sight.

"Mahkicw Egroeg!" Elizabeth called out bravely. Darcy wondered at her words.

Then he heard the voice he most dreaded in such a situation. "Gibberish, Mrs. Darcy? You are grasping at straws, my dear." Then Wickham continued speaking, but Darcy could not make out his words.

Elizabeth paused, seemingly at a loss. "Georgiana!" she called out again, as Darcy edged close enough to see Elizabeth's profile. She stood with his crucifix dangling from a chain in front of her. "You can see Wickham has no power to defeat the crucifix. You must believe, Georgiana," Elizabeth urged her. "You must believe in your brother and in me."

Darcy wondered where she got her courage; Elizabeth Bennet Darcy was facing Wickham's demonic possession armed with nothing more than a jeweled cross.

Elizabeth took another step forward, and Darcy nearly groaned, knowing the danger she was in. He wished he could see his sister—see the situation in which Georgiana found herself. Georgiana had not spoken, so she might be gagged. "Release my sister at once, Sir!" Elizabeth demanded. Darcy winced, knowing how Wickham detested orders and those who dared to issue them.

Intuitively, Elizabeth became aware of Darcy's presence. He made no sound nor could she see him, but just the same, she knew he was there. Emboldened by his nearness, she sidestepped farther, hoping to pluck Georgiana from Wickham's grasp. "I will tell you one last time, Wickham; your plan is madness. You will be found and punished."

Desperately trying to formulate a plan as she moved, she thought once more of the book, and immediately Elizabeth recognized her error. The foul monster's name was not really George Wickham; he was Seorais Winchcombe. George Wickham was his Anglicized name. She needed to use the correct one before the spell could work. Again, she visualized his name. She thrust the crucifix forward, extending her arm as far as the chain would go—

taking the jeweled cross itself into her palm.

"*Ebmochcniw Siaroes!*" The words shot through the darkness, and with a gust of wind, Wickham flew backwards, slamming against the brick wall behind him.

Instantly, Elizabeth grabbed Georgiana and tumbled with the girl to the ground, anticipating that Darcy would step forward from the shadows. Darcy fired the gun, aiming for Wickham's heart, as the demon slid down the wall.

In triumph, Darcy strode forward, adjusting the sword in his grip as he moved, planning to decapitate the beast lying at his feet. Poised above the limp body of his enemy, he could not have anticipated the attack.

In the shadows of the alley, a figure waited for an opening. Phantomlike, it clung to the side of the building, blending in with the faded wooden slats. Following Wickham's orders, Amelia Younge had tracked Darcy's carriage back to the bookstore. She had seen him enter the alley and hide in the darkness created by the haphazard stacking of discarded boxes.

So when Darcy stepped out of his hiding place and fired on Wickham, Mrs. Younge reacted in the only way she knew. She attacked the assassin attempting to kill the *man* she had followed into hell. Like a wild animal, she charged forward, taking Darcy by surprise, clawing at his back and ripping his coat to shreds with just a few swipes.

Dropping the sword, Darcy hit the ground and rolled, trying to escape the claws and the fangs snapping at him with great force and speed. His face sustained a raking from the tips of her nails, but he fought on. Calling forth his own powers, he pushed against her chest, shoving the woman back far enough that he could extend his arms. Blue light streamed from him, wrapping the vampire with a force she had not expected.

Yet energized by her need to help Wickham, the lamia valiantly led another attack. Again, she pressed Darcy back, her fangs dangerously close to his neck and ear. He struggled to right himself, but the she-devil drove a knee into his chest as she mounted him, forcing Darcy's shoulders to the ground.

As they wrestled for control, neither Darcy nor Amelia Younge saw Elizabeth move; their struggle was too intense. Elizabeth grabbed the sword discarded during the battle and, with a sweep and a lunge—a perfect *envelopment*—she came down upon the woman with all her might. "*No...o...o!*" Elizabeth screamed as she thrust the sword through Mrs. Younge's back, sending it all the way through the woman's body.

A blood-curdling scream reverberated throughout the small space. With the evil released, the body of Amelia Younge shriveled, becoming an empty shell. The blood drained from her instantly, and her skin began to decay before their eyes.

Darcy scrambled to his feet, scooping the cowering Georgiana into his arms as he moved. "Hurry!" he called to Elizabeth over his shoulder. Without thinking, she hiked up her skirts to follow him, glancing back only long enough to see Wickham lean over Mrs. Younge's festering body and then disappear in a puff of smoke.

Entering the nearly deserted street, Darcy bolted towards the waiting carriage, unceremoniously dumping Georgiana onto the floor of the coach before shoving Elizabeth in after her. Heaving his own scratched and bruised body onto the seat, he pounded on the roof, and the coach lurched forward, throwing Darcy and Elizabeth into each other's arms. Righting himself, but not releasing Elizabeth, he called out, "Pick up Belton!" Then he turned his attentions to his wife, without whom, he would, undoubtedly, be dead. His hands slid up and down her arms—her back—searching—trying to assure himself of her safety. "Tell me that you are all right," he demanded.

"I am," Elizabeth said, her voice raspy.

The air rushed from him in relief. "Thank God."

Then Darcy quickly untied Georgiana's hands, and both he and Elizabeth helped her to a seat between them. "Are you hurt?" he asked as he massaged her wrists.

"I am well, dear brother," she responded. "Thanks to you."

Turning her head to Elizabeth, she said, "And thanks to you, dear sister." She leaned against Elizabeth's shoulder and sobbed.

Darcy cupped Elizabeth's chin with his palm and, leaning across his sister, kissed his wife's lips tenderly. "Thank you for saving *both of us.*"

Tears misted Elizabeth's eyes as he pulled back to gaze at her. Georgiana sobbed, but Elizabeth raised her chin in defiance. "I could not become a widow so soon after my marriage," she declared. "Nor could I lose a sister I had so recently gained."

Georgiana released her hold on Elizabeth and sat back quietly in her seat. By and by, Elizabeth picked up Georgiana's right hand and Fitzwilliam her left. All three held hands in silence—united as one, with one purpose—for the rest of the trip.

Arriving at Overton House, Darcy sent servants scrambling for the ladies' pelisses and his overcoat before they departed the carriage. It was a façade of normalcy, played out for the benefit of the neighbors. What each of them wore under their outer garments might be tattered and torn—might be smudged with dirt and blood—but no one else would know.

He helped first his wife and then his sister depart the coach, and, leisurely, Darcy followed them into the interior of the house. They would deal with this together and in their own time. "Mr. Frasser, please have tea and some brandy sent up to Mrs. Darcy's sitting room. And each of us would like a warm bath." Elizabeth and Georgiana did not stop in the foyer. Instead, they ascended the main staircase, heading towards the personal quarters. We will need privacy after that. I will ring when we wish supper." Both women turned towards Elizabeth's suite of rooms.

"Certainly, Mr. Darcy." The butler bowed as Darcy followed the women.

Elizabeth waited patiently for Darcy's staff to set up the tub before the fireplace and bring in the water. Then she helped Georgiana undress for a bath. Neither woman wanted a maid's service on that day. They said little to each other, too tired to chat. Once the water was changed out, Georgiana returned the favor.

As Elizabeth slid into the warm water laced with lavender oil, the realization of what she had done finally hit her. She submerged herself in the water, needing to wash away the horror, trying to make herself clean again. *How long?* she wondered. *How long will it take before the mental images of this ghastly incident fade? Will they ever go away?* The water washed over her, caressing every inch—invading every crevice; and she wanted to stay there forever—under the water—where purity still lived.

She counted. How long could she hold her breath? What would happen when she ran out of air? Would she shrivel up like the woman in the alley? Yet no matter how much she wanted to stay under the warm water—stay where sins were washed away—Elizabeth's body forced her to come up, gulping for air, sputtering water. She pulled her hair away from her face and wiped the water from her eyes, trying to clear her thoughts, attempting to obliterate the images lodged behind her lids.

Then Elizabeth sat quietly in the lukewarm water, fingertips stroking her lips, seeing herself from a distant vantage point, stabbing the woman—again and again.

Painstakingly, Darcy completed his own ablutions. This evening he would go without the customary cravat and jacket, and opt instead for a loose-fitting shirt and waistcoat. His appearance was the least of his worries.

He, Elizabeth, and Georgiana had survived. Needing to reassure himself, Darcy moved towards his wife's room. The thought of what had happened that day compelled him to be where she was—confirming she was safe.

Georgiana sat sipping tea in Elizabeth's sitting room. "Where is she?" he demanded, too consumed by his fears to be his normally polite self.

"Elizabeth is bathing." Georgiana did not look up, and he noted that she shivered.

Her distress pained him, and Darcy leaned over to caress her face and kiss the top of his sister's head. "I am sorry," he whispered before he moved on to find his wife. His need to see Elizabeth immediately outweighed even his duty to comfort his sister.

The screen blocked his view, but nothing moved in the water, and Darcy momentarily wondered if she was finished and dressed. Then he heard Elizabeth break the water's surface. A quick intake of air and a choking gulp frightened him. He rushed forward, expecting to have to pull her from the tub. But as he reached the screen's edge, Darcy held back. Elizabeth swept her hair from her face. Ringlets of auburn curls streamed down her back, but his wife did not move. Elizabeth sat in the cooling water, lost in thought.

Darcy could not disturb her. Instead, he enjoyed the view of Elizabeth's nude body—the curve of her spine and the perfect swell of her hips.

Then Elizabeth began to sob. At first, he thought to let her have her cry—but then she purposefully submerged herself again. Her limbs twitched as Elizabeth mourned for someone she had not known, and she opened her mouth to let the sorrow out. Water rushed in, and Darcy moved immediately to halt her madness.

Hands reached into the tub, lifting her from a watery grave. She choked, coughed violently, and spit water. Darcy firmly pounded on her back, forcing her to spew the last of the liquid. Then he pulled her to her feet, and, immediately, Elizabeth felt the warmth of a large towel surround her before Darcy lifted her from the tub.

Elizabeth tried to swallow—to clear the burn from her throat—to say *something* to him—but all she could do was to cough again before leaning against his chest—into his love—into his protection.

"I have you," he murmured as he took another towel to help dry her. "I will never let you go."

Elizabeth nodded, unable to speak, but thankful for the strength of his arms.

"Do not leave me, Elizabeth," Darcy whispered close to her ear. "I cannot live without you." Elizabeth nodded mutely. Darcy sat in a nearby chair and settled her in his arms. "Please, Love; you are everything to me." Darcy tilted her chin up to where he could see her face. "Never leave me."

"Never," she said as she kissed his lips, eager to be a part of him.

CHAPTER 15

Darcy lost track of how long he held her to him. The damp towel slid away from her back, and he knew nothing but the feel of Elizabeth's skin on his fingertips. He caressed the smoothness of her spine, leaving a trail of fire along the curve of her back. "*Fitzwilliam,*" she whispered as she showered feathery kisses along his chin line.

Darcy's hands searched her body, needing desperately to possess her in every way. "You are exquisite," he murmured as her body arched into his hand. The back of his hand brushed against her breast, and her nipple hardened instantly. "I want to make you mine," he groaned.

"I want to be yours, Fitzwilliam," she breathed.

Elizabeth's surrender was a red flag. Darcy loosened his embrace, but he did not withdraw. "How—how could I?" he stammered. "How could I take the chance of turning my darling ...my darling Elizabeth into the kind of beast we met today?" He lightly stroked her chin as he spoke, captivated by her nearness and appalled at what he desired.

"There is no way...no way our passion could produce evil," she declared.

"My loveliest Elizabeth," Darcy whispered. He traced her lips, wishing to return to them and to drink his fill. "What we possess *is* pure, so pure I cannot destroy it to satisfy my hunger."

Darcy read the disappointment written on her face. He wondered for a moment if Elizabeth might actually love him. They never spoke of love—at least, not between them. Their story to everyone else was one of undying love for each other, but he and Elizabeth had never said such words. Did he love Elizabeth? Since he had met her, Darcy could not breathe unless she was close.

Without her, his life would be a shell—a pretense of living. She was *his Elizabeth.* Even though it was selfish of him,—for she deserved better—Darcy had never been happier since the day Elizabeth had appeared before him at the Meryton assembly. Aloud, he said, "It is time to dress for dinner, Elizabeth."

"Of course." Elizabeth blushed, pulling the towel closer to cover her nakedness. She tried to scramble to her feet, but Darcy caught her to him again.

"You know that your wishes are my own." He kissed the top of her head, while playing with one of the rapidly drying ringlets of her hair.

Elizabeth sighed, as if accepting her fate. "We tarried too long." Her voice held sadness, and Darcy felt his heart lurch with self-contempt.

Elizabeth moved away quickly. "I will need someone to lace my dress; possibly Georgiana would favor me." She did not look back at him; he was too tempting. Instead, she slipped behind another screen to don her undergarments.

"I will send Georgiana in." Darcy's eyes followed his wife's retreat. It hurt to think he embarrassed her with his actions. He needed to get his emotions under control; yet unfortunately, where Elizabeth was concerned, he showed little restraint.

As she stepped behind the screen, Elizabeth's distress was acute. Her hands shook and her knees nearly buckled. When she was near Darcy, she surrendered to her basic need for him. His touch—his well-being—only those things possessed her. *Is this love?*

She was married to one of the wealthiest men in England. She had exceeded everyone's highest expectations, but she wanted more. Elizabeth wanted Darcy's heart. *I love him.* Elizabeth wanted Darcy to love her as much as she surely loved him.

"Elizabeth," Georgiana's soft voice came from the other side of the screen. "Fitzwilliam sent me to help."

Elizabeth took a deep breath and reached for her chemise. "I will be out in a moment, Georgiana."

★ ★ ★

Wickham crawled through the window on Edward Street. He could not stay there for long, but it would be a day or two before Darcy would come; and Wickham knew, at last, Darcy would come. The man would no longer accept Wickham's intrusions without a response. Since Darcy had connected with Elizabeth Bennet, the man was uncannily lucky. That day, Darcy and his new wife had worked in tandem to defeat poor Amelia and seriously weaken him.

Elizabeth Darcy's mumblings had seemed to be nonsense until her last pronouncement had sent him flying through the air like a kite caught by a swift breeze. *How in the name of all that is evil did she know what to say?* Even he had not known a reversal would have such a profound effect! Wickham laughed bitterly at the irony. *Are the fortunes of Elizabeth and Fitzwilliam Darcy intermingled with my own, our destinies intertwined?* He snorted at the distasteful thought.

Wickham settled himself in the room in which he had previously slept. The bullet Darcy had fired had lodged in his shoulder, but the rejuvenating powder of his father's ashes and the earth from his homeland would heal that wound quickly. Fortunately, Elizabeth Darcy's incantation had sent him sliding down the wall before Darcy fired. If his enemy had taken the time to aim at his heart, he might have suffered a different outcome.

Lying back on the bed, Wickham contemplated his next move. He had to find a way to stop Elizabeth Darcy's influence over her husband. What could he do to make her turn against the man she had married? What could he do to force Elizabeth Darcy to either turn from the man or, at a minimum, refuse to help him any longer? Wickham's success depended on his separating the Darcys. Together, they were too powerful.

As he closed his eyes and welcomed a restorative sleep, his mind filled with images of the past few weeks. Suddenly, an idea surfaced—one so brilliant that he congratulated himself on it. He was still an officer in the militia—a very agreeable young officer, by all accounts, and Elizabeth Darcy still had sisters at Longbourn whom she loved. Wickham doubted that Mrs. Darcy had shared what she knew of him with any of her family; to do so would give away Darcy's secret. Wickham had watched the manor house from a safe distance and had seen Mr. Bennet enter to look for his daughter. As Wickham had, Darcy could have disappeared if he wanted to, but the damnable man was too honorable for that. Perhaps Darcy did *not* love Elizabeth Bennet, but married her only because his presence in the same room with her threatened her good reputation.

Such thoughts allowed Wickham to relax. It would be easier to drive them apart if Darcy had married Elizabeth Bennet out of duty, rather than out of love. Their union simply needed a reason for a withdrawal. Taking one of Mrs. Darcy's sisters as a replacement for Amelia Younge could be the perfect revenge on Elizabeth Darcy for her interference with his mission; plus, it was an inventive way to deny Fitzwilliam Darcy the one thing he most needed: his wife. Wickham had made his decision—he would travel to Meryton on the morrow.

★ ★ ★

Elizabeth and Georgiana joined Darcy in the sitting room; Darcy ordered fresh tea, and then they were alone. They sat in silence for several uncomfortable minutes before Darcy found his voice. "We need to discuss what happened today."

"I do not think I can," Georgiana protested.

Elizabeth moved to the mahogany desk. "Of course, you can, Georgiana," she asserted as she took the chair behind it. "There is but one way to end this madness, and that is to consult together. I am more determined than ever to finish what we began." She took out several sheets of paper from the drawer and prepared her pen. "I propose we organize what we know about George Wickham— what works and what does not work against the wretched fiend."

"Please start with your thoughts, Elizabeth." Darcy stood to pace. He thought best on his feet. "How did the two of you come to be in the alley with Wickham?"

Elizabeth looked imploringly at Georgiana, and Darcy's sister reluctantly began her tale of injuring her foot and of Wickham's abduction. "I am sorry I did not react when he first appeared; I am helpless." Tears formed in the girl's eyes.

"You are not helpless!" Elizabeth declared vehemently. "You are young. And you did what was necessary to survive."

"Your courage, Elizabeth, gave me hope."

Elizabeth shot a furtive glance at Darcy. "That was not courage, Georgiana. That was faith in your brother's protection."

"How did you know Fitzwilliam was there? You could *not* have seen him from where you stood."

"I knew," Elizabeth said softly. "I knew your brother would come for us, and I sensed his presence. We have a deep connection. I have no other way of explaining it."

Darcy cleared his throat self-consciously. "In the alleyway… what was that you chanted?" he asked.

"Georgiana and I visited the same bookstore that I was at the other day. We found several books dealing with spiritualism and with Celtic tales. One mentioned saying the vampire's name backwards. I was desperate for ways to stall until you arrived, so I tried it. When I reversed the name George Wickham, nothing happened. Finally, I remembered that name was not his real name." Elizabeth recorded something on the paper as she spoke.

"What are you writing?" Georgiana asked curiously.

Elizabeth looked up from her task. "I want to write down everything that seems pertinent to Wickham. We can add information found in the books. That way, maybe we can solve the puzzle of how to defeat him."

"Then add the iron cross," Georgiana said, brightening.

"The iron *retards* Wickham's efforts," Elizabeth observed, "but it does not stop him or kill him."

Georgiana thought aloud, "Was that why you begged me to also believe in Fitzwilliam and in you?"

"I suspect the power of the crucifix lies mostly in our belief—

first in God, and second, in the truth of the Baobhan Síth legend. The power comes more from our faith in the item protecting us than the item itself."

Stunned by his wife's analysis, Darcy paused in his pacing. "If what you say is true, then we must discover what Wickham believes in. Your theory makes sense; two hundred years ago, Christian ideas readily mixed with tales of the supernatural. Why did I not see that before? Elizabeth, you are brilliant."

Elizabeth's eyes softened. "I do believe we previously approached this the wrong way." Elizabeth's voice held her anticipation. "If we discover what protects Wickham, we can use it against him."

"Was there anything else in the books we should note?" Darcy leaned over the desk, as caught up in the possibility as she.

"I do not know," Elizabeth confessed. "I sent the majority of them to Pemberley. We will have more time to study them there."

"Fewer prying eyes." Darcy recognized the sensibility of her action. "Right now, we should spend our time making lists of what we know of the ballad—of the curse—of Wickham's habits. Then we can compare them with the folklore. Perhaps a pattern will appear."

"Fitzwilliam," Elizabeth interrupted, "who was that woman today?" Although it pained her to recall her part in the woman's demise, Elizabeth had to know why she had the sense that Darcy was acquainted with the woman.

He glanced quickly at his sister. "It was Mrs. Younge."

"Mrs. Younge?" Georgiana was on her feet also. "Are you sure, Fitzwilliam?"

"Who is Mrs. Younge?" Elizabeth demanded.

"Yes, Georgiana, I am positive the woman I fought today was Mrs. Younge." The girl gasped in disbelief and sank into the nearest chair. Darcy returned his attention to Elizabeth. "Mrs. Younge was once Georgiana's governess. I believe it was through her that Wickham was able to exact his revenge on my sister."

Georgiana's head snapped up in attention. "You told her?"

"Elizabeth is my wife, Georgiana." Darcy understood his sister's embarrassment, but he had no time for such propriety. "If she knows of Wickham, how could I keep anything from her? I trust her with my secrets and with my life."

"What do we know of Mrs. Younge since Wickham's attack at Ramsgate?"

"She lets lodgings in a less-than-desirable area of London," he impulsively blurted out, before adding quickly, "I had her investigated after Georgiana's attack. I thought Wickham might follow the woman to London, so I hired some Bow Street runners to find her. Wickham never appeared, however."

"Do you know where this Mrs. Younge lives?" Elizabeth needed to know every detail.

"I do not recall the exact address, but it is in the report," Darcy assured her. "Do you think Wickham is *there?*"

"Wickham likely took shelter with Mrs. Younge after your last battle. I suspect you injured him seriously. I doubt he is there now. He disappeared as we ran away today. He was bending over the woman's body when I looked back—and then he was gone. He probably would be afraid to return there, but he might if your bullet hit him as I suspect it did. He must know you would make the connection; however, we should check it out just the same. Do you not think?"

"It is too late to safely enter that section of London this evening," Darcy reasoned. "We will pay a visit to Mrs. Younge's address tomorrow."

A small voice came from behind them. "Fitzwilliam, when may we return to Pemberley?"

Darcy sought his new wife's counsel. "When might you wish to leave, Elizabeth?"

"We have commitments to family in the next few days. Plus, if you whisk me away to the country so soon, it might appear you wish to hide me from the *ton*. I want no rumors to follow our union."

"I agree. If we withdraw after two days, gossip will run unchecked."

Elizabeth noted Georgiana's dissatisfaction with her brother's response. "Possibly our sister could accompany His Lordship to Mat-lock. We could retrieve her from there on our way to Derbyshire."

"Could I?" Georgiana begged. "I do not wish to be here if Wickham is about."

"I will arrange it," Darcy assured her. "Now, we will go down to supper, and then we will return here to finish our discussion. I asked Mrs. Annesley to join us this evening. The two of you will stay here tonight, Georgiana."

"Thank you, Fitzwilliam."

"I will send to Steventon House to have your things packed. His Lordship plans to depart tomorrow, as soon as our aunt sees fit to leave Bond Street." Darcy helped his sister to her feet. "You will be safe with Damon at Matlock."

"And you and Elizabeth will be safe here together?"

Darcy glanced at Elizabeth. "We will…most definitely, we will."

★ ★ ★

She opened the door to a seedy-looking house on a nearly desert-ed street. Darcy circled towards the back of the building as she pushed the door wide, fearing someone might lurk behind it. The sound of the frame banging against the wall reverberated through the empty entrance hall. They came had come to find Wickham. Clutching the iron crucifix in her fist, Elizabeth moved cautiously.

She peered into each room, surprised by the tasteful décor. The dining room, for example, held fine china on a table set for twelve. Elizabeth wondered how anyone who might stay in this neighbor-hood would react if he saw such elegance. Such a disparity in eco-nomic situations must make for fine dinner conversation. Plus, if Mrs. Younge could afford such furnishings, why would she take up residence in the recesses of filth? *Wickham.* When Elizabeth consid-ered what Wickham's deviance had done to the woman, the situa-tion made more sense.

Finding no one on the lower level, Elizabeth began making her way slowly up the staircase. *Odd that no one, not even a servant, has appeared.* Her eyes searched the shadows for any movement. *Where is Darcy?* she thought. They had agreed he would come through the servants' entrance.

Elizabeth paused on a landing, debating whether to proceed without him. She looked anxiously at the way she had come in, expecting him to turn the corner at any second, and then she felt it—Wickham stood at the top of the stairs. His steel grey eyes devoured her as he stood in the shadows.

"Mrs. Darcy." Wickham's voice sent a cold shiver down her spine, and automatically Elizabeth began to edge her way back down the staircase.

"Mr. Wickham," she answered, taking note that he kept pace with her retreat. It was one of his favorite cat-and-mouse games; for her every step, he took a matching one, keeping the distance between them constant.

Wickham's satisfaction showed on his face. His smile increased, and for the first time, Elizabeth noticed his protruding, fanglike teeth. *How is it that I never took note of them before?* They were exactly like those in the drawings she saw in the books found in the bookstore. All her senses on alert, Elizabeth watched him, anticipating a cobra-like assault. He took each step that she did—challenging her—testing her—preparing to tame her.

Wickham tormented her by lowering his foot ever so slowly before letting it come to rest on the hardwood of the staircase while leaving his other on the previous step. Elizabeth never looked away from Wickham's stare, allowing her foot to seek the depth of the next stair on its own.

"Do not tell me you plan to run away?" Wickham asked smoothly, and he smiled. He narrowed his gaze and edged forward. "Really, Mrs. Darcy, you should know by now that I prefer my conquests with a little more spirit; I prefer when they fight for their lives. It is *so* much more satisfying that way."

"I will fight you," Elizabeth declared, "but you will find no satisfaction in the results."

With Elizabeth's threat, Wickham now took two steps to each

of hers, quickly closing the gap as they neared the bottom of the staircase. "Now, that is the Elizabeth Bennet Darcy spirit I have grown to admire!" he declared. "Taking you from Darcy will increase my pleasure immensely."

At last, Elizabeth felt her foot touch the floor of the hallway, and, intuitively, she turned towards the still-open front door, hiking up her dress and sprinting away with all her might. She heard Wickham's footsteps quicken behind her, first on the last of the stairs and then in the hallway. A few more steps to the outside—for her, everything seemed to move in slow motion except Wickham's advance. She felt him so close to her that she was sure it was his breath on her neck. Then, to her horror, a gust of wind slammed the door closed just as she reached it. Frantically calling Darcy's name, she pounded on the frame, pulling and twisting the knob, but it did not give.

Finally, she turned to face the demon at her back. Her right hand continued to turn the knob, but the rest of her prepared for Wickham's assault.

Wishing to feel the pleasure of her complete defeat, he stopped a few feet away from her. "Leaving so soon, my dear?" he hissed. "And I thought we had an understanding." He moved in closer and braced his arms against the door, effectively penning her in.

Breathing deeply to keep her emotions in check, Elizabeth tried the knob again, but to no avail. Resigned to what she must face, her body stiffened. Would Wickham pounce on her or approach more slowly? Out of the corner of her eye, she sought some sort of weapon—something that might penetrate Wickham's heart, for nothing else seemed to affect him for long. She found nothing that could help—she saw a clothes tree and a broken umbrella stand in the corner next to a bench, which was likely used for muddy boots. A vase of flowers rested on a table to the left. She backed as far away from him as possible as Wickham's gaze taunted her, playing with her fear. With all exits blocked, Elizabeth dreaded what was to come.

Patiently, Wickham waited for her survey, allowing time for

panic to set in, and watching her slender neck bob as she swallowed deeply. He relished the moment when his victims realized they would have to fight. He licked his lips in preparation for the taste of her, but then something behind him told Wickham they were no longer alone.

"You will deal with me first, Wickham." Darcy's voice echoed through the empty house.

Elizabeth gasped.

"Killing both of you on the same day will be a memorable occasion." He turned slowly to face his greatest adversary, determined to gain the upper hand. Then, as if possessed, Wickham lunged forward, a maelstrom of power hitting Darcy full force and sending them both flying through the air, landing with a crash on the lower stairs.

Darcy answered with an energy of his own, propelling Wickham across the room, slamming the devil against the far wall.

The air filled with the smell of decay and death. Thus assured that Elizabeth's fear would not quickly dissolve, Wickham purposefully righted himself and then dusted off his sleeves before making his next move. Elizabeth watched in horror as Darcy staggered to his feet, preparing for a new offensive. Elizabeth edged to the left, but a raised hand from both Darcy and Wickham stayed her movement. With a flair she could not have expected, Wickham snapped his fingers, and three pale figures appeared in various doorways. One of them looked vaguely like the woman from the alley. Elizabeth felt her body contract in response. *Is not Mrs. Younge dead?* Then she realized, *They are all dead! How does one kill something already dead?*

Before she could reason how that might be, everyone seemed to move at once. Elizabeth saw Darcy knocked to the floor as the three ghostly figures swarmed over him. Like wounded animals mad with rage and blood lust, she heard his cries and the sound of tearing flesh; yet she had her own problems. As Wickham advanced towards her, Elizabeth grabbed the nearest thing—the broken umbrella stand. Flipping it over, she heaved it at him, hoping to retard his progress. She had no time to assess the appalling futility of the act, for a cry frightened her, and Elizabeth looked to see a blood-covered Darcy beset by ghoulish figures who were draining his life blood. "No!" she screamed, and charged forward to save the man she loved. "Enough!" Time stopped as she bent down to wipe the blood from his face. Moments they had spent together flashed through her memory—waltzing in an empty ballroom, holding each other during the night at Longbourn, and kissing for the first time. "Oh, Fitzwilliam," she moaned. "Do not die. Do not leave me."

"*Elizabeth!*" Darcy shook her shoulder lightly. "It is all right; I am here. I will not leave you." He moved the hair draped across her face. "It was only a dream, Sweetheart."

Elizabeth's heart raced as if still in the middle of a life-or-death fight, and her breath came in short, ragged bursts, but the reality of what he had said sank in, and she clung to him for reassurance. "I thought you were dying," she whispered close to his ear.

Darcy caressed her cheek and clutched Elizabeth to his chest. "I will die of old age, my love. We will spend many years together." He kissed the top of her head. "You dreamed of Wickham, did you not?"

"We went to Mrs. Younge's house, and Wickham was there." She still whispered, afraid to voice her fears aloud—afraid of making them real. "Mrs. Younge and two of Wickham's followers attacked you. I saw it all." Again, Elizabeth shivered with the image of Darcy's bloody countenance.

A light tap at the door interrupted her words. Elizabeth sank back against the pillows. "I will see who it is," Darcy assured her. "I shall be right back." Elizabeth gave a quick nod, but she, intuitively, clung to him for as long as possible.

Cracking the door only a little, Darcy peered out into the candlelight. Georgiana and Mrs. Annesley both stood there, wrapped in robes. "Yes, what is it, Georgiana?"

"We heard someone scream." Mrs. Annesley moved closer. "Is Mrs. Darcy well?"

"It was a nightmare," he said, attempting to assuage their concerns. "It makes sense after what happened today."

"Of course," Georgiana said, and she started back to her room. "Tell Elizabeth I will see her in the morning."

Darcy started to close the door, but Mrs. Annesley's hand shot out to stop him. "Find out about what Mrs. Darcy dreams," she said. "Her dreams bear moments of truth."

"How can you be so sure?" Darcy implored her. "Have you seen something else?"

"No, Mr. Darcy, I have not; but Mrs. Darcy has."

"I do not understand. Does Elizabeth have the Sight also?"

The old woman paused for a long moment before answering. As if in a trance, she said, "Not in the traditional sense. Your wife is not just your future; she has the ability to *see* the future. Look at her eyes. Nearly catlike at times, are they not?"

Darcy's mind flashed to the many times he had considered the compelling effects of his wife's eyes—how the depths of them amazed and enthralled him from the beginning. "Yes, they are, Mrs. Annesley."

"Ask Mrs. Darcy to relate her recent dreams, especially ones of Mr. Wickham. Something in them is the key to this madness."

"Thank you, Mrs. Annesley." He watched as the elderly widow followed his sister back to the room they shared that evening. As he turned back to find Elizabeth curled up in their shared bed, he thought about what his sister's companion claimed. Years of dealing with the unknown told him to listen to his intuition and to pay attention to Mrs. Annesley's advice. He would find out about Elizabeth's dreams and prepare himself for his future.

CHAPTER 16

The door to the Edward Street address stood ajar, and they slipped in unnoticed. Darcy had hired a hack rather than taking his private coach, and he and Elizabeth had dressed inconspicuously to avoid being noticed by Mrs. Younge's neighbors. No one seemed to be about in the house. Elizabeth called out to servants, but none responded as they made their way from room to room.

In her dream, Mrs. Younge's décor had demonstrated the woman's good taste, but, in reality, the furnishings were shabby. The cushions showed threadbare sections, but the place was clean. No dust rested on the cheap figurines nor were there spots on the carpeting. Looking at the economy with which the woman lived made Elizabeth pity the late Mrs. Younge. The woman's descent into hell had started with Wickham's seduction.

"Someone is in the kitchen," Darcy whispered into her hair. "Let us see who."

He pushed open the door, and the smell of porridge filled the air. An old woman with white hair stood with her back to them, fussing over the food preparation. Darcy cleared his throat to get her attention. She turned quickly and was surprised to see Darcy and Elizabeth occupying the doorway. "Oh, goodness gracious me." The woman wiped her hands on her apron. "He'p you, Sir? Ma'am?"

"We are friends of Mrs. Younge. Might she be about?" Darcy tried to keep his tone amiable. He had no idea whether the woman was a vampire. He would take no chances with Elizabeth here. He moved to shield his wife from a possible attack. Elizabeth had shared part of her dream with him, and after Mrs. Annesley's words of advice, Darcy knew not which "reality" to trust.

"Have yet to see her, Sir. Mrs. Younge come and go as she please. I hep out here couple days a week with cleanin' and cookin'." The woman adjusted the lid of the soup pot. "She be havin' guests later. I fix soup for 'me."

"Are there guests in the house now?" Elizabeth ventured from off Darcy's right shoulder.

"Mr. George left hours ago. He be it."

Darcy shot a quick glance at Elizabeth out of the corner of his eye. "Mr. George?"

"He be an ole friend of 'Melia's, too. My, Mr. George kin sleep—sleep for two days stright, he did." She chuckled as she bent over and pulled two loaves of bread from the oven. "You be stayin' tonight, Sir? Ma'am? I fix mighty fine soup."

"We are considering it." He took Elizabeth's hand to edge her back through the door. "Would you mind if we looked around?"

The woman looked up suspiciously. "How be you know 'Melia?"

Elizabeth responded casually, "She and I worked together before she was governess for the Darcy family. I taught school for a year before I hooked up with my mister."

"This be yer mister?" The old woman eyed Darcy appreciatively.

"Yes, he is. We just came to London to make our way. I thought Amelia might have a place we could afford until we got a nest egg of our own." Elizabeth snuggled into Darcy's arm in a possessive way.

"Well, seein' as how you know 'Melia, I be supposin' you could choose yer room of those empty ones. All be clean 'ceptin' Mr. George's."

"We will not bother anything," Elizabeth assured her, "just look around."

"That be fine, Ma'am." The woman turned back to her work.

Darcy and Elizabeth slipped from the room and headed towards the main staircase. "Does this resemble your dream?" Darcy wondered aloud as they ascended the hardwood steps.

"Only in the angle of the curvature of the staircase," she said, trying to downplay the vivid dream, which still clung to the recesses of her mind.

"The old woman said Wickham is no longer here."

Elizabeth murmured, "What if she was wrong?"

"She is not." Darcy touched the knob of the only closed door in the hallway. "I am able to sense Wickham, and I have no such feeling right now."

Elizabeth sighed audibly, accepting his reasoning. "I hate it when you are right," she joked, trying to ease the tension.

"You must accustom yourself to it, my love. I am rarely wrong."

"Open the door, Mr. Darcy," she said, "so we can find what we need and then leave this place."

Darcy turned the knob slowly; the click of the release made Elizabeth jump, but he let the wood swing away from the frame, revealing a darkened room. Cautiously, Darcy moved to the windows, pulling open the drapes to let the natural light pour in. Finally able to see, Elizabeth tiptoed into the space.

Nothing seemed out of place; the water pitcher, the glass, the hairbrush, the folded towel—everything appeared to be ready for the next guest. They surveyed it all—every inch of the room. Elizabeth's gaze fell on the chintz-covered bed. "What is that?" She pointed to dark streaks on the pale yellow cloth.

They cautiously approached the four-poster from either side—the drape, a dark guillotine blade, seemed to separate them from reality. "I do not know." Darcy touched the black streaks spread in a curving pattern across the flat surface of the bed cover. He touched the smudge with his finger, brought the flakes to his nose, and sniffed. "I think it is dirt."

"Dirt?" Elizabeth questioned. "Why would there be dirt all over the coverings? It makes no sense. Even if Wickham had mud on his jacket, it would not be in a definite pattern. Step to the foot of the bed. Can you not see it is an outline of someone lying here?"

Darcy did as she suggested. "It is indeed; you have a good eye, Elizabeth."

"Did Wickham sleep here on this dirt-streaked bed?"

Darcy walked away to examine the rest of the room. "As clean as the other rooms are, the bed seems out of place. It must have something to do with *him*."

"Is there anything else? This room is most unwelcoming." Elizabeth closed her eyes and shivered. "Wickham slept here after both of his attacks on us."

"The only other thing that seems out of place is the hand towel. All the others are neatly folded, but this one is twisted and placed next to the bowl. It has a smear, as if someone wiped their soiled fingers on it." Darcy held the towel aloft.

Elizabeth came forward for a closer look. "This does not look like the same dirt as is on the bed. It is greyer in color and has an odd smell—more like ashes."

"Earth and ashes," Darcy summarized. "I suppose we will add them to our growing list of vampire theories."

"These different concepts must all fit together somehow," Elizabeth warranted.

"Let us depart, my love. We have seen enough." Darcy reached for her and, hand in hand, they left the house. Elizabeth wondered what would become of the old woman and even the house when Amelia Younge did not return. Sitting in the hack Darcy had flagged down for their return to Overton House, she could not control her tears. Imprisoned by her thoughts, she again grieved for a woman she had never known.

Entering their town house some thirty minutes later, Elizabeth quickly slipped away to freshen up and add their findings to the list she had began begun the previous evening. Darcy squeezed her hand in parting and headed towards his study to complete some estate paperwork.

"Mr. Darcy," whispered Mr. Frasser as he passed through the foyer, "you have a visitor."

"A visitor?" Darcy asked, annoyed.

"It is Mr. Bingley, Sir. I assumed you would wish me to admit him."

"You are quite right, Mr. Frasser. Where is Mr. Bingley?"

"The gentleman waits in your study, Sir. I took the liberty of ordering tea upon your return. I will serve it momentarily."

"Thank you, Mr. Frasser." The inevitable moment had arrived.

Instead of going directly to his study, Darcy stepped into a nearby sitting room to gain control of his nerves. For some time, Caroline Bingley had seemed to expect him to reciprocate her attentions to him. However, he had never found Miss Bingley appealing. In fact, there had been only one or two others throughout the years with whom he had considered marriage, but that had been before he understood the full ramifications of the Darcy hex. With Elizabeth, he had lost his head immediately, despite her less-than-stellar social connections. The situation was an awkward one for both men. Darcy had delayed as long as he could. He walked quickly towards his private room, a sense of guilt permeating every step. He should have sent Bingley word of his marriage, but he had avoided acknowledging his obsession with *his Elizabeth*. Would Bingley understand? "Bingley," he called out as he entered the room, "why are you in London? I thought you to be in Hampshire!"

Bingley sprang to his feet and shook Darcy's hand. "We heard nothing since we left you along the London Road. I came to assure myself that you had suffered no harm."

Darcy motioned to the chair Bingley had just vacated and then took the one opposite, behind the desk. "I am ashamed to put you through such trouble, Bingley. As you can see, I am well."

"I am relieved to confirm just that, Darcy." Bingley shot a quick glance at his friend before adding, "You were in some distress when we parted."

Darcy cleared his throat, preparing to confess everything, but before he could speak, Mr. Frasser carried in a tray of tea and cakes. Both men waited for the butler to deposit the refreshments on a nearby table. "Thank you, Mr. Frasser, I will pour," Darcy said.

"May I pour instead?" Elizabeth stood framed in the doorway. She had changed into a deep green day dress, which complemented her eyes, making them more intense, and her complexion glowed with their sudden scrutiny.

Bingley sprang to his feet and bowed. He stammered, "Miss... Miss Elizabeth! I did not expect to see you at Overton House."

Darcy slowly rose from the chair. His whole body responded to her entrance. Like the flame and the moth, she enticed him simply by walking into the room. Speaking softly but firmly, he said, "Bingley, may I present my wife."

"Your *wife?!*" Bingley exclaimed. Before he could recover from the shock, he asked, "When?"

"Three days ago," Elizabeth said sweetly, a hint of amusement playing across her face as she moved to where Darcy stood. "Please return to your seats, gentlemen. I simply came to welcome you to our home, Mr. Bingley." She stood beside Darcy as Bingley sat back down quickly.

Darcy took her hand and brought the back of it to his lips. "I was just about to divulge our surprise to Bingley when you joined us, my dear."

"I apologize for interrupting you, my Husband."

Darcy led her to a nearby chair. "Please join us, Elizabeth." He seated himself across from her and next to Bingley.

Elizabeth poured the tea as Darcy began his explanation. "Bingley, I should have shared my situation with you before we left Netherfield, but being in such an emotional upheaval, I could *not* speak of it. I presented my plight to Elizabeth the night of the ball, having found her an irresistible force over the weeks we were in Hertfordshire. However, because of the gruesome discovery of Miss King's body, she did not give me an answer." He paused to accept the tea Elizabeth offered him. "Knowing I was leaving with you, Elizabeth sent her response by courier. Luckily, the man she dispatched met Lucas along the road. Lucas, sent on another task, brought me news from Georgiana of my uncle, the Earl of Matlock, coming to London on family business. She had no idea we had left Netherfield on the same morning. As fate would have it, coincidentally, we all met on the London Road. When I read Elizabeth's message, I immediately returned to claim her hand. Once I held Mr. Bennet's permission, I moved heaven and earth to make the wedding happen before Christmas. Mrs. Darcy's aunt and uncle graciously allowed her to marry out of their home, and my aunt and uncle were able to witness our joining."

Darcy's convoluted tale amazed Elizabeth. She wondered if he had planned the story prior to Bingley's appearance or whether it was purely extemporaneous. "My Husband, Mr. Bingley, can be very persuasive." Elizabeth dropped her eyes in feigned embarrassment.

"Mrs. Darcy," Bingley said, having regained his composure, "may I wish you much happiness. Darcy is an exceptional friend, and I am sure he will make you a *fortuitous* match."

"It is *fortunate*, Mr. Bingley," Elizabeth said calmly, "that my dear Fitzwilliam and I care so deeply for each other. My regard for Mr. Darcy grows daily. I have no doubt about our match."

Bingley flushed in embarrassment. "Oh, Mrs. Darcy, I meant no offense."

"No offense is taken, Mr. Bingley," Elizabeth reassured him. "I expect you are simply surprised by the speed of our courtship."

"My regard, Bingley, began with the many meetings between Elizabeth and me during our stay in Hertfordshire. It grew rapidly when she came to stay at Netherfield with her sister. I cannot fix on the hour, or the spot, or the look, or the words, which laid the foundation. I was in the middle before I knew I had begun." He sipped his tea.

"After Fitzwilliam and you saved me from my attacker, I became dependent on him. I think his tender care during that time finally won me over," Elizabeth added. Elizabeth knew—because Darcy had told her—that if Mr. Bingley thought more about the matter, he would remember Darcy had *avoided* her after that attack, saying he did not want her to think he was courting her. But Elizabeth was confident a man would never think of such a thing. Those comings and goings were in the realm of female thoughts.

"Mrs. Darcy and I married while His Lordship was in town. Colonel Fitzwilliam stood up with me, as he and his parents insisted on being here for the ceremony. In fact, Georgiana returned to Matlock with my aunt and uncle earlier today. Elizabeth and I will leave for Pemberley the first part of next week. I was remiss in informing you, Bingley, of my change in marital status; it was shameful of me. I became so engrossed in our first few days as man and wife I neglected my friends. Forgive me, I pray you."

Bingley shifted uncomfortably, not accustomed to Darcy's humility. "It is perfectly understandable, Darcy. Besides, you realize I also needed a few days away from my sisters. Seeking you out was a reasonable excuse to allay Caroline's censure. In reality, I should thank you for aiding my escape."

Elizabeth stood. "I will leave you two to renew your friendship." She returned her cup to the tray. "Mr. Bingley, I hope you will join us for supper."

"Mrs. Darcy, I cannot intrude on *newlyweds*."

"Nonsense, Mr. Bingley. It is the least my dear Fitzwilliam can offer you after your trip to town." Elizabeth winked at Darcy when Bingley looked away. "Besides, my Husband graciously encourages me to share our new home with my aunt and uncle. He realizes I will miss my family when we return to Pemberley. With your permission, Fitzwilliam, I would ask my family to join us."

"Charming idea, Mrs. Darcy. Shall you send word to the Gardiners and Miss Bennet, or shall I?"

"Miss Bennet is in London?" Bingley asked, surprised.

"My sister accompanied me to my uncle's house. My father, obviously, could not allow Fitzwilliam and me to travel to London alone."

"I will be pleased to see Miss Bennet again."

Elizabeth smiled at Darcy knowingly. "If you would see to the invitation, Mr. Darcy, I will go to the kitchen and speak to Mrs. Perkins about the menu."

"I will see to it immediately, my dear." Darcy stood and escorted her to the door.

"I will be in my sitting room if you have need of me. I must wrap the packages to send home with Jane." Elizabeth touched Darcy's cheek before turning to his friend. "Until later, Mr. Bingley." She made a curtsy and was gone.

Darcy gazed after her retreating form. Elizabeth had assumed the role of his wife in a natural, easy manner. It was pleasant to observe her in action. Speaking to their cook would go a long way in appeasing Mrs. Perkins for such short notice of a dinner party. "Bingley, how about a game of billiards?" Darcy asked suddenly.

"Splendid, Darcy."

Nearly an hour later, Elizabeth sat staring out the fogged windows of her bedchamber. So far, her life with Darcy amazed her. Today alone, they had seen his sister off to Matlock. Then they had taken public transportation to Edward Street to track down a vampire. Now they entertained Darcy's best friend and her family.

Elizabeth's thoughts drifted to her husband. She missed him. He was downstairs with his friend, but she missed him. *It is ironic that the man I once loathed has become the obsession of my heart.* Elizabeth had come to depend on him—to need him—she felt truly alive only with Darcy close by.

She sighed deeply and peered down into the withered garden. Just then, a light tapping on the door caught her attention. "Come," she said, assuming it to be her maid.

She glanced up to find Darcy standing in the doorway. Just his presence brightened the room, and she bestowed a full smile on him. "Mr. Darcy," she greeted him, coming to her feet.

Darcy drank of her presence. *Everything seems brighter when Elizabeth is near.* "Ah, there you are, Elizabeth."

"You needed me, Sir?" She gazed at him lovingly.

Slowly he closed the door behind him and returned the look, taking in her beauty. "Mrs. Darcy," his voice came out a bit raspy, "I always need you."

Elizabeth rushed into his welcoming arms. Darcy lifted Elizabeth to him and held her close; she snuggled into him, resting her head against his chest. "I know it is the most absurd *foolishness*," she whispered as he lifted her higher, "but I was just considering how very dear you are to me."

Darcy's heart skipped a beat. Elizabeth rarely spoke of her affection. He often felt selfish for marrying her; she would have been happier, he thought, with a man with a less tragic family. It gladdened him to hear her declaration. Instantly, Darcy's mouth found hers. "Oh, my dearest Elizabeth," he murmured, his lips resting above hers. "Nothing is as right as you in my arms."

"Do you think me foolish?"

Darcy smiled down at her. "I think you exquisite." He sat her gently on her feet in front of him before using his fingertips to brush an errant curl back from her forehead. He lightly kissed the place his fingertips had touched. "I heard from your uncle," he said, his voice caressing her as much as his hand or his lips.

"Will they join us this evening?" She did not move, needing to feel his warmth.

"Actually, I have a surprise for you, my love. After you left Mr. Bingley and me downstairs, he suggested an evening out, as well. So when I sent word to Mr. Gardiner, I requested that your family attend the opera as our guests this evening. Your uncle accepted for the family; we will dine here and then enjoy the musical entertainment from our box."

"We have a box?" she asked and giggled.

Darcy traced her lips with the tip of one finger. "We do indeed have a box."

"Oh, Fitzwilliam!" Her arms laced around his waist. "You are the most generous man!" She hugged him tightly.

He bent slowly, forcing Elizabeth to anticipate the kiss. "Then you are happy, Sweetling?"

"Happier than I have ever been."

That was all the confirmation he needed. His tongue traced the outline of her mouth before her lips parted and welcomed him. She moved closer, and Darcy caressed her hips and groaned as he held her tightly against him.

"Fitzwilliam, what about Mr. Bingley?" she inquired provocatively.

"Let Mr. Bingley find his own wife." Caught up in the heat of the moment, all reason left him. He backed Elizabeth towards the bed and pinned her down there. He kissed her mouth—her temple—her ear—her neck. Instinctively, her hips moved against him, seeking something she desired. Darcy's mouth traced lines of heat across the swell of her breasts before returning to her mouth.

He palmed her breast as he released the kiss, recognizing her growing need for him. Looking deep into her hypnotic eyes, he said hoarsely, "It is wrong, but I must touch you. Please allow me." As he spoke, Darcy edged her skirt tail up, exposing Elizabeth's legs; yet he never looked away from her eyes. "You are so beautiful." His hand slid up the inside of her calf, and a small warm pool formed inside her body.

Darcy lowered his head and sucked gently on the side of her neck. His fingers massaged the back of her thigh, increasing his hunger, and so he sucked harder, lightly raking his teeth over his favorite spot. His breath on her skin brought her a new shiver of pure desire.

Totally involved, neither of them initially heard Morris's knock. "Mr. Darcy, Sir," came the familiar voice.

Darcy closed his eyes. Then he lowered his wife's skirt. "Just a moment, Morris," he called out in a strained voice, but Darcy and Elizabeth did not break their gaze. "I apologize," he whispered, preparing to roll away from her.

But before he could do so, Elizabeth caught the lapels of his jacket and pulled him back. "If you apologize, my Husband, for having to stop what we began, then I accept your regrets." She turned his chin to her. "However, do not ever make amends for showing me your affections. Touch me—kiss me. I am yours." Her lips brushed against his lightly.

Darcy swallowed hard, taking command of his body. He did not respond to her declaration; he would think on it later. He simply nodded, moved away from her, and straightened his waistcoat and combed his fingers through his hair. Reaching the door, he released the lock; cracking it open only a few inches, he looked out into the worried eyes of his valet. "What is it, Morris?"

"Mr. Redford reports, Sir, that he found your gun and your cane in the recess off the main street where you dropped them while assisting Miss Darcy yesterday. But he found no traces of the sword. I placed the items in your chambers, Sir."

"Thank you, Morris."

Darcy closed the door as his manservant strode away. Immediately, Elizabeth was beside him. "You sent someone to retrieve your weapons?"

"I could not go myself. I sent one of the Bow Street runners. Wickham disappeared and Mrs. Younge crumbled into decay before our very eyes. I feared someone might have taken notice of our altercation—the sound of gunfire—the screams. That is why I rushed you and my sister from the scene—to protect both of you. I wanted no evidence to link us to that battle. Could the sword have disappeared with Amelia Younge? Could Wickham have taken it? Or could someone else have taken it after we left?"

"What did you tell the runner?"

"Georgiana hurt her ankle, and a nefarious character tried to take advantage of her before I brought the carriage around. I chased the man into the alley, and we fought. I was defending my sister's honor. I dropped my weapons when I carried my sister to safety, totally forgetting about them in my concern for her."

Elizabeth chuckled with a new realization about her husband. "Another half truth, Mr. Darcy?"

"It is the way of high society. One becomes accustomed to such shades of verity. People believe what they want to believe. A man would protect his sister's honor by chasing her attacker into a service alley. No more needs to be said." He closed his eyes briefly, and when Darcy opened them again, Elizabeth looked into blue pools. "I tell others what they wish to hear. I tell you the truth; you know me as no one else does. I hide nothing from you, Elizabeth—not my fight to end the curse—not my need to protect those I love—not my barely controlled desire to possess you."

Elizabeth caressed his chin line, and Darcy turned his head to kiss her palm. "I know you, Fitzwilliam," she whispered in a thready voice. "You are like me. We neither of us want anyone to really know us for fear we will be found wanting." She squeezed her eyes shut to control the tears forming behind her lids. She felt a not unfamiliar constriction in her throat. *Darcy said, "My need to protect those I love." Does that mean he loves me? Does he love me with the same depth of devotion I feel for him? Or did he marry me only because it was the honorable thing to do?*

Elizabeth opened her eyes to find his eyes had turned nearly transparent and were rimmed with an icy blue. It was the color she knew well—it was the color of his eyes when he looked at her with desire. In such unguarded moments, Elizabeth actually believed he did love her. He held her gaze. "You, Mrs. Darcy, could never be found wanting." He kissed her tenderly.

"Be careful, Mr. Darcy," she said playfully. "Such *half truths* will lead me to try to convince you to finish what we started here."

Darcy's large palm held her chin, and his thumb touched Elizabeth's lips—moving gently across them. "Ah, what a tempting minx you are; but we have guests to attend to. Mr. Bingley would wonder at my absence."

"*Mr. Bingley* will forget all our offenses once he lays eyes on *Jane,*" she claimed.

"You may be right, my Love. Perhaps all the Bennet sisters have such powers." Elizabeth swatted his chest, and Darcy chuckled as he stepped away from her. "I will send Sally to help you dress. Wear one of your new gowns."

"The emerald-colored one?"

"Yes, my darling. No one who beholds you this evening will forget your beauty. I will be considered to be most astute for having carried away the brightest jewel of the country." He kissed the tip of her upturned nose and was gone.

Elizabeth leaned her back against the door and smiled. Somehow, they would survive the evil of George Wickham; the dangerous darkness of the odious creature would be a shared secret taken to their graves.

CHAPTER 17

Elizabeth heard laughter coming from the drawing room as she approached the open door. She paused to catch her breath before making her entrance. The dress was cut lower in front and in back than any she had ever worn, and she felt ravishing in it. The sound of her uncle's deep, rolling voice brought her back to reality, and Elizabeth swept into the room, awaiting their evaluation. Conversation stopped when they caught a glimpse of her.

Jane gasped, "Elizabeth!"

Her aunt uttered what they all were thinking, "You are dazzling."

Elizabeth smiled, but she waited for the reaction she cared about the most. She turned to face Darcy, but the intensity of his gaze caused her to lower hers and look away.

Darcy moved quickly to take her hand and raise it to his lips. "Mrs. Darcy, you look extraordinarily lovely," he said into her ear.

"Thank you, my Husband. As foolish as it may seem, I require your approval."

"You have it and more, my love." Darcy placed her hand on his arm and led Elizabeth forward to greet her family.

"You look stunning, Lizzy," Mr. Gardiner said as he kissed her cheek.

She beamed. "Thank you, Uncle."

Darcy pressed her arm to his side, pulling Elizabeth closer to him. When she had entered the room, passion flooded his body and need drove him to her side. Absurdly, he could not force himself away from Elizabeth. Impulsively, he kissed the back of her hand again and watched her blush. He enjoyed making *his Elizabeth* blush. And she *was* his; she had said so that very afternoon. *Touch me—kiss me. I am yours.*

"Supper awaits everyone in the dining room, Mr. Darcy," Mr.

Frasser said softly at his side.

"Thank you."

Darcy informed the others and then led Elizabeth to the head of the table. Before taking his seat, he sent a footman to find Morris.

Conversation flowed at the table. Bingley devoted his attention purely to Miss Bennet. Their brief separation had told him that Jane Bennet owned his heart, and the man was determined to use their time together to his advantage.

Elizabeth bubbled to Mrs. Gardiner about her first few days as Darcy's wife. Mr. Gardiner consulted with Darcy on a new business venture he was considering.

When Morris appeared at the door, Darcy motioned the man forward and whispered instructions to him. No one about the table took note except Elizabeth, who raised one eyebrow in curiosity, but all Darcy offered was a raise of his glass and a slight nod of his head.

With the last course, Morris reappeared, slipping something into Darcy's hand before bowing out of the room. As they each finished the cheese and fresh fruit, all eyes fell on Darcy, expecting him to take the lead in their evening plans. He cleared his throat. When he spoke, his eyes rested on his wife. "Mrs. Darcy and I thank you for sharing our evening. As we are expected at the theatre soon, we will not retire to the drawing room. I thought, perhaps, to lead you on a tour of Overton House before we depart."

"Yes, please!" Jane said. "Mama will expect a full report upon my return."

Mr. Gardiner added, "As we will accompany you, my dear, it would be beneficial to give a like account to my brother Bennet as to Lizzy's well-being in her new life with Mr. Darcy. Thank you, Sir."

Bingley added, "Pemberley is likewise impressive. It is one of the most renowned estates in England."

"Aunt Merry is from Lambton," Jane lightly reminded him. "She is familiar with Pemberley."

"It will be satisfying to know Lizzy is its new mistress, however. I have had no opportunity to visit Derbyshire for many years, but

Mr. Darcy has kindly extended an invitation to visit in the summer," said Mrs. Gardiner.

"Mrs. Gardiner speaks of little else, Mr. Darcy," Elizabeth's uncle informed the table.

Mrs. Gardiner chuckled. "As is only fitting, Sir. I look forward to seeing Lizzy well settled, along with the opportunity to renew long lost acquaintances."

Darcy came slowly to his feet. "Before we share our home with your family, Elizabeth," he said as he moved closer to where she sat, "I have a surprise for you. As this is our first evening out together, I chose a gift to match your beauty." Darcy reached into his pocket and removed a palm-sized black velvet cloth. He knelt on one knee at Elizabeth's chair. "This was my mother's." He extended his hand, and Elizabeth gingerly took what he offered, laying the velvet box on the table.

With trembling fingers, Elizabeth untied each of the strings. Darcy remained on his knee beside her. Tears of happiness misted her eyes.

Then she rolled back the last of the black cloth, and Darcy watched her chest rise with a quick intake of air. Joy filled her face. "Fitzwilliam!" she gasped, and her arms encircled his neck and a kiss landed on the side of his cheek. He drew Elizabeth to him and to her feet.

Both Jane Bennet and Mrs. Gardiner dabbed at their eyes, assured of Mr. Darcy's affection for Elizabeth; Mr. Gardiner beamed with pride, observing the match his niece had made.

Darcy picked up the emerald-and-diamond necklace and draped it around her neck, fastening it in back.

Her sister declared, "Lizzy, you are as beautiful as a princess!"

"My husband," Elizabeth looked lovingly at Darcy, "is most generous." She turned her attention back to the man. "Fitzwilliam, there are no words to express my gratitude."

"My mother would be pleased to see these jewels find such a beautiful home." Then he took Elizabeth's hand and wrapped her arm about his. "Let us show the house, Love." The others rose to their feet and followed Darcy's tour, but they watched the newly married couple as much as they observed their surroundings.

At this time of year, the theatre crowd consisted mainly of lords and ladies who turned over the running of their estates to their eldest son, widows who preferred the draw of Bond Street and London's cultural attractions to a dowager house, and second sons who would never have their own estate, but who lived happily in their family's town house. Darcy introduced Elizabeth to his circle of acquaintances. For the past six years, he had spent the winters in London, socializing with many of these same people; although they were not first-tier *ton,* they would write to those who were and describe the woman Fitzwilliam Darcy had chosen for his wife.

"Ah, Darcy," Lord Eddington said, approaching them as they reached Darcy's private box. "I heard you gave up the ghost, old boy."

"Your Lordship," Darcy said as he offered a quick bow. "How are you, Sir?"

"I will be of excellent standing when I have met this lovely young lady holding so tightly to your arm." The white bushy eyebrows rose and fell playfully.

"Mrs. Darcy, may I present Lord Eddington of Edsterton Abbey in Dove Dale, a distant neighbor in Derbyshire. Your Lordship, this is my wife, Elizabeth Darcy."

Elizabeth dropped a quick curtsy before Lord Eddington took her free hand in his and brought it to his lips. "My pleasure, Mrs. Darcy." The old man gave Elizabeth a wry smile before returning his attention to Darcy. "I heard you recently married, Darcy. Does this mean that you will be spending more time at Pemberley?"

"That is our plan, Your Lordship," Darcy said as he recaptured Elizabeth's hand.

"We are glad to hear it. It is time you made Pemberley your home—your dear parents are gone and life is for the living. Raise a family!"

Darcy motioned to Bingley to lead the others to their seats. "Mrs. Darcy and I will do our best to live up to your expectations, Sir."

Lord Eddington puffed up with self-importance. "James Darcy and I were at Oxford together. He was a fine man, and he would want this for you. I never saw a man so proud as the day you were born. It was as if the world had righted itself."

"Thank you, Your Lordship. Your words are balms to my grief. Now, if you will excuse us, I believe the performance is about to start."

"Of course, Darcy." The man eyed Elizabeth again. "Mrs. Darcy, your beauty is such that I understand why this scoundrel hid you away until he secured your hand." He winked conspicuously at Darcy. "Your wife is lovely, Darcy." He bowed to them both and made his way to his seat.

Elizabeth leaned in close to Darcy as he held the curtain leading to the private box. "Lord Eddington is quite the character."

"An old man can get away with outrageous remarks," Darcy commented.

"Do *you* not think I am lovely, my Husband?" Elizabeth asked flirtatiously.

"You know perfectly well that I find you to be the most exquisite of God's creatures." His breathing was shallow, and he felt her closeness in every fiber of his being.

Elizabeth stroked his arm lightly; then she entered the box as Darcy closed the curtain. Bingley placed Jane and the Gardiners in three of the lower-level chairs before taking the seat next to Jane. Darcy seated Elizabeth behind her sister and took the chair to her right. Then he took Elizabeth's hand into his large grasp.

Elizabeth leaned forward to whisper in Jane's ear, "Do not forget to tell Mama we have a private box, but be sure to have a bottle of vapors close at hand when you do."

Jane smiled brightly. "Mama will tell all of Meryton and probably several strangers passing through."

Elizabeth patted her sister's shoulder before leaning back into Darcy's nearness. Her family meant everything to her, but now Darcy was her world. Only when *he* was near did she feel complete. Automatically, she tightened her grip on his hand, and he answered by pulling their clasped hands to his lap. Elizabeth leaned against his shoulder as the lamps darkened, allowing his warmth to fill her.

When the performance began, she turned her head to him. Only inches apart, she whispered, "I wish we were alone so I could thank you properly for all of this." She gestured first to the theatre, and then to her family. Then she allowed her fingers to touch the necklace.

"I will accept your gratitude later," he teased her.

"Guaranteed." She winked at him before turning towards the stage.

Darcy gazed at the effect the dampened lamps had on her eyes. They glowed with the shaded light, as if every point of brightness in the room began and ended in her eyes. They were the green of limes and of new leaves and of moss, all at the same time. In the light of the nearest sconce, he could see the indentation of her neck. The diamond and emeralds glistened there, sparkling at the spot he most desired, a spot that was now slightly reddened from his earlier attentions to it.

Darcy smiled at her when she looked back at him. Her eyes danced with happiness, and he knew he had married the right woman. Without Elizabeth, Georgiana might now be dead, and he *surely* would be. Plus, she brought hope with her—hope for a different way of life. Just for a moment, Darcy wondered, *If we destroy Wickham, will I change, too? Will I still carry the curse? Will I still create another vampire if we have a son? Or*—He dared not finish his own thought.

At the intermission, Darcy and Mr. Gardiner sought refreshments while Bingley escorted Jane about the building, showing her the architecture of what was once a royal residence. Alone with her aunt, Elizabeth could not resist asking, "Do you still suspect Fitzwilliam of crimes most heinous?"

"I no longer believe Mr. Darcy could take a life violently because I believe in *you,* Lizzy. You could not love the man as you do if there were such evil in him." Mrs. Gardiner patted Elizabeth's hand.

Elizabeth looked about to see if anyone might hear her confession. "Aunt Merry, I do love Mr. Darcy, and I do not speak of the man who gives me diamonds. I speak of the man who holds me when I have a nightmare—of the man who buys a horse from his friend because I love the animal—of the man from whose eyes I cannot look away."

"The necklace is enchanting." Mrs. Gardiner reached out and touched the jewels with her fingertips. She spoke in a lower tone: "I noted the red mark on your neck, Lizzy."

Elizabeth's fingers shot to the spot. "Does it show, Aunt Merry?"

"Your husband cleverly covered it with the necklace. I, too, have the mark." Her aunt rolled back the netted scarf draped around her neck and tucked it in at the bodice of her gown.

"Uncle Edward?" Elizabeth could not believe her own ears. Her uncle could not be a vampire, too. Besides, he was her *mother's* brother, not a relative of Lord Thomas.

Mrs. Gardiner blushed. "Your uncle enjoys my *femininity,* as he calls it."

"Are you saying, Aunt, that my uncle—your husband—*kisses* you in such a way?"

A bit sarcastically, Aunt Merry responded, "Yes, Lizzy, your uncle and I still share a bed, even after all these years."

Elizabeth's mind churned—turning faster and faster. What if what Darcy thought to be the perversion of the curse was actually just part of what he desired during lovemaking? What if he was not a vampire? But he *was* a vampire, she reasoned. She had witnessed his supernatural powers. *But what if he is not?* Aloud, she said, "So every time you wear a scarf, it is to cover up Uncle Edward's affectionate attentions?"

Her aunt laughed. "Not *every* time, dear Lizzy."

Elizabeth's eyes danced in delight. "Aunt Merry, I love you," she said and gave her a hug.

"I love her, too," Uncle Edward attested as he entered the box, followed closely by Darcy. He handed his wife a glass of punch. "Of what were you two speaking?"

Elizabeth shot her aunt a shy glance. "Of Pemberley, Uncle. Of your trip to Pemberley."

"I should have known." Mr. Gardiner settled himself next to his wife. "Shall I have no peace until summer, Merry?" he teased.

"None whatsoever."

Bingley and Jane returned just in time for the lights to go down. Elizabeth sipped the lemonade Darcy had brought her. Throughout the second act, she could not help sneaking peeks at her husband. Perhaps she knew something he did not.

★ ★ ★

They spent four more days in London, visiting museums and art galleries and allowing Elizabeth time to learn the city. They would not return until the season; then she would be on display at all times—a daunting thought. Elizabeth thought she might rather face Wickham's wrath than come face-to-face with the *ton*. Bingley chose to remain in town as long as Jane Bennet resided at Gracechurch Street. He called on her daily, and they often joined Darcy and Elizabeth at Overton House or out for the evening.

The newlyweds' private time became more routine, even though Darcy continued to fight his desires for Elizabeth. When they were out on the town as a couple, he could almost believe the lie they presented. He and Elizabeth were in love and were planning a family. He would have his heir for Pemberley. But Darcy knew that although he loved Elizabeth, they would never produce children; nor would life be routine until he and Elizabeth had disposed of Wickham. It made his heart ache to know Elizabeth had given up so much by becoming involved with him; therefore, he threw all his energies into gratifying her with little things. Sometimes he wondered if he should tell her that he loved her. Would that knowledge please Elizabeth? Could she ever return his love? Would such a declaration make a difference to her? Darcy's pride would not allow him to take the chance of Elizabeth rebuking him; he would settle for her loyalty and her devotion. It would be enough. Being with her forever would be enough.

On the way to Pemberley, they spent two days at Matlock with his aunt and uncle. His family welcomed Elizabeth, and she sparkled when she was with them. The Earl offered Darcy his approval before their departure. "It will be good to have you at Pemberley. Your estate needs you; the country needs you. Mrs. Darcy will bring you contentment at last, my boy. You will see what a good woman can bring to a man's life. You were never known as a rakehell, but you always seemed to lack a focus. Now, with Mrs. Darcy, you appear finally ready to meet your destiny."

"You are astute, Your Lordship."

"Your aunt is quite taken with your bride, Fitzwilliam. I dare say my sister would approve most wholeheartedly."

A week from the day they had spent an evening at the opera with her family, Darcy's coach arrived at Pemberley. Elizabeth, as they drove along, watched for the first appearance of Pemberley Woods with some perturbation, and when at length they turned in at the lodge her spirits were in high flutter. This was her home—their home—where she would spend her days and nights with Darcy.

Looking out the coach's window, she noted the expanse of the park. They entered it in one of its lowest points and drove for some time through a wood stretching over a wide extent. "Pemberley in the spring and summer is the most beautiful of places," Georgiana assured her.

Elizabeth nodded. Her mind was too full for conversation, but she saw and admired every remarkable spot and point of view. They gradually ascended for half a mile, and then found themselves at the top of a considerable eminence, where the wood ceased and Pemberley House instantly caught the eye. She remembered Darcy's words from that first night in the Netherfield library. *It is a large, handsome stone building, standing well on high ground and backed by a ridge of high woody hills with a stream of some natural importance in front. Its banks are neither formal nor falsely adorned.* He had described it perfectly, and Elizabeth was delighted. She had never seen a place for which nature had done more, or where natural beauty was so little counteracted by an awkward taste. At that moment she felt to be mistress of Pemberley might be something. "It is magnificent, Fitzwilliam," she said.

Darcy allowed himself to breathe and to release the tension he held high in his shoulders. He had waited and watched for Elizabeth's reactions as the coach drew nearer to the house. "Your approval is important to me, Elizabeth." He clasped her hand in his. If Georgiana and Mrs. Annesley did not travel with them, he might have pulled Elizabeth onto his lap and kissed her properly. Instead, he leaned across her and pointed out places along the route where he planned to make improvements. He spoke of maintaining the natural order of the land. Finally, they descended the hill, crossed the bridge, and drove up to the door.

Once the coachman let down the carriage steps, Darcy descended first. He helped Georgiana and Mrs. Annesley alight, and then he reached into the coach to take Elizabeth's hand. "Welcome to your new home, Mrs. Darcy," he said softly.

She glanced up at the pink gold brick façade of the house; the late afternoon winter sun reflected off the rows of windows, making the place glow with light. "What is the superlative form of magnificent?" she murmured. She took his proffered arm, allowing him to lead her forward, all the while keeping up a litany of adjectives to describe Pemberley, intent on finding the right one. "Splendid—resplendent—glorious—grandiose—sublime—stately—superb—imposing—radiant."

Darcy chuckled at her nervousness. "I believe the house cannot live up to such praise," he whispered close to Elizabeth's ear.

"Was I saying those words out loud?" Elizabeth was shocked.

"You were, my love." He locked her arm close to his side. "Let us meet the assembled staff."

Elizabeth glanced up to find two lines of servants gracing the entrance steps to the house. She took a deep, steadying breath and allowed Darcy to usher her forward. With each of the servants,

Elizabeth took the time to look them in the eye and to address them courteously. She told them all she would learn their names in time and begged for their patience while she learned about the estate and about them.

"Behold the conquering hero," Darcy joked after excusing the staff to their various duties. He lifted her gloved hand and planted a kiss on the inside of her wrist. Then Darcy replaced her hand on his arm to make the last of the introductions. "These three, Elizabeth"—he gestured to the remaining servants in the front foyer— "are the real experts on Pemberley. Among them, they have nearly seventy years of service to the Darcys. They keep the house and land running in my absence. This is Mr. Harold, my steward; Mr. Lockwood, my butler; and Mrs. Reynolds, the housekeeper." The men bowed and Mrs. Reynolds curtsied. "It is with great pleasure that I present my wife, Elizabeth Darcy."

Mr. Lockwood spoke first. "Mrs. Darcy, we were elated to hear of the master's marriage and the fact of his return to Pemberley for Christmas. I speak for the entire staff in saying your presence here is a welcome renewal of this household."

"That is very kind of you, Mr. Lockwood." Elizabeth fought back tears. These people loved Darcy and wanted the best for him; they wanted to see him well settled, with children in the nursery. She regretted that part of their dream would never happen. She made a silent vow to help Georgiana marry a man she adored and find domestic happiness. Pemberley would lose the Darcy name, but Georgiana's children would bring the estate what Elizabeth's marriage could not give it.

She received like praise from the other two before they all returned to their tasks. Georgiana withdrew to her quarters, followed closely by Mrs. Annesley.

"Alone, my dear," Darcy leaned down to whisper close to her ear. Then he winked at her before saying loudly, for the sake of the servants, "May I show you some of the lower rooms before we freshen up?"

"That would be pleasant." Her voice trembled. With the departure of the servants, Elizabeth let her guard drop and, naturally, her energy seemed depleted.

"Would you rather see your chamber first?" Darcy felt her sag against him.

Elizabeth looked up at him sheepishly. "Would you be offended? I do want to see the *entire* house, but it is a bit daunting. Might I bolster my reserves first?"

"We will change for dinner and then call upon Georgiana to add her insights about Pemberley. I am eager for you to see the house and grounds, but we will have a lifetime together. The house and grounds can wait."

"A lifetime? A lifetime with you, Fitzwilliam—how horrendous, my dear!" She winked at her handsome husband.

He chortled and bent down to kiss her on the cheek. "Yes, my darling, it will be horrendous for me, too." They ascended the main staircase, arm in arm.

CHAPTER 18

Wickham waited in one of the out buildings of the village of Meryton. By changing himself into the image of a new recruit, he had discovered there were no productive clues into the deaths of the dark-skinned bar maid or the recently dowered Miss King. One of the noncommissioned officers had told him there had been no repeat attacks and Colonel Forster felt the deaths were the crimes of a drifter who had moved on. Wickham found such conjectures amusing. The average British citizen held *no* understanding of the evils of the world. And it gave him some sense of security to know no one looked for him in these cases.

After determining that his acquaintance James Denny was on assignment out of the country—and no one would be the wiser—Wickham waited for one of the Bennet sisters to attend their aunt in town. As far as he could tell from his first stay in the area, one or more of the Bennets came to the township daily; but although he had waited for several hours, none of the Bennets appeared on that day.

Finally, he spotted Charlotte Lucas and one of her sisters entering the outer limits of the village. Assured of his appearance, Wickham stepped from behind the door and strode towards the Lucas sisters.

"Mr. Denny," Charlotte Lucas greeted him and offering him a curtsy. Wickham smiled at her. "It is pleasant to meet you today."

The woman was plain—as plain as they came. He preferred his converts to be attractive. From the Bennets, he would choose the oldest sister, Jane Bennet, or maybe the buxom Lydia Bennet. As far as he was concerned, Elizabeth Bennet Darcy's beauty ranked third of the five sisters. However, he needed to keep all his options open. Wickham thought that if he could not capture one of Mrs. Darcy's sisters, Charlotte Lucas might do. She was known as Elizabeth

Darcy's best friend. Wickham bowed. "Miss Lucas," he said, "you are looking well today."

"Thank you, Mr. Denny. You are most kind." Charlotte blushed.

"May I walk with the two of you?" He offered an arm to both ladies, but he paid little attention to the younger sister. Although the girl was much more attractive than her older sibling, Charlotte Lucas had what he needed right then: intimate details of Elizabeth Darcy's life.

They walked the length of a street, and Maria Lucas pleaded to be excused to the local mercantile. Wickham hated niceties: He thought of himself as a man of *action*. Societal demands bored and irritated him—too many rules. He had to keep reminding himself that, to Charlotte Lucas, he was James Denny. He waited with seeming patience while Miss Lucas agreed to excuse Maria, and then Wickham began a *seduction*. Today, he would seek only information, nothing more. Alone with Charlotte, he favored her with one of his best smiles. "Have you had word from Miss Elizabeth?"

Charlotte waved to an acquaintance before turning her attention to the junior officer. "Oh, yes, Lizzy writes of her marriage plans. Of course, I have had no news from her in several days, but that is to be expected." She relaxed in his presence. Wickham thought how foolish that would be under normal circumstances.

"Then you approve of Miss Elizabeth's marriage?" Wickham knew all about the wedding, but he needed to make small talk—needed to continue building her trust.

"Lizzy always said she would marry only for love, and although Mr. Darcy is quite wealthy, I must believe Elizabeth feels deeply for the man. As Lizzy's intimate friend, I cannot see her marrying, even for a man of Mr. Darcy's consequence, without true affection between them."

Despite how much he hated to admit it, Wickham held similar assumptions. From what he knew of the Darcys, they held each other in high regard—although he hoped to change that. "With such a fortuitous match, Mrs. Bennet must be beside herself with happiness."

Charlotte laughed. "So she told my mother—several times."

"It is a shame Mrs. Darcy's family and friends were denied the pleasure of sharing her special day."

"Miss Bennet was with Lizzy, and her mother's brother lives in London. I am sorry not to have been there, but if Lizzy is happy, then I am satisfied. Mr. Darcy did not want to wait, as Christmas approaches. I imagine that with the winter, the roads to Derbyshire are often not passable. He wanted no delay once Lizzy agreed to his suit. It was all very romantic; after leaving with his friends, Mr. Darcy rode back to Longbourn to claim her heart. What woman could resist such gallantry?"

The retelling of the romance irritated Wickham, and he fought to hide his feeling. Darcy had returned to Netherfield to thwart Wickham's plans for revenge. *Somehow,* Darcy had learned of his abduction of Elizabeth; Wickham still had not solved that mystery. Darcy had married Elizabeth Bennet because her father had found them together in the deserted house. He had witnessed the scene himself. Darcy's constant need to do the honorable thing sickened Wickham. Again, he reminded himself he was James Denny, who would be happy for the couple. Aloud, he said, "Mr. Darcy's behavior surprises me; I never suspected his preference for Miss Elizabeth."

"None of us did, Mr. Denny, but we share in their joy just the same."

"Did Miss Bennet remain in London after the ceremony?" On his way to Meryton, Wickham had worked out a detailed plan to claim one of Elizabeth Darcy's sisters as part of his reprisal and as a warning to the woman to withdraw her support for Darcy. He had decided on Jane Bennet, who appeared to be Mrs. Darcy's favorite sister; she was also the prettiest one. *Do I need to make another choice?*

"Mrs. Bennet reports that Mr. Bingley returned to London. I am sure Jane's mother would not allow her eldest daughter to leave if it meant a like withdrawal from Mr. Bingley's attentions. Mrs. Bennet has never hidden her desire to marry off each of her daughters to a suitable match. Mr. Bingley would fill that role admirably."

Although he took no interest in local gossip, Wickham chuckled. "I dare say he does." They now sat together on a public bench outside the village church. "I have not seen any of the Bennets in the village for nearly a week. Has there been a falling out with Mrs. Phillips?"

Charlotte appeared amused. "You seem awfully interested in the Bennet family."

Wickham shifted uncomfortably; he must not raise her suspicions, especially if he wished to abduct one of Elizabeth's sisters. He forced his body to lounge back, giving the impression of being perfectly at ease, although his mind speculatively weighed all she shared. "They are lively girls and gentlemen admire such amiability, but my real concern comes from their sudden withdrawal from the company of men such as me. You would tell me, Miss Lucas, if you knew of any offense I unknowingly offered the Bennets. I would need to beg their forgiveness if that be so."

Charlotte looked shocked by his words. "Heaven forbid, Mr. Denny! I hear nothing but praise on your behalf," she protested.

Stepping up his game, Wickham assured her, "It pleases me to hear so; I would be chagrined to know otherwise."

"I would say Mr. Bennet's concern for his daughters' safety outweighs Mrs. Bennet's search for husbands for her girls." Charlotte laughed, as if sharing a well-kept secret.

Glancing at his hands, Wickham's heart pounded in panic. The crown marking on the back of his hand was becoming clearer. He normally wore gloves to cover the mark, but he removed them when he sat with her on the bench. He needed to withdraw; his ability to shift to James Denny was coming to an end. "Even that opinion gives me some comfort, Miss Lucas."

Charlotte now stared at him.

Wickham smiled, although her close inspection made him uneasy. *Has the image faded?* "Is something in error, Miss Lucas?"

Charlotte snapped out of her deep thoughts and flushed with color. "It is nothing really; just a trick of the light. I know you to have brown eyes, but just now they appeared a storm-cloud grey."

Wickham forced the panic away, but he did not break their

gaze. "The light washes them out? It must be the red of the jacket, overpowering everything else."

"I suppose," she mumbled, but did not look away.

Wickham removed the fob and glanced at his watch. "Unfortunately, Miss Lucas, I must report back to the barracks. I hope you will excuse me." He stood and offered her his hand. Charlotte rose, too. "I hope to see you and your family at some of the entertainments in the coming weeks."

"I would expect so, Mr. Denny."

"Until then." Wickham executed a quick bow and strode purposefully away. He needed to find cover; the spell slipped as he walked.

Ducking into the stable, he darted behind some tackle, before leaning over at the waist and gasping for air. *What happened?* he wondered. Never before had the image faded until he was ready for it to do so. He had escaped just in time. The woman noted his eyes—the difference. He had counted on the ability to shape shift to dupe his prey. He might need to rethink his plan for the Bennets.

A few minutes later, from the protection of the corral, he watched Charlotte Lucas make her way towards the village center. The woman was very common—sharp intellectually—but never attractive. He suspected, however, she would make someone a good wife—the plain ones always did. They possessed no other hold on a man. Sometimes he regretted not having chosen a woman like Miss Lucas, but he had fallen in love with Ellender D'Arcy, a striking beauty like none other—a witty, sensual woman—indulged and pampered—elegant and arrogant. He loved her even now, but she had never returned his regard. Seorais Winchcombe lacked the breeding—lacked the name. Ellender D'Arcy had decided on Arawn Benning, a man with a title, and she had traded Wickham's life to save her precious Lord Benning. It still pained him to remember how she had betrayed him. Ellender D'Arcy had doomed him to an endless life—one of fiendish desires—of a ghoulish hunger—a brutish monster.

Pushing the memories aside, Wickham turned in place twice

before disappearing in a rush of wind—it was time to call on the Bennets.

Although he watched the Longbourn estate for two days, the Bennet girls strayed no farther than the gravel walk that led to the copse. He decided on the youngest girl, Miss Lydia. Mary Bennet, a studious girl, even less comely than Miss Lucas, would never do, and the one they called Kitty, although mildly attractive, much along the lines of her sister Elizabeth, was too moody—too difficult to determine what might tempt her.

No, Lydia would be the one. Being the youngest, she was sure to be a favorite among the family, although he found her continuous chatter and flirtations annoying. But Lydia Bennet would make an easy mark—gullible—unsophisticated—foolish.

He noted with approval that Miss Lydia was friends with Colonel Forster's new wife. Only that afternoon he had witnessed Lydia Bennet's silliness. Lurking among the trees, disguised as a stray dog, he had eavesdropped on their conversation.

"Good heaven! What is to become of us? What are we to do?" she had exclaimed with girlish woe to Mrs. Forster.

"Whatever do you mean, my dear?" Mrs. Forster had captured Lydia's hand and patted it in sympathy.

Lydia whined, "My sisters are still able to eat, drink, and sleep, and pursue the usual course of their employments, but I take no pleasure in such pursuits. I would prefer a ball every night for entertainment. Papa is so cruel!"

"Do not fret so, my friend, for I will send my husband, the colonel, to speak to Mr. Bennet. Surely he can convince your father to let you accompany me to the Christmas festivities. The colonel will vouch for your safety."

Lydia collapsed on a bench next to her friend. "Oh, I do hope so!"

Wickham had withdrawn before they had spotted him. He had an outlet—a way to get to Lydia Bennet! He would call on her as himself, establish his interest in a relationship with her, and when he knew all the details of the military celebration, he would spring the trap. Only a few more days, and the happy situation for the Darcys would change dramatically.

★ ★ ★

The tour of the house resumed as Darcy led Elizabeth into the dining parlor. It was a large, well-proportioned room, handsomely fitted up. Elizabeth, after surveying it, went to a window to enjoy its prospect. The hill, crowned with wood, which they descended, receiving increased abruptness from the distance, was a beautiful object. Every disposition of the ground was good, and she looked on the whole scene—the river, the trees scattered on its banks, and the winding of the valley, as far as she could trace it—with delight. As they passed into other rooms these objects were taking different positions; but from every window there were beauties to be seen. The rooms were lofty and handsome, and their furniture suitable to the fortune of their proprietor; and Elizabeth saw, with admiration of his taste, it was neither gaudy nor uselessly fine with less of splendor and more real elegance than she had anticipated.

Darcy came up behind her and wrapped her in his arms; they spoke not for several minutes. "Dare I ask your thoughts?" he inquired.

His voice—rumbling and masculine—stirred her, making her stomach fill with butterfly wings. Automatically, Elizabeth leaned back—sealing her spine to his chest—and Darcy hardened with her closeness.

"And of this place," she spoke with disbelief, "I am to be mistress?" She turned in his arms, burying her face in his chest. "At Overton House, I stood a chance of being an acceptable wife, but how am I to be that here?"

Darcy tightened his hold on her. What could he say to allay her fears? He did not marry Elizabeth to make her mistress of his estate; he married her to protect her and because of the need he held for her. "I am away from Pemberley for months at a time, but the estate continues to function without my presence."

"Then you have no need of me!" she wailed.

Darcy chuckled. "I did not consider whether you could run my household when I became obsessed with kissing your luscious lips." To prove his point, he raised her chin and lowered his mouth to hers.

When they separated, she said, "At your club, they will ask, *Mr. Darcy, how is your new wife?* And you will reply, *She is a terrible mistress of my estate, but Mrs. Darcy is the best kisser I have ever known.*"

Darcy smiled wickedly. "I did not say you were *the best I have ever known.*"

Elizabeth suddenly shoved against him, ready to escape his taunt, but Darcy clamped his hands together behind her back. "You are a cad, Sir—a true blackguard!" she retorted hotly.

"Methinks the lady doth protest too much," he joked, holding her tightly to him. Darcy took one hand to cup her face, turning it to him. "Elizabeth, I married you because I need you—beyond reason—I need you." His breathing became shallow with desire.

"You *need* me—for what, Mr. Darcy?" Her lips took on a slight pout.

"I need you to…you are the one I turn to when I need reason…when I need courage. I need your kiss—your touch—your empathy. I need the excitement I see in your eyes when you practice fencing or riding Ceres or waltzing. I need to feel alive, and only you, my dearest, loveliest Elizabeth, can do that. I could hire someone to run the estate, but no one could take your place. Do you understand that?"

Elizabeth blushed in embarrassment. "Yes, Fitzwilliam, I understand," she said meekly. She added wryly, "You do not need a mistress of your estate, but you do need a fencing partner, a riding mate, and someone with whom to dance."

"Do not forget that I need someone to kiss." Darcy gently brushed his lips across hers.

Elizabeth provocatively walked her fingers up his chest before grasping his lapels. "Then if I am to be your playmate, Mr. Darcy, play on." She caught his hair and pulled his head closer. "Play on."

Darcy took her mouth possessively, the hunger filling him, both a sexual desire and an animalistic need taking hold of him. "Elizabeth," he murmured, "you are everything." His fingers traced the indentation of her neck, caressing it before scraping his nail across his favorite spot. "It is the middle of the afternoon," he whispered close to her ear before sucking the lobe with his lips and tongue, "and I can think of nothing but touching you." His mouth trailed a line of fire down her neck. A moan escaped his lips before he kissed the spot between the swell of her breasts. He heard her quick intake of breath as he returned his head to suck gently on the side of her neck.

"Ah, you enjoy my *femininity*," she whispered.

"Femininity?" Darcy barely got the word out; his hunger was driving him on.

Elizabeth leaned her head back to welcome his continued possession. "That is what my uncle calls it when he kisses Aunt Merry as such."

The words she spoke invaded his passion-filled brain. "Your Aunt Merry?"

Elizabeth enjoyed taking him by surprise. "Aunt Merry wears a scarf to cover Uncle's lovemaking."

"And how, Mrs. Darcy, would you know that?" Darcy sounded both suspicious and amused.

"Aunt Merry noted how you judiciously covered my mark with the emerald necklace. She shared her diversionary techniques at the opera."

Darcy smiled good-humoredly, suppressing the image. "I believe that I will never be able to look your aunt in the face again."

"I feel the same about Uncle; Aunt told me too much and not enough, both at the same time."

Realizing that the moment had passed, Darcy released his hold on her and straightened his waistcoat. "I suppose we need to think about this."

Elizabeth looked down shyly. "I suppose."

Before Darcy could respond, Mr. Lockwood tapped on the

door. "Enter," Darcy called out.

"Mr. Darcy, a large box arrived for Mrs. Darcy from London. Shall I place it in her room?"

"It is the books, Fitzwilliam," Elizabeth said from behind him.

"The library will be more appropriate, Mr. Lockwood."

"Yes, Sir." The man began to back out of the room.

"Mr. Lockwood, would you place a small table, several straight-backed chairs, paper, and pens and ink in the library also. My wife and sister have studies they wish to pursue."

"Certainly, Mr. Darcy." The man exited immediately.

"Well, my love, shall we see what insights the books have brought? I will send for Mrs. Annesley and Georgiana to join us."

"I can think of nothing I would enjoy more." They moved towards the door. Suddenly, she stopped in her tracks, and turning to him, she blushed profusely. "Well, I can think of one thing, but it must wait."

★ ★ ★

Wickham lounged leisurely in the corner of Mrs. Phillips's drawing room. He held a glass of port, but he did not drink; it was all part of the illusion. The Bennet ladies had arrived five minutes earlier. Now, Wickham waited to greet them; he anticipated it taking at least a fortnight for him to maneuver Lydia Bennet, his intended target, away from her family. Discreet inquiries had told him that the Forsters planned to travel to London for a Christmas military ball, and Mrs. Forster wished Lydia Bennet to be her special friend and join the party. Wickham could simply take Lydia, but that would not serve his purpose. Instead, he wanted to spirit her away from her family, letting Elizabeth Darcy rue the day she aligned herself with Fitzwilliam Darcy. Because of her choice, Elizabeth's sister would die. It would be enough to force the Darcys apart, leaving Fitzwilliam Darcy vulnerable once again.

"Mr. Wickham," Lydia Bennet called out loudly when she spotted him, "it has been a lifetime since we last saw you."

Mrs. Bennet allowed her youngest daughter too much freedom in her deportment, and this annoyed him. Wickham always preferred refined ladies to the "working" girls he often took on the street. His tastes had been established two centuries earlier with Lady Ellender D'Arcy. The image of his first love flickered momentarily in front of his eyes. He thought of her often of late—especially since seeing Georgiana Darcy—as if he were coming full circle, back to where it all began. Shaking off the image, Wickham pushed away from the wall and strode forward to meet them. "Miss Lydia," he said, bowing before taking her hand and bringing it to his lips. "It is a pleasure to hear that you missed my company."

"You are a tease!" Lydia playfully struck his arm with her fan before twining her arm about his forearm. "You remember my sisters, Mr. Wickham."

Wickham offered Mary and Kitty Bennet an abbreviated bow. "How could I forget such beautiful ladies?"

Lydia pulled him after her. "You will sit with me, Mr. Wickham." She led him to a card table, and, dutifully, he gave in to her request.

Over the next hour, much to Wickham's chagrin, Lydia Bennet talked incessantly of lottery tickets and of the fish she lost and fish she won. Although her immaturity irritated him, he made sure that his manners recommended him to everybody. Whatever he said was well said; and whatever he did, done gracefully. He did not leave Lydia's side, not even during supper; he tolerated her childishness. Throughout the excruciating evening, he took pleasure in visualizing her end. *It will be satisfying to finally silence her.*

"Miss Lydia," he said as he prepared to take his leave, "may I call on you day after tomorrow?" If he was to stay in the area over a period of time, he would require some time away to replenish his hunger for blood. He would take his desires back towards London, away from the local officials.

Lydia giggled with excitement, her head full of his attentions. "I look forward to it, Mr. Wickham."

★ ★ ★

"Fitzwilliam." Elizabeth kissed his ear, trying to wake him. Darcy knew he should open his eyes, but having Elizabeth seek his affection gave him too much satisfaction. He kept his breathing even and his eyes closed tightly. She pulled on the lobe with her lips, sucking, the way he had taught her. Darcy's shaft grew as she blew lightly in his ear. "Fitzwilliam," she tried again, this time actually sliding her tongue in his ear. A jolt of desire shot through him. He had not taught her *that!* Unable to withstand her seduction, Darcy pulled her atop him as he captured her lips with his.

When he finally released her, she giggled and said, "Good! You are awake."

"Did you think I could sleep through such an exhilarating *Good morning?*" he inquired froggily.

"It is snowing," she declared. "There are several inches on the ground."

"Welcome to Derbyshire winters." Darcy pulled the blankets tighter to keep them both warm.

Elizabeth pushed the hair from his eyes. "I love it when it snows; it makes Christmas seem so near. It rarely snows this early in Hertfordshire." She rolled from his embrace. "Shall we go for a walk in the snow?"

"We have not yet broken our fast, Elizabeth," Darcy protested.

"I do not want breakfast."

Darcy laughed. "I cannot recall the last time I purposely went walking in the snow."

"Then it is about time you did it again," she reasoned.

"All right," he said and reluctantly threw the blankets aside. "You win, my love."

"Oh, good, I almost never win." Elizabeth scrambled from the bed before Darcy changed his mind.

Twenty minutes later, they emerged from a side door of Pemberley and started off across the south lawn. The snow was a hand deep and still coming down steadily. Darcy expected the snow would reach the middle of his calves before the storm finished. The last blades of grass poked through the smooth surface sloping away from the house, and a few tracks of rabbits and squirrels touched the icy white covering, but even they were soon filled in with new flakes.

"I love it when the snow is so smooth." Elizabeth stood wrapped in Darcy's arms, looking out over the lawn's coating. "It was so beautiful from our bedroom window that I could not resist coming outside to experience it firsthand."

"It is as if God is wiping everything clean," Darcy said, looking over Elizabeth's shoulder at Nature's perfect picture. "Pemberley is beautiful in the spring and summer, but newly fallen snow has its appeal as well."

"Mr. Wickham told me it would be so." The words escaped involuntarily; she had not planned to say them.

"*When* did Mr. Wickham offer such observations?"

Elizabeth turned to face him. "I forgot the conversation. It was after you shunned him in Meryton—before he attacked me. Wickham said terrible things about you—things I knew to be false. Wanting to know if Wickham was in Derbyshire when you were, I asked about his time in Bakewell, where he said he had resided for some time." Elizabeth strolled away from Darcy, needing to gather her thoughts. "I asked Wickham what he knew of Derbyshire, speaking under the guise of wanting to know more about Aunt Merry's childhood home. He told me the terrain was more rugged, with thicker vegetation, colder winters, and milder summers. He said he preferred the wildness of the Peak District because it reminded him of Scotland. Next to Northumberland, he preferred the Peak District to the rest of England."

"Could Wickham still have a home in Bakewell?" Darcy mused aloud.

"It is possible—or even in Northumberland."

Yesterday in their readings, they felt they had uncovered the mystery of the dirt in Wickham's bed. One text claimed a vampire could sleep only if he had his coffin. The account said the beast

needed to transport the coffin loaded with dirt from his homeland; a like report said the earth was more important than the
coffin itself. If so, finding Wickham's home would aid in their pursuit. Darcy strode towards her. "Was not Northumberland once
part of Scotland?"

"I am not sure, but I do know there have been enough border
wars that at least part of Northumberland must consider itself to be
part of Scotland. All I know of Northumberland is that our breakfast kippers come from Craster. What did you learn of it at the university?" Elizabeth walked in a circle, scraping the snow with the
toes of her ankle boots.

Darcy tried to remember his history lessons. "The area came
under English rule with King Edwin. Northumberland stretches
from Newcastle upon Tyne to Tynemouth. It is quite undevel-
oped—sparse high moorlands. There were famous battles, such as
when Malcolm II annihilated the Northumbrian army at Carham
on the Tweed, but under James I and VI, the Scottish and English
claims were united. However, even as late as the early 1700s, there
was trouble during the Jacobite rebellion." He recited the lines as if
he were back in school and studying for an exam.

"A house in Northumberland would fit in with Wickham's
need for isolation," Elizabeth reasoned. "Could we find out where
Ellender and Lord Thomas lived? It would tell us from where
Wickham originally came—where he was buried—from where he
derives his home earth."

"We can check Dugdale's catalogue or Debrett's *Baronetage of
England* or even the *Doomsday Book*. Surely one of them lists Lord
Arawn Benning." Darcy's excitement grew; it was their first real
lead. "When we have a possible location, I will send out investigators before we make a move."

"Fitzwilliam, do you realize what this means? Wickham's hold
on the family could be coming to an end." In complete happiness,
Elizabeth turned in a circle, arms spread wide and face raised to
meet fresh flakes of newly fallen snow. "I have never felt freer!"

CHAPTER 19

Darcy watched her spin around and around, pure joy streaming from her face, and all at once his heart swelled, too. Suddenly, he felt the weight lift from his shoulders, and it was all because of her—because of *his Elizabeth*. He did the only thing he could under the circumstances.

"Elizabeth!" he called out.

She recognized the warning in his voice and turned to him. He stood playfully tossing a snowball into the air and catching it once again. Her light green eyes widened in disbelief, turning a forest green in recognition. "Fitzwilliam, you *would not*." She began to back away, a hand held out as protection.

"I *would,* my dear." He lifted his arm as if to toss the snow at her, and she broke into a run, heading for the tree line.

Elizabeth heard Darcy's laughter behind her and the sound of snow crunching under his pursuing feet—and then the snowball smacked her shoulder, spraying icy streams down her neck.

Without thinking, she bent as she ran, scooping up a handful of snow in her glove, squeezing the snow tightly. It was not a very big ball, but it was solid. Stopping suddenly, she turned and let it fly. Darcy, in his chase, did not expect the densely packed ball, which hit his ear and spattered across his cheek. "Why, you…!" he threatened, still advancing.

Catching her up in his arms, he swung Elizabeth around, both of them laughing helplessly. He pretended to drop her just to hear her cry of alarm, and when he sat her down again, he scooped up an armful of snow and dumped it over her head, covering her with frozen flakes.

Elizabeth flicked the cold away from her face with snow-covered gloves and came at him, bent on vengeance. Darcy sprinted to the safety of a copse of trees, darting behind one to hide from her on-slaught of poorly formed snowballs. She circled around the tree, trying to entice him away from the safety of the trunk. "Come, Fitzwilliam, we will call a truce."

"Why is it I do not believe you, my love?" He switched directions several times to fool her, but each time Elizabeth responded accordingly.

"Fitzwilliam, I am getting cold," she said at last, and dropped the snowballs to the ground in defeat.

Darcy came from behind the tree and enveloped her in his arms, opening his greatcoat to bring her closer to him. "I am sorry, Sweetling. I should have thought as such. I will warm you." Darcy lowered his mouth to hers, tasting Elizabeth and snow and happiness. He sighed with desire. She loosened her grasp on him and stepped back. Then he felt it. Snow rained down on his bare head, sinking into his shirt and sliding down his back. He looked up to see the last of the flakes cascading from a low-hanging bough. Elizabeth's laughter faded away as she sprinted from him.

"I *will* get you, Mrs. Darcy," he warned and lunged after her, icy streams reaching the band of his breeches.

She knew she stood no chance. Darcy's long legs and knee boots put her at a disadvantage, so she turned on him and started frantically throwing snow in the air, covering them both in a pow-dery spray of frosty crystals. Darcy fought his way through the snowy cloud, grabbing Elizabeth up by the waist and dumping her none-too-gingerly into a snowy heap. "You deserve this," he asserted, as he unceremoniously fell on top of her, wrestling with her in the snow. His weight held her down, although she continued to squirm against him. The snow had nearly frozen his back mus-cles, but Elizabeth's grinding hardened him instantly.

"Give up," he said as he pressed harder.

"Never." Elizabeth shoved a handful of snow into an opening in his shirt.

Darcy let out a gasp of surprise and a shudder before catching her wrists in his large palm, locking them above her head. "Should

I do the same to you, Vixen?" It was the first time he had called her Vixen since before they married. "Would those lovely breasts like a cold shock?"

"Only if you warm them for me afterwards." Elizabeth arched forward, seeking his mouth for comfort.

Darcy brushed his lips across hers. "Woman, what are you trying to do to me? Such words!" His pulse raced.

"I am *trying* to make you love me, Mr. Darcy," Elizabeth blurted out without thinking. Her words brought their struggle to a standstill.

Darcy gazed into her eyes, heavy-lidded with desire, and he lost all sense of reason. "Cease trying, Mrs. Darcy," he whispered. "I loved you from the beginning." He wondered about the sanity of admitting his true feelings. *What if she does not share my love?* He kissed her, parting her lips with his tongue. Coming to himself, he whispered, "What am I doing?"

"Kissing your wife. In public." Her voice was breathy with desire and raspy with pent-up emotion.

Darcy chuckled with the realization. "I suppose we will be the talk of the servants' quarters tonight."

"So much for my hopes of being a model of decorum," Elizabeth observed. "Do you think we should return to the house now?"

"We have done enough damage to our reputations." He rolled from her and rose swiftly to stand before her. Extending his hand, he waited for her to join him, but Elizabeth continued to lie in the snow, staring up at him. "Come, Elizabeth," he demanded, reaching for her.

"No." She did not move.

"No?" He looked confused. "Why ever not?" He let his hand drop to his side.

Elizabeth licked her lips; surprisingly, she felt nervous. "Because I did not get the chance to tell my husband that I am completely and hopelessly in love with him."

Darcy's heart leapt in his chest. He extended his hand again, and this time Elizabeth took it. They walked silently back to the house, arms wrapped around each other. At the door, he turned Elizabeth to him and tenderly kissed her lips. "You are everything—my world—my love," he whispered.

Elizabeth kissed him back and wondered, *Could I really be married to this magnificent man? A man to whom I give my heart—my body—my soul?*

If the young master had scandalized his staff by kissing his new wife on the south lawn during a snowstorm, the next few days kept the gossips even busier. Darcy and Elizabeth resumed their fencing lessons, using the ballroom as the arena for the activity; and if that was not outrageous enough, Mr. Darcy procured a pair of breeches, a shirt, and a waistcoat from one of the young groomsmen for Mrs. Darcy's use. The lady dressed as a gentleman, tying her long hair back with several ribbons.

"What do you believe Mrs. Darcy will do *next?*" one of the chambermaids asked as she slid into her place along a bench in the kitchen.

"That is enough, Milly," Mrs. Reynolds warned her. "It is not our place to judge the Darcys."

"But Mrs. Reynolds," the girl retorted, "even *you* must think this beyond reason."

Mrs. Reynolds gazed firmly at the girl, but everyone in the kitchen knew it was meant for all. "Reason means knowledge, so I will tell you, Milly, what I know of the man who is our master. I have never known a cross word from Mr. Darcy in my life, and I have known him since he was four years old. If I were to go through the world, I could not meet with a better. I observed that they who are good-natured when children are good-natured when they grow up, and he was always the sweetest-tempered, most generous-hearted boy in the world. His father was an excellent man, and his son will be just like him—just as affable to the poor. He is the best landlord and the best master that ever lived. Not like wild young men nowadays, who think of nothing but themselves."

Mr. Lockwood joined the conversation, "Mrs. Reynolds is correct. There is not one of Mr. Darcy's tenants or *servants* but what will give him a good name. Some people call him proud, but I am sure I never saw anything of it. To my fancy, it is only because he does not rattle away like other young men."

"Whatever can give his sister any pleasure is sure to be done in a moment. There is nothing he would not do for her." Mrs. Reynolds set down her teacup. "And just as with his sister, Mr. Darcy gives his wife freedom to be who she chooses to be. I do not believe every woman should pick up a sword, but Mrs. Darcy wishes to, and she does so with her husband's permission and his participation. And as far as Mrs. Darcy is concerned, she treats each of us with kindness. I am impressed with her civility."

"That she is, Ma'am," one of the footmen added. "Mrs. Darcy was all apologies when we moved furniture for the Master."

Mrs. Reynolds nodded in agreement. "He is exactly the man who, in disposition and talents, most suits her, and she him. The man is happy—at last, after all these years of loneliness, he is happy, and I would tolerate the worst harpy to see him such. Thank the heavens that all I have to do is look the other way when the Master playfully shows affection for his wife. When Mr. Darcy is contented, so are the members of his staff."

Milly blushed with the reprimand. "Of course, Mrs. Reynolds. I meant nothing by my remark."

"Then it is best not mentioned."

"Yes, Ma'am."

★ ★ ★

He sat in the Bennets' parlor, paying homage to Lydia Bennet while other officers from the troop flirted with Kitty and Mary Bennet, along with Charlotte and Maria Lucas. Wickham hated such dalliances; he preferred the feast to the hunt. Yet he wanted no one suspicious until he reeled in his prey—until it was too late for the Bennets or the Darcys.

"Will you travel with the Forsters, Miss Lydia?" As usual, he held a glass of port for effect. It amazed him that no one ever noticed he did not drink.

Lydia frowned in response. "Papa has not relented."

"I do so hope you attend the ball, Miss Lydia, and I wish to claim the first set." Wickham gave her one of his best smiles.

Lydia batted her eyelashes at him and fanned her face. "You will be in London, Mr. Wickham?"

Now, Wickham thought, *now, she is ready*. As if to entice her, he lowered his voice. "*I* will be in London if *you* will, Miss Lydia, and it would give me great pleasure if I might take you to see the sights. Of course, none of the beauties of the city will be able to compete with your beauty. If I might be so bold, I would like to take you riding in Hyde Park or to the theatre while you are in town. Anything you wish, Miss Lydia."

He thought she might rebuke his forwardness, but Lydia Bennet relished his attentions. Wickham knew wedding bells rang in her head, but as it was for many others, marriage to him would be *more* than a life-long commitment; it would be eternal damnation.

"Mr. Wickham, I would entertain your wishes most readily."

He could barely keep a straight face when she rolled her eyes up to his. If he could get her alone, Lydia Bennet would easily succumb to his temptations. "Then, Miss Lydia, we need to do what we can to convince your father to change his mind. Our happiness depends on it."

Wickham captured her with his gaze, thundercloud grey eyes promising things of which she had no knowledge. "Oh, Mr. Wickham," she said with a sigh.

★ ★ ★

The day that the Darcys admitted to their growing love, the forces holding them together changed dramatically. For Fitzwilliam, his need to touch her became even more intense. For weeks, he had cautiously guarded his emotions. Yet each resolution to ignore her disappeared the moment Elizabeth swept into a room. Her presence created a response deep within his being. He knew Elizabeth would not deny him if he approached her with his desires; sometimes the knowledge of her agreement thrilled him as nothing ever had before. At other times, the recognition of her certain consent tortured his body and his mind. In fact, for the past two evenings, he had left her bed in the middle of the night because the need to possess her was too strong. Lying beside her created a fire that was impossible to ignore.

For Elizabeth, dreams of a family permeated her waking and resting moments. These dreams made her more aware of Darcy's masculinity—made her want to act in a manner such as her Aunt Merry had described in her motherly talk before Elizabeth married. She found that she flirted more than ever with Darcy, never passing up a chance to wrap her arms around him or to kiss him.

For both of them, their desperation to defeat Wickham increased. By silent assent, they set the day of Wickham's demise as the day they would begin their "real" life. Their need for a normal life together fueled their daily search for facts in the books that she had purchased in London. When Georgiana tired of reading passage after passage, Darcy and Elizabeth pressed on, as did Mrs. Annesley. It was a matter of life and death.

"It says here," Elizabeth summarized a passage, "that vampires often have the ability to physically transform themselves. This is obviously true; I thought I followed Fitzwilliam through the woods, but it was really Wickham."

"That does not make me feel safer," Georgiana commented before adding *transformation* to their growing list of characteristics.

"Repeat what we have on the list so far," Mrs. Annesley said, and she sat back to listen to Georgiana's recitation.

"Let me see—does not eat or drink, has the power of the wind, can disappear, probably carried forward at a great speed, has no reflection, is affected by iron and by holy objects, needs native soil to rest." Georgiana laid the paper down.

Darcy repeated what he had learned about his enemy. "We think Wickham is from somewhere in Northumberland because Arawn

Benning's estate was near Forth, along the Scottish border. It only makes sense that he and Ellender D'Arcy were close, and if Winchcombe was one of Ellender's suitors, he must come from the same area. People did not travel as extensively two hundred years ago."

Georgiana picked up another list. "To kill a vampire, the number of ways grows. A stake through the heart, cut off and burn the head, pile stones on the grave, place a coin in the mouth, drive a nail through the neck, use a silver bullet. The list goes on and on."

"If I find Wickham, I will use them all for good measure," Darcy asserted.

Mrs. Annesley read from the book currently in front of her. "Burn the heart, producing a plate of ashes. Mix those ashes with local well water to create a drink to cure those infected by the beast." She laughed. "Sounds delicious. I still think your best bet is to apply Mrs. Darcy's dream to interpret what we read."

"I dreamed of Wickham before my dream in London," Elizabeth interjected.

Darcy demanded, "When?"

"The day of the attack at the manor house."

"Why did you not tell me before?"

"I suppose it just slipped my mind."

Mrs. Annesley interrupted, "What do you remember, Mrs. Darcy?"

"Well, …I was running through the woods, trying to escape. Wickham did not run, but he kept pace with me. The wind carried him forward or perhaps he floated." Elizabeth looked up at Darcy, ashamed of the next part. "Wickham bade me to come to him, and I could do nothing else. Then it began to rain, but only on me; only *I* was tormented by the wind and the rain."

Darcy sat down beside her. "Go on."

"The mud was pulling at my feet and legs, but I kept trying to reach where Wickham stood, waiting for me. My body moved on its own. Finally, a gigantic deer stepped from the shadows. He had your eyes, Fitzwilliam, so I trusted him implicitly. Then he lowered his head, and I took hold of his antlers. Easily removing them, I charged at Wickham, and the horns pierced his chest.

Blood of all different colors came pouring from him. The blood covered my hands...."

Georgiana leaned forward, anxious to hear the rest. "Then?"

"Then nothing." Elizabeth looked around sheepishly. "Then I woke up."

Georgiana wrinkled her nose in disappointment. "What could such a silly dream mean?"

Mrs. Annesley's gentle eyes told them she had her own opinions. "It seems to me that Mrs. Darcy's dream tells us that the legends of vampires not tolerating running water might have some merit, as well as what we read yesterday about driving an ash or white thorn stake through the heart with a single strike to destroy them. We just need to figure out the deer and the many-colored blood. All the answers are there; I am sure of it. We just need to ask the right questions."

★ ★ ★

It was Christmas Eve, and Wickham knew that he need not spend it in Meryton, trying to woo the youngest Bennet sister. Miss Jane Bennet and the aunt and uncle from London had arrived several days earlier, along with a houseful of nieces and nephews. He would make little progress in his quest, so he took himself off to one of the gaming halls peppering the London back streets. Even with the religious holiday on the next day, patrons packed the place. He supposed it was because the Black Ghost served as both a tavern and a gaming establishment. The tavern, with its locals and its lowlifes, was filled with boisterous drunks, while the three private rooms in the back burst with some of the *ton's* finest. Men won and lost fortunes while laborers and sailors pissed away their hard-earned money on a tankard of watered-down ale. The owner of the Black Ghost thought of everything.

Wickham did not gamble—just as he did not eat or drink. He had no need for such activities, but he took a jaunt through the gaming rooms, seeing if anyone interested him. It did not matter whether the victim was male or female; the only difference lay in how he handled them. With a woman, his natural persuasive charisma made her an easy mark; he simply needed to seduce her with a few precisely placed caresses. Often the woman did not realize her mistake until he snapped her lovely neck with a well-planned crack of the tendons. If he found the woman to be especially attractive or potentially useful, Wickham would often not kill her before he drank. Sometimes he simply facilitated an exchange, filling his victim with the power he possessed and taking her life blood. That was what he had done with Amelia Younge, keeping her as a follower, a soul imprisoned to fulfill his needs. That was his plan for Lydia Bennet; Wickham would bind her to him forever as part of his revenge. He fancied his actions made him a *consummate* lover.

However, if no woman was available, a man or a boy would do, and it was more an issue of brute force. The feasting became an act of base survival, like an animal overcoming its prey. Actually, he hated it when he took someone simply because he hungered for him like a lion claiming a gazelle as food in the wild. Wickham preferred a woman. With a woman, he considered himself an artist.

Finding no one whom he thought might consider leaving with him, he returned to the public rooms. Laying on a good one for the holidays, probably to cover their loneliness, drunken louts spoke loudly and shoved each other. Aware of the alcohol-induced happiness circulating around him, Wickham found a small table in a darkened corner, where he could watch the goings-on. As he settled himself, he took on the image of James Denny. He could not be seen leaving the bar as himself.

In a few minutes, a busty bar maid, no longer young, came to the table, swiping at it with a none-too-clean rag. "Need some Christmas cheer, Guv'nor?" she asked as she circled the table a second time with the cloth.

"A tankard of ale, if you please." Wickham's eyes found hers. She was not what he would normally choose, but as he knew the Christian holiday kept many people at home, he would make do. The woman's breasts swelled from the tight-fitting bodice of an equally tight dress. He let his eyes trace them and then slide up her neck, where he would have her. "You do not know where a man might find some company for the evening? I have no desire to be alone."

The woman took full note of his appearance, and Wickham offered up a lonely smile, playing on her pity. He usually took more time with his seduction, but after what had happened in Meryton, the possibility of his disguise fading played on his mind.

The chaos swirled behind her as she made the mistake of looking deeply into his eyes to judge his character. He changed instantly from affable gentleman to supreme seducer. "I might be persuaded, Dearie, if ye be interested." Her voice cleared away the inebriated din of the room.

Wickham's hand lightly stroked her bare forearm. "May I ask your name, Sweet Lady?"

Enthralled by the gleam in the swirling grey of his eyes, the woman did not move. "Me mama named me Lucinda. Most call me Lucy."

"I will call you Lucy or Love or my Heart." The words made little difference because she could not withdraw even if she wished to do so. "When do you leave work, my lovely Lucy?" His voice was sweet.

"Me thinks it be mighty soon. I come in early today." She leaned into his light touch.

Wickham winked at her, solidifying his hold. "You have a place we might visit?"

"It be just a sleeping room."

"I have no desire to sleep." Wickham leaned back in the chair to release his hold on her. "Say we will not sleep, my lovely Lucy."

The woman shook her head, trying to clear it. "No, Guv'nor, we will take no sleep." She gave him a smile, showing one missing tooth. "I will bring ye the tankard. I be askin' Harry about leavin'."

"That would be capital, Lucy."

The woman disappeared into the crowded room. As she departed, Wickham visualized what he would do to her. Getting her to a room, he would make her submit to him with a twitch of his eyes.

His body would perch over hers, while he held her down, clasping both of her hands in his grasp. Then he would take her leisurely.

Surprisingly, Lucy appeared at the table in less than a quarter hour. "Ye be ready, Guv'nor?" She extended a hand to him.

Wickham, as Denny, took the hand and brought her to him as he stood. "Never been more ready, lovely Lucy."

He slung his arm about her shoulder and maneuvered the bar maid out into the crisp December air. "Whew," she uttered, her breath forming a solid film, "it be colder."

"I will keep you warm," he growled close to her ear.

Lucy laughed, a bit nervously, but she never paused or faltered as they crossed the intersecting streets. "I live just down here." She pointed to a row of tenements, shabby-looking buildings even in the daylight. In the cold night, they seemed to huddle together to keep themselves warm. "Ye be tellin' Lucy yer name, Guv'nor?"

"I am James," he said as he followed her up the narrow stairs of the second row house.

"James be an honest-soundin' name," she observed as they reached her door. Unlocking the bolt, Lucy opened it to a darken-ed room. "I find us a candle." She fumbled along the mantelpiece.

"Allow me." Needing no light to see clearly, Wickham managed to find the flint and the stub of the candle easily.

Lucy removed the scarf she wore around her neck for warmth. "My, ye be handy."

"I am here to please." He gave her an exaggerated bow. "You settle yourself, Lucy, and I will stoke the fire."

When the fire was blazing, he came to where she stood. He did not kiss her, as she had anticipated, but Lucy knew some men pre-ferred not to kiss—too intimate. She found that amusing. Instead, Wickham caressed her jaw line and raised her chin to look into her eyes. He would do nothing else but rest his intense gaze upon her.

Lucy felt the heat all the way through her, although he barely touched her. With a slight tilt of his head, Wickham indicated the bed, and Lucy backed towards it. Besides the caress of her cheek, he had not touched her. She lay back, and he straddled her, taking both her hands in his large grasp. With the other hand, he traced circles across her breasts with his fingertips. He heard a quick intake of breath from his captive.

Now as caught up in the act as the woman, Wickham lowered his mouth to the side of her neck. She smelled of sweat and of tobacco and of cheap liquor, but Lucy also smelled of life and of iron-filled blood, and Wickham needed what she offered. He raised his head to stare at her with another spellbinding gaze. Then came the snap of her neck, a quick movement of his hands, placing the thumbs at the indentation before giving a lethal jerk. Lucy's eyes rolled back in her head, the life leaving her immediately.

Slowly, finally enjoying himself, Wickham lowered his head again, drinking his fill of Lucy's blood—feasting on her existence. The act of tasting her in the most personal of ways brought the erection the woman had thought to enjoy, and Wickham sated himself with a copulation with her lifeless, rapidly cooling body.

It was pure power—this lustful lapping of the woman's life fluid. It was the taking of a human life; it was the build-up of emotions—the control—*his* control—and the submission—*her* submission. The exhilaration of the absolute power he held inflamed him more than did the sex act. Wickham lived for that one split second before they died—the moment his victims knew the folly of their decision.

Wickham considered the act very much like the Christian Eucharist—a sacrifice inasmuch as it is offered up and a sacrament inasmuch as it is received. *Whoever eats my flesh and drinks my blood remains in me and I in him.*

CHAPTER 20

After the storm, the days warmed quickly, unseasonably so for December. The weather allowed Darcy and Elizabeth to escape the house and resume the riding lessons. They had left Ceres in the London stables, so Darcy introduced Elizabeth to a new horse, the gelding Apollo he had considered for her back at Netherfield. Apollo was more spirited than Ceres and would challenge Elizabeth to use her natural skills.

"Straighten your back," Darcy reminded her when she began to bounce in the seat.

"He is so powerful, Fitzwilliam!"

"No more so than Ceres; Apollo is just different—not as comfortable as your favorite, but he is a better horse for the rolling hills of Pemberley. Ceres is better for the city—not as skittish with the noise and the traffic."

"You know so much about the nature of animals," she observed, while automatically relaxing into the horse's gait. Darcy's words gave her the confidence to handle the reins admirably.

For nearly half an hour, they rode leisurely. The ground was still muddy and soaked from the melting snow. "Do we have a destination?" she asked.

"I thought that we might call on a few of the tenants; and maybe the vicar if there is time."

"I would take pleasure in that." Elizabeth shot him a quick glance. "I was thinking." Suddenly, she seemed tongue-tied.

"Dare I ask of what?" Darcy found her embarrassment endearing.

Elizabeth breathed deeply. Apollo tossed his mane and pranced. The deep breaths calmed her, and she carried on. "I considered where I might find my place as your wife—as the mistress of this estate. Back at Longbourn, I often handled the tenant affairs for my father. He chooses his books so as to avoid such *trivial* confrontations, and my mother's nerves make the confrontations too tedious. I flatter myself that I have a way with the workers—at least, I seemed to at Longbourn. Pemberley is much bigger, of course."

Darcy pulled up on his horse, stopping at the crest of a hill. He gave her a level look. "What would you do at Longbourn? For the tenants?" he asked seriously.

Elizabeth sparkled with his interest. "Papa trusted me to settle the disputes and such matters. And at this time of year, I would arrange a basket for each family. It was not much; Papa is not wealthy, but everyone appreciated our acknowledgment."

Intrigued, Darcy asked, "What kind of basket?"

"Simple gifts: cold meat, bread, a few potatoes, a candle, and a branch of consecrated mistletoe." Her eyes searched Darcy's for his thoughts.

"We could do something similar. Why do you not consult with Mrs. Reynolds when we return to the house? It would give you a chance to establish your place in my life, giving it your own *Elizabeth* touch. I like the idea. For some time, I took care of the overseeing of the land, but I neglected the personal aspects of being the master of Pemberley. It would do wonders in strengthening bonds." Darcy smiled at her in approval and then nudged his horse ahead again.

Elizabeth kicked at her horse's side, lunging forward to catch up with him. "Thank you, Fitzwilliam," she said when she came abreast of his mount. "I will make you proud of me."

Christmas at Pemberley must resemble *heaven*, the rooms aglow with light and the smell of cinnamon and fresh pine and nutmeg and everything good of the season. Unlike the hustle and bustle of Longbourn, with family and children underfoot, Pemberley, in its majestic realm, held court for the community, and, especially this year, as the Darcys, including the new mistress, held *court*.

After the morning service, they received tenants and villagers for several hours in their home. People came to see the splendor of the house; they came to learn more of the master's new wife. Elizabeth Darcy would affect their lives for many years, and they were all curious about the nature of the woman. The neighborhood wanted to know how much influence she would exercise over her husband, and they were surprised and thankful to find not only Mr. and Mrs. Darcy affably receiving each of them but bestowing a gift on each family.

"The workers are grateful for the charming baskets," Darcy whispered into her hair as the latest arrival curtsied before his new wife. Darcy paid the staff members extra to work the holiday hours involved in opening Pemberley to the country.

Elizabeth's viridescent gown with golden threads shimmered in the soft light reflected through the amber-tinted windows; she sparkled as brightly as the ornaments hanging from every available cornice and stairwell. "Mrs. Reynolds outdid herself. Georgiana and I helped, but Mrs. Reynolds is phenomenal. She even added tea and some candy for the children." Elizabeth smiled happily.

"I am sure Mrs. Reynolds saw the idea as a way to promote the Darcy family; she is very protective of the name," he observed.

Elizabeth added before greeting the next family, "As it is now *my* name, so am I, Mr. Darcy. So am I."

Elizabeth and Georgiana surprised Darcy with the gifts of the riding boots and riding crop. Darcy was delighted beyond reason with the presents. Elizabeth had taken close note of his appearance, sought out his favorite boot maker, and enlisted Georgiana's help in having the boots delivered to Pemberley. She had personalized her choice by thinking of the man who would receive the gift.

"They fit well." Darcy took a few steps about the room in the new boots. Elizabeth had insisted that he try them on immediately, even retrieving a boot pull from his private chambers and helping him remove the old ones.

"You look very debonair, Fitzwilliam," Georgiana half teased when she handed him the riding crop.

"You are astute, Georgiana. I am fortunate to have earned your brother's affection before all the ladies of the *ton* saw him so bedecked. Otherwise, he would pay me no regard, being so beset with admirers."

"I would find you, Mrs. Darcy, despite the biggest crush at the grandest ball," he asserted.

Elizabeth smirked and said, "Assuming you found my appearance *tolerable,* Sir."

"I would choose you for the liveliness of your mind," he countered.

Elizabeth laughed out loud. "Clever rejoinder, my Husband," she congratulated him before handing another package to Georgiana.

Late Christmas Day, Darcy relaxed on the settee before the fireplace in his sitting room, sipping a brandy. Elizabeth lay on the settee, her head in his lap and bare feet draped over the arm of the furniture. Darcy absentmindedly stroked her hair, letting the silken curls trail through his fingers. "It was a good day," he observed, setting his glass on a nearby table.

Elizabeth closed her eyes and sighed. "I have never knew known such peace—such contentment."

Darcy should have listened to his uneasy feeling, which mutely warned of a shadow spreading across his life. For a time, he had thought such tranquility of spirit could not exist, but now that he had tasted it, he hungered for it—craved the normalcy that a life with Elizabeth offered. He feared speaking of it—feared he might jinx it if he acknowledged too loudly how happy she made him. Some men prayed to go to heaven, but Darcy prayed to remain contentedly on earth with her. Knowing Elizabeth loved him was his heavenly reward—his life began and ended with her. More than anything else, now that he knew *his Elizabeth,* he feared losing her and returning to the emptiness of his earlier existence. He ached with a hunger to claim her—to possess Elizabeth completely.

Eyes closed, Elizabeth returned to the image of Darcy standing majestically in his new boots and wielding a crop. A smile turned up the corners of her mouth as she thought of loving him. Despite his weaknesses—despite his foibles—she loved Fitzwilliam Darcy. She knew the worst of him—knew of the curse—knew of how he released the souls of Wickham's victims—knew his stubbornness—knew his vulnerability—but saw only the best of the man.

Unfortunately, thinking of Darcy led her to thoughts of George Wickham. With eyes still closed, she thought out loud, "I was encouraged by what Mrs. Annesley discovered yesterday. It helps to explain the symbol of the pitchfork—or crown—or burn mark I observed on Wickham's hand and confirms my belief that he cannot be killed by our religious icons."

More tenacious than Georgiana, Mrs. Annesley spent hours poring over the literature for clues to destroying Wickham. On the previous day, she had discovered a Celtic pagan god known as Cernunnos, or the Horned God. He wore a crown of branching antlers, symbolizing his animalistic nature. To the Darcys, that explained part of Elizabeth's dream, but more noteworthy was the fact that Cernunnos could be found traveling with Owl, the Crone of the Night, and with Eagle, the Lord of the Air. The Stag of Seven Tines, the Master of Time, had left his service because Cernunnos became known as the "All-Devourer." Wickham's largely female following, as well as his power over the wind, now made more sense. If the deer in her dream represented Darcy, then Darcy's ability to control time also seemed logical. According to the book, Cernunnos possessed shape-shifting powers, as a shamanic god of the Hunt.

Elizabeth found it fascinating that Cernunnos's life was one of sacrifice; this explained Wickham's role with Ellender D'Arcy. According to the legend, it was through Cernunnos—as a courier to the Underworld—that old life passed away and new life began. He was known for fits of violence and the panic he instilled in his prey as the Hunter. As a Celtic god of the afterlife, Cernunnos was described as the god who never died because his flesh was rejuvenated with a "reservoir" of sacred fluids. Knowing the source of Wickham's revitalization sent a shiver through all three women and reminded Darcy of his own deviation.

But tonight, Darcy wanted none of that. "If you do not mind, Elizabeth, I would like a holiday from thinking of George Wickham or the curse. Could we not today just be the Darcys of Pemberley?"

"Certainly, Fitzwilliam. I would enjoy that also." Impulsively, she sat up and turned where she might reach him. Recognizing his pensive mood, Elizabeth wound her arms around his neck before meeting his lips with hers. "I believe that the Darcys of Pemberley have a great love. What do you think, Sir?"

Darcy tightened his hold on her. "The Darcys of Pemberley could be one of the great love stories."

★ ★ ★

Appearing in the Longbourn foyer the day after Christmas, Wickham, as Colonel Forster, asked to speak to Mr. Bennet. After waiting a few minutes, Mrs. Hill ushered him into Mr. Bennet's study.

Mr. Bennet came to his feet as the man entered the room. "Colonel Forster," he said, "I am happy to see you again, Sir." Bennet offered his hand and then motioned to a nearby chair. "How may I help you, Colonel?"

Wickham settled himself comfortably in the wing chair, placing his gloves in his hat and then resting it on his knees. "I will get right to the crux of my visit, Mr. Bennet; I come on behalf of my wife, Mrs. Forster. My Anna has become very fond of your youngest daughter, Miss Lydia. Mrs. Forster hopes that you will allow Miss Lydia to accompany my wife and me to London for the annual Festive Ball."

"When is the ball?"

"The day after tomorrow, Sir. We leave today and return the morning after the New Year's. We shall take rooms at the Whitmore, a hotel only two streets from the hall. Of course, Miss Lydia will be staying with Mrs. Forster, as is only proper."

Mr. Bennet paused for a long moment before stating, "You will forgive my prudence, Sir, in wishing to keep my daughters close.

After all, I had a daughter directly involved in two of the three recent attacks. My Lizzy discovered the body of the first victim, and the assailant took her captive. If not for Mr. Darcy, God only knows what might have happened." He gave Wickham a level look. "Do you believe that there is no longer a threat to the neighborhood, Colonel?"

"We had the three attacks within a few days, but for a fortnight there has been nothing." Wickham toyed with his gloves. "The magistrate and I believe the perpetrator was someone passing through the area, probably committing other crimes along the way."

Mr. Bennet leaned back in his chair, weighing what the colonel had said. "As a man I respect, you will understand if I insist that Lydia not go anywhere without you or Mrs. Forster."

"Of course, Mr. Bennet; I would expect nothing less. Miss Lydia is so young. I guarantee that your daughter will never leave my sight." Wickham relished making such statements—they were perfectly true, but not the way the hearer presumed.

"I would never consider this, Colonel, if not for your impeccable reputation, and if not for the fact that I would not hear the end of it from Mrs. Bennet if I denied Lydia a chance to meet an eligible young officer. Mrs. Bennet reminds me every day of our duty to find husbands for all our daughters, as my estate is entailed upon a distant cousin. However, Lydia shall travel to London with my wife's brother. Then you and Mrs. Forster may retrieve her from her uncle's home. That way, you will not have to bear my youngest daughter's silliness for your *entire* journey." He took out a piece of paper and began scrawling the Gardiners' address. "And my brother Gardiner plans to leave within a few hours."

Wickham had not anticipated such a turn of events. He tried to figure out how to explain the absence of Mrs. Forster when he returned for Lydia in a carriage. "How fortunate," he interjected, "to have relatives in London. Then my wife and I will call for Miss Lydia this evening and take her with us. I wish to reach London before nightfall today." Wickham picked up his hat, needing to make his leave as quickly as possible, having felt the *image* beginning to fade. He stood and extended his hand to Mr. Bennet.

Bennet rose to his feet also. "I will give you time to escape the house, Colonel, before I tell Lydia," he said with amusement. "It will save your ears the shrill of happiness to which we shall be subjected." He took Wickham's hand in farewell. Turning the hand, he commented, "That is odd, Colonel. You have the same marking on your wrist as the one I noticed on Mr. Wickham's."

Wickham laughed nervously; apparently the shapeshift had lost some of its originality. "Mr. Wickham is one of many soldiers who chose to display their loyalty to the Crown with this symbol; it is our pledge to defeat French tyranny."

"How interesting," Mr. Bennet mused. "I thought Mr. Wickham's to be a birthmark."

Wickham shifted his stance and headed towards the door, pulling on his gloves as he walked. "More than likely, Mr. Wickham earned his as I did—a few too many drinks and an Indian Punjab skilled in the art of tattoos."

"I imagine so, Colonel," Mr. Bennet said wryly as he followed Wickham to the door. "I wish you a safe journey, Sir."

"Thank you, Mr. Bennet. We will see you on the New Year's." Wickham left quickly, striding from the house and mounting the horse without looking back. Before he could reach the outer rim of the property, his disguise gave way to his own face and body. "That was close," he mumbled to himself. "Would that I could predict the shape change. It must have something to do with Darcy's attack at Netherfield. I had no problem before that time. Maybe Amelia did not get out the entire silver shaft."

Leaving Longbourn, Wickham turned his horse towards London. He held the address of Lydia Bennet's uncle in Cheapside and the means with which to destroy Elizabeth Darcy, and, ultimately, Fitzwilliam Darcy. In two hundred years—since Ellender D'Arcy and Lord Benning—no one had challenged him as these two did.

CHAPTER 21

Late in the afternoon, once more shifted into the image of Colonel Forster, Wickham released the knocker on the Gardiners' town house door, and a maid admitted him immediately. "Ah, Colonel," Mr. Gardiner extended a greeting as Wickham stepped into the drawing room. "Prompt, as predicted. Have a seat, Sir. May I offer you something to drink or some other refreshment?"

"Thank you, Mr. Gardiner. Although I do not wish to offend your hospitality, if you do not object, I would retrieve your niece and be on my way. I left Mrs. Forster at the hotel to freshen herself for dinner, and I am eager to do the same, as I am sure will Miss Lydia. I brought a carriage for your niece, and I will ride beside it for protection."

"Of course, Colonel. Let me send for Lydia. We did not unpack my niece's trunks in anticipation of your arrival." Mr. Gardiner rose from his seat to ring for a servant.

Wickham remained standing, anxious to be gone. "As I hired a coach, and one has no idea about the true abilities of such workers, I will take my leave of you, Sir, and oversee the securing of Miss Lydia's belongings. I prefer things done properly the first time." He made his way to the door, bowed, and stepped into the hallway.

Assuming the man's abruptness was a result of Colonel Forster's military efficiency, Mr. Gardiner simply followed him into the foyer. "Lydia will be out in a moment, Sir." Mr. Gardiner shook hands with him once again and disappeared into the recesses of the house.

Meanwhile, Wickham instructed the servants in storing Lydia's baggage. When the girl in question appeared, along with her aunt and uncle, Wickham helped her into the back of the hired carriage before mounting his horse. Lydia waved farewell to her family and giggled with the prospect of balls and parties and fawning soldiers.

His plans nearly complete, Wickham felt the expectation of taking her and destroying the Darcys at the same time.

"Colonel!" Mr. Gardiner called as the coach began to edge into traffic, and Wickham reined in the animal to hear the man's parting words. "Mrs. Gardiner and I plan to take our niece shopping tomorrow. We will come by the Whitmore at noon. Please tell Mrs. Forster we would be pleased if she could join us."

"I am sure my wife would take great delight in relieving me of my purse, Mr. Gardiner. I will inform Mrs. Forster of your plans." With a tap of his crop to his hat as a parting salute, Wickham nudged the steed forward in an obvious need to be gone, and then he galloped away to catch the rapidly vanishing coach.

When she peered out the coach's window, finding George Wickham riding beside it surprised Lydia. "Mr. Wickham!" she exclaimed after moving the drape aside and lowering the window. "What on earth are you doing here? And where is the colonel?"

Wickham offered up his most seductive smile. "Colonel Forster wanted to find a special gift for his wife before returning to the hotel. I believe the good colonel plans to woo his lovely bride this evening." He edged the horse closer to the coach. "I assured him I would happily see you to your destination."

Lydia dropped her eyes, blushing. "That is most kind of you, Lieutenant."

Wickham paused, increasing the drama. "It is not so kind, Miss Lydia; I did it for very selfish reasons."

"What type of selfish reasons, Mr. Wickham?"

"If you allow me to ride with you, Miss Lydia, I would express my deepest regard to a beautiful woman." To emphasize his sincerity, he touched the window where her hand rested upon the opening.

"That would be a great break with propriety, Sir." Although she was young, Lydia Bennet was well schooled in how to tempt a man and then withdraw. Unfortunately, with Wickham, her wiles on a *man* were worthless. He would get what he wanted, whether she chose to offer it or not.

"I promise I have only the highest opinion of you, Miss Lydia. I would wish to express my plans for my future and my ardent admiration for one of God's most beautiful creatures." Such niceties never failed to make a woman let down her guard, whether she be a working-class bar maid or a lady of the realm.

Lydia bit her bottom lip, debating the sensibility of allowing a man to share her carriage. She believed she had good reason to hope for a proposal of marriage from Mr. Wickham. So she said, "As you wish, Mr. Wickham."

Wickham called up to the coachman and reined in his horse. Dismounting, he tied the animal to the back of the coach and climbed in, seating himself across from her. Lydia settled back into the cheap seats of the letted coach. She smoothed the creases of her dress and tried to look prepared for what she hoped would happen.

Once the coach rolled again, Wickham leaned forward and took Lydia's hand in his. As he made small circles with his fingertips along her wrists, he beckoned her to look at him. His gaze would solidify his control over the girl. "Miss Lydia," he said slowly, giving himself time to enthrall her, "I wish to keep you with me through eternity. I would give you a love no one else can. I would welcome you into my arms nightly; we would be partners in the oldest game known to man." With what ability to think she still possessed, Lydia envisioned balls and kisses and wedding dresses. "Instead of the Forsters, please say you will let me take you to Scotland, where we may join forever. I have a home of which you will be mistress in your own right."

Lydia Bennet simply nodded her agreement. His eyes held her, and she could no longer generate an independent thought. Wickham enjoyed this moment, the one when his whims became his victim's actions. Whatever he wanted would occur. He could manipulate Lydia Bennet as he chose. Wickham knew better than anyone how all humanity fed on the power of one another. Every minute of every day, people tried to *best* their neighbors—to suck the life from those less fortunate, leaving the weakest drained and ruined.

Darkness filled the windows as Wickham moved to the seat

beside her. "You will look good in my house," he whispered close to her ear before starting to trace light kisses down Lydia's neck. Using his thumb against her chin, Wickham tilted Lydia's head back to give him access to the veins in her neck—an unnatural kiss of eternal life.

When he sank his teeth into the spot, she flinched but then relaxed into his arms. This moment always amazed him, because as the victim's life became his to use as he saw fit—as the fluid flowed into his innards—the stranger's life moved through him—all their memories were now his. Lydia left him with stolen kisses behind the stable from a knock-kneed storekeeper, with games of hide-and-seek with her sisters, with the frustrations of useless music lessons, and with boisterous laughter to hide her own insecurities.

He did not drink enough to kill her outright, just enough to change Lydia Bennet forever. He did not break her neck but instead gently released her, laying the girl back along the seat. He lifted Lydia's feet onto his lap and removed her slippers; then he absentmindedly stroked her leg from ankle to knee. Being given such liberties would sexually arouse a man, but Wickham was more interested in the texture of her skin, making sure it retained its softness. He would exchange fluids with her several more times over the next couple of days on their way to Northumberland. The lights of London faded into the distance. The coach isolated them from the outside world; he no longer heard the click and the clack of the wheels on the roadway. He sprinkled some of his home earth on the opposite seat and settled in for a long rest. The coachman was one of his followers. There would be no need to stop for food or drink. Changing horses would be the only delays. They would return to his home and wait for what Fitzwilliam Darcy would do next. By noon tomorrow, when her aunt and uncle discovered that Lydia was gone, there would be no turning back. He had instigated a last stand—a final battle with Darcy—one from which only one of them could walk away.

★ ★ ★

"What does it say, Fitzwilliam?" Elizabeth watched him as he read the latest report from one of the many investigators he had hired to find Wickham. It was two days after Christmas, and by silent agreement, they had not discussed Wickham or the curse since his declaration on Christmas day of wanting time away from the obsession.

He tossed the paper on the desk with disgust. The information brought his reprieve to a close. For those few hours, he had enjoyed being simply the master of Pemberley, overseeing his properties, scouring the newspapers for political pieces that would affect his tenants or his business holdings, treating Georgiana in an attentive way, and stealing romantic moments with his wife. This could be his life if not for an ancient hex, and Darcy did not want it to end. "We have news from one of Bramwell's agents. He located Wickham's home."

Elizabeth moved quickly to grab the letter. "Where?" Her eyes searched the words for the answer.

"Near Chillingham." Darcy crossed the room, putting space between him and the damnable missive. Hands resting on the sill, he took up a sentry position at the window overlooking the south lawn, where he had wrestled in the snow with Elizabeth only a week earlier.

Recognizing his foul mood, Elizabeth first put the offending letter in her pocket so that she might read it more closely later. Then she encircled his waist with her arms and rested her head against the lean, strong muscles of Darcy's back. "What causes your grief, my Husband?" Elizabeth knew the letter to be related to his discontent, but she knew not the exact reason. "Did not Bramwell's men do a thorough job?"

Darcy sighed. "On the contrary; they were very professional."

"Then I do not understand. Are you not happy to know where we might find Wickham?"

Darcy held her to him, clasping her hands tightly. He did not answer for several moments, choosing instead to keep up his vigil and to enjoy the warmth of Elizabeth's body along his back. "I cannot in all honesty say I find the report fortuitous."

Elizabeth released her hold and came to stand in front of him. "Will you not search Wickham out?"

"For what purpose? The chance to get myself or you killed?" He looked away, not wishing to see the censure in her sea-green eyes. "I will not put you in danger again, Elizabeth. *I will not risk it.* You are too precious to me."

Elizabeth's hands balled into fists at her sides, her frustration evident. "But we *must* stop him!"

He frowned. "Why is it *my* duty to protect everyone from Wickham?" Darcy, at a loss to explain why things had changed, stalked away from her, horribly and disturbingly uncomfortable. "I willingly accept the responsibility of safeguarding my family and my tenants. I would even defend the village. But how can I accept the responsibility for all of England?"

Elizabeth stormed across the room. "You sound like those weak-willed members of Parliament who are eager to forgive the French just for the sake of peace!"

"Even England cannot protect the whole world, Elizabeth. It can only effectively protect its own borders. That is what I want; I want to preserve what we have. Do you not understand? Am I not defeating Wickham simply by doing that very thing? By not letting his evil overtake me?"

"We have done all this just to *let Wickham go?*" she asked and burst into sobs.

Seeing her so distraught, Darcy scooped her into his arms and took Elizabeth onto his lap as he sat down in a nearby chair. "Have not the past few days been glorious? Just you and me and the hope springing from every wall of Pemberley? We can have that *every day,* Elizabeth. Wickham cannot reach us here."

"He brought his destruction to the neighborhood before. Why would he not come again?" she countered.

"Because when he was here before, it was when I was learning about Wickham and he about me." Darcy lifted her chin with the first two fingers of his right hand. "I would never allow that to happen here again. Wickham cannot take me by surprise; I am an opponent he does not wish to face."

Elizabeth's bottom lip trembled. "Then we just...*go on* with our lives?"

Darcy traced her lips with his fingertips. "Do you not want a family, Elizabeth? I have thought of little else for days. We could adopt, just as you said before. We could make everyone think you to be with child—a pillow for padding—then off we go to one of the hundred foundling homes in London or Brighton or even Edinburgh. It will be our secret."

"What of my maid? Would she not know?" Elizabeth inquired skeptically.

Excited by the possibilities, Darcy now kissed her freely. "We pay her extra to keep our counsel, or I become your handmaid for several months. Our servants would view me as an eccentric, doting husband and father. After all, I have been seen upon numerous occasions kissing my wife. As your time for delivery draws near, we will be called away on a family emergency, or we can go abroad, and you will deliver before we return."

"But I will have no milk for the child!"

"We will employ a wet nurse," he said. "Choose a son or a daughter; I do not care. We can repeat the process again in a year or two. How many children would you like? I considered two, but a half dozen would make me even happier."

"You wish me to miraculously have six children?" Elizabeth wondered aloud.

"We will need to come up with creative tales, but I have no doubt we can do so."

"Georgiana's children would be denied their birthright with such a ruse."

"My sister has a large dowry. She will marry well, and her family will not suffer. We can leave them an inheritance. Think about it. We end the curse with my passing, and the children we raise with a responsibility to the land will carry on—keeping Pemberley and my family's legacy great. We have the resources to raise a large family." He seemed to have considered everything.

"What if I want my *own* children?"

Darcy looked serious. "Then I will swallow my pride and allow you a discreet assignation."

"I do not want to make love with anyone but you, Fitzwilliam." Elizabeth felt like screaming.

He lowered his voice to share a delicate secret. "I have been thinking about that also. There are ways, Elizabeth,…ways I could pleasure you without…without our being…*together.*"

What he said both embarrassed and excited Elizabeth. "I said I wanted to *make love* with you, Fitzwilliam," she asserted.

"Then we *will* make love, Vixen. I will send for one hundred French letters. They will prevent your ability to conceive a child—or we can use treated sponges."

Elizabeth slid off his lap and strode away from him. "I was thinking of something more intimate—something spontaneous shared between a husband and a wife."

Darcy rose to his feet to follow her. Coming up behind her, he started to embrace her, but then thought better of it. "Elizabeth, do you not understand?" His voice sounded calm, but his hunched shoulders and taut expression said otherwise. "It can be however we want it to be. We will name our own terms."

"This is madness!" Elizabeth threw up her hands in exasperation. "What have you done with my sane and sensible husband?" She started for the door.

"Please, Elizabeth,…I am begging you," he called after her.

Elizabeth stopped suddenly and whirled around to face him. "Begging? That is not begging, Fitzwilliam. That is demanding—it is *manipulating!*" And she strode off.

She was nearly to the door when his voice, so soft and so full of grief and pleading, froze her in her place. "*This* is begging."

Elizabeth turned and the sight of her proud, powerful husband on his knees immediately brought tears to her eyes. She looked on in silence. "Oh, Fitzwilliam," she sighed before rushing forward and dropping to her own knees in front of him; her arms encircled his neck while she peppered his face with an array of kisses. "I love you," she assured him before starting the barrage of kisses again.

Darcy made the decision the moment she stormed for the door. He would do anything to keep her with him. Their weeks together were the only joy he could remember. Elizabeth offered paradise; without her, there was no hope—no happiness.

For Elizabeth, the sight of Darcy on his knees ripped her heart in two. She knew him—knew what it cost her husband to beg her to agree. She also knew deep in her heart she could never deny him. She existed only to please him—to worship the man she embraced. Darcy pleaded in supplication for her agreement, and Elizabeth met his prayers with those of her own.

The next two days unfolded blissfully; they were some of the best of his eight and twenty years. Nothing troubled the exquisite serenity. He rode out with his steward to inspect several of the storage barns for possible repair, settled a tenant dispute over property lines, and listened to the new vicar's plea for a village school. In the early afternoon of the second day, Darcy sat with Georgiana at the pianoforte while she practiced a new piece, even joining her on the more difficult parts. They then played several duets.

At night, although they still did not consummate their marriage, he held Elizabeth close and indulged in new intimacies. He knew it was only a matter of time and of trust before they knew the full range of pleasure. He once again experienced her *femininity,* as Elizabeth now playfully called it. In fact, he left a distinctive red mark at the base of her neck—his badge of love. Surprisingly, she returned the favor, seductively nibbling at the nape of his neck, leaving a raw place, which nearly drove him insane with passion.

She sat in a winged chair looking out over the prospect, attempting to embroider a handkerchief for Darcy, but Elizabeth's mind rested purely on the man himself. It might shock him to realize that she found his laugh soulful—and addictive. She would do anything to make him laugh out loud. Her husband was a tall, supremely masculine man of impressive figure and imposing assurance, and an unexpected glimpse of him could be exhilarating.

"Ah, there you are," the image spoke from behind her, and Elizabeth turned her head slowly to look into ocean blue eyes, the kind in which one could drown.

Elizabeth shook her head to rid herself of the vision and focus on Darcy's countenance as he approached. "Do you need me, Sir?"

A smile turned up the corners of his mouth. "I *always* need you, Elizabeth." Darcy's voice warmed her as much as his smile did. "Actually, I thought we might share a walk; the sun warms the day."

Elizabeth scrambled to her feet. "I would enjoy just that. Wait while I find a pelisse and a scarf.

"I will be in my study when you are ready." She started past him and then stopped suddenly to caress his cheek before hurrying on her way. Watching the sway of her hips as she left the room, Darcy chuckled. Elizabeth's spontaneity gave life to his household.

"I am ready," she announced as she bounded into the room a quarter hour later. Seeing Darcy deep in thought, reading a letter, she paused close to his desk. Unable to interpret his expression, she asked, "Bad news?"

"Not exactly," he mumbled, but did not put the letter down. "It is from Miss Bingley."

"Caroline Bingley?" Elizabeth sat down suddenly. "Is it to do with Mr. Bingley?"

Darcy looked up, hearing the anxiety in her voice. "No," he tried to assure her. "I suppose it is Caroline's *congratulations* upon our marriage." He tucked the letter into an envelope. Then he opened his desk drawer and placed the letter inside.

Elizabeth recognized how Darcy avoided speaking the truth. "I am sure Miss Bingley extended no such feelings towards me. Wishing me congratulations after I stole the *prize* upon which she had set her heart is unlikely."

Darcy's eyes sparkled. "The prize? Shall I consider myself so worthy?" he half teased.

"I am certain Miss Bingley held you, my Husband, in high regard. As for me, I took pity on you; as I recall, you were quite insensate." She lifted her chin in challenge.

"I suspect I was." Darcy winked at her. "Thank you for your humanity, my love."

"Well, tell me." Elizabeth sat back in her chair, straightening the seams of her outer garments. "I must hear of Miss Bingley's felicitations."

"Are you confident that you wish to hear what she writes?" Darcy leaned back, retrieving the letter from the desk. "It will likely give you some offense. Miss Bingley often lacks tact."

Elizabeth took a position—straight-backed and haughty, even defiant. "There is little Miss Bingley could say that would surprise me."

"I never doubted your lack of surprise, but I would not intentionally give you displeasure, Elizabeth. Some parts of the letter will annoy you, at the least."

"I would still prefer to hear it, Fitzwilliam."

Darcy sighed with resignation. "If you wish, my love."

23 December

Mr. Darcy,

As the holiday looms upon us, I reflect on the many times your family and mine joined for the celebration. Those days serve as a measure of how Christmas should occur, with good friends and family warmly enjoying one another's company.

Out of the corner of his eye, Darcy could see Elizabeth arch an eyebrow. Elizabeth and Caroline Bingley had a rivalry when they were at Netherfield together. Used to having her way, Miss Bingley often took offense at Elizabeth's frankness and open, natural manner.

This year, our days will seem less lively, as you and dear Georgiana are at Pemberley, and we reside at Mr. Hurst's estate in Hampshire.

Charles shared your precipitous news upon his return to Langley

Hall, and both Louisa and I were taken aback to not be included in your solemn, although obviously rushed, exchange of vows with Miss Eliza Bennet. Although we noted your preference for the lady, neither of us suspected your motivations when you returned to Netherfield. However, Charles swears he saw firsthand your affection for the new Mrs. Darcy; therefore, we offer our congratulations and wish you happiness.

Darcy looked up from the letter when Elizabeth snorted in disgust. "Let us leave this." He began to rise from behind the desk, but Elizabeth waved him back to his seat. Stalling, he pretended to look for his place again before he read once more.

We were equally chagrined by the fact that Charles spent time with Miss Bennet and her family in Cheapside. My naïve brother does not understand, as you now must, how such connections very materially lessen the Bennet sisters' chances of marrying men of any consideration in the world. Mrs. Darcy must thank her lucky stars under the circumstances. We suppose Charles purposely chose to not share news of your nuptials for fear we would disapprove; he originally sent word only of finding you in health.

"Disapprove?" Elizabeth protested. "More than likely, Mr. Bingley simply wanted a few moments of peace and quiet without the harpies…." She broke off the rest of her retort when she noted the warning in Darcy's eyes.

"I told you this would be a source of irritation. I suggest we go for our walk instead."

Elizabeth tried to look ashamed of what she had said and thought, but she did not feel as such. "How can Miss Bingley carry on so in the name of civility and manners? I understand her disappointment in losing your attentions to me, but I do not understand the venom she spreads in the name of *courtesy.* Jane was nothing but kind to the woman."

Darcy put the letter in a drawer, placing it out of Elizabeth's sight. "Let us forget Miss Bingley's pettiness." He came from behind the desk to take her hand.

Elizabeth reached for him, but then stopped. "Why do you wish for me not to read the end of the letter?" she said accusingly.

Darcy forced his countenance and his voice to remain calm. "I have no reason but your peace of mind."

"Fitzwilliam, we do not lie to each other. Why do you do so now?"

Darcy knelt beside her chair. "I do not wish you to read the letter because Miss Bingley disparages your looks and your manners and attributes such censure to me as its source. I would not have you doubt my true feelings. I sincerely wish only your happiness; you must believe me. Let me place the letter in the fire, and let nothing come between us."

Elizabeth caressed his cheek. "I should not allow the woman to goad me so."

He kissed the tip of her nose. "A walk will do us both a service."

"Burn the letter, Fitzwilliam." Elizabeth made the decision before standing. "I need some fresh air."

Darcy took her hand and headed towards the door, but he pulled up before they crossed the threshold. Looking back at the desk, he flushed for his absentmindedness. "I forgot. You have two letters from Miss Bennet."

Elizabeth considered returning to read the family news in her sister's letters. She missed her family, more than she would admit to Darcy, especially her father and Jane. Sometimes she wished they were nearer, so she might discuss her marriage with one of them. She and Darcy could use the sensibility of her sister and the quick perceptiveness of her father. At barely twenty years, she often felt inadequate to be Darcy's wife. With a look of longing, she said, "They will wait. I need time with my husband right now."

Darcy smiled down at her, slowly tracing the outline of her face with the tip of his finger. "Your husband is blessed by your amiability, Mrs. Darcy. His affection for you deepens by the day."

CHAPTER 22

A little more than an hour later, Elizabeth wandered back into Darcy's study. Finding the letters from her sister still lying on the silver salver, she picked them up and headed to her favorite chair. Missing her family, she brought the letters to her nose and sniffed, hoping to find the scent of her sister there. Holding them close to her chest, she relished the anticipation of reading the latest news. Finally, slipping off her shoes and curling her feet up under her, she snuggled into the warmth of the chair. The letters remained on her lap for several minutes; she purposely waited to open them, enjoying the knowledge that in a few minutes she would connect with her former life.

Finally, she took both of them into her hand and tried to determine which was written first. Noticing one letter was marked as being missent elsewhere, Elizabeth was not surprised, because her sister wrote the direction remarkably ill. The one missent must be first attended to. The beginning contained an account of all their little parties and engagements, with such news as the country afforded, but the latter half, written in evident agitation, gave more important intelligence.

Since writing the above, dearest Lizzy, something occurred of a most unexpected and serious nature; but I am afraid of alarming you—be assured we are all well. What I have to say relates to poor Lydia. An express came from our Uncle Gardiner at twelve last night, just as we were all gone to bed.

Against his original inclination, Papa agreed to allow Lydia to accompany the Forsters to London for a military ball and other festivities. Lydia traveled with our aunt and uncle to Cheapside. Uncle Gardiner reports the colonel retrieved Lydia from his residence the day after Christmas, and all seemed well.

However, the next day, he and Aunt Merry meant to take Lydia and Mrs. Forster shopping, but when he called upon the hotel, the Forsters had just arrived, and there was no Lydia. In fact, the colonel denies having even approached my father about the possibility of Lydia accompanying him and his wife, and as they had just arrived in London—although Uncle swears the man's appearance to be uncannily like the colonel's—the colonel could not have been the one who rode away with Lydia in his coach.

Uncle Gardiner ascertained the direction the coach took, but found no trace of Lydia at the posting inns. Because the carriage departed along the North Road out of London, we assume this is some sort of elaborate hoax—an elopement. Yet with whom, we do not know. Colonel Forster gives us reason to expect him here soon. I must conclude, for I cannot be long from my poor mother. I am afraid you will not be able to make it out, but I hardly know what I have written.

Without allowing herself time for consideration, and scarcely knowing what she felt, Elizabeth, on finishing this letter, instantly seized the other, and opening it with the utmost impatience, read as follows. It was written a day later than the conclusion of the first.

By this time, my dearest sister, you received my hurried letter; I wish this may be more intelligible, but though not confined for time, my head is so bewildered I cannot answer for being coherent. The mystery of Lydia's flight increases. I know not what to think. After making every possible inquiry on that side of London, Colonel F. came on into Hertfordshire. With the kindest concern he came on to Longbourn and broke his apprehensions to us in a manner most creditable to his heart. I am sincerely grieved for him and Mrs. F., but no one can throw any blame on them.

This is what we do know. A man presented himself to Papa as Colonel Forster. He convinced Papa to allow Lydia to attend the military entertainment in London. That same man repeated his performance at our uncle's home. Because of the colonel's superb reputation, neither our father nor our uncle doubted the act.

Compound this with two other unexplained occurrences, and we are at a loss as to how to approach this break with propriety on Lydia's part. Following on the colonel's return to Hertfordshire, a constable came seeking the colonel. The constable held a summons for Mr. Denny; he is charged with the murder of a bar maid near Limehouse. The constable produced a drawing based on witnesses' accounts of the man with whom the woman left the Black Ghost, where she worked. The thing is, the colonel sent Mr. Denny to Dublin nearly a fortnight ago on military business; he heard regularly from Mr. Denny and is sure that there is a grievous mistake. Mr. Denny could not have been in London at the time of the woman's death. However, Charlotte Lucas reports talking to him shortly before the incident occurred. Mr. Denny allegedly accompanied her and Maria one day in Meryton, but this was after Mr. Denny's first report arrived from Ireland—so it would be impossible. Upon questioning Charlotte, she commented on the man having grey eyes, rather than Mr. Denny's brown ones; Maria confirms her sister's assertions.

What we fear, Lizzy, is improbable; but we have no other solutions. Our sister has, of late, been the exclusive recipient of Mr. Wickham's attentions.

Elizabeth's heart leapt to her throat. *Wickham?* She and Darcy had assumed he had left the Hertfordshire area after they encountered Wickham in London. Why had he returned to the village—to the shire? Her eyes returned to the page.

When the colonel met with Papa, the only indication that something was amiss was that the man had an unusual marking on his hand; but this was easily explained away at the time. But this marking on the man's hand pretending to be the colonel was the crown found on Wickham's hand. Mr. Denny has brown eyes, while Mr. Wickham has grey ones. As such, we conclude that somehow—somehow!—Mr. Wickham disguised himself as both the colonel and as Mr. Denny. At first, as bad as it seems, we assumed it was so they could go off to Scotland to marry. So imprudent a match on both sides! But could Mr. Wickham have more nefarious motives? The woman...the bar maid was killed in a manner most heinous. The constable explained it to Papa and the colonel, and they confirmed her death to be in the same manner as the woman you nearly tripped over and of Miss King. They now believe Mr. Wickham to be the perpetrator of these crimes and are actively searching for him. We fear Lydia might be his next victim. As you know my nature, you can suppose that I wish this to be something it is not. If it were but truly an elopement, we would rejoice. Can I suppose her so lost to everything? Impossible! I grieve to find, however, that Colonel F. is not disposed to think marriage a possibility; he shook his head when I expressed my hopes and said he feared W. was not a man to be trusted.

My poor mother is really ill and keeps to her room. It was her encouragement by which Papa let Lydia leave. Could she exert herself it would be better; but this is not to be expected; and as to my father, I never in my life saw him so affected. I am truly glad, dearest Lizzy, that you were spared something of these distressing scenes; but now, as the first shock is over, shall I own that I long for your return? Circumstances are such I cannot help earnestly begging you all to come here as soon as possible. My father is going to London with Colonel Forster instantly, to try to discover Lydia's trail. What he means to do, I am sure I know not, but excessive distress will not allow him to pursue any measure in the best and safest way. As the colonel has obligations, my father and uncle will carry on without him.

Elizabeth darted from her seat, in all eagerness to be with her family at once. Without losing a moment of time so precious, she reached the door, but Darcy opened it instead. Her pale face and impetuous manner told him instantly that something was amiss. "Good God! What is the matter?" he cried.

"I must go!" She started past him, but Darcy caught her arm to stay her retreat.

"Go where?" he demanded.

Still in a state of shock, she mumbled, "Longbourn...home... Wickham has Lydia." Elizabeth hesitated, her knees trembling under her; and despite her need for action, she sagged against Darcy before he caught her to him.

"Wickham has abducted your sister?" He said the words without believing their truth.

Elizabeth shoved the letters into his hands as she pushed away from him, needing distance from the man she loved. "She is probably dead…or worse, poor, innocent, silly Lydia is one of Wickham's *minions* by now!" Her voice rose in volume and in shrillness as acknowledgment of the situation settled in.

Darcy started forward, but her hand stopped him in midstride. He searched Elizabeth's face to detect her emotional state and then tried to scan the letter for information. "We will leave at once." He moved to the bell cord to summon a servant.

"No!" The word resonated throughout the room.

Darcy turned to her, hoping to reason with his obviously distraught wife. "We should return to Longbourn; your family needs us."

"*We* are the *reason* for their anguish." The words hung in the air between them. "What would we do at Longbourn, Fitzwilliam? Set up armed guards around the estate? Talk all my family into wearing cloves of garlic around their necks for protection? We did this to them—*you and I*. We defied the Fates by thinking we could find love and end the curse simply by being together."

"I am…so sorry, Elizabeth. So very sorry."

"*Sorry* is not meaningful, Fitzwilliam. Wickham did this to take revenge on *you*. I chose to be with *you* because I thought we would make a difference, but all we did was destroy my family. First, Georgiana. Now, Lydia. Who is next? Will it be Jane or Kitty or Aunt Merry? How many more before it stops?" She wrapped her arms around herself, closing off any contact with him.

"We will find a way…we will make this right, Elizabeth." He wanted desperately to hold her—to feel her closeness.

"I do not want to find a way to fix this! I simply want to go home. I want this to end!"

Her words frightened him. Did Elizabeth want to end the curse or did she want *their marriage* to end? "I will send Morris and your maid to pack our things."

Her chin rose in defiance. "You are not coming with me."

"Elizabeth, this is madness. You are my wife; I will help you find your sister." He edged forward, hoping to bring her into his embrace, where he might convince her.

"And what will you *do*, Fitzwilliam, when you find Lydia? Take an ax to her head like you did the others? Free her soul?" Her voice quivered with rage.

Darcy flinched from the accusation. "I will do whatever is necessary to end your sister's wanderings." He tried to stay calm—tried to make Elizabeth understand.

"Do not dare to take that self-righteous attitude! If we had pursued Wickham, *as I wished*…" she charged. Her eyes burned with resolve, and he watched the color rush to her cheeks.

"It would have made no difference," he countered. "The letter says he came for Lydia the day after Christmas. We had not even discussed whether to continue our pursuit at that time."

Elizabeth shook her head. "It lacks significance; I cannot do this any longer!"

The words hit him harder than any blow he had ever taken from an opponent. Cautiously, he asked, "Cannot do what any longer?"

"This!" She threw her hands up in a gesture of frustration. "This…us!" The silence deflated her spirits. "Us," she whispered. "I cannot do *us* any longer." Tears filled her eyes, and Elizabeth's bottom lip began to tremble. "If I had not allowed myself to be seduced by the idea of helping you, my family would be safe from danger.…I would be back at Longbourn, listening to Lydia rattle on about the latest militia officer to catch her eye. Instead, she is probably calling George Wickham *my lord*. I cannot forgive myself for my weakness. I want to go home, but how will I ever face my parents with the knowledge that my arrogance cost them their youngest child? How will they ever forgive me? How can I explain without being disloyal to you? My keeping your secret allowed Wickham the opportunity to exact his revenge."

"I cannot let you go alone." Darcy was clutching at a straw. He knew, deep in his soul, that she meant to leave him forever.

Elizabeth turned on him, eyes ablaze. "How will you stop me from going alone, Fitzwilliam? Will you keep me under lock and key? Will you follow me and drag me back here against my will? If you do, I will escape again and again, and one of those times *I will* make it to London, and *I will* find a solicitor who will take my case; and although I, as a woman, cannot seek a divorce from *you,* I will let it be known that we never consummated our marriage. The *ton* will shun you, thinking you perverted in your tastes." Elizabeth did not know why she said such awful things; she would never purposely hurt Darcy. Even with Lydia's abduction, she, truthfully, did not blame Darcy as much as she did herself. *She* had let down her guard, and Wickham had swept in for the kill.

Darcy stepped away from the door, resigned. Elizabeth would never forgive him. He had lost her—lost the only woman he would ever love. "I will not stop you," he muttered, "and not because of your threat, but because I will not see you hurt by me any longer. Send word where you choose to go, and I will have my man provide for you. Whatever you need—tell him; I will not deny you." He stepped purposefully behind the desk, as if negotiating a business arrangement. "If you wish to leave today, I shall have the coach readied." Deflated by his loss, Darcy sat down heavily.

Elizabeth nodded before moving to the door; yet she paused with her hand on the knob. Her voice trembled. "I am sorry, Fitzwilliam," she said softly, as if offering a caress, but she did not turn around. Tears flowed freely down her cheeks.

"I will think otherwise," he said from somewhere behind her. Elizabeth heard the emotion in his voice. "I will never be sorry for loving you, Elizabeth. Even with everything that happened, I do not regret one moment I held you in my arms. I only regret that I brought you pain. It was not a fair exchange for the joy you gave me."

Imagining the danger in which she placed her family by being with Darcy, Elizabeth forced herself to turn the handle—made herself leave him. Closing the door behind her, she leaned back against it for a moment, considering returning to his embrace. "I love you." The words barely escaped her lips, but her heart screamed them. Tears choked her as she pushed away from the entrance and ran towards her chamber. In that instant, her life ended.

The tap on his study door was insistent, but Darcy made no move to respond. Elizabeth had departed more than two hours earlier. He had watched her board the coach—watched as she left, never to return again. Even if he had not seen her leave, Darcy intuitively would have known Elizabeth was gone forever. The house was a crypt; all the sunlight that had filled it for the past few weeks had departed on the back of the carriage that took her away from him. He now stood leaning against his forearm, looking deeply into a fully engaged fireplace, but feeling the chill of an empty heart.

"Fitzwilliam?" Georgiana knocked again and tried the knob before pounding with her fist. "Fitzwilliam, open the door! Elizabeth left, Fitzwilliam. Will you not go after her?"

Georgiana waited for an answer, but Darcy did not move. He had locked the door when Elizabeth walked out of it two hours and thirteen minutes earlier. He counted it off in five-minute intervals, wondering how long it would be before he died of a broken heart. How long could he survive without breathing? What had he done before Elizabeth? Was there anything prior to when Elizabeth Bennet had danced into his life?

His sister's voice came again, but this time it was softer and more pleading. "Fitzwilliam, please. Brother, we need her. We need Elizabeth."

"Go away, Georgiana," he called over his shoulder. "There is no more Elizabeth."

"But, Fitzwilliam…" She jiggled the door handle again.

"*Damn it,* Georgiana; I said there is *no more Elizabeth!*"

His sister heard the glass shatter as it hit the door and felt the wood vibrate from the impact. That was followed quickly by three thuds in close succession and then an inhuman cry of pain emanating from the room. If she could have seen behind the door, Georgiana would have observed her brother first sink to his knees in defeat and then roll over onto his side to lie in a crumpled mess. Darcy pulled the carpet upon which he lay around him, over his shoulders and around his body. He thought, *It is so cold. Why is it so cold?* before he closed his eyes and let the blackness overcome him.

★ ★ ★

As the carriage pulled away from the steps of Pemberley, Elizabeth hoped Darcy would stop her. All along the lane, she imagined his riding up like a highwayman, stopping his coach, and demanding that she return to him. Before she left, she had tried the door to his study, but found it locked. *Is he behind the door? Does he not care enough to even say his farewells?* Secretly, she regretted her impetuous stand in his study; she should not have accused him of causing her family's grief. Assuredly, he had played a part in it, but so had she, and so had Lydia, and—most important—so had Mr. Wickham. It was no more Darcy's fault than it was Lord Thomas's fault for catching Leána's eye two centuries earlier. Possibly Ellender D'Arcy shared some of the blame for her decision to trade Seorais Winchcombe for Arawn Benning, but as a woman in love she could easily visualize that she would go to such extremes to save Darcy's life if faced with a similar situation.

Now, as the carriage rolled towards London, Elizabeth urgently wanted to order it to turn around. Yet how could she admit she was wrong? And how could she be sure that Darcy would welcome her return? Elizabeth wanted what *he* wanted—a family, even if they adopted them, and the estate, and lying in each other's arms, legs entangled and bodies touching. She groaned in acknowledgment of her stupidity.

Where will I stay? When she left Pemberley, she had planned to return to Longbourn, but upon reflection, Elizabeth did not see how she could do so. She certainly could not share with anyone what she knew of Darcy and of Wickham. And what other reason could she give her parents for her return? They would welcome her, of course, for a few days while Lydia's disappearance was investigated, but she could not return in shame—having left Darcy would bring more notoriety to her family. Jane, Kitty, and Mary would suffer, never finding husbands of their own. In addition, her presence at Longbourn might draw Wickham there.

So where else was there? She could not stay with her aunt and uncle. Wickham might choose to strike their household also. Elizabeth would never risk the lives of her niece and nephews by returning there.

Overton House? At least, there her presence would not place a loved one in danger. Her father could stay with her while he looked for Lydia. Although Elizabeth knew his search would prove fruitless, her father would know all the comforts that Darcy's money could provide. Plus, if he was with her at Overton, she could tend to her dear Papa and ease his pain.

Afterwards, she would go far away—a just punishment for her conceit—for being the source of so much pain—and as a way to forget Darcy, as if she ever could. It would be like trying to forget how to breathe. Being at Overton would be a constant reminder of the man who had haunted her every thought for months now. She let the misery of missing him break over her. She would have to learn to play on the safe side in the future.

Darkness crept into the carriage. Elizabeth knew that making it to London in one day was impossible, but she hated the idea of staying anywhere alone.

The coachman opened the slot in order to speak to her. "Mrs. Darcy?" he said.

"Yes, Peter?"

"There be a storm stirrin' up the leaves. Might be best if'n we stop at the next inn. You can seek shelter there."

Elizabeth could hear the wind whistling through the opening. "I trust your judgment, Peter."

"Yes, Ma'am. We should be there in a quarter hour or so." He slid the slot closed and called to the horses.

Elizabeth felt the coach lunge forward with the effort. She would spend the night without Darcy—her first since they had wed. It seemed unnatural somehow, but she would learn to control her thoughts of him. She had no choice. She brushed a tear from her cheek, only to find another one to replace the one she had wiped away. Another and another followed that one. *Why bother?* she thought. There was no controlling how many tears she would shed over Fitzwilliam Darcy.

A little after midnight, Darcy emerged from his study. The household had slept for at least two hours. He wanted to see no one. Taking a single candle from one of those left burning in the entrance foyer, he made his way to his chambers, the ones connected to *hers*—to Elizabeth's. She had been gone twelve hours and forty minutes, and unbelievably, his heart still beat and his mind still remembered. Elizabeth had left him. He had known from the first moment he desired her that this was inevitable, but he had succumbed to the hope that the outcome would be different. Yet how could he expect otherwise? He was an aberration, and he had brought evil into her life. Elizabeth was the perfection that he had held in his hands for a few precious moments. She deserved the best, and he had foolishly thought he could *buy* her things…and that would be enough. He had never considered the fact that Elizabeth's goodness—her loyalty—her empathy—all those intangibles she offered in return—were priceless abstracts.

Sometime over the past few hours—after openly prostrating himself at Misery's feet—he had formulated a plan—a plan to die. He knew where to find Wickham, and with the first streaks of dawn, Darcy would set out for Northumberland. For months now, he had set his estate—his papers—in order, and everything was ready for his death. Wickham had thrown down the gauntlet, and he would respond. Lydia Bennet's seduction was a message—a warning—that George Wickham would not stop until one or both of them no longer existed. His enemy had chosen the girl as a symbol of his own strength—and, as usual, he had succeeded.

Responding in kind, Darcy would release Lydia Bennet from her eternal grave. He owed Elizabeth that much, and if he died in doing so, his effort would be well worth giving back to *his Elizabeth* the only peace he could. Then she could go on with her life— a life without him. Even if he survived—and Darcy held no illusions in that area—Elizabeth would never love him again. What woman could love the man who was the means of ruining a most-beloved sister? He wrote Georgiana a letter explaining his departure. He left specific instructions for his solicitors to execute the dictates of his will, leaving the estate and the care of his sister to Elizabeth, with Damon's help, until Georgiana married. When Georgiana's children came of age, Elizabeth would hold the dowager house.

Of course, the possibility existed of Elizabeth's choosing to remarry, but he felt confident that she would not bring another man into his house. If the situation were reversed, Darcy would never have another woman at Pemberley. It would be a break in the natural order.

Reaching his quarters, he stripped down to his breeches and shirt before falling across the bed in exhaustion. Tomorrow he would leave to find his enemy. After several tomorrows, he and George Wickham would face the ultimate battle—a battle of strength, of endurance, and of fate.

★ ★ ★

The shadows draped the hedgerow surrounding the community cemetery as Darcy edged along its perimeter. The graveyard backed up to the land identified as belonging to Wickham. Hot and sweaty and dust covered from his four-day ride, he wanted a bath and a warm bed, but death waited in a place where appearance made no difference. A deep hushed silence permeated the air. Darcy would cross the cemetery to circle behind the house that Wickham occupied.

Weaving his way among the headstones, an eddy of soft mist dampened his boots. The moonlight, shredded by the bare-leafed boughs, flickered off the granite, allowing him to read bits and pieces of epitaphs: Loving Father, Angel, Dearest Child, Peace. He crept now, on all fours, to the center of the graveyard. Resting his back against the cool stone, he caught his breath. "Elizabeth," he groaned. It was for *her* that he had come—for her more than anything. Closing his eyes, her tear-stained face rose in his memory. Darcy hated the fact that his last image of Elizabeth was one of her in tears—tears he had caused.

Pushing the picture of his wife back into his heart, he shoved away from the stone while allowing his fingers to trace the engraving. A cloud moved aside, and the words glowed: Ellender D'Arcy Benning. The irony of finding the stone that signaled the beginning of this madness rang wildly with mimicry. "Let us end this," he whispered, and moved forward again.

Finally, he made his way through the hedge shrubs, moving cautiously through the shadows. He would sacrifice himself for Georgiana, for his family name, but most of all, for Elizabeth. Up until this moment, a feeling of doom had followed him, but now tranquility came. If it was his fate to die here on this day, then die he gladly would.

A window glowed faintly with light, and Darcy crawled unevenly along the ground until he crouched beneath its sill. Unsurprisingly, the house itself smelled of old blood and bones. Peering inside, Darcy thought it all looked eerily ordinary, like a country manor house, except for the fact that a phantom circle moved about the middle of the room—trancelike—maintaining their distance from one another and from a center ornate chair occupied by Wickham himself. No one spoke, yet mumbled chanting—rhythmic and haunting—filled the air.

Looking closer, Darcy could see that the *throne* chair was an uncommon furnishing; it was made of earth, rich with decaying matter and coated with the same grey ashes he and Elizabeth had found at Amelia Younge's house. Wickham, intent on the display, simply smiled and looked all-knowing. Then his gaze fell on the window where Darcy watched, and Darcy knew they saw each other as clearly as if daylight shone. The moment they had both anticipated was upon them.

In a flash, the shades, which had looped around Wickham, formed a semicircle, enclosing Darcy in a ghostly prison. Pathetic monsters, they waited for him to react—to move—ready to respond with a sad compulsion not their own. Darcy recognized Lydia Bennet among them and murmured a prayer for her salvation. Among all these, she would be his target. He would use what skills he had to free Elizabeth's sister from a macabre immortality.

Sounds and sensations came from the distance—from the graveyard behind them—a graveyard full of the same kind of souls dancing to an eerie tune. Wickham appeared on the periphery of his vision as Darcy surveyed the scene. "Ah, Darcy, you came." He floated among those swaying in place, waiting for his command.

"You knew I would."

Wickham nodded, a vacuous smile clinging to his face. "For you, at last, it all comes down to this. I must admit you were a worthy opponent; I almost hate to see it end."

A loud rushing in his ears told Darcy that the chanting had increased. Riveting his attention on those closest to him, Darcy extended his arms, letting the energy flow outward, but it made no difference. His power could not stop the dead, and Wickham's followers pushed forward, crowding Darcy against the wall.

"Farewell, Darcy." Wickham offered a brief salute as he turned towards the cemetery.

Darcy pulled the iron crucifix from his pocket, holding it in his left hand, and he raised the silver sword in the other. A few of these apparitions would know heaven tonight, starting with Lydia Bennet. He angled his body to meet her assault first. The others did not matter.

From the right, he felt the skin along his arm tear as the claws of one of the coven slashed him, but Darcy did not even lower the sword. His attention rested purely on Lydia's approach. He held the crucifix higher and began his prayer. "Our Father, who art in heaven." His voice rang out clearly, resonating in the night air. Lydia Bennet's specter moved closer, near enough for Darcy's reach, and in a moment of triumph, he touched the relic to her forehead and continued the prayer. The others tore at him, but Darcy concentrated all his power on Elizabeth's sister. "Hallowed be thy name." Claws crisscrossed his cheek, tearing at his eye socket, but he steadfastly pressed the holy symbol against Lydia's head, demanding that the demons be exorcised forever. "Thy kingdom come, thy will be done." Still he held Lydia to him. "Deliver us from evil," he shouted; as her scream exploded, a bloody swirl of vapor poured forth from her mouth before crystallizing and falling to the ground. The shell of her body turned leathery and shriveled as Darcy pressed her downward.

Now, the others attacked him with full force. He spun and turned and twisted, fighting one after another. The sword and the crucifix took their tolls, but the combined effort was too much for him. They tore at him, blood gushed everywhere, tongues lapped at his wounds, and still they pressed him harder against the grey stone wall. Unable to see any longer, he leaned his head back and slid down the wall in defeat. The ghoulish apparitions covered him, tearing away his skin and sinking in their teeth to drain away what was left of his soul. As they smothered him, his mouth formed one last word: Elizabeth.

She bolted upright in the bed, her gown soaked with sweat. Elizabeth brought her trembling hand to her face, shoving the hair away. The image of Darcy's blood-spattered face still hung in the air. Her jagged breath was the only sound in the inn's small bedchamber. Elizabeth fought to control her breathing, gulping air into her lungs. A cold shiver shook her as tears erupted from the corners of her eyes. It was all so real; unable to stop herself, Elizabeth glanced at the foot of the bed, half expecting to find Darcy lying in a bloody pool at her feet. Feeling the coolness of the room, she pulled the blanket around her like a shawl and began to rock herself back and forth, in the same rhythmic swaying of the souls in her dream. The beating of her heart slowed, but the image did not fade. For hours, she remained as such, seeking warmth that was not there and trying to wash away the dread that suffused her every thought.

CHAPTER 23

Streaks of sunlight cleared away clouds from the late December sky as Darcy slipped into his sister's room. Only the dying embers of the fireplace provided warmth, and he was half tempted to stoke the fire so Georgiana might be more comfortable, but he would not wake her. Standing by her bed and looking down at her, he noted how she grew lovelier every day, looking very much like their father's forebearers. There were portraits in the gallery of some of the earlier Darcy households, and he saw the resemblance in many of them. When he was younger, he had searched the faces, looking for someone who he resembled. He had to go back five generations to find his eyes and his chin line. These thoughts on such a day were silent ramblings, but somehow they gave Darcy a sense of completeness. He belonged to this family—to this girl—to this curse.

He gently pulled the bed linens over her shoulders and tucked them in about his sister before placing the letter on the nightstand. "I love you, Georgie," he mouthed and then turned for the door.

When he was nearly out of the room, her sleepy voice stopped his progress. "Fitzwilliam?"

Darcy returned to her side. "I am sorry I woke you, Sweetling. Go back to sleep." He moved a strand of her hair away from her eyes. "I am to be away from Pemberley for a few days; I left you a note explaining everything."

"Will you go after Elizabeth?"

Darcy shook his head. "I cannot. Elizabeth must be with her family now."

Georgiana struggled to sit up in bed. "Elizabeth will return?"

He looked away and forced himself to swallow the hurt. "It would be my wish, Sweetling, that you and Elizabeth share a life together…best friends. You can learn a great deal from my wife."

"But not without you?" she insisted.

"Unfortunately, Elizabeth possesses reasons to hate me. I am not under the persuasion that she will return." How could he explain? "Georgiana, George Wickham took Elizabeth's youngest sister. The girl is now one of the walking dead, and Wickham did it as revenge against our family—against me, specifically, because I foolishly challenged him. How could Elizabeth forgive my arrogance?"

Realization of what he planned hit the girl full force, and she clutched at his hand. "Fitzwilliam, you cannot go off alone to find Wickham! How will I face this without your guidance?"

"It is the only thing—the only honorable thing—I can give Elizabeth…the only thing I can do for this family."

"Elizabeth loves you, Brother; she would argue against this for you."

Darcy caressed her cheek, feeling the warmth of her skin against the coolness of his palm. "Elizabeth's loyalty remains true, which will strain her relationship with her parents and her sisters. She cannot tell them the reason for Lydia's demise or admit her share of the blame. I know Elizabeth; she will exile herself from her family. She will need someone to whom to turn. Be that someone, Georgiana; Elizabeth will respond in kind. The two of you will be a formidable pair. I have outlined what must be done for the estate and for your future. You and Elizabeth will want for nothing; I have seen to it all."

Georgiana's tears escaped, although she fought to be strong for him. "Do not go," she whispered.

Darcy wiped away her tears with his thumbs. "I will make you one promise before I leave you, my darling girl. If somehow I survive this confrontation, I will find Elizabeth, and I will beg her on bended knee to return to us. I will humble myself at her feet and not take *no* for an answer."

"You *do* love her? I *knew* you did!" The tears began again.

"With all my heart." Darcy pulled his sister to him. "With all my heart that I have not given to you." He kissed the top of Georgiana's head. "I will journey far and the weather may not hold, so I must be on my way. Stay here where it is warm. Smile for me, my girl. That is the picture of you I wish to take to Northumberland with me."

Elizabeth traveled for nearly two hours, but the previous night's rain, leaving large ruts in the road's normally smooth surface, slowed her progress. She asked Peter to stop at the next inn; she desperately needed to stretch her legs. A dull headache remained from the nightmarish images, which had haunted her aborted sleep. She could not shake the image of a bloody Darcy speaking her name. *How much of the dream is true?* That question troubled her waking hours. With the other dreams, parts of them were predictions that were fulfilled, and parts were events that had already occurred. She could not *bear* the thought of what she had seen happening to Darcy. Yet what could she do? She needed to go to her family. Besides, her helping Darcy only put him in more danger—dividing his priorities. At least, that was what she told herself.

The carriage, thankfully, rolled to a stop. As Peter scrambled down from the seat, Elizabeth righted herself and straightened her clothing. Peter jerked open the door and let down the steps. "Here we be, Mrs. Darcy." He offered her a hand down.

Elizabeth took a few gingerly steps, testing her legs. "Thank you, Peter." She patted his hand before stepping away. "I promise that I will not be long. I just need some tea to settle my stomach." She motioned to Hannah, her maid, to follow her once she checked on the belongings.

"Of course, Mrs. Darcy. I will just be tendin' the horses. We can start out again whenever you be ready."

"You get something, too, Peter. Tell them to put it on my account." She walked stiffly towards the inn. Few horses or carriages were in the yard, and Elizabeth thought she might find the peace and quiet refreshing. The rattle of the carriage seemed deafening today.

A stout innkeeper rushed forward when he saw her enter. Well-dressed women tended to demand immediate attention, and the man recognized the quality of her clothes. "Good day, Ma'am, may I be of help?"

"I just need some refreshment. Be sure that someone aids my driver and my maid, and see that they get something also." She took off her gloves and her bonnet. "I will sit over there." Elizabeth gestured to a table along the wall.

"Yes, Ma'am," he said and gave a thick-waisted bow. "Me wife will be right over."

Elizabeth settled herself at the table, placing her outer garment on one of the chairs. She shrugged her shoulders several times to loosen the tension. It was not a big inn, but everything appeared clean and well polished.

A stout woman waddled towards the table. "What might we be gettin' you, Ma'am?"

Elizabeth recognized that it was unusual for a woman to travel alone, and it was important to let everyone know with her tone that she was no fool when it came to proper service. "I would like some tea, and if you have some sweetmeats or tartlets, that would be wonderful."

"I be findin' you some of the best sweetmeats in the country, Ma'am." The innkeeper's wife took off at a trot.

Elizabeth sighed deeply. She really did not care for the sweet refreshments, but she would eat a few and box up the rest. Her maid had a sweet tooth and would appreciate the gesture. In only a few minutes, the tea arrived, and she sat stirring it mindlessly.

Engrossed in her own reflections, Elizabeth took no note of the gentleman striding purposefully towards the door upon leaving the taproom, but just as he reached the exit, he realized he had dropped one of his gloves. Turning quickly in place, the man searched the floor in the direction from which he had come. "Ah, there it is." He bent to retrieve the item, but then his eyes drifted to the woman seated alone. Shocked to see her there, the words burst from his mouth. "Elizabeth...I mean, Mrs. Darcy?" He made a quick bow from across the room. "What in the world are you doing here?" He came forward as he spoke.

Elizabeth jumped to her feet upon hearing her name. "Colonel Fitz—Fitzwilliam!" she stammered.

Immediately, he took her hand in his two large hands and gestured to the chair. "Please be seated." He looked around, as if expecting Darcy to come through the door. "May I join you, Ma'am?"

"Certainly, Colonel." Elizabeth looked away in embarrassment. She would need to explain to Darcy's cousin why she had left Pemberley without her husband.

Damon Fitzwilliam sat next to her. "I am in amazement to find you in this out-of-the-way inn, Mrs. Darcy. I would not think my cousin would allow you out of his sight so soon after your nuptials." He gestured to the innkeeper to bring him another tankard of ale.

Elizabeth stalled; she took a sip of her tea before she answered. "My mother is ill, and my papa is distraught. We have experienced a family tragedy, Sir."

"I offer my condolences." She acknowledged his words with a slight nod. "Yet I am still at a loss as to why your husband does not travel with you. There are many things one might say about Darcy, but ignoring his responsibilities is not one of them."

The reappearance of the woman with her sweetmeats and his tankard gave Elizabeth a moment to decide how to answer. The truth—as much as she could offer—seemed the best bet. Obviously, Darcy's family would soon know of their separation. "How candid might I be, Colonel?"

"Personally, I can think of only one reason for your separation from my cousin. I asked Darcy before he married if you were aware of his unique situation, and he assured me that you knew *everything*. Darcy loves you. Otherwise, he would not have brought you into his life." His words demanded she speak honestly.

"My husband, I assure you, Colonel, owns my heart!"

He took a drink of the ale and studied her closely. She was not what he had considered her to be when he met Elizabeth Bennet in London. "I have all the time in the world, Mrs. Darcy, and sometimes it is best to get another opinion."

Elizabeth nibbled on the sweetmeat, and although it had nothing to do with the woman's cooking, it certainly tasted bitter. "May I assume, Colonel, that you know of the pox which haunts my husband?"

"As I share guardianship of Georgiana with Darcy, he confessed his concerns to me about the Darcy legacy. No one else in the family knows. My father is a Fitzwilliam, as was Darcy's mother. The aberration travels through the Darcy line, and I doubt my father would welcome the knowledge of what James Darcy did to his sister. It would explain Lady Anne's withdrawal from her husband and also her weakened condition." He leaned forward to ensure secrecy. "My cousin has not infected you, Madam?"

"No...no, Colonel. My husband refuses to continue the family curse over to another generation." She blushed thoroughly at sharing such intimacies. "Mr. Darcy is a man of honor."

"Then you must explain what caused this sudden departure. You do sound as if you wanted this removal. I will not judge, so please be honest. I cannot imagine how both of you must suffer with such an arrangement." He cradled her hand in both of his as he spoke.

Tears misted Elizabeth's eyes. It would be helpful to share some things with another, even one of Darcy's family—to speak some of her thoughts aloud. "Do you know of Mr. Wickham, Colonel?" Her bottom lip trembled with the memory.

"I am aware of the menace that Mr. Wickham created for my cousin." He guarded the emotion shooting through him.

"Yesterday, I received two letters from my eldest sister, the one you met at the wedding. She reported the disappearance of Lydia, our youngest. A man disguised as Colonel Forster, the commanding officer of our local militia, convinced my father to allow Lydia to attend Christmas festivities in London with him and Mrs. Forster. Through putting details together, it is quite obvious that the man who took my sister was no man at all; it was George Wickham. My family, at first, suspected an elopement. But as another officer is accused of a heinous murder similar to the ones that brought your cousin and me together, Mr. Darcy and I are sure Wickham committed that murder and also made my dear, sweet Lydia one of *his own*."

Colonel Fitzwilliam added cautiously, "And this brought unfair accusations on both your parts?"

"Oh, Colonel, I said the most *hurtful* things to Fitzwilliam." Her tears flowed easily now. "How could I have been so stupid? It was not my husband's fault, but I stormed out, and now I know not what to do."

"I suspect we should order you more tea, and you will tell me everything." He handed her his handkerchief and motioned the innkeeper over. "Mr. Witherspoon, Mrs. Darcy is my cousin's wife." He needed to prevent rumors as to why they might be together. The colonel stopped regularly at this inn, and he wanted no gossip about an assignation. "Imagine my meeting her along the London Road! We will catch up on family news for a few minutes, so please freshen the lady's tea and ask your good wife if she has any of those delicious rolls I love."

"Immediately, Colonel." The man made his way to the back of the inn.

For the next hour, Elizabeth told Darcy's cousin how her own family was part of the curse, how she had met Darcy, how Wickham had killed the bar maid and Miss King in Meryton, how she and Darcy fought Wickham and Amelia Younge in London, how they had studied the books for knowledge of vampires, and how Mrs. Annesley believed that Elizabeth's dreams were the key to defeating Wickham. "The dream from last night haunts me even now. Fitzwilliam fought Wickham's followers and lost. It was so real, Colonel, that I expected to see a bloody body at the foot of my bed." She shivered in remembrance.

"Where is Wickham?" Colonel Fitzwilliam demanded.

"His carriage was seen leaving London and heading north. Recently, Mr. Darcy received a report from Bramwell's men saying that Wickham has a house in Stanwick, above Chillingham. Fitzwilliam did not want to follow Wickham there; he feared putting me in danger. I read the report, though. Wickham keeps himself isolated from the village; he would not need supplies like a normal man would, and the village took note of his hermitlike habits. Reportedly, the neighborhood burned down Wickham's ancestral home two hundred years ago—or at least, that is the legend—when Leána's hunger became his. They tried to burn out the evil. Of course, no one in the hamlet realizes it is the same creature of old. They think the current Mr. Wickham is a descendant of the one their ancestors tried to destroy. His new house is built on part of the original land, which makes sense because of how a vampire needs earth from his homeland to survive. Fitzwilliam and I thought the ashes we found in the room that Wickham used in Mrs. Younge's house must be from the foundation of that original house. It was after the fire that he swore revenge on the D'Arcy family."

"Then my cousin has left for Stanwick?"

Elizabeth froze with his words. "He would not! Fitzwilliam cannot face Wickham alone!" She started up from the table, but the colonel's hand on her arm stayed her.

His words were ominous. "Mrs. Darcy, you know my cousin as well as anyone. Can you imagine his sitting at Pemberley while Wickham flaunts his possession of your sister?"

"I taunted him about removing Lydia's head to release her soul." She sat down, as if in a trance, as she recalled her cruel words. "Fitzwilliam said he would do whatever was necessary to end her wanderings." Elizabeth grabbed the colonel's hand. "We have to help him. Fitzwilliam cannot defeat Wickham by himself. My *dream* says so. I must return to Pemberley immediately."

"Darcy is not there!" His words spoke the truth that she did not want to acknowledge. "If you left Pemberley by noon yesterday, I would venture to say that Darcy left for Northumberland shortly afterwards—by this morning, at the latest. Our going all the way to Pemberley would be fruitless."

Agitated, Elizabeth asserted, "I must go to Northumberland."

"*We* will go," the colonel said, taking command. "First, we need to lighten your coach so we travel faster. Have your maid pack you one case, enough clothes for a week's journey. Darcy will have gone by horseback, which means he will arrive at least a full day before us, but he must come across Derbyshire; we have more of a straight shot to Newcastle." The colonel was planning battle maneuvers. "We may have to stay together at some inns along the way, so I pray, my dear, that you are not prudish. I will make a pallet on the floor. In some areas, it would not be safe for you to stay alone." He began picking up his gloves. "I assume Darcy provided you funds before you left Pemberley."

"I have my pin money, and Fitzwilliam had Mrs. Reynolds bring me five hundred pounds."

"Perfect! We will leave your maid and the excess baggage here. I will send word to Pemberley for someone to come and retrieve her and the baggage. Your coachman and I will take turns driving the carriage. Even with that, it will take us four to five days to reach the Scottish border. Hurry, Mrs. Darcy. We must be on the road."

He took over the dismissal of the maid's services, over the woman's protestations. Elizabeth paid for their food, the horse's feed, and a room with board for the maid for two days. She asked the innkeeper to make a basket out of which the three of them—she, the colonel, and Peter—could partake on the road.

Within thirty minutes, they were headed north. "Thank you, Colonel." The words broke the smothering silence.

"My dear, no thanks are necessary. Darcy is my family." He changed his seat to sit beside her. "What I am going to need, Elizabeth, is for you to tell me everything you know about vampires. I want to know what the books say, what your intuition tells you, and what Mrs. Annesley believes to be your role in Darcy's fate."

Elizabeth realized the colonel had assigned her a job in asking for her insights. He would keep her focused on the task at hand, and she was thankful for his interference. How much she had learned of vampire legends and facts amazed her. After two hours, he took over the reins, and Peter climbed into the carriage. The coachman made his apologies to Elizabeth, but explained that the colonel wanted him to rest, for they would not stop until nightfall. Then the man curled up on the opposite seat and went immediately to sleep.

Elizabeth followed suit. She had slept very little the night before, and she would need all her wits to help Darcy defeat Wickham. She settled back into the luxurious seats of Darcy's coach. They reminded her of him—warm and comfortable. Automatically, she turned her head into the material and inhaled deeply. She fancied that she could smell the man she loved—sandalwood and masculinity. Breathing in deeply again, she closed her eyes and tried to feel Darcy around her—the muscles of his arms tight and pulling her closer—the heat of his breath hot on the back of her neck—the hunger of his mouth as he kissed her. "Please, God," she whispered, not wishing Peter to hear her prayer.

That evening, the colonel registered them as man and wife at a rowdy inn along the main road. They took a room over the bar, both of them expecting little sleep because of the noise. They had dinner in a semiprivate room with two other couples, so their conversation remained on mundane subjects—mostly his family in Matlock.

"Will they not wonder what happened to you?" she whispered.

"I sent word that I was called to Newcastle unexpectedly. My parents are used to my position interfering with family obligations."

She blurted out, "Would you tell me about Fitzwilliam's life? Surprisingly, I know little of his childhood."

"My cousin was groomed from an early age to be the Master of Pemberley...." Elizabeth listened for three quarters of an hour as Darcy's cousin lovingly shared anecdote after anecdote about a young Darcy and the mischief the two of them often found themselves a part of. "Unfortunately, much of that carefree youthfulness left him at sixteen. My aunt, Lady Anne, never recovered from giving birth to Georgiana, and when the girl was but age four, their mother passed. Darcy felt the loss deeply. He promised his mother on her deathbed to protect Georgiana. Filled with guilt, Lady Anne begged Darcy's forgiveness for allowing the curse to continue—for plaguing him with such a blighted future—for permitting her weakness to ruin her son's life. It was the moment the epiphany came—the moment all those misgivings about his own sanity—about any deviation he might possess—became clear. Darcy's life changed with her words. He was no longer free to consider a life every other man might choose. There would be no wife—no children—no future. Everything he did would be for Georgiana. Shortly after that, he withdrew from society as much as possible, except to give Georgiana a passage into a world he would never know. He swore on all that is holy, he would never bring a child of his own into this world. For twelve years, he adhered to that promise, but then you entered Darcy's life." He cast Elizabeth a glance.

"I am sure, Colonel, that my husband explained how we were caught in a compromising situation." Elizabeth blushed with her own admission.

"Mrs. Darcy, you fool only yourself if you believe that your situation would have forced my cousin to do something he did not want to do. He could easily have thrown enough money at it to make it go away—money enough for dowries for you and all your sisters, for example. And although Darcy is the most honorable of men, you were not ruined in the worst sense. In the country, rumors might persist, but censure is not so daunting. There was something more, and Darcy knew it."

"Would you not consider, Colonel, the possibility that Mr. Darcy married me simply to protect me from a danger he had brought into my life?"

"I have no doubt, Elizabeth, that Darcy pondered that fact when he first considered your union, but he could have protected you by simply withdrawing from you, taking Wickham's interest with him. Darcy married you because he saw *hope* for his life in your eyes. With you, he knew some sort of unvarying viability." Damon took her hand in his before adding, "You should have seen Darcy's hot-blooded reaction when my father questioned his motivation for marrying you, my dear. Truthfully, Darcy's reaction delighted my parents and me. We had watched him become more and more reticent—disavowing all human feelings in a permanent ebb of emotion. Finally, he showed anger, but also he laughed.... Darcy became the passionate, although a bit selfish, man we all knew he could be if given a chance to love, and his family rejoiced in a way we had never thought possible."

His honesty disturbed her, and Elizabeth stood upon this proclamation. "You have provided me much food for thought. If you will excuse me, Sir, I will prepare for sleep." She leaned in, as if to make a private remark to her husband. "I will make you a proper pallet in front of the fire if you give me a few extra minutes."

"With pleasure, my dear," he said loudly enough to maintain the illusion.

Thirty minutes later, the colonel slipped into their room. Elizabeth had dressed modestly for the night and burrowed under the blankets. Only the fire from the fireplace provided light. Damon chuckled when he saw how she had used the furniture to build a wall between them—to maintain privacy. He undressed down to his breeches before wrapping himself in the blankets and cushions she had placed in the makeshift bed. "We will leave early tomorrow. I told Peter to have the carriage ready by seven." He spoke to the darkness surrounding them, but the colonel knew she did not sleep.

Elizabeth pushed herself up on one arm. "Colonel, will we get there in time to help Fitzwilliam?"

It was the words he knew they had shoved to the backs of their minds since the moment they decided to follow Darcy to Northumberland. "I certainly hope so, Elizabeth, for I fear Darcy's recklessness could have dire consequences otherwise." He heard a quick intake of breath, as his prediction became a reality for her. Trying to change the serious atmosphere, he teased, "Mrs. Darcy, are there any more like you in Hertfordshire?"

Elizabeth relaxed back into the bed, recognizing the ploy. "Your cousin thinks I am unique—more adventurous than proper young ladies of the *ton*."

"Then I dare say, Mrs. Darcy, my cousin took the best of the litter." With that, he pulled the blankets around his ears and pre-tended to drift off to sleep. Elizabeth Darcy was a mystery; for once, he actually envied his cousin's life.

Four hours north of where they slept, Darcy settled onto a lumpy mattress in an attic room of a cheap country inn. He had ridden across back roads most of the day, angling his way from the westernmost part of Derbyshire towards the Lake District and then still farther north and east. As he tried to force sleep to come to his exhausted frame, he pictured the face of Elizabeth that day in the snowstorm when he told her he loved her. *Because I did not get the chance to tell my husband I am completely and hopelessly in love with him.* "Ah, Elizabeth," he whispered while trying to maintain the picture in his head. Within a few days, she would be free of him forever.

CHAPTER 24

The second evening on the road, Elizabeth realized early in the day that it was New Year's Eve. Since her marriage to Darcy, she had developed an idealized concept of what ringing in the New Year with her husband would be like. She marked it as a new beginning for their shared life. Darcy had admitted his love for her, and Elizabeth believed the date would change things for the better, making them truly husband and wife. Instead, she found herself in a country inn, trying to make conversation with her husband's cousin, and despite her gratitude to the man for his help, he simply was not Darcy. She feigned a headache from the exhausting ride and retired early, but when the colonel finally joined her in their shared room, he could not help but hear the muffled sobs that broke the silence. Elizabeth cried for the loss of a great love, and the colonel wondered if he would ever know such torment and such pleasure.

For three days, Elizabeth taught Damon Fitzwilliam everything she knew about George Wickham and how to vanquish vampires. At each of the stops, they took on weapons and supplies as they found them. Silver and iron, and staves of ash and white thorn were bundled into blankets and tied securely to the Darcy carriage. In small villages, they bought several crucifixes, cloves of garlic, bags of salt, and wooden stakes. Even buying several bags of millet seemed prudent at one such stop. By silent agreement, they prepared for war, knowing that if Darcy failed, only *they* stood between Wickham and a continuation of evil.

They expected to be in the area described in Bramwell's report by late the next afternoon or early evening, depending on the weather. It was significantly colder than in Derbyshire, but to their surprise, they met no snow or rain. The colonel and Peter kept a steady pace with the horses, not pressing them too strenuously, knowing Northumberland and the counties surrounding it to be some of the least-populated land in England. Inns were fewer and farther between, and the opportunities for changing the horses for fresh ones were scarce. They traveled to an area nearly halfway between Alnwick and Berwick.

"A stake through the heart, a coin in the mouth, decapitate with an ax, boil the head in vinegar, chain to the grave with wild roses, bury at a crossroads—my God, the list goes on and on. How will we *ever know* what to do?!" The colonel began to feel the frustration she had known weeks earlier.

"We will listen to our intuition. Actually, I have a theory about all this. It depends on when the person died. What I mean is, different generations placed their beliefs in different symbols; that is why so much is unknown about how to do this. Besides, it is not as if there exists a vampire hunter instruction book!"

The colonel laughed at her assertion. "Do you suppose there be a market for one? We might be able to author such a tome after this." He settled back into the cushions of the carriage. "Maybe it is the nationality difference of which you speak, rather than a generational one," he mused. "It seems that many of the items have some relationship to purifying wounds or curing illnesses."

Elizabeth weighed what the man said. Over the past few days, she had developed a real respect for her husband's cousin. If she had met the colonel first, she might have set her sights on him. Shorter than Darcy, but not by much, the colonel was well made. Long, dark lashes capped dark brown eyes, which matched his head of thick brown curly hair. He possessed a compelling, almost sensual, masculinity. She appreciated his logic and his amiability and his arresting wit. Damon Fitzwilliam was not as intense in his interactions as her husband, but he was attractive, although for her, Darcy spoke of manliness and charisma and love. She shook her head, trying to clear her thoughts. They avoided speaking of the possibility of Darcy's already being in Stanwick. Meticulously, the colonel silently estimated how long it would take Darcy to reach the former Scottish territory from Derbyshire. He determined how long Darcy might spend in the saddle each day, and he was sure that his cousin would be there by that very day, if not already in residence in the area. Yet they would not speak of that probability. Elizabeth and the colonel would either find Darcy a victor or find Darcy dead or find the battle still in progress. They would react accordingly.

"One of the things of which I am relatively sure is that Wickham does not believe in the Trinity. I have witnessed how he *retreats* from symbols of Christianity, but they do not *destroy* him. Fitzwilliam threw holy water on him in the confrontation over Georgiana, but all it got him was a scream, the smell of burning skin, and a momentary withdrawal on Wickham's part. I had more success with the name reversal in London than my husband did with his attempts at Ramsgate. The crucifix will work on my sister, but not on Wickham."

"Is Wickham that close to the Devil to be immune to symbols of God?"

"Wickham is closer to his own gods. Mrs. Annesley discovered the god Cernunnos, a classic stag-horned god of Celtic origin. The crown everyone describes as a mark on Wickham's hand resembles the ram-horned serpent of the Meigle stone in Perthshire, which everyone identifies as Cernunnos. Some believe Cernunnos is the figure encountered in the tale of King Arthur and the Lady of the Lake. Even Shakespeare mentions Cernunnos as Herne the Hunter. Anyway, the ash stakes should be effective in that realm."

The colonel looked out the carriage window, noting that Peter had turned off the main road and was headed towards the inn they had discussed earlier. "What will you do if we find that Darcy did not survive?" The words hung in the air, a curtain of doubt between them.

"I will try to recover both my husband's and my sister's bodies and put them at rest. Then I will return to Longbourn."

"You will not go back to Pemberley?" He turned his head to look closely at her.

"Pemberley belongs to Georgiana," she argued.

Colonel Fitzwilliam returned his gaze to the window. "Darcy would provide for you. I am sure he would want you to be a part of his sister's life."

"Georgiana has you, Sir. She does not need me. I barely scratched the surface in making my way there. In fact, the staff members probably find me most scandalous."

The colonel chuckled at her assertion. "Perhaps. If…if my cousin cannot be saved, as Georgiana's only other guardian, I would be grateful if you would return to Pemberley, Mrs. Darcy. Your intuition is good, and I am sure my young cousin could learn much from you."

Elizabeth was silent, but she was touched by the sentiment. Aloud, she said, "Let us not face that decision until it is necessary, Sir."

★ ★ ★

Darcy scouted the area after his arrival at the local inn. It would be dark soon, and he needed to become familiar with the lay of the land before it was too black to see the details of the buildings. A several-hours' ride northeast of Chillingham, the village of Stanwick was little more than a turning-off point for Edinburgh.

Wickham's residence could be accessed only by one of two ways: through the churchyard and cemetery and then down a treacherously steep hill and through a wooded field or the direct route of over a drawbridge, across an open courtyard, and through the front door of the moderate-sized house. Darcy could not get close enough to see into the house, but some carefully placed questions told him that the few steps led to an unadorned open hall, evidently used as the center of activity for Wickford Manor. A few of the more adventurous youths gladly told him how the pantry in the kitchen was totally bare and the well was only for show, because no water was ever seen within it. From the road, Darcy could see that the garden and the lawn, although naturally dormant in winter, still showed signs of neglect and overgrowth.

Thinking the churchyard a better choice for his approach, he tried to appear casual as he strolled through the graveyard, pausing periodically to read epitaphs: *Make Wisdom Your Provision for the Journey from Youth to Old Age* and *Ye Shall Know the Truth* and *True Nobility Is Exempt from Fear* were mixed with *The Music of My Life, Matthew Horace* and *Charles McDane, Loving Father* and *Behold the Child, Mary Adams.* Circling the perimeter of the cemetery, he stumbled across the Winchcombe headstones of Mairte Rosin and Domhnall Neill. He suspected them to be those of Wickham's parents, because they were the last ones before one exited the rear of the neighborhood's churchyard. He would not find Wickham's grave here. The great evil associated with George Wickham prohibited his inclusion in consecrated land. More than likely, Wickham's house was designed to embrace his own grave.

Then his eyes fell upon the dual crypts dominating the center of the site. Without reading the engraving, Darcy knew to whom they belonged. These two faced in towards the center of the cemetery, as if they stood staring into each other's eyes for eternity. Darcy could see them in his mind's eye—Lady Ellender D'Arcy and Lord Arawn Benning, circling each other on the dance floor… preparing to rush into each other's arms in a moment of passion… arguing heatedly over some domestic matter.

Slowly and methodically, Darcy made his way around different mounds until he stood reverently before the locked gate of the memorial to the woman who had begun this madness with her beauty: Ellender D'Arcy Benning. "Would you do it all again?" Darcy murmured, but he knew the answer—she would. Ellender D'Arcy did what she did for the love of a man, the one person who completed her—the way Elizabeth completed him. Darcy had no doubts that he would risk it all for *his Elizabeth.* He turned to stare at the other crypt, the one belonging to Elizabeth's ancestor. The irony of how Fate brought him to this moment and to loving Elizabeth could not ignored.

Sighing, Darcy strode away from the all-too-raw memories of his wife. He worked his way down the well-worn path leading away from the graveyard towards the wooded field, which he crossed quickly, wanting to see the back of the house before the dark set in.

Finally satisfying his need for information, he retreated to the inn. Tonight, while the village slept, he would return to find Wickham and to finish their *battle,* one way or the other.

Near midnight, dressed all in black except for a loose-fitting shirt he had bought in the village store, Darcy made his way through the graveyard once more. Instead of hiding behind headstones and staying in the shadows of the hedgerow, he strode proudly through the center of the land of the dead, crossing the point where the crypts might touch. He carried a silver sword and wore the iron crucifix, but his true weapon, he told himself, was his determination. He had come to end the plague on his family, and, one way or the other, Darcy would know peace at last. Two hundred years of demonic hatred and fear would end with this confrontation.

Edging his way down the steep slope, his boots loosened pebbles, which cascaded in a rain of dirt down to the bottom. He cared not whether someone might hear. The living were safe in their beds, and Darcy was sure Wickham knew that eventually he would come.

He slowed his steps as he emerged from the woods. Only fifteen paces away, a dim light reflected off the windows of the central room. Darcy moved more cautiously now—weaving his way to where he might see what the room offered. Plastering himself against the grey stone of an exterior wall, the cold shale caused a shiver to run the length of his spine. The shutters were slanted outward, but the openings between the slats provided a clear enough view of the interior. Wickham sat at the end of an expansive table, facing the window. As if on cue, he raised his hand in a salute, the way he always did in farewell; and then Wickham's lackeys, who had materialized out of the mist creeping along the ground, surrounded Darcy.

Darcy smiled, despite the danger. After all, this was why he had come. Wielding the sword in his right hand, he stepped away from the house, although he left his back to the wall. When the first apparition stepped menacingly in front of him, Darcy simply swung the sword, arcing in a downward thrust, hacking at the woman's neck. A second whack from the opposite direction took off the head a few inches above the shoulders. Years of removing the heads of Wickham's victims provided him enough practice to be somewhat efficient in the motion. A shrill cry of despair filled the air as the body turned to a skeleton. A bloody mist, smelling of decaying waste, floated upward before congealing and drifting away like fiery embers in a breeze. "One down," he said as he smirked.

Boldly reciting "The Lord's Prayer" as he stepped now to the left, Darcy swung the crucifix he carried from its chain, keeping the next set of attackers at a healthy distance. A parry and a basic thrust through the heart sent another soul to heaven. The crucifix smacked an abandoned spirit, and a repugnant somnambulist screamed out, as if burned, and then followed the fate of those struck by Darcy's blade.

Inflamed now with success, Darcy attacked more diligently, striking first with the sword and then with the holy relic, but with each release, two more dusky fiends took its place. "It is too late, Darcy," a cold breath whispered in his ear, but still he fought on. He tried desperately to stave off the encroaching *army*, but a vaporous stench surrounded and smothered him, and one final blow to the back of his head—one snapping his neck violently forward—sent him first to his knees and then into a complete darkness.

He did not know how long he remained unconscious, but when he opened his eyes, greyish blue ones, only inches from his face, stared back at him. It took several blinks of his lids before the reality of his situation became evident. He was not dead, but he was Wickham's prisoner. His arms ached from the battle, and Darcy tried in vain to move them, only to find them presently lodged behind him. Wickham's face withdrew, and Darcy struggled to right himself.

"That was a fine display, Darcy." Wickham found his enemy's grappling to be amusing. "You took more than a dozen of my favorites with that exhibition of your swordsmanship."

Darcy licked his lips, tasting his own bloody inner jaw. "I would have preferred twice that many." Darcy forced himself to return Wickham's smirk. "I hoped you would be among them, Wickham."

"I am sorry I could not accommodate you." Wickham sat down in an ornate chair, leaned back in it, and crossed his legs at his ankles.

Darcy looked about him, trying to assess the depth of his situation. "Where am I?"

"In the house's root cellar." Wickham gestured at the bare walls. "I am afraid that I entertain so very little, and my lack of hospitality must be evident."

Darcy tried to look over his shoulder to see what bound him. He shook his hands and heard the rattle of chains. "And why am I so restricted? Do you fear me so, Wickham?"

"Your power increases, Darcy, since your alliance with Mrs. Darcy. Your once-latent interest in your abilities blossomed with the appearance of Elizabeth Bennet in your life." Wickham appeared to be amused again. "*Unfortunately* for you, and I suppose *fortunately* for me, you chose not to refine those innate skills." He gestured towards the chains binding Darcy to the wall. "I took note of your ability to manipulate time and space. I also noted that to do so, you must extend your arms to the sides; therefore, your current bonds."

Darcy nodded in a respectful acknowledgment of his opponent's intelligence. "How long will I be here?"

"I am not sure exactly, Darcy. I suppose it will be, at least, until your lovely wife and maybe your sister make an appearance. Someone is sure to try to save you. I will wait until I capture the whole lot. Then you will receive the pleasure of witnessing my repeatedly taking the two of them and claiming your loved ones as my own." Wickham paused suddenly and looked off wistfully. "I wonder, Darcy, if you know how much your sister resembles Ellender?" He seemed momentarily sad, but then he returned to his threat. "You will beg me to let you die, seeing Mrs. Darcy and the innocent

Georgiana willingly coming to me to feed, and only then will I grant your wish."

Staring absently at the void between them, Darcy looked off, seeing something Wickham would never recognize: the love of a fine woman. He returned his gaze to his opponent. "Elizabeth will not come. She left me, Wickham. You will be satisfied to know your maneuverings were quite successful. When Elizabeth discovered you had taken Lydia and would continue to torment those she loved because of me, she turned on me. She could not love a man who had brought such evil into her life."

Wickham allowed his eyes to betray his true pleasure. "But it was *I* who brought the evil."

"Because you hated Ellender D'Arcy for what she did to you," Darcy retorted. "My *family* brought on Elizabeth's grief."

"Actually, it was as much your *wife's* family as it was your own. Arawn Benning took everything I wanted, and then, because of his treachery, I was sacrificed. It was not bad enough that he had won Ellender; he took away my chance of finding someone else and caused the death of my parents."

"The village?" Darcy probed.

Wickham's eyes flashed. "I came back to Stanwick because I wanted retribution against the descendants of those who had turned on my parents and sent them to a fiery grave."

"An avenging angel?"

Wickham offered an honest smile. "I like that, Darcy—an apropos signature. I believe I may steal it from you. You will not mind, will you, as you will be dead by then?" He gestured at the ceiling. "Those sounds you hear above are my *pupils* dancing a waltz of sorts about the main hall. They gather there nightly, these henchmen of mine—many of them descendants of those original villagers. I have my revenge, you see. They took my parents, and, just as with your family, I choose among them. I studiously avoid the families who moved here *after* my parents' death. It is often a purulence, because I hunger for some of the more *delectable morsels,* shall we say, but it is an indiscretion I do not allow myself."

"Well, unfortunately, Wickham, you will need to be satisfied with my death only. Elizabeth has exiled herself from her family and from me. And like me, she would gladly die to end the curse." Now it was Darcy's turn to laugh. "Have you considered, Wickham, what happens to you when I die? The curse involves all of us. Even if you were to capture Elizabeth, she would, as I am doing, sacrifice herself. Then there would be no more bonding of the D'Arcy and Benning families. The curse on the D'Arcy family exists only as long as we produce first born sons. I am the last of the male line, and I refused to allow my wife to produce another. There will be no more, and soon no more villagers. Then what happens to you? If two sides of the triangle are broken, the third collapses into nothingness. It has taken two hundred years to eradicate you, but the evil will stop."

Wickham feigned nonchalance. "I thought of all this, Darcy." He stood quickly to make his departure. "I will do a little reconnoitering this evening—see if you lie about your wife's presence in the area. I am sorry to say I must lock you in. Some of my imitators might consider you an appealing meal. You are quite the delicacy. As the majority of them were brought up with Christian beliefs, I will hang your trusty crucifix on the door to dissuade them of any overwhelming desires they might have to feed on mixed blood." He hooked the chain on the latch. "Rest now, Darcy. It shall not be much longer."

Darcy leaned his chair against the wall to relax the tension on his arms. His shoulder joints throbbed from overextending the arms for so long. At this moment, he was happy Elizabeth had deserted him. She would not witness his death nor would she be in danger. He would die by Wickham's hand or by the strategy of one of those who rhythmically danced to an unknown tune above him; or he would die by his own devices. It was not likely Wickham would think to feed him, so he might starve or die of thirst or smother in his own waste, but Darcy *would* die, and there would be no more first born sons to carry on the curse. The thought satisfied him, and he closed his eyes to find some pleasure in the idea and to do as his enemy suggested: rest.

Wickham moved through the inn like a cold breeze let in through an open window. One of the women who Darcy had dispatched during the night once resided here and had foolishly invited him in. Now, he checked each of the rooms, finding no signs of Elizabeth Darcy, only the remnants of Darcy's toilette. In some ways it pleased him to know his subterfuge had played out so well, but he also regretted the possibility of meeting the formidable Mrs. Darcy again. The most recent time they met, her incantation had sent him slamming into the back wall of a bookshop, and while he recovered, Elizabeth Darcy had set Amelia Younge free with a powerful thrust of Darcy's sword. The woman was no wilting violet, that was for sure; in fact, she was a briar rose, just like the one in the accursed ballad about the love between Fair Ellender and Lord Thomas.

Satisfied for the moment, he returned to the house. He would check again tomorrow before he would believe Darcy completely. Wickham had witnessed the love Elizabeth Darcy tried to conceal even before the man married her—as far back as those initial meetings in Hertfordshire and definitely when she followed him to the Netherfield Manor House. She did not fear Wickham, even then, because the woman knew Fitzwilliam Darcy would protect her. Darcy had given her that damnable crucifix, and Elizabeth Bennet put her trust in the symbol of her God and in the man she adored. Wickham avoided touching the necklace that day because of the love associated with it. Darcy had never…never…succumbed to any of the women who threw themselves at his feet, but a saucy maid from a country estate had brought the man to his knees. Originally, Wickham had thought she would be a weapon he could use to defeat Darcy. Little had he known at the time, the reverse was true: Elizabeth Bennet Darcy would give her husband the strength to bring about closure for all of them.

Wickham took up his favorite chair and observed the ritual

movement about the room. The mesmerizing mist filled the hall. These souls belonged to him, and he controlled when they hunted and when they fed. As the first streaks of dawn lit the upper panes of the windows, they drifted away. They would return that night, leaving their graves to congregate in his home. The only disciples remaining throughout the day were Lydia Bennet and an opera singer he brought to his house a little more than a year earlier. Neither woman had a grave to which to return. They had never known the blessing of a funeral. Instead, they were among the walking dead—those who would have no peace.

★ ★ ★

Elizabeth hurried from the room she shared with the colonel. She had put away all the bedding had managed to get the various maids to bring her, knowing that her husband's cousin had spent the past five nights sleeping on hard floors. She was thankful for the man's intrusion, but tonight she wanted to sleep in her husband's arms and feel his breath on the back of her neck.

The colonel met her in the open dining room, took her hand, and pulled her towards the private one. "Is something amiss?" she whispered when the door closed behind them.

"The carriage has a problem. A mail coach lost a wheel, and it struck our livery, breaking some of the spokes. It will take several hours to repair." He still held her hand, expecting Elizabeth to respond impulsively.

"This cannot be!" she protested, breaking for the door before the colonel tightened his hold. She spun back on him. "We have to go today! Fitzwilliam is there, and we both know what danger he is in!"

With his thumbs the colonel wiped away the tears now streaming down her face. "What other choice do we have? My cousin is a strong man; he will not do anything rash. We will make it to Stanwick today, but it will be later than we anticipated. Luckily, we are on the eastern side of the shire, traveling along the coastal way, whereas Darcy had to cross the entire country. Possibly, he was detained, as well."

Elizabeth strode away from him in agitation. "Why do we not take the horses? I can ride."

"We have but one saddle, the one from my horse, and even if we could find another, it certainly would not be designed for a lady." He moved to where she now stood looking out the window. He was absolutely certain she was terrified by what she could not control. "Be reasonable, Elizabeth. We are seven to eight hours away in the carriage. That translates to around six hours in the saddle. Even an experienced rider has difficulty maintaining such a pace."

Elizabeth now bit her bottom lip, considering all possible scenarios. Finally, she made her decision. "I will give it two hours. If the coach is not repaired by then, I am hiking these skirts to my knees, and I am riding off on the best horse I can acquire. You may join me or choose to wait for the coach, Colonel."

He laughed at the stubbornness he heard in Elizabeth's voice. "Two hours, Mrs. Darcy," he repeated. Then he took two steps towards the door. "Elizabeth," he said to her back, "my cousin is wealthy in more ways than one."

Elizabeth heard the door close behind her. Darcy's cousin was an exemplary man, someone to whom she would always be grateful, but he did not understand. When a person loved as she loved Darcy, a life without that love was impossible. How could she explain that she could not breathe without Darcy? Could not exist without him? He was her other half. Elizabeth's whole heart belonged to Fitzwilliam Darcy.

CHAPTER 25

"Yes, Ma'am." The innkeeper bowed to Elizabeth upon her entrance. "May I be of assistance?"

"I am looking for my husband, Sir." She demanded immediate attention with her tone.

The innkeeper gave her a critical look, thinking her a spurned wife seeking to catch her husband in the mix of a dalliance. "I assure you, Madam, I do not tolerate such use of my establishment."

Elizabeth looked momentarily confused, and then she flushed with color, recognizing the innuendo. "You misunderstand, Sir; my husband is not that type of man. We were to meet him here. This is his cousin." She gestured to Colonel Fitzwilliam as he stepped up beside her.

"Of course, Madam." The man bowed once again to guarantee he offered no offense. He took up a position behind the registration book. "Your husband's name, Ma'am?"

"Fitzwilliam Darcy."

The man ran his finger down the page to find Darcy's name. "Yes, Ma'am. Mr. Darcy is a guest. Might you wish to join him?"

"Naturally," Elizabeth said, "and my cousin will also require quarters."

Colonel Fitzwilliam took control. "Please see that the lady's luggage is placed in Mr. Darcy's room, and that our carriage and coachman receive proper care."

"Immediately, Sir."

"Is my husband in his room?" Elizabeth now felt the anticipation of finding Darcy and of assuring herself that he was well.

The man looked about for a servant to retrieve their baggage. "I do not believe so, Ma'am. Mr. Darcy walked through the village earlier today, and then he took a light meal in the private dining room. I believe he was going to enjoy the evening at the assembly hall. It is an acknowledgment of our Viking influence in these parts. Our village is recorded in the *Anglo-Saxon Chronicles* as the site that saw the beginning of the Viking Age. We take our heritage very seriously. St. Cuthbert's body was once entombed on Lindisfarne Island, and we do not forget it."

Colonel Fitzwilliam looked amused. He turned his head to the side to whisper in her ear, "Did he just use the words *enjoy* and *assembly hall* in the same sentence with Darcy's name?"

Elizabeth laughed lightly. "They seem incongruous terms," she said without moving her lips.

"It appears, Cousin, that we will be attending an assembly in the good village of Stanwick." The colonel brought her gloved hand to his lips. "I hope, my dear, that we have something appropriate to wear. I will meet you here as soon as you freshen your clothing."

"I suppose we will simply have to attend the dance ourselves to determine my husband's motives." Elizabeth reached for his arm.

The colonel patted her hand. "Let us be about it, Mrs. Darcy. We did not travel this far to falter now."

Elizabeth rushed after the boy toting her baggage to Darcy's room. She shook out one of the clean gowns, working the wrinkles free. In less than thirty minutes, she rejoined the colonel in the inn's entranceway. "Do you suppose Mr. Darcy will be surprised by our appearance?" For some reason, Elizabeth's courage wavered.

"If Darcy is surprised by the fact that the woman who loves him traveled halfway across England to find him, I am sure it will be pleasantly so." The colonel placed her hand on his arm. "To the next adventure, Mrs. Darcy."

They walked the quarter mile to the village assembly hall. Light filtered through every window, and the sound of instruments, sometimes poorly played, filled the chilly night air.

"Do you see him?" Elizabeth stood on tiptoes, hoping to spy Darcy.

Although the colonel was not as tall as her husband, he still cut a fine figure. "I have a better idea. In a crush like this, we could circle each other for hours. Darcy hates cards more than he does dancing, so we will not find him in the game rooms. I suggest we take to the dance floor and let *him* find *us*."

"Will it work? I do not see Wickham either, although he can change his appearance. I could be looking right at him and not know it to be him." Elizabeth took the colonel's proffered arm.

"If not, we will try something else," he guaranteed.

The music changed suddenly to a waltz, and Elizabeth looked about in surprise. "A waltz? At a country assembly?"

"Maybe the Scottish are more progressive than we Brits—even northern England must be a bit less censorious," he teased. "Will you still honor me with a dance, Elizabeth?"

"My wife waltzes only with me, Cousin." Darcy stood in his usual haughty stance, waiting for the colonel to relinquish Elizabeth's hand.

The colonel chuckled. "You always claimed the pretty ones for yourself, Darcy. Where am I to find another partner who knows how to waltz?"

"I fear I do not care, oh cousin of mine." He took Elizabeth's hand and led her around the edge of the floor and brought her close, resting his hand on the small of her back.

When the music began, only six couples dared the dance; however, all eyes remained on the Darcys. Darcy held Elizabeth next to him, but she arched her back so she could see his eyes, and then they stepped into the dance, and magic happened. They were in each other's arms once more. "I missed you," he murmured close to her ear as they swirled around the floor's corner.

"I feared I had lost you." Elizabeth's eyes drank in the face she craved.

"You are mine, Elizabeth Bennet Darcy." He spoke softly, but there was no doubting his words. "When you waltz, you waltz with me; and when you love, you love only me."

Elizabeth's face lit up. She let her hand inch up to his shoulder, where she could play with the hair at the nape of his neck. "I will waltz only with you, my Husband, and our love binds us across time." She tilted her head back farther, as if to accept his kiss. Darcy lowered his head....

The coach jostled her awake. Elizabeth shot a quick glance at her husband's cousin. Although he pretended to sleep also, Damon Fitzwilliam scrunched his eyes shut; it was not the relaxed face of someone truly asleep. She realized she had spoken the words of her dream aloud, and the colonel had heard her declaration of love, but he pretended ignorance of it. Such speech should embarrass her, but Elizabeth was beyond denying her love.

Elizabeth had waited three hours for the wheel's repair, but not before she had tried to let or even buy a horse of her own. Without an alternative, she reluctantly yielded to the only choice available.

Ignoring the colonel's pretense, Elizabeth asked, "When shall we reach Stanwick?"

The man sat up immediately, overlooking how they had both chosen not to speak to her discomforting intimacy. "I estimate it will be several hours after dark. Peter is a skilled coachman and will get us there safely, but even he will need to exercise more caution on unfamiliar roads after nightfall."

"Will Fitzwilliam be there?" Again, Elizabeth bit her bottom lip in distress.

The colonel wanted to lighten her mood by telling Elizabeth that her dreams always came true, but his earlier deception precluded it. "I am incontestable in my belief of my cousin's speedy arrival in Stanwick; yet I cannot warrant his safety in doing so."

Elizabeth looked out the window at the passing countryside. "This land has a savageness about it—not necessarily sinister—but definitely a harsh, unbroken fierceness."

"Aye, it does. It is as if a person steps back in time to when life itself was ruthless." Fearing he had said too much, he tapped on the carriage's roof to tell Peter to pull up. "I think I will spell Peter for awhile; I want him well rested for the last part of the trip."

★ ★ ★

Wickham patiently watched at the village inn throughout the day, but there was no sign of reinforcements on Darcy's behalf. Darkness had surrounded the village for at least two hours, and no one any longer traveled the roads. Feeling more secure, he sauntered off towards his house. Evidently, Darcy had told the truth about Elizabeth Bennet's withdrawal of her affection. Wickham had once thought that impossible, and had even considered how he might kill the two of them together. Now his only problem was how to dispose of Fitzwilliam Darcy. Wickham did not want to allow Darcy to become a vampire, because Wickham did not want to continue the struggle between them. He preferred to rule *the kingdom* alone. That meant killing Darcy the traditional way, without the benefit of feeding. Of course, that also meant he must keep the others away from his prisoner.

★ ★ ★

A little after nine o'clock, the Darcy carriage rolled into the courtyard of the Blue Dragon in Stanwick. With the stops and the darkness, the seven or eight hours they had estimated had turned into nearly ten. "I will see to the room," Colonel Fitzwilliam muttered as he helped the rumpled-looking Elizabeth from the coach.

"If Fitzwilliam has a room, I will be staying with my husband." The colonel recoiled, as if slapped.

As they had on several occasions during this trip, they both pretended not to notice the exchange. "Ah, I no longer need to sleep on a pallet."

Elizabeth blushed, although with the darkness, no one saw. Impulsively, she caressed his cheek. "I am sorry, Damon. I will forever be grateful for your interference and your gentlemanly concern. Although it was a bit awkward the first evening, I truly took comfort in knowing you were so close. I will never be able to repay you for your kindness."

Damon Fitzwilliam fought the urge to turn his head and kiss Elizabeth's palm. She was *Darcy's* wife, but for the past few days, he had found himself wishing she were not. *She is phenomenal*, he thought. "I could not let you travel halfway across England alone. The Earl of Matlock would disown me for sure, and as I am a second son, I cannot afford to be in his disfavor." He tried to cover his growing feelings with a jest.

"Let us go inside and see what we can learn of my husband." Elizabeth took the colonel's arm as they entered the inn.

Just as with all the other places they had frequented over the past few days, the innkeeper greeted them at the door and jumped to meet their needs. They had decided prior to leaving the coach that the colonel would ask discreet questions. "My cousin and I were to meet in Stanwick," he began a bit aristocratically. "I escorted his wife, so that they might enjoy a holiday in Edinburgh. Would you tell me, Sir, if Fitzwilliam Darcy is a guest at this inn?"

The innkeeper glanced at the registry. "Let me see. We have a Mr. D'Arcy." He turned the registry so the colonel could see the name. "He registered yesterday. Be that whom you seek, Sir?"

Damon was momentarily flustered, but he recovered quickly. "That appears to be him."

"Very good, Sir. I be afraid no one saw Mr. D'Arcy today. The maid reports his bed remains unused. Yet Mr. D'Arcy's belongings be still in the room. He paid for three days, so I kept the gentleman's personal things intact."

The colonel could feel Elizabeth's fingers tighten on his arm, and he brought his free hand to rest on hers. "Did my cousin speak to anyone whom you noted?"

"The gentleman, he walked 'bout the village upon his arrival. He sat for some time with Mr. Bruce. Bruce be pro'bly the most knowledgeable man in the area, lived here forever he has." The man puffed up with importance. "We be thinkin' Mr. D'Arcy be attendin' the St. Cuthbert dance last night at the assembly, but old Bruce say he not there. You not be thinkin' somethin' bad happen, do ye, Sir?"

The colonel smiled with confidence. "Of course not. My cousin is a learned man—very interested in history—more than likely, he found himself in conversation and forgot where he was. I am sure he will return later with tales of the Highlands and border wars with which to regale us all."

"Mr. D'Arcy be findin' plenty of those." The innkeeper chuckled as he made arrangements for their baggage. "I be puttin' the lady's things in her mister's room. You be needin' one of yer own, Sir?"

"That would be excellent. A comfortable bed would take care of all my travel woes."

"Ye be starvin', too, I 'magine."

Elizabeth looked about her. "If it would not be too much trouble, something hot would be most appreciated."

"Ye and the lady take yerselves into that there room. Me wife find ye some meat pies and some tea. She be happy to serve ye there."

"Thank you, Sir," the colonel responded. "Ask your kind lady to make my tea into ale, if you would." He maneuvered Elizabeth towards the private room. "And our coachman needs provisions, as well as our cattle."

"No problem, Sir. All be seen to." The man moved away to do their bidding.

When they were seated in the private dining room, they were able to drop the pretense. Elizabeth released her breath. "At least, we know Fitzwilliam is here. I was surprised that he used the old spelling of the family name."

"Very astute of Darcy, in reality—he can blend in better."

Elizabeth looked anxious. "I suppose so."

"It seems I will be spending time in the taproom after we eat. A few rounds of drinks should loosen the local tongues."

"Where do you suppose Fitzwilliam is now?" She spoke softly, although they were the only two in the room.

The colonel took her hand in his. "I doubt if Darcy waited for long before he approached Wickham's coverture. Knowing your husband, he went through the front door, *guns blazing,* like one of those tales of the Archibald Montgomerie and the 77th Regiment of Foot."

"How would you handle it, Colonel?" she half teased.

"Years in the military would make me a *Cherokee,* not one of the Royal Scots. I would wait and watch and choose the right moment." He laughed at himself. "I suppose Darcy's way is the more honorable one."

"But not necessarily the more prudent one." Elizabeth squeezed his hand. "No one who ever met you, Colonel, would think you anything less than honorable."

The innkeeper's wife interrupted their conversation. "Hopin' the meat pies serve ye," she said as she placed the tea service on the table next to the colonel's tankard.

"They smell delicious, Ma'am. Thank you for all your trouble." The colonel and Elizabeth were ravenous, immediately attacking their fare.

The coachman appeared at the door, and Elizabeth motioned him forward. "Yes, Peter?"

"Mrs. Darcy, I be takin' note, as ye asked. The Master's horse is in the stable."

"Trident?" Her excitement rose.

"Yes, Ma'am. Trident glad to see me—gave him a randy apple, likin' I always do."

"Watch Trident for us, Peter. Let me know if anyone goes near him." The servant looked pleased with the new responsibility. "We will be staying here for a few days, so use the time to make whatever repairs are needed."

"Yes, Ma'am." He bowed out of the room.

The colonel had already consumed a goodly portion of his meal. "You get some rest tonight, Elizabeth, and I will find where Wickham is and how we might best approach him."

"You will be careful, Colonel?"

"I have not my cousin's powers. Like you, my dear, I am very much a human, and I must depend on my wits to survive. Trust me, I will not do anything foolish. As soon as I know something, we will act."

"Make it soon, Colonel. I fear Fitzwilliam needs our help."

The colonel nursed his drink as two men shared their stories of how each night those foolish enough to be out after midnight took the chance of meeting what these men simply called "bloodsuckers." He also learned that the whole neighborhood "knew" the source of these diseased creatures to be the master of Wickford Manor.

"He be the family of Seorais Winchcombe," the one called Gordy told him, "the one who be lovin' Lady Ellender. The lady and Lord Benning be buried up in the cemetery with all them others. It be odd the man came here."

"How far is it to Wickford Manor?" the colonel asked casually.

"Half'n mile back towards the church. Wickford Manor is not much by London standards, but it got some land. The thing is, it sit right on the back of the line where be the church's graveyard. Like Wickford Manor takin' in them souls."

His partner offered his own insights. "Some be sayin' them bloodsuckers dance in the hall every night. I nary believe it, but everyone be sayin' it so."

Finally, having all the information he needed, the colonel bid the two farewell. "It is near eleven, gentlemen. I shall not detain you any longer. I thank you for sharing your local legends." Damon Fitzwilliam knew he should go and share what he had discovered with Elizabeth, but if what these men said was true, he needed to act now, before the "dance" began.

A quarter hour later, he stood before the church's graveyard. Everything still seemed quiet, but after the past hour of listening to two grown men excitedly share what they knew of the grave sites looming before him, Damon Fitzwilliam had to steel his nerves before proceeding. As rambunctious children, he and Darcy had often played soldiers, hiding behind family headstones in a pretend battle; and in the military, he had spent more time than he cared to remember with the dead. Yet this was different, and the colonel sensed it. In this cemetery, death *lived*.

He chastised himself for his fear and quickly crossed the mounds to exit through the hedge shrub outlining the graves. A glance over his shoulder showed him a low, creeping fog spreading across the granite memorials.

His drunken informants had told him the house was behind the cemetery; they had forgotten to mention the hill and the wooded field. Luckily, light streamed from the house's windows, serving as a beacon for him as he took unsteady steps on the hill, and the colonel made his way stealthily through the forested area to come out where the steps led to the kitchen. In the back of his mind, Damon reasoned how country homes would never be lit up as such at that time of night, but this was no ordinary household. Armed with cloves of garlic and a crucifix purchased in one of the small villages through which he and Elizabeth had passed, he edged the kitchen door open and slipped into a perfectly clean room. At first, its pristineness shocked him, but then he remembered Elizabeth had told him that Wickham never ate regular food. The pots and pans and kettle were purely for show—Wickham's playing at being the master of his small estate.

Leaving the kitchen behind, Damon followed a staircase leading to the private living quarters, but again these offered no insights into how to defeat Wickham, because they stood unused—sparsely furnished—a mausoleum to an unemployed life. Only one room was locked, and although he wished to force his way into it and see what it might hold, a pulsating cadence caused him to curtail his search and find his way towards the center of the house. Drawn by the unusual sound, he felt compelled to find its source. Creeping on all fours, Damon edged forward to where the upper floors overhung the center hall. He glued himself to the wall, crouched so he might respond if necessary, and looked for what he could not explain. The sound increased as he peered between the slats of the railing to the room below. He feared his presence might affect the show, but nothing stopped the accentuated movements as one after another shadowy eidolon entered a spiritual gambol. They turned and twisted and oscillated to an undulating rhythm. Periodically, one pasty form would hazard a challenge to another, and the room would fill with squeals of despair and of yearning before returning to the murmured chants.

Then a creature as pale as the colonel had ever seen got out of his grotesquely adorned chair. He held out his hand to a pretty sort of girl with curls pinned tightly to her head. Then, horror of horrors, the image the colonel assumed to be George Wickham looked on in infinite sadness as the girl slid into his embrace. Wickham brought her closer still, swaying with her in a primitive invitation to passion. His hands searched her body, and then wordless voices rose in exultation as Wickham lowered his head and drank the girl's blood. Damon bit back a cry of dark, piercingly pure contempt for the display. He shuddered in anguish at his inability to change what was happening to the girl. With a despairing gesture, he withdrew to the servants' stairs. He had to escape before the surging call of the coven pulled *him* in.

Slipping cautiously down the passageway, he rested a split second with his fingers on a door's handle, before a muffled sound on the other side sent his heart racing. Damon froze with fear, unable to move, and prayed that what was on the other side would not find him. He pressed his ear to the door, listening with all his senses, but he heard only a soft wind. A mysterious presence moved through the closed portal, and the colonel could feel it so exactly, it was as if he saw through the door. He knew the moment it moved on, and he eased the handle to the right, sliding the door aside only far enough to fit his body through before silently resettling it.

Clinging to the wall, Damon stepped softly, trying to escape his fear and what happened in this house. On the battlefield, he knew death was all around him, but he had never *felt* it before, never knew it to fill his lungs like acrid smoke, never smelled the stench of decay so clearly. He felt totally unprepared for this battle.

A door stood ajar on the other side of the hearth—a door not open before, and despite his desperate need to flee the room and the house, Damon made himself move to where he could see into the space. Before him, Wickham paced to and fro, and then he stepped to the side, and the colonel stifled every impulse to rush forward to save his cousin. Darcy slumped back against the wall, held in place by attached chains. *Darcy is alive!* Damon's first instinct was to storm the scene and fight Wickham to the death, but how did one kill something already dead? From a distance, he heard the murmuring increase, but Damon continued to watch as Wickham bent to taunt Darcy. The tension rose between the two, and for a moment, Damon thought that Wickham would attack Darcy also, but then he realized, *He just fed; Wickham will not feed again so soon.* And despite the number of vampires dancing ceremoniously in the main hall, Damon knew Wickham would allow no other to touch Darcy. Wickham would want to destroy his enemy himself. If he wanted Darcy dead, his cousin would no longer be breathing.

Assured that he could do nothing that night, he let himself out the kitchen door. He still was not safe if what his drinking consorts said was true. Damon slipped the crucifix from his pocket and lifted his sword in readiness for any attack. He wove his way among the trees and climbed the hill, but when he reached the cemetery, Damon circled the hedgerow on the outside. Loudly repeating every prayer he could remember, he vigilantly watched as the fog he thought to be part of the countryside congregated solely in the church's cemetery. From it, specters formed and disintegrated before his eyes. Some challenged his progress, but all retreated from the raised silver weapon he carried and from the sign of the Lord's forgiveness.

Reaching the road to the inn, he followed the embankment; the mist trailed him, but the spectral provocations—strange, unheard presences—kept their distance. He congratulated himself for leaving the horses at the inn. A nervous mount would serve no master. Damon kept up his litany of invocations and refused to look about to see what might await him. He figured the prayers would not hurt, and they definitely made him feel safer.

When he arrived at the inn, Peter let him in through the door. Damon had set the man on guard when he left for Wickford Manor, and he was thankful for his foresight. He handed the garlic and the crucifix to Peter. "Keep them close," he warned.

"I saw what followed you, Colonel. If these keep that *evil* away, ye will not be able to pry them from me." The coachman bolted the door. "Will they not try to come in?" He listened closely to the howls of the night.

"This is more than that for which we all bargained, Peter, but those creatures must be invited in by someone who lives here. No one will do that." Damon leaned back against the door to steady his nerves.

The servant moved closer, fearing that someone might hear. "Did ye find him, Colonel? The Master? He be alive?"

Damon gave a curt nod. "Now I must figure out how to get Mr. Darcy out of that hellhole."

"Bless you, Sir." Peter started for the pallet he would sleep upon that night. "When ye be ready, I be ready, Sir. The Master be a good man."

"That he is, Peter." Damon moved towards the stairs. "I need to tell Mrs. Darcy what I know."

"The Mistress will certainly be glad to hear it." He settled onto the straw-stuffed mattress.

Damon let his gaze travel up the stairs, resting on Elizabeth's door. "Mrs. Darcy is an exceptional woman. Good night, Peter." He knew she would be awake, waiting for his news. Slowly, he climbed the steps; they had a daunting task ahead of them. *What if we cannot save Darcy?*

★ ★ ★

"Someone looks for you, Darcy." Wickham paced the room, agitated by the intrusion into his home.

Darcy tried not to react; he forced his breathing to remain even, but the joy of knowing another knew of his capture played havoc with his composure. He kept his eyes closed, fearing Wickham could read his countenance.

Wickham leaned down, his face only inches from Darcy's. "Do you want to know who it was?"

Darcy opened his eyes slowly and smiled. "As you appear intent on telling me, I see no reason to waste my energy with guessing."

Wickham walked away casually, although he knew apprehension. "It was your beautiful wife, Mrs. Darcy." Wickham straddled a straight-backed chair, turning it to where he could watch Darcy's reaction.

For a split second, Darcy's heart skipped a beat. He did not want Elizabeth to put herself in danger for him, but then the truth flashed in Wickham's eyes. "You are quite amusing, Wickham, but the thought of my wife being here is ludicrous. I told you from the beginning, Elizabeth left with your seduction of her sister. However, if that were not true, and my wife were here, you have not enough ghouls in your *congregation* to hold me in these chains, for she would not stop until I was free. Trust me, Wickham, there is no way you could defeat her. She is more than either of us can handle."

Wickham sat in complete silence; Darcy chose to ignore him and closed his eyes again. Finally, Wickham barked out a forced laugh. "You have me there, Darcy. Your rescuer was a man. Maybe you would have been better off with your wife; at least, *she* would not turn tail and run." He stood with that statement. "The man favored you in some ways, Darcy—not quite as tall, however. Should I send for reinforcements?"

"Probably a stranger enticed by tales of the unknown." Darcy hoped to convince his enemy to ignore the incursion.

"I can smell human blood." Wickham looked off, as if no longer seeing Darcy. "Did you know that? I smell it as easily as I once smelled a rose. It is metallic and bittersweet. Have you ever tasted it, Darcy? It is addictive."

At first the words were offensive, but then Darcy's pity replaced his anger; and despite his personal loathing of Wickham's baseness, Darcy suddenly felt empathy for what once must have been a proud and handsome man—a man who loved a woman too well and lost everything because of it. "I have not tasted it—at least, not in the way you mean," Darcy spoke softly, not wishing to break the understanding between them.

Wickham laughed lightly at his own show of weakness. "That was a foolish question, was it not? Of course, you never succumbed to the noxious hunger that consumes me. You are too honorable to allow the poison to cross your lips."

Darcy shook his head, a deep sadness overcoming him. "I simply want it to end, Wickham. It is not honor which drives me; it is the fear that my child—my son—could know such *despondency*—could live an *inconsolable* life. I would not term that honorable—it is pure cowardice."

Wickham watched as Darcy once more took up his resigned vigil against the wall. An understanding passed between them; he imagined that in another lifetime, he and Darcy might even be friends, but circumstances prevented that ever becoming true. Wickham respected Darcy as much as he abhorred him. "Never fear, Darcy," he said as a way of parting. "I may yet choose to do the honorable thing and fight you to the death, so to speak."

Darcy tried to relax the pain in his shoulders and arms. Wickham had imprisoned him twenty-four hours earlier, and other than the occasional break he negotiated to meet his personal needs, he remained restrained by the shackles. Wickham, as he suspected, brought him no food or drink; he was to die of starvation, and Darcy accepted it. "You will let me know when you choose, Wickham," he mumbled, closing his eyes and trying to welcome sleep. He heard the door close in front of him and knew when the bolt slid into the latch, but Darcy remained in repose. Images of Elizabeth filled his mind; remembrances of their time together overspread his thoughts as sleep found him.

CHAPTER 26

The door opened before he knocked, and Elizabeth reached out immediately and pulled him into the room. "You promised," she lambasted him, "you would do *nothing* to put yourself in *danger!*" Elizabeth swatted at the colonel's chest. "I have been at my wit's end with worry since I learned of your excursion."

It pleased him that Elizabeth worried on his behalf. "Then you do not wish to know what I learned?"

Elizabeth pulled him to the table, forcibly shoving the colonel into a chair. "Tell me you found Fitzwilliam." Her voice held her fears.

"My cousin is alive."

Elizabeth collapsed, burying her face in her hands; sobs of joy racked her shoulders. "Thank God," she moaned. The colonel rested his hand on her back in comfort. Allowing herself the moment of relief, she dramatically caught her breath, dashing away her tears with the knuckles of her hands. Raising her head, her eyes fell on Damon's countenance. "Tell me everything."

The gentleman in him told Damon Fitzwilliam to protect her from the terror he had experienced in Wickham's house, but he held nothing back. He described the horror of the lost souls found in the cemetery and the compelling dance in the Wickford hall. He told her in detail of the young girl's seduction and of Wickham's bloody feast.

Elizabeth gasped, "It must be Lydia!" Her voice shook with anger and with remorse. "My poor dear Lydia; she knows no rest."

"We will tend to your sister, Elizabeth."

"Go on," she insisted.

Then the colonel related what he had seen of Darcy's bondage. Elizabeth continued to fight back the tears, but she listened closely to what he said. "It is my opinion that we need to find a way to release Darcy before we do anything else. He appeared weak and in some pain."

Elizabeth half smiled. "This tells me that Wickham fears my husband more than Fitzwilliam had realized. Over the past few months, Mr. Darcy has opened himself up to his once-latent powers. Wickham has my husband's hands chained behind him because if Fitzwilliam extends his arms to the sides, he can control light and time—freezing the latter in place. Wickham has the power of the wind."

"That explains the sound I heard while in hiding."

Elizabeth glanced at the mantel clock. "Then we are agreed; we will go after Darcy in the morning after Wickham's followers return to their graves."

"Is there some way to lure Wickham away from the house?" The colonel considered all the options.

"My dealings with Wickham are limited," Elizabeth thought out loud, "but what I know of him is that he is a performer. He pretends to be a regular man, one owning a well-run household. In just the same way, he put on a display for your eyes. He used Lydia as a warning. I suspect Wickham *knew* you were in the house."

"Then you think he will come looking for us—for me?" Damon began to think as she did.

Elizabeth sat back in satisfaction. "While you were enjoying the taproom, I questioned the maids and the hostler. The master of Wickford Manor watched this inn from early morning until well after dark. Wickham suspected that someone would come for Fitzwilliam. Luckily, we arrived so late that he had no time to prepare. I believe we should set a diversion for tomorrow."

"Excellent! I excel at diversions." The colonel rubbed his hands in anticipation. "The way I see it, Wickham knows I am here, but he probably does not realize who I am. We have had no direct encounters before now. Why do we not send him on a wild goose chase? If he likes public displays, let us send a pretender riding towards Berwick. I suspect that Wickham will follow—at least, initially. That should give us time to get to Darcy."

"Whom should we trust with the task?"

"Peter." The colonel knew that without a doubt. "He is most eager to be of service. I will put him in one of my uniforms; he can take Trident. We just need Wickham away for a few minutes."

Things settled, Elizabeth moved to end their discussion. "We need some rest." She stood and offered her hand.

The colonel followed her to his feet. "Will you be well alone, my dear?"

"I will, Colonel. Find yourself a real bed tonight. You deserve a proper sleep." Elizabeth led him to the door. "I will be ready in the morning, Sir."

Damon opened the door and edged out, not wanting anyone to see him. "Rest well, Elizabeth."

From the upper window, they surreptitiously watched Wickham try to blend in with the villagers moving about the area. He dressed in plain clothing, but he did not assume another's identity, and Elizabeth easily recognized his awkward movements as he pretended to be a farmer herding sheep through a series of pens.

"Peter knows what to do." The colonel stood behind her.

"He is brave to face this. Mr. Darcy needs to reward him accordingly."

The colonel walked away. "I am sure my cousin will be generous." He picked up his gloves. Today he dressed, as did the local gentry, in a loose overcoat and a plain waistcoat. They wanted as little attention as possible.

"The stable hand has brought out Trident." Damon returned to the window just in time to see Peter stride from the inn. He wore the colonel's uniform, belted and tucked in to give the appearance of fitting, along with a hat pulled down over his forehead and a scarf covering the lower part of his face. He used a mounting block to settle himself into the saddle. Although no horseman, Peter knew horses well enough to create an illusion, and he kicked Trident's flanks to edge the horse out onto the road. Recognizing a friend—one who regularly offered him a treat—Trident responded by dropping into a lazy gallop.

"I hope Peter is able to walk tonight," Elizabeth mused.

"It is for a good cause." Damon watched more intently. "Come on, Wickham," he thought aloud, "take the bait."

They waited for several long moments, and then Wickham moved to a waiting gig. The colonel heard Elizabeth let out her breath. "We are on, Elizabeth." He moved swiftly towards the door. "We have very little time."

Nearly at a run, they cut across several fields to make their trek shorter. The innkeeper pointed out the way and within less than ten minutes, Wickford Manor loomed ahead.

"You are very adept at moving through the countryside," the colonel murmured close to Elizabeth's ear as she knelt beside him, observing the house for occupants.

She smiled brightly. "I am often criticized for being a good walker."

"Not today, my dear." Damon touched her hand and pointed to the kitchen door he had used the previous night.

Elizabeth nodded in recognition; he expected her to follow him. Less cautious today than during the night, the colonel opened the door, and both of them moved through the portal. He motioned for her to wait while he scouted the area, taking the servant stairs once again and moving quickly through the house.

However, Elizabeth chose not to wait; impatient to see Darcy, she discovered the door by the hearth. The crucifix affixed to the handle—which she intuited that Wickham had hung there for his own nefarious purposes—told her that she found what she sought. She tried the handle but, as expected, it did not move; Elizabeth though, was not the type to allow that to stop her. She began searching for the key. *Could Wickham have it on him? Not likely. It was not in his character. Wickham loved the melodramatic—the manipulation, the puzzle. He would hide the key in an obvious place to see if anyone were smart enough to outwit him.* Realizing the truth of the matter, Elizabeth began to frantically turn over cups and bowls, assuming Wickham would put the key in a unique, but less than subtle, place.

Finding nothing above, the colonel returned to the kitchen. "Do you see anything?" he whispered, but she shook her head as she continued to search everything in sight.

Damon moved to the door and tried physically to force the lock. "We need to do something *now*," he insisted, but Elizabeth ignored his urgency and continued her search.

"It *has* to be here." Elizabeth turned over the kettle—and then she saw it, lodged between the logs ready for a fire. "I have it!" She was all excitement as she scrambled to recover it.

Coming to the door, she handed the key ring to Damon, who quickly opened the cellar. And then Elizabeth saw him, crumpled and broken looking. "Fitzwilliam!" she exhaled his name as she rushed forward, nearly bounding down the steps. Reaching him quickly, she cradled his head in her hands, covering his face with a battery of feather-light kisses. "Oh, God, Fitzwilliam, speak to me," she pleaded.

His mouth parched from a day and a half of no nourishment, he managed, "Are you real? I dreamed of you."

"Very real, my love." She kissed him again. "Let us help you out of here."

The colonel had already begun to work at the locks of the shackles. Not expecting anyone to stage a rescue, Wickham had foolishly left all the keys on the same ring, and so the colonel released the first lock and gingerly lowered Darcy's arm to his side. "Easy, Darcy," he whispered before moving on to the other lock.

Darcy tried to turn his head towards his liberator. "Damon?" he mumbled softly as he slumped into Elizabeth's arms.

"In the flesh, Cousin." He released the other binding before helping Darcy to his feet. "Hopefully, your legs work, because I do not choose to carry you." But the colonel bolstered his cousin's weight and started Darcy's unsure footsteps to the door. Elizabeth led the way, but as she reached the top stair, she halted suddenly in place, refusing to move from the portal.

Pushing her aside, Damon leaned Darcy against the frame as

he assessed the room. Before him stood the girl from the previous evening and another, older temptress. "Take care of your husband, Elizabeth," he murmured softly. "When I tell you, get Darcy out of here."

Elizabeth did not answer, but Damon knew she had heard by the slight nod of her head.

"You will take my lord's friend nowhere," the older woman hissed. She was beautifully handsome—buxom, with raven black hair and pale violet eyes; yet Damon knew she would ravish him without a thought.

"Unfortunately, we differ on that." He noted how the girl he now recognized to be Lydia Bennet edged to the side.

Then before he could stop her, Elizabeth faced her sister. "Lydia, listen to me; you cannot do this." When the apparition who once was her sister made no response, Elizabeth tried again. "I will not let you hurt Fitzwilliam or the colonel, Lydia. I love you, Lyddie, but I will *not allow you* to destroy others."

Lydia, a bit taller than her older sibling, turned her head slowly, as if observing a fly on the wall. "Then I will destroy you, Elizabeth." Not only were the words bone-chilling, but the tone told Elizabeth that nothing of her sister remained.

Darcy gave his senses a shake, knowing he must intervene. He could not let Elizabeth fight her sister. In pain, he lifted his arms and turned once in place. "Heads down!" he ordered his rescuers as the weak flow of energy temporarily blinded the two vampires. Intuitively, the colonel ducked his head and tackled Elizabeth around the waist, dragging her away from their assailants; then he, too, spun a half turn, bringing the sword high as he did so.

Still weak from his confinement, Darcy's arms soon lowered, and the energy waned, but a different type of energy—one of pure evil—replaced it. Instantly, the women attacked, first knocking the enfeebled Darcy to the floor and then turning their full vengeance on the man.

Elizabeth watched in horror as the colonel arced his sword through the air, hacking at arms and legs as sharp claws dug at his skin and clothing. "Get Darcy out!" he ordered between strikes, and Elizabeth moved at once to pull Darcy to his feet and towards the exit.

Jerking the door open with one hand, she shoved her husband through. He landed on all fours in the dirt, and then she turned back to the melee. "Lydia!" she screamed as she picked up a poker and challenged her sister.

The being who was once Lydia Bennet turned immediately, giving Damon Fitzwilliam a reprieve, the thing for which Elizabeth had hoped. Behind Lydia, the colonel still fought with a frenzied older woman, but Elizabeth's attention rested purely on the creature who had been her sister. Gaping stab wounds now crisscrossed the countenance she loved, and slash marks laced the girl's arms. Elizabeth groaned in pain, witnessing the evil that controlled her younger sister.

Lydia now advanced, backing Elizabeth to the wall. "You wanted me, Sister?" Surprisingly, the sinister words drowned out the shrieks and grunts of the fight raging over Lydia's shoulder. "My lord will welcome you among his followers, *Elizabeth*."

"Mama and Papa grieve for you, Lydia." Feeling guilty, Elizabeth tried to reason rather than fight.

Lydia bared her fangs. "I grieve for no one." The girl took a step closer. "I will not grieve for you, Sister."

"But *I* will grieve for *you*, Lydia." Elizabeth intuitively raised the poker in a defensive stance.

Meanwhile, Damon fought for his life. With no experience in fighting vampires, at first, he underestimated the brute strength of the animals he encountered, seeing only a beautiful woman and a pretty girl. But a few well-placed blows from his attackers told him that he fought more than the shell in which each was encased. He fought unearthly demons determined to strip him of his very soul. Knowing Elizabeth's life was in danger, he redoubled his efforts. Finally, the woman charged, and he thrust at the same time.

When the sword pierced her heart, a blood-curdling shriek filled the room as her momentum impaled her all the way to the blade's hilt. Instinctively, he jerked upward, ensuring his hit incapacitated his opponent, and then he looked again into the violet eyes of the woman he had just killed. She had died before, but now she was at peace. A smile turned up the corners of her mouth as she closed her eyes and welcomed heaven.

"Lydia, no!" he heard Elizabeth warn behind him as he pushed back on the woman's body, following her to the floor.

Screams continued as Damon frantically wrestled with the woman's limp form to free the sword, finally placing his booted foot on her chest and yanking at the handle with all his might.

Darcy, hearing Elizabeth's calls of distress, fought his way to his feet. Reeling from exhaustion and desiccation, he knew he must find some way to reach her. He must stop Elizabeth from being the one who hurt her sister. She would never forgive herself, no matter how justified the action. Staggering back through the open doorway, he battled for some sort of control.

Elizabeth had reacted too late to fend off Lydia's attack, assuming she could rekindle the goodness she had once known in her sister, and now she struggled to keep Lydia's claws from tearing at her face and neck. Lydia's inhuman strength surprised Elizabeth as she twisted and turned, trying to wrench herself free of the viselike grip of the being's hell-bent fury, but Lydia's demonic possession pushed Elizabeth farther against the wall, effectively pinning her and allowing Lydia to move in for the final mastication.

Elizabeth's scream shattered the near silence of the room as Lydia lowered her head. Darcy raised his arms, and everything moved in slow motion as Damon pulled the sword free and turned, preparing to charge across the room. Propelling himself forward to help Elizabeth, Darcy reached the point of contact first, and the colonel automatically released the metal, sending it turning end over end.

The twang of the silver as it sliced the air mixed sharply with Elizabeth's screams and Damon's fight for breath. Darcy paused, focusing all his energy into one movement. Growing up, he and Damon had fought local bullies in tandem; and without a doubt,

Damon had placed all his trust in Darcy to finish the battle. The glint of the silver as it caught the refracted light of the morning sun resembled a flash of lightning in a storm, and Darcy's arm shot out to catch it as it wobbled towards him. Without thinking, he lunged forward, recognizing his target—Lydia's heart—from behind, and the blade again found its mark.

Lydia Bennet slumped forward, clinging to her older sister as they both collapsed to the floor, Lydia lying face down in Elizabeth's lap. With the last of his strength, Darcy pulled the sword free as Elizabeth rolled Lydia to her back.

"Lyddie." Elizabeth caressed her sister's cheek, but there was no response. Darcy had released her from hell, and Lydia rested at last.

"We need to get out of here," the colonel said as he pulled Darcy to his feet.

"Elizabeth." Darcy reached for her.

"I cannot leave her, Fitzwilliam…not like this." Elizabeth's eyes pleaded with him to do something.

Darcy turned to his cousin. "Can you carry her, Damon?"

Frustrated by the change in the dynamics and his own feelings of inadequacy, Damon unwillingly agreed. "I can carry her long enough to keep her body safe. I will come back for her later." The colonel hoisted Lydia Bennet's limp body onto his shoulder as he led the way out the door. They left everything else in shambles, the quickly decaying body of the once-beautiful opera singer prostrate on the hardwood floor.

Making their way in the open again, Elizabeth hurried between the colonel's steady footsteps, carrying the dangling limbs of her sister, and her husband's faltering footfall. In retreat, they were slower than in their advance. At last, they reached the final field. The inn in sight on the horizon, Damon laid Lydia's body under a cluster of trees, while Darcy also sat to rest.

Bent over in fatigue, Damon stated the obvious: "We look bad enough as it is. We cannot go waltzing in with a body slung over our shoulders."

Darcy and Elizabeth took a close look at each other. All three of them, they realized, were covered in blood and dirt and sweat; clothes were torn and tattered. "Fitzwilliam, Damon and I left together. It is probably best if he and I return at the same time. If anyone asks, I fell down the hill behind the church, and the colonel scrambled to save me."

"We will freshen up and come back for you." Exhausted, Damon now leaned against a tree.

Elizabeth knelt beside her husband. "Will you be safe?"

"I have the sword, and a few minutes to rest will do me well." Darcy touched her face. Like a man starving for what he could not have, he traced her lips with his fingertips. "You will hurry?"

"I will bring you clean clothes. Peter led Wickham on a merry chase, but we should still have time to get you to the inn." Elizabeth's eyes searched his face, needing to convey her undying love. "Not long, Fitzwilliam."

"Damon," Darcy said as he turned his attention to his cousin, "make arrangements to send Lydia's body to Longbourn. It is the least we can do for her parents."

"Certainly, Darcy." He reached his hand down to help Elizabeth to her feet. "Come, Elizabeth, we must make haste."

She kissed Darcy's cheek before following the colonel across the field. She ran the few steps it took to catch up with him. Impulsively, Elizabeth's hand touched his arm. "Thank you, Damon, for everything—for Fitzwilliam's life, for my life, and for my sister's peace."

He chose not to look at her, the domestic scene of the past few minutes too raw for his sensitivity. "Your husband saved you, Elizabeth, not I."

"With your weapon and your help," she insisted. However, they continued their torrid pace because he wanted to put distance between himself and his mixed feelings. Although she had to take two steps to every one of his, Elizabeth did not falter. She knew the source of his frustration and would voice what neither of them had said before. "Damon," Elizabeth begged, "please do not do this. You knew my marriage to Fitzwilliam was not one of convenience when we met again on the London Road. I cannot lose *you* in my life because of something that cannot be, and I will *not* be the cause of a rift between you and Fitzwilliam."

Elizabeth's words shook him; Damon knew his behavior to be out of bounds. It was not like him to act so impulsively. He did not respond; he did not want to recognize the truth of her words. Yet he did slow his pace, letting her know—in the only way a man of honor could—that he would deal with her heartfelt sentiments. Just before they crossed the stile leading to the inn's road and courtyard, he caught her hand. "Let me help you," he said as he lifted Elizabeth over the opening. Setting her down gently in front of him, Damon murmured, "It will all be well, Elizabeth; Fitz-william is my best friend."

"Thank you, Damon." Elizabeth looked away. Too much was happening for her sensibilities. She could not deny her dependence on her husband's cousin. Without him, Darcy's life would still be in danger. For his efforts, she was eternally grateful; but *Darcy* was her sun and her stars.

The rest of the way, they did not speak. When they reached the inn, always the perfect gentleman, Damon blocked the view of bystanders, sending Elizabeth hurrying to her room before he casually followed.

Twenty minutes later, Damon tapped lightly at Elizabeth's door. "I am off to make arrangements," he said as she opened the door. He looked presentable once more. "I will meet you and Darcy in the fields. Make haste. Peter just rode back into the courtyard. Wick-ham will be going home."

Elizabeth nodded and grabbed a shirt and overcoat from among Darcy's things. She also took a flask of water, afraid to give him anything else for the moment. "I am going out the back of the inn. Should I take Trident?"

"No, it will draw more attention." He left her standing in the doorway and headed towards the village after saying something to the innkeeper.

Elizabeth watched him go and then took the back stairway. At this time of the day, no one was around, so she darted out a side door, which was blocked from the front view by a lean-to, and scooted across the courtyard, crossing to the field once again.

Watching her approach, Darcy wondered about the exchange he had observed as his cousin and Elizabeth left him. Something happened between the time she touched Damon's arm and the moment he helped her over the stile. Whatever it was, they had made their peace in those few minutes. *Has Damon developed an affection for Elizabeth?* The thought kept returning to Darcy's mind. *If so, would it not be better for her to spend her life with him? Damon Fitzwilliam would provide for her and treat Elizabeth with respect; but even more important, she would no longer be involved in the madness of* my *life. She would be* safe *with Damon.* Darcy fought back the jealousy seeping into his heart. He knew neither his cousin nor his wife would ever act on any growing regard between them as long he lived. *As long as I live.* Despite the knot forming in his stomach with the thought of Elizabeth being with anyone else, he reconciled himself to the knowledge that, at least, with Damon, someone he trusted could be a part of Elizabeth's life if things turned bleak for him.

Darcy got to his feet and made the effort to smile upon her approach. "You are beautiful, Mrs. Darcy," he said as he painfully lifted her off her feet, welcoming her into his embrace.

Elizabeth laughed, despite the horrors of the morning. "I am happy to see you, my love." She let her fingers trail down his face, as if memorizing it. "I am afraid, Mr. Darcy, that you will not have the comfort of a fire by which to change your clothes, but as your wife, I will enjoy watching you just the same."

"*Wife,* you have no idea how I missed your relentless teasing." Darcy set her on her feet and took the shirt and coat and water she offered. Before he did anything else, he gulped down about half of the flask. Wiping his mouth with the back of his hand, he leaned his head back in relief. "Thank you for thinking of the water, Elizabeth."

She nodded her head to acknowledge his thanks before noting, "You may add the waistcoat and cravat at the inn." Moving away from him, Elizabeth intentionally sat some distance from her sister's body.

Darcy stripped off the torn shirt and donned the clean one. Despite what she had said, Elizabeth did not look at him while he changed. Instead, she forced her eyes to look at Lydia's face. "Thankfully, Lyddie did not shrivel up like the other woman."

Darcy went quiet. "I suspect your sister still retained some small part of her humanity. She was under Wickham's control for only a short time."

"My parents will appreciate our efforts. I will write them when we reach the inn." Elizabeth stood up and brushed the dirt from her skirt. "I was to be with them by now. I thought I might tell them we had a lead on where Wickham could be found, but we arrived too late. Does that sound reasonable?"

"Your parents will be thankful we recovered Lydia's body." Darcy paused, wondering if he dared hope that she would accept his next suggestion. "We should follow and go to Longbourn." Darcy watched her face to see how she would react. Less than a week earlier, she adamantly refused the same offer. "Would you like that, Elizabeth?"

She waited, ashamed of how cruelly she had treated him previously. "Yes, Fitzwilliam." Then, two heartbeats later, she rushed to encircle his waist with her arms, needing to find comfort. "I never meant all those awful things I said."

Her tears now stained his clean shirt, but Darcy paid no mind. Elizabeth sought solace in his arms, and the world was good. "I am sorry about Lydia—what I had to do back at Wickford Manor. I could not stand by and let her hurt you."

Elizabeth swallowed. She was grateful for Darcy's action. Without it, Lydia's attack would have been Elizabeth's downfall, but she could not be happy for Darcy's involvement. "That was not Lydia; that was one of Wickham's monsters. I have to think of it that way. The girl lying under that tree is the *true* Lydia."

She leaned into his closeness, and Darcy settled his hands at her waist. "Damon and two other men are approaching," he murmured into her ear. Then he reluctantly released her so he could put on the coat she had brought him. They stood side by side and waited.

Damon told the undertaker that they had been looking for Lydia, originally suspecting she had eloped to Gretna Green. Darcy and Elizabeth came from Derbyshire, and he had traveled from London, trying to follow her trail, but, unfortunately, they had been too late. Lydia had slept out in the cold when she ran out of money. A legitimate physician would not be available to inspect the body, and the exorbitant fee the colonel promised would ensure that the story of a disgruntled runaway would be repeated. These were the same people who allowed the bodies racked by the evil that Wickham brought to be buried in consecrated land. Why should they take note of a stranger? No one would know what Lydia Bennet had endured as one of Wickham's disciples, and the Bennets would be relieved to at least have a body intact, which they could bury and grieve.

"Thank you, Damon." Darcy offered his hand.

Damon Fitzwilliam took it, as he always did, knowing that somehow they would get back to where they had been.

"You are not going back to that house tonight!" Elizabeth threw her napkin onto the table in frustration. They dined in Darcy's room, needing the privacy to plan what to do next. "I will not have it, Fitzwilliam! Do you hear me?"

"I am afraid I agree with your wife, Darcy. You can barely move your arms. How can you face Wickham?" The colonel speared another slice of ham and lifted it from the platter.

Darcy knew they meant well, but he also recognized how Wickham would respond. The entire neighborhood would suffer. "If I do *not* face Wickham, he will wreak havoc tonight. He and his followers will feed on the innocent."

"Darcy," his cousin began to reason, "these people know the dominion that Wickham holds over them. It is an unspoken reality. I believe if the word is passed, some livestock may suffer, but no person will."

"How would we go about doing that, Damon? How might we sound a warning?"

The colonel leaned back in his chair. "I know just the men... my drinking companions. Let us send them out on some horses to the neighboring farms. It is only ten in the morning. We have at least seven hours until dark, and many more before Wickham's ghouls dance."

Elizabeth began to process what Damon suggested. "What do we tell them? How will we explain we know what Wickham plans?"

"I suggest we tell them the truth. Obviously, we have to do more than eliminate Wickham. He has a graveyard full of ardent imitators. Yet many of those mimics are the loved ones of these very villagers." Damon waited for them to comprehend his line of thinking. Many times in battle, the army first had to win the good-will of the people they wished to help. As a soldier, he found the truth to be the most beneficial weapon in winning the war of wills. "We openly declare you are both a dhampir and a vampire hunter, and you came to free this village of the hold that Wickham has over it. However, you recognize that your challenge will likely infuriate your enemy, and you wish to warn them to protect themselves for tonight. Tomorrow night, you will lead a full assault."

Darcy asserted, "You are absolutely mad, Cousin!"

"Actually," Elizabeth began tentatively, "I *like* Damon's idea. His assumptions are correct; we have to do more than address Wickham."

"Neither of you understand," Darcy argued. "You saw only two of Wickham's underlings. I fought an army of them, and for each one I vanquished, another took its place. We cannot possibly overcome the number under Wickham's control."

"I disagree." The colonel leaned forward to speak directly to Darcy. "Elizabeth knows more things about vampires than anyone could imagine. She knows ways to dispatch them. We can control how many we fight at one time, using the old military adage of divide and conquer. You need to listen to your wife *and* to me. We have skills that you do not, and despite all your powers, you will lose if you do this alone."

Silence filled the room as Darcy assessed what his cousin declared. Obviously, Damon held a special fondness for Elizabeth, but the man had put that aside and would not act upon any blossoming feelings. Instead, he wanted Darcy to accept Elizabeth's love without question and to accept her as an equal. What choice did he have? Following Damon's lead, Darcy turned to his wife. "Are you sincerely of the persuasion we can do this?"

"Damon speaks the truth, Fitzwilliam. We have the means by which to end this nightmare, but we need time to put everything in place and to give you time to heal. You cannot face Wickham in your weakened condition."

Darcy took a close look at his wife. He had always known her to be an exceptional woman, highly perceptive and quite opinionated, but it took his cousin's acceptance of Elizabeth for Darcy to actually see her as a partner, someone he not only must protect, but also someone he must trust as an independent thinker. Deep in his soul, his heart leapt with joy; maybe hope still lived, beautiful—selfless love. Elizabeth trusted him, and she would always stand by him. He nodded his head in agreement. "Put everything in motion, Damon." He spoke the words, but did not remove his eyes from Elizabeth's countenance. She had changed somehow.

"I will find Gordy immediately." Damon stood to take his leave. "You two need some time to talk. I will let myself out." Then he was gone, leaving Darcy and Elizabeth to reconcile their differences.

Neither of them moved, but instead spent time memorizing the face of the other. "I have thought of little but you since you left Pemberley." Darcy's breathing became shallow. "Tell me that we still have a chance."

Elizabeth dropped her eyes, needing to speak the truth, but not sure Darcy would accept the person she had become since she met him. She was not the perfect model of a lady. She could not give full control to her husband. "It seemed so simple at the start," she began.

Darcy swallowed the emptiness filling his heart. Unable to look into those emerald green eyes any longer, he rolled his own up in an act of supplication. "I understand. We will do what is necessary, and then I will make arrangements for your protection."

Elizabeth was on her feet immediately, taking his face in her hands and forcing him to really see her. "Fitzwilliam Darcy, some-day you will let me finish a thought before you jump to a conclu-sion. I am saying that I cannot be a passive female, waiting for my husband to tell me what to think or how to act. Do you really believe you are so unworthy of a person's love? If so, I have an ordeal of my own after we finish this one, because I must convince you that I love you beyond reason." She leaned in to kiss him. It was an act of tenderness—but also an act of incomplete submission.

Darcy pulled her onto his lap, but he never released the kiss. Instead, he deepened it. Like a starving man, he took her mouth fully. Nothing satisfied him; he could not get close enough—could not let Elizabeth leave his embrace. When she breathed out, Darcy breathed in—needing to fill himself with her. He hungered in a way he once would not have believed possible. It was a sexual thing, but it was more than that. True, Darcy wanted to ravage her, but he wanted to possess her—to cherish Elizabeth and bind her to him forever in an all-encompassing love. Darcy's lips rested above hers. "How have I lived without you?"

"My love, neither of us lived before the Meryton assembly."

CHAPTER 27

Tremulous cries of mortal terror reigned during the night. If anyone slept, he was the exception. Wickham led the attacks himself, and nary a house in the village or countryside was spared. Shrills of death filled the air as the mist moved progressively over the landscape. Those brave enough to watch it likened it to the finger of God and the plagues of Egypt, and—similar to God's Passover—each household marked their door frame and all windows with signs of Christianity and crudely made crosses of ash, along with garlic, in the pagan way. Prayer vigils continued throughout the night, and the blessed streaks of dawn brought shouts of joy ringing from household to household.

Even more effective, the colonel placed sentries throughout a five-mile radius to keep anyone from entering the area during the darkness. No loss of human life occurred, and they congratulated themselves on their small victory. Darcy promised to replace the few farm animals lost, and most were satisfied with how well their precautions had protected them.

Besides the other safeguards, Elizabeth placed a score of salt outside each door of the inn, and she put a line around the barn to protect the animals and the stable hands. Yet no one celebrated at the inn. Few boarders stayed with the preparations, and those who did huddled together. Throughout the night, faces and hands clawed at the windows, glazed eyes pleaded for admittance, and bloody mouths sang out in warning. Darcy heard the innkeeper comment on being the proprietor of hell.

He and Elizabeth watched it all unfold from their bedroom window. Elizabeth leaned into his shoulder for comfort. "Will it ever end?" A blood-curdling scream caused her to start in fright.

"It is like something out of Exodus, but it will end with the dawn." He stroked the back of her head. "I never expected such a scene of horror. How did evil get such a foothold?"

Elizabeth traced his jaw line with her fingertips. "No one would take a stand before now."

"Am I up to this, Elizabeth? I mean, can I change this for these people? I am not some gypsy claiming vampiric powers in order to swindle good people out of their money. I came here to save *my* family, but now the blood of more than *twenty* families is my responsibility."

She stroked his chin with the back of her hand. "You cannot, my love, take such thoughts into this battle, or failure will be assured. Instead, do this for me, for Georgiana, and for yourself. Everyone else will benefit from your triumph."

Damon tapped on the door. "Everything is in place," he informed them when Darcy bid his cousin to enter. "This will be the last night these people live in fear."

"I sincerely hope so." Darcy's doubts still played havoc with his resolve. "Damon, would you stay with Elizabeth for a few minutes? I wish to speak to the innkeeper. This hurt his business, and I want to assure him we will make restitution." He handed off his wife to the colonel. Darcy noted how they both stiffened with the gesture, but he made no comment.

Judiciously, Elizabeth moved back to the window to watch the road and the countryside. She hugged herself, looking for comfort. "How much longer before dawn?"

"Less than an hour." Damon moved behind her and rested his hands on her shoulders.

She forced herself to relax into his touch. The colonel was a gentleman, and even without Darcy as an impediment, he would treat her appropriately—with respect. They would come out of this trying situation as good friends. "Are we doing the right thing?"

"We are fighting for your husband's life."

Elizabeth simply nodded. "He is a good man."

"The very best."

She turned to face him. "Will we prevail?"

The colonel tilted his head as he pondered her question. "I have been in situations with less preparation and fewer options for victory. Maybe I underestimate our opponents, but we have the means to hold sway."

"Then Fitzwilliam and I will put our trust in you, Sir."

★ ★ ★

"They dare to defy me!" Wickham shouted in the empty hall. His emulators had returned to their graves, and he remained alone to face his own *demons*. Furious with how Darcy's family had tricked him, Wickham steamed before exploding. A tornado unleashed itself within the hall, as Wickham stood dead center in the room and let the wind carry the tapestries and the furniture in a crazy swirl of color and power and deafening noise. His hair whipped about his face, but Wickham was lost in the impregnability of the display, allowing the blast to steadily increase in strength, rebuilding his confidence with the sheer brute force of it. "*Aaaah!*" he yelled at the top of his lungs before letting his arms lower and the whirlwind subside. "They will *rue* the day they dared to question my order!"

Rushing up the stairs, he hit the door to his private room with a blast of air, tearing it from its hinges. Then he stilled himself, reverently entering his shrine. Here he might find serenity. Everything he loved—except Ellender D'Arcy—could be found in this room. The sun, the moon, and the stars—three turning gold circles—hung overhead, directly above the moss-covered coffin. A misty cauldron, whispering of time and night and blood, sat in the corner, while an ivy-covered crown of antlers stood in the center of the altar. Candles lighted in veneration highlighted a torque of gold, a symbol of his sacred pledge, while five serpents, embodying the five rivers, slithered among his treasures. "Welcome home," he whispered to the room. The open coffin spoke of longing, and Wickham moved to it. Stepping within, he laid back against the satin-covered interior. Within moments, he slept deeply—chest rising and falling in a slow, sustaining rhythm. "Tonight," he murmured in his dreams. "*Tonight,* Darcy."

★ ★ ★

"Will this work, Colonel?" Gordy unloaded bundles of white thorn and ash staves. It was high noon, and the Darcys prepared for the evening.

"A dhampir knows how to drive a vampire away, and this is one of the steps." The colonel placed a stave horizontally across each of the marked and unmarked graves.

Gordy followed Damon's pattern. "What will them staves do?" he asked, bending over to place the wood carefully on the mounded dirt.

"The soul cannot leave the grave if the stave lies across it."

"All them creatures be stuck in the ground?"

Damon responded, "Until we decide to let them out."

"That be somethin' to see, Colonel." He picked up another bundle and moved to the other side of the cemetery.

Damon watched as Elizabeth struggled with the large bags of salt and millet. "Gordy, leave those if you would, and go and help the lady. She will explain what she needs for you to do."

Damon's newest recruit did what he was told. "Let me be helpin' ye, Ma'am." Gordy took the heavy bag from Elizabeth's arms.

"Oh, bless you, Gordy." She wiped perspiration from her forehead with her handkerchief.

"Ye jist be tellin' Gordy what to do, and I be doin' it. Colonel there tell me to he'p ye."

Elizabeth looked up to see Damon continuing to place the staves. "I will thank him later. Now, Gordy, if you will follow me, we want to place a stream of salt all around the inside of the graveyard."

"Seem like a mighty big waste of salt, Ma'am, but I be doin' what ye ask." Using a knife, he cut a small hole in the bottom of the bag and walked slowly around the perimeter of the site.

"Make at least two rounds, Gordy. The spirits cannot cross the salt line, so I want no breaks in the markings," Elizabeth instructed him.

"Yes, Ma'am." He continued his slow trek, meticulously filling in the uneven flow.

Darcy came up behind her. "Where shall we place the millet, Elizabeth?"

"Have Peter use a ladle to scoop millet onto both the head and the foot of each grave and in front of the gate of each crypt."

Darcy smiled at her, squeezing her hand. "Yes, my love."

They brought in wooden stakes and several bags of coins to hide in a church alcove until they needed them. "Everything is set!" the colonel called out to the group. "Gordy and Peter, you two stay here. We will send food and drink. You are to make sure that no one else enters the cemetery. The three of us will return long before it is time for the confrontation."

"Yes, Colonel."

"Gordy," Darcy asked, "do the villagers understand that they must rebury those we release tonight?"

"I be tellin' 'em all. We be not understandin' how ye be doin' all this, but they come on the morrow. I'se sees to it."

Darcy, Damon, and Elizabeth returned to the inn. Not wishing to talk about what the night might bring, they took their meal in Darcy's room, away from curious travelers. They ate in near silence, each one consumed with his or her own thoughts.

Finally, the colonel could take no more. "I believe I shall take to my bed for a few hours. It is likely to be the last rest I will have for some time. If you two will excuse me." He left with a half bow.

Yet still they remained silent. Finally, Darcy spoke his thoughts. "I wish I had not agreed to this. How can a man place his wife in such danger and still call himself a man?"

"I am not a weak woman, my Husband. You, in fact, taught me to use a sword and to ride," she protested.

Darcy looked contrite. "I should not have encouraged your behavior."

"Mr. Darcy, you fell in love with me because I was different, not part of the *ton*. Did we not settle this earlier?"

Darcy moved to kneel in front of her. "God help me, Elizabeth, I truly do love you, and although I know you to be more capable than many men with whom I am acquainted, I cannot bear to place you in danger."

"If you worry, remember, Damon will protect me, Sir."

Darcy felt a pang of jealousy at hearing her refer to his cousin on such intimate terms, but he tried to push it aside. "It is my province to protect my wife."

"We keep coming back to this sticking point. Damon Fitz-william recognizes that I am *more* than what *you* see. Maybe it is his experience on the battlefield that allows him to see a person's true worth; even though you profess to know my worth also, you cling to antiquated ideas. I gave you my heart months ago. May I remind you, my Husband, it is my love for you that brought me here!"

Darcy closed his eyes in submission. "Is there nothing I may say to change your mind?"

Elizabeth gently touched his face in a soft caress. "No, Sir. Your cousin will go tonight, with or without me. I cannot let him do this alone. You must concentrate your efforts on Wickham. Damon deserves some consideration for all he has done for us." Elizabeth brushed her lips across his. "Now, I will follow your cousin's example. I intend to take to my bed. Would you join me, my Husband?"

Darcy emitted a deep sigh of resignation. He was not sure he could ever be the type of man Elizabeth needed, but he was sure he could not let her out of his life, so he would try to emulate his cousin's approach. "Holding you is exquisite, my love. How could I refuse?" Darcy scooped Elizabeth into his arms and carried her to his bed. He reverently lowered her to the pillows, following her down. "Remind me why I should stop the curse," he murmured as he trailed a line of kisses down Elizabeth's neck. He hovered over that one spot, which possessed him, sucking gently with his lips and then expelling his breath over it to make her shiver with desire. Her breathing became shallow, and she let her head fall back to give him easier access. Then boldly she slid her hand down his back, and

Darcy groaned. He returned to her mouth and, with lips hovering above hers, he growled, "Elizabeth, you consume me." The kiss that followed became a promise of love—love they would share when the insanity ended.

Darcy and Elizabeth arrived at the church a few hours before midnight. They planned to run through every possible scenario they could anticipate with the colonel. They sent the others away, not wishing to involve innocents in what could potentially be indiscriminate slaughter. It would be difficult enough for the villagers who had already mourned the loss of their loved ones to do so again. Those defeated tonight must be staked and reburied tomorrow.

The colonel looked up from the pew upon which he reclined when the Darcys made an entrance. He had returned several hours earlier to check the security around the church and the gravesites.

Elizabeth's appearance brought a smile to his face. "Mrs. Darcy, you look fetching," he teased.

Elizabeth donned the breeches, shirt, and waistcoat Darcy had given her to facilitate their fencing lessons, along with a loose-fitting coat, probably belonging to one of the stable hands. She turned in place and made a deep curtsy, as if dressed for a ball. "Thank you, Colonel, for noticing."

A bit possessively, Darcy caught her around the waist and pulled her to him. "I was thinking, Cousin, all women should dress as such."

"Heaven forbid, Darcy! Could you imagine Lady Anne or *my* mother dressed so? Besides, if we accepted women wearing breeches like a man, what else might we have to accept?"

His good-natured taunt did not offend Elizabeth, as she added her own thoughts. "The right to vote? Control of our own money? An honorable occupation besides being a wife?"

Damon laughed out loud at her disputation. "This is sacrilege, Madam!" he said, feigning ridicule.

Darcy relaxed into the repartee, watching his cousin's attentions to Elizabeth. Damon placed any feelings he possessed for Darcy's wife behind him. The two of them would be friends.

Suddenly, reality returned. In a short time, they would face the possibility of death.

"Is everything in place, Damon?" Darcy's arms encircled Elizabeth, needing to feel her closeness for what could be the last time.

"Elizabeth and I will open graves until we defeat each of Wickham's followers. The salt and the millet will affect their assaults. We have crucifixes and holy water strategically placed throughout the headstones. We will work together to do this. Wickham will have no reinforcements tonight; it will be just the two of you. We have contained the others to this earth. By the way, the priest left you several vials of holy water by the back door of the church. He said you asked for them."

Darcy signaled an acknowledgment of what his cousin told him. "Have we forgotten anything?" Darcy now thought out loud.

Elizabeth moved away from Darcy's embrace, placing importance on what she said. "Fitzwilliam, you must use your wits. Wickham hides something in that house. You must find his *grave* and destroy it, the same way that Damon and I will vanquish those within the cemetery. Without his grave—his coffin—Wickham cannot survive."

"I understand, Elizabeth." Darcy seriously listened to her instructions. Damon trusted her knowledge enough to place his life on the line, so Darcy would also.

"Might we share a prayer?" The colonel moved to the front of the church.

"I believe it appropriate."

The three of them joined hands and bowed their heads. The colonel lowered his voice in worship. "Dear Lord, protect us and guide us in this endeavor. As your humble servants, we pray to release these souls once more into your hands. Allow us to prevail and lead us to do the honorable thing. In the name of the Father, and of the Son, and of the Holy Ghost. Amen."

"Amen." Darcy's and Elizabeth's voices echoed in the silence.

They remained locked in a circle of love for several minutes, each resolving to do their best by the other two.

When Darcy raised his head, he turned to embrace his cousin. Privately, he whispered, "Damon, I know I need not say this, for you will understand even without my words, but I charge you to protect Elizabeth and Georgiana if something goes awry."

"Of course, Darcy."

"Now, if you will excuse us a moment, I need to speak to Elizabeth."

The colonel simply saluted cordially and walked away. "I will check the weapons one more time," he called as he went towards the back of the church.

In semiprivacy, Darcy took Elizabeth in his arms. "You are to be careful, Elizabeth; I cannot live without you. Defeating Wickham would be a sour victory without you by my side." He brushed Elizabeth's hair away from her face. "I love you, Elizabeth Bennet Darcy."

"Then I charge you, Sir, to protect yourself. My happiness depends upon your being my husband. You are not to leave me at twenty years to find my way in this world alone."

"Are those orders, my love?" he said as he smiled down at her.

Elizabeth traced his lips with her fingertips. "They are, Mr. Darcy, and you need to address your bride's wishes."

"Might my bride wish to kiss me?" His voice sounded suddenly less sure.

"*Wish* to kiss you?" She shook her head. "*Need* to kiss you." She went up on her tiptoes as Darcy lowered his head. It was a kiss that bound them to each other—not ravenous—but tender and giving, and, above all, loving. "Godspeed," she whispered as they parted.

Almost instantly, the colonel returned. "It is time." He handed Elizabeth a sword as Darcy took up one of his own. "Come, Elizabeth." The colonel took her hand. "We will see you on the other side, Darcy," he called as he led her away. Darcy prayed his cousin's words had no double meaning.

He watched them exit the side entrance to the church. Just as they reached the door, Elizabeth's catlike eyes caught Darcy's—speaking of commitment and of tenacity. "Protect her, God," Darcy pleaded and then turned to the back of the church. Grabbing the vials of holy water, he directed his attention to Wickford Manor.

Still a few minutes before midnight, Darcy circled the graveyard on the outside of the hedgerow. Reaching the hill's well-worn path, he glanced over his shoulder to where Damon lifted Elizabeth over the hedges, not wishing to disturb the salt line. He waited for his cousin to place her safely on the ground. They turned to face where he stood. Damon gestured with the sword, but Elizabeth simply stood tall and gazed at him. Through the dark, Darcy saw her every feature, the look of undying love clearly visible, and then he turned to make his descent. Tonight, no light came from Wickford Manor, but Darcy knew Wickham waited within. The full moon helped to illuminate the way as Darcy moved cautiously through the wooded field.

Reaching the house, he tried each of the doors and the windows, seeking an entrance, but each one was bolted shut. He preferred not to break in, not to sound an alarm, although he intuitively knew Wickham expected his arrival.

Circling the house, Darcy hid behind a large bush to observe the front of the manor; yet nothing moved within. Guardedly, he climbed the outside steps, trying to remain in the shadows. *I can smell human blood.* He heard Wickham's words clearly now as he approached the front door. A shiver shook Darcy's spine when he saw the door standing ajar. *He waits for you.* A warning rang in his head: *Death calls you.*

Shoring up his resolve, Darcy used his shoulder to push the door wider. For some reason, he did not fear Wickham's lying in wait, hiding behind the door or some other darkened passageway. It was not of Wickham's nature: They would face each other in a pivotal arena.

Waiting for his eyes to adjust to the dense darkness of the entranceway, he cautiously stepped inside. The moon reflected through the left-hand windows, creating a latticework of light and dark patches across the hardwood floors, a luminescent carpet leading to the main hall.

Darcy warily moved to the room described by his cousin—the hub for the dance. He had seen it only briefly the night he came here alone. For two nights Darcy had listened to the cadent shuffling of feet—unaccented pulsations. He imagined the sway of the banshee-like disembodied spirits bending to Wickham's gestures as his enemy orchestrated an improvised promenade.

Now he stood where those lost souls had stood. The double doors, fully wide, opened to a grand hall. The expanse of the room spoke of Seorais Winchcombe's desire to be the gentleman he never was. Darcy again felt a twinge of empathy for the man who had lost everything because he loved Darcy's relative. Finding a candle by the door, Darcy lit it, compelled to see the hall for himself.

Lighting it, Darcy held it aloft. Again, he knew Wickham was not in this room, but he moved guardedly. Broken and twisted furniture filled every corner and was piled high in the room's center. Fine tapestries depicting forested scenes of animals and of pagan gods hung precariously from light fixtures, shredded by the force of what must have been a violent storm. Darcy recognized the destruction, knew automatically that it had come from Wickham. Every pretense his enemy had put in place lay destroyed, except for an ornately carved, thick-legged chair, resting in the dead center of the room. Moving to it, Darcy's fingers traced the etching found in the wood, a horned god—resembling a human—surrounded by animals. The branching antlers stretched like treetops as the god sat, legs spread wide and holding a torque in one hand and a horned serpent in the other. Above the scene was the name Cernunnos, written in gold. *Elizabeth and Mrs. Annesley were correct*, Darcy thought.

Darcy circled the chair once, admiring its craftsmanship, and then moved to the doorway. *Upstairs*. He heard the word as if the walls spoke it. Setting the candle on the table, he took a fresh one and lit it from the first.

Taking a deep breath, he placed his foot tentatively on the first step and straightened his knee to move his weight upward. Darcy repeated the process, slowly approaching a final counterpoint. Step by step, he soon stood at the top of the staircase. Knowing that most people would turn automatically to the right, Darcy chose the passage on the left.

Again, the moon lit the way, a beacon in the night, to another open doorway. Unlike the rest of the house, this room radiated light; yet it was cold and uninviting all the same. The door tottered on its hinges, but Darcy moved through the doorway anyway, now drawn by a hypnotic spell.

The coffin was there, and Wickham was in it. Tantalized by the tranquility of the scene, Darcy first set down the candle and then reached for the sword by his side. Inching slowly towards the target, he overcame a powerful urge to run from the room and the scene depicting what he could easily become.

Wickham rested in his coffin, arms crossed about his waist, his eyes wide open, but as if seeing something not there. Darcy's hate controlled him; this was the creature that had filled the lives of generations of Darcys with fear. Wickham left chaos and death wherever he looked. A beast of the night, Wickham indiscriminately discarded his victims, leaving them torn and broken, great gashes ripping apart their necks, or he took them as he had Lydia Bennet, small puncture wounds draining their life, one drop of blood at a time.

Impulsively drawn to Wickham's figure, Darcy now stood over it. Poised, he placed the tip of the sword above the braggart's heart and prepared to end it all. Wickham's steel grey eyes told a tale of despair and of rage—and as they turned deathly pale, Darcy felt a fizzle of excitement course through his veins. Minutely, he shifted his weight and prepared to plunge the blade into Wickham's flesh, but as he watched, silently, a serpent slithered forth from under Wickham's arm and wrapped itself around the sword's tip. In a fraction of a second, panic shot up Darcy's back, and he snapped a quick glance at Wickham's face, only to find the grey eyes closed and a grim smile adorning the mouth. Knowing Wickham's penchant for show, and needing to act immediately, Darcy flicked his wrist to adjust the paik, but before he could thrust, a wrist shot out and caught his arm in a viselike grip. Seeing Darcy's face again, Wickham's eyes—now blackened pools of timeless death—glowed.

CHAPTER 28

Damon and Elizabeth stood in the middle of the headstones, waiting for they knew not what. "Stay close," he cautioned.

"Count on it." Elizabeth turned slowly in a circle, scanning for a possible attack. "When do you suppose…?" She did not need to finish the thought; the colonel understood.

"Any moment now," he whispered.

Almost as if the earth heard them, the ground beneath their feet began to vibrate so violently they barely could maintain their balance, and they jumped to safety. "They want out," the colonel gasped as he caught Elizabeth before she fell. Shrieks of pain rang from the earth; chasms of sorrow—eerie howls of anguish begging to be set free. "So it begins," he murmured to himself. "One at a time, Elizabeth," Damon warned as he reached for a white thorn stave, seesawing on the nearest mound.

They stepped back as a deliciously beautiful young maid, dressed innocently in a white gown, like one for a girl at her debut, rose from the mist seeping from the center of a grave. Her features became more defined as the breeze lifted the vapor until she floated alluringly only inches from the ground. She smiled seductively at Damon and rolled her shoulder, letting the bodice of her dress sag, exposing the curve of her breast. "Would you like to come with me, Sir?" she purred. "It is my introduction to society."

The colonel simply nodded and gestured for the spirit to lead the way. He followed her at a healthy distance. Behind him, the shrill drone continued. He could see Elizabeth out of the corner of his eye paralleling his movement on the other side of the markers.

When the girl reached the back of the site, she paused, swaying to a silent tune.

"Is something amiss?" Damon asked behind her.

The girl did not turn, but she spoke. "Someone blocks my way." Sadness laced her voice.

Damon steadied himself, expecting an attack. "*I* do."

"Why?" A man's deep voice boomed, but it was the girl who threw her head back and howled.

Elizabeth jumped with the verbal explosion, but the colonel simply waited. Within a split second, she was on him, pushing Damon back with savage force. Her jaw snapped as she lunged for his throat, but he used his own weight against her, sending the girl flying through the air and crashing against the side of a mausoleum.

Immediately, she attacked again, climbing on his back while clawing at his arms. Damon struggled to throw her off, but suddenly, Elizabeth appeared from nowhere. She scooped a handful of millet from that placed about the graveyard and unceremoniously threw it in the girl's face.

Instantaneously, the girl released her hold and dropped to the ground on all fours. Using her fingers, she began to separate the seeds, lining them up and organizing the grain in structured piles.

Meanwhile, Damon staggered forward a few steps, trying to recover from the intensity of the fight, but then he turned, ready to begin again, only to see the girl's spirit groveling in the dirt.

Elizabeth seemed as stunned as he. "What do we do?"

"Put her to rest forever." Reverently, he bent over the girl and plunged the sword deep within her, aiming for her heart. The vapor rose from the wound, and with its exodus, the girl's shape disintegrated into the night air.

Elizabeth's mouth fell open. "Mercy."

"Amen."

"No more waiting for them to attack." Elizabeth moved to the next grave.

The colonel half laughed. "I wanted to see what would happen when she reached the salt line."

"Admit it, Damon. You were enticed by the girl's *beauty.*"

He took a fighting stance before Elizabeth reached for the stave. "How could you think so, Elizabeth?" Damon smiled at her mockingly. "You are the most becoming *Scottish laddie* I have ever seen."

Elizabeth removed the stave, and they waited, but nothing happened. "That one is clear," Damon noted. "Put the stave in the ground like a spear next to the headstone. That will be the mark tomorrow to pass over this one."

Moving down the row, Elizabeth lifted the next stave. This time, the mist took on the visage of an old man. Once he stood before them, Damon struck out with the sword, hitting this one in the side of the neck. The revenant lashed out at Damon, as Elizabeth, on the other side, swung an arcing stroke of her weapon, also slashing at the man's neck. He growled at her and bared his teeth, preparing to strike, but Damon lunged and hit the heart once again. The man fell backwards across the grave and disappeared into a bloody haze.

"That was better," Damon commented as they moved to the next mound.

"Look at the size of this graveyard!" Elizabeth peered around them, realizing what they still faced. The vibrations continued, but the corner in which they stood no longer rocked. They had checked twelve graves and fought two apparitions.

The colonel moved around the last headstone of the row. The upright staves marked all those safe from Wickham's evil. "The next row," he said ominously.

"Where do you suppose Fitzwilliam is?" She glanced towards Wickham's house.

"My cousin is well, Elizabeth," he assured her. "Are you ready for the next one?" She signaled her agreement as he bent again. "We have our job, and Darcy has his. It is up to us to ensure that Wickham has no reinforcements. One on one, Darcy will prevail."

* * *

The skeletal hand tightened on Darcy's arm as Wickham sat up, like Lazarus rising from the dead. "I knew you would return." The ominous words ricocheted off the walls, and momentarily Darcy did not respond. He simply stared dumbly at the bony fingers encircling his wrist and the slow, gravity-defying climb of the snake up the length of the sword.

Elizabeth's voice rose in the silence. *Because I did not get the chance to tell my husband that I am completely and hopelessly in love with him*, it called out, and Darcy reacted. Jerking his arm vehemently from the force holding it, Darcy spun quickly away, bringing his arms to his sides as he did. The rotating force sent the serpent flying through the air, carrying it through the open door and out somewhere into the bowels of the house. An overwhelming energy filled the room, pressing Wickham's coffin against a far wall and tilting it on its end.

Incensed by the intrusion, Wickham answered, delivering a show of his own. The cauldron—the antlers—the engraved gold plates—and even the snakes swirled around Darcy's head, dipping dangerously close in a maelstrom of power—an obvious threat.

Yet Darcy did not falter. He stood proud and strong, now beginning to understand that Wickham's power was a great deal of smoke and mirrors, depending on his victim's fear—on intimidation—and as he watched, the tornadic winds died out, and everything came crashing to the floor between them. Not waiting for Darcy to respond, a quick flick of Wickham's hand sent the cauldron cannonballing into Darcy's midsection, knocking him to the ground and leaving him gasping for air.

Struggling to his knees, Darcy answered with his own display by powering the antlers—a barbed spear—which barreled down on Wickham. A quick sidestep kept it from impaling him, but not from ripping open several points along Wickham's left side. Miraculously, as Elizabeth's dream had predicted, the wounds oozed with blood, each a different shade of red, as if it did not belong to Wickham at all—he had only stored it to sustain his existence. With his right hand, Wickham pulled the bony points from his shoulder and cast them down to join the debris accumulating on the floor. "Your accuracy improves, Darcy." Wickham used a crossover step to keep facing his enemy, but allowing the distance between them to increase. "We have crowed like the rooster," he said and smirked. "Shall we now fight like cats and dogs?"

Darcy never let his eyes leave Wickham's face, but he was very aware of every object in the room. One of the snakes slithered into the discarded cauldron, and another followed the flying one into the darkened hallway. In his field of vision, Darcy could not see the other two, but he did not worry about them. Even though he knew little of snakes, he suspected Wickham kept them, like everything else, purely for show—to instill fear in anyone who might invade his privacy. If a person was to die in this house, it would be at Wickham's hands, not from being bitten by some poisonous snake.

In a mimicking pattern, Darcy also used a grapevine step to adjust to his enemy's new position. "What now, Wickham?"

"We finish it, Darcy—only one of us."

★ ★ ★

"Wait, Elizabeth!" Damon called from the end of one row of graves as she moved around a particularly tall headstone, which completely blocked her from his sight. He delayed; the last specter had come close to escaping before he threw holy water on it. The shriek of pure pain still resounded through every bone in his body. He would not forget the sounds and the smells associated with this night for as long as he lived. It was worse than the slaughters at Talavera and at Salamanca. The metallic smell of so much blood sickened him, and the fact that he and Elizabeth were bringing forth the demise of so many ate away at him. Yet he judiciously carried on, trying to spare Elizabeth as much of the slaughter as possible. *He* understood the destruction of war, but Elizabeth was an innocent. He would not let *her* suffer such nightmares.

Elizabeth's scream jolted him from his thoughts, and instantaneously, Damon was at a run to reach her. A hulk of a man, perhaps twice Elizabeth's size, pinned her to the side of Lord Thomas's crypt and pressed her lustfully to the wall, meaning to have her in a primitive coupling. Enraged, Damon sprang forward, and with a powerful attack of his own, stabbed the creature through the back, perforating his chest with the rapier. Now the scream came from the demon as he stumbled away from a very shaken Elizabeth. The mist rose again and was sucked back into the earth as Elizabeth propelled herself into Damon's waiting arms.

She shook from sobs of joy and of fear. Damon's breath rasped in exhaustion as he held her close. "I am so sorry, Elizabeth." He caressed her hair, stroking gently as he held her head to his chest. "I should have protected you."

Elizabeth pressed her face against his shoulder. "It was my fault; I should have waited for you. I foolishly put both of us in danger."

Damon tightened his embrace and gently kissed the top of her head. Elizabeth's arms encircled his waist, and they stood as such, hearts pounding from the unbelievable terror.

Breathing normally at last, Damon loosened his grip, but did not release Elizabeth. "Do you hear what I hear?" he whispered close to her ear.

Elizabeth tilted her head back to listen carefully. "I do not hear anything."

"Exactly." Damon smiled down at her.

Elizabeth pulled away and looked around her. "But we are not finished."

"Maybe we are. This is the newer part of the cemetery—more than likely containing families not from this area originally. We will still check each one, but I suspect we have finished our task." Triumphantly, they shifted between the last two rows of headstones, but nothing happened when they lifted the staves.

"No more!" Elizabeth nearly cackled when she speared the last stave into the frozen ground. "What of Fitzwilliam?" she asked in surprise at having forgotten her husband's ordeal in the midst of her own struggles. Turning curiously towards the house, she called to the colonel, "My God, Damon, look!"

★ ★ ★

"We finish it, Darcy—only one of us."

The words still reverberated in the room when Wickham threw himself at Darcy, clawing at him like a wild animal. His nails shredded the sleeve of Darcy's coat and ripped the skin along his forearm. Like a rabid wolf, Wickham's jaw snapped viciously, trying to reach Darcy's face and neck.

Overpowered by the sudden attack, Darcy, knocked from his feet, braced his arms, holding back the sheer monstrous force of the beast. All of Darcy's other dealings with Wickham had been with a mildly taunting gentleman vampire, who used his powers to strike quickly and then escape. This Wickham tried to tear Darcy limb from limb. This animal felt no remorse—just the compulsion to kill its prey. Finally able to wedge his knee between them, Darcy used his legs to hurl Wickham across the room, where he landed on all fours.

Immediately, the wolflike Wickham rebounded, crouching in preparation for the next attach. Like him, Darcy rolled from his back to a semiclosed position, grabbing the sword as he did. Straightening slowly, he shifted the sword to his other hand, and then made a come-hither motion, a silent challenge. Unhurriedly, Wickham began to circle, a bestial specter needing to hunt—needing to kill and feed. His eyes, now coal black, flashed with a fiery glow, as if coal tar burned within them. "You cannot win, Darcy," he growled.

Warily, Darcy turned in a slow circle, keeping Wickham always where he could see him. Like the dance he arranged each night, Wickham turned in a definite pattern, and Darcy adjusted accordingly. As he turned once more, he began to search the room behind Wickham for weapons he could use. Surprisingly, just as in the great hall, Wickham's earlier windstorm had left much of the periphery untouched. The candles still burned and the golden torque still rested on the altar. The three golden plates, which once hung above the coffin, now lay flat on the floor and off to the right. The cauldron, turned on its side, spilled out its contents: a layer of grey ashes, just like those Darcy had found in London; and then there was Wickham's coffin. *Wickham hides something in that house. You must find his grave and destroy it.... Without his grave—his coffin—Wickham cannot survive.* As he surveyed the room, Elizabeth's instructions meant even more. Watching. Waiting. Wary. They circled each other cautiously.

Two more steps and Wickham sprang again. Darcy spun just as the creature leapt, leaving his opponent lying face down among the ashes. Using the sword, he hacked twice at his adversary's left side, hoping to open further the previous wounds. As Wickham tried to recover, Darcy darted to the coffin, still sitting askew on its base, and with a gargantuan effort tipped it over. The dirt sprawled across the floor in dark streaks of decaying matter, and Wickham crawled to it, scooping it up with his right arm, trying to repair his home. "*No...o...o!*" he screamed as he dumped handfuls back into the opened front.

Hoping now to destroy it all, Darcy poured one of the vials of holy water on the satin as Wickham used his body to protect his grave. Darcy waited, but nothing happened.

Wickham, covered in earth and ashes, looked up with amusement. He rubbed the dampened dirt between his fingers. "It is oil, Darcy. You fool," Wickham charged. "You poured oil into the dirt." Triumphantly, Wickham stood, brushing his hand against the side of his pants. "You will pay for this degradation." The ominous words became Wickham's challenge.

Realizing he needed to retreat before he could attack again, Darcy began to edge along the wall, backing away from the advancing, infuriated Wickham.

"I plan for you to suffer long and hard." Wickham hissed the words. "You will pray for hell's relief."

"What makes you think, Wickham, that I am not already in hell?" As he spoke, Darcy moved slowly in the direction of the burning rows of candles. He knew he carried another vial from the church in his pocket; he said a silent prayer that the second one contained anointing oil, as well. "In fact, hell is right here in this room." With that, he threw the second vial against the wall; the glass broke and oil spattered across the fire. Flames leapt and fizzled and began to creep up the dried ivy left strung across what remained of the antlers. The bones of the stag ignited and crumbled. Now, fed by the kindling, the flames moved faster.

Not caring about death, Wickham dove for Darcy's legs, knocking him to the floor, where they rolled in the dirt again. The beast of a few minutes ago returned, and Wickham bit down on Darcy's leg, only to find part of his boot. Darcy used his other leg repeatedly to kick relentlessly at Wickham's face, tearing chunks of skin away from his enemy's eyelid and cheekbone. Fists landed. Cries of pain split the heated air. Their gazes met and did battle.

Darcy's assault forced Wickham to release his hold, and uttering a curse, he clambered to his feet. Picking up the sword that Darcy had dropped, he began irrationally swinging the blade in arcing figure eights, slicing at everything in his wake. Darcy scooted backwards in a crablike manner, trying to evade Wickham's demonic fury. "Hell! Darcy, we are in hell!" he howled, his voice grating.

Reaching the wall closest to the door, Darcy shoved to his feet, sliding his back up the smooth surface. Half the room was now engulfed in flames, but Wickham still railed, screaming of hell and damnation. He caught the tip of the blade on the satin lining of the coffin, pulling part of it free and dragging it through the fire. The material caught the flames, and in his choler, Wickham flung it from him, sending it through the open door to land on the carpet found there.

Out of control, Wickham stalked Darcy, herding him, blocking his every move to flee. Darcy reflexively worked his way sideways along the wall. Heart pounding, he tried to recover from the attack and to judge how to escape the fire and Wickham's wrath. He shifted his weight several times, but each time Wickham countered with a move of his own. Then it happened: The flames reached the coffin. As the fire spread to the lining, the wood popped and cracked from the heat. Wickham spun around to see the damage, and Darcy took his chance and dove out the door, barely missing the flames now crawling along the carpet runner and skipping up the wallpaper and tapestries.

Clumsily, Darcy struggled to his feet and broke into a run, heading for the staircase.

"Darcy!" Wickham boomed as he menacingly stepped into the hallway.

Without thinking, Darcy knelt down and jerked hard on the runner, pulling it from under Wickham's feet and sending his opponent tumbling backwards. Throwing the flaming runner over the banister, Darcy shot a quick glance in Wickham's direction before taking the steps, bounding over the landing. Hitting the main hallway at a run, he looked around frantically for a weapon, hearing the ominous sound of Wickham's boots on the upper stairs. The great hall loomed to the right, and Darcy madly ducked into the room, looking for safety, but Wickham followed only a few heartbeats later. "Darcy!" he bellowed.

Finding no immediate escape, Darcy nonchalantly stepped from behind the pile of broken furniture. "I am here, Wickham."

"So you are." Wickham's eyes glowed red in the darkness as he slowly brought the sword to Darcy's chest. "I expected more from you, Darcy." He moved the blade in a gesture towards the debris. "Have a seat."

Darcy warily moved to the ornate offering, the only piece still intact.

"It seems I no longer have my followers." Wickham looked about the room, feeling anger well up again. "I suppose you had something to do with that."

"You suppose correctly." Darcy watched the flames behind Wickham scatter about the entranceway, jumping from item to item.

"Then I will start over." Wickham pressed the tip of the sword to Darcy's chest. "In fact, I will leave tonight—your wife has three more sisters, if I recall, and there is always sweet Georgiana." The words incensed him, but Darcy realized he needed to keep control; he squeezed the arm of the chair in disgust.

He expected Wickham to run him through, but his rival did not. Instead, a strong right caught Darcy's jaw, shoving it upward and driving his head into the back of the chair. A momentary blurriness became complete blackness. The last thing that Darcy saw was Wickham closing the door behind him.

How long he was out, Darcy did not know, but long enough for the fire to spread, because when he touched the door, the heat told him not to open it. For the second time, Wickham had left him in a burning house. Grabbing the back of a broken chair, Darcy struck the window through which he had spied Wickham that first night. He hit it full force, and it shattered into hundreds of pieces. Using the chair's leg, he battered away at the shards. Climbing out the window, his eyes fell on a shadowy figure, silhouetted in the moonlight, mounting the hill to the cemetery. "Oh, God, not Elizabeth," he murmured and took off at a run.

★ ★ ★

"My God, Damon, look!" Elizabeth stood transfixed by the fiery glow in the sky. "It is the house!"

She was running as hard as she could in the direction of the hill—towards Wickham's house—towards her husband. With each step, her eyes filled with tears. She could not lose Darcy now.

Damon caught her around the waist just as Elizabeth reached the back of the graveyard. She fought him like a wildcat, kicking and screaming for him to release her. "Let me go!" she pleaded, but the colonel pulled her away from a house now fully consumed in flames. Pungent smoke filled the air, and burning embers showered down on them as they clung to each other and stared at the inferno.

"He got out." The colonel said the words aloud, trying to convince himself.

Elizabeth shivered and collapsed against him, defeated. As they watched, the walls began to give way, leaving only a shell.

Then they heard it, running steps coming their way.

Elizabeth broke away from Damon's grasp and, cutting through the barriers they set up to contain those they hunted, she rushed to the edge of the rise, screaming her husband's name—expecting to see his face; but when George Wickham appeared in front of her, Elizabeth could only stare. When he pointed the sword at her, she did not move. Then he jabbed her gently with the tip; Elizabeth responded by stepping back gingerly.

The colonel skidded to a halt behind her. Annoyed by the new configuration, Wickham insisted, "Do you care to introduce me, Mrs. Darcy?"

Elizabeth took another step back. "Where is Fitzwilliam?" she demanded.

"What? No manners, Elizabeth?" Wickham amusedly nudged her with the blade again. "I expect the gentleman knows *my* name. After all, he broke into my house twice, and I have no need of his name."

Damon caught Elizabeth with his left hand and placed her behind him, offering his chest as Wickham's target. "Answer the lady, Wickham," the colonel pressed.

Sinisterly, he complied. "I believe I left Darcy in the grand hall."

Elizabeth caught her breath, and Damon could feel her trembling hand on his back. He reached behind him and caught that hand; he needed for her to move before Wickham charged. He guided her backwards with a tighter-than-usual squeeze of her hand.

Wickham watched the interaction closely. "Does Darcy know how you feel about his wife?" Wickham enjoyed being in control, and this situation played to his conceit. He flicked a finger in the direction of the gravesites, and the colonel stepped back into the arena, but he carefully kept Elizabeth out of Wickham's way. She now lightly rested her hand on his back and stepped in unison with him.

Seeing the graveyard adorned with the perpendicular markings, Wickham actually laughed. "This was *your* idea, Mrs. Darcy? How very astute of you! I knew you were trouble from the beginning. Truthfully, taming you would have been much more pleasurable than bringing that insipid sister of yours to heel." Damon knew when Elizabeth's ire began to rise. With a slight touch of his hand and a shift of his shoulders, he willed her to hold her tongue. "So there is no one left?"

"No one," Damon responded.

"Your husband warned me as such, Mrs. Darcy, but I thought he bluffed, though not so well. You are more tenacious than I expected."

Interrupted by the sound of running feet behind him, Wickham automatically spun to meet the new provocation.

Darcy cleared the rise of the hill, only to once again be at Wickham's disposal. He caught his breath in a great gulp when he saw his wife and cousin safe, and he forced calm into his body although he faced the tip of a sword. He took Wickham's attention from Elizabeth, and that was all that mattered.

Seizing the opportunity, Damon caught Elizabeth up and carried her to safety. She began to resist, but a slight shake of Darcy's head told her to stay, and she let Damon drag her behind a massive memorial. "Stay put," he warned her and began to circle to the far side of the line of graves.

"Darcy?" Wickham said as he smirked. "We return to where it all began."

"Where it began for *you*, Wickham," Darcy countered, "but not for me. My life began only a few months ago when *hope* walked in."

"Ah, is that not sugary sweet! Did you hear that, Mrs. Darcy?" he called out to Elizabeth. "Your husband speaks of your love." Using the sword, Wickham herded Darcy in the direction of the cemetery's center. "You may be right, Darcy. Maybe this is only my personal hell."

They now stood directly between the two crypts, which anchored the site. "Let me show you something." Although barely able to move on his left side, Wickham raised his hands and with a quick burst of air, the lock of Ellender D'Arcy's burial chamber exploded, and the iron gate swung open. "Step next to the gate, Darcy." Darcy moved slowly, not knowing what to expect. "Do you remember the part of the legend where Lady Ellender gave me to Leána?" Darcy nodded as he took up a position next to the opening. "The legend says that I then exacted my revenge on the lady. Watch and see." Then Wickham unveiled the inner door and called out.

As if a supernatural force carried her forward, Lady Ellender D'Arcy appeared in the door of the open vault. "Come, my dear." Wickham extended his hand, and the lady placed hers in his.

Darcy swallowed hard. Lady Ellender D'Arcy was Georgiana in ten years. Long blonde locks adorned her head; the square chin was softened by the high cheekbones and eyes the color of sapphires. "I brought someone to meet you, Ellender." Wickham treated the apparition as if she were his lady. "This, my dear, is Fitzwilliam Darcy."

"The last name is familiar, Sir." The lady curtsied.

Wickham ordered, "Speak to the lady, Darcy."

"Lady Ellender."

"Mr. Darcy, Lady Ellender, came from Derbyshire, his family seat, to make your acquaintance."

"Charmed, Mr. Darcy." Lady Ellender swayed to the same unknown tune that the others had.

"Is she not beautiful, Darcy?"

"How could I deny it, Wickham? My sister is the spitting image." Out of the corner of his eye, Darcy noticed Damon moving quietly to the right.

Wickham glanced back at Ellender. "I thought so also. Georgiana is Ellender as a young girl, when I first fell in love with her."

How gently Wickham treated Ellender surprised Darcy. The man that this creature once was still loved this woman, despite the havoc she had brought to his life. This was a new aspect of Wickham, and Darcy hoped to use it against him.

"The gentleman has his own lady love, my dear." Wickham brought Ellender's delicate hand to his mouth and kissed the back of it; then he called out, "Will you not join us, Mrs. Darcy?"

"Stay where you are, Elizabeth!" Darcy ordered.

"If you wish to see me end your husband's life on the spot, then ignore my bidding." Wickham purposely nicked Darcy's neck to let the blood bubble there.

Darcy warned, "It does not matter, Elizabeth; Wickham plans to kill me anyway."

Wickham jabbed Darcy again, and a second stream worked its way towards his shirt's collar. "Enough!" Elizabeth ordered and stepped from behind the granite. She walked slowly to where Darcy stood, taking his hand as she defiantly took her place beside him.

"That is more like the Elizabeth I have come to know and despise," Wickham growled. "Now, play nice, Mrs. Darcy, and acknowledge *my* Lady Ellender."

"I gladly acknowledge Lady Ellender," Elizabeth contended, "but she is not *your* Lady Ellender, Mr. Wickham. She belongs to *my* ancestor Lord Arawn Benning." Elizabeth watched with some satisfaction as her declaration caused Ellender to drift away towards Lord Thomas's crypt. She now swayed to her own silent music, tracing Arawn's name with her fingertips.

"Ellender!" Wickham roared, but *the lady* heard only her own longing. "Ellender!" he repeated. Then he turned on Elizabeth. "You…ruin…everything!" he roared, stressing each word, loading them with vehemence. With his injured left arm, Wickham lashed out at her, catching Elizabeth's neck with his large hand, his bestial claws returning.

Elizabeth's hands tore at his fingers, and, instantly, Darcy reacted, his own high dudgeon exploding as he hit Wickham full force in the chest with instant power. The potency of the impact sent Wickham reeling backwards as Darcy caught the slumping Elizabeth in his arms and knelt lovingly over her. "My love," he cajoled as he pushed her hair from her face. "Speak to me."

But before she could respond, Wickham charged again, and this time he did not stop—plunging the rapier into Darcy's back. Darcy collapsed on top of his wife's body as blood oozed from the entry and exit wounds in both his back and his side. They laid perfectly still, arms and legs entangled in an intimate moment of ghostly love.

CHAPTER 29

Damon Fitzwilliam saw it all, but was too late to stop Wickham's potentially fatal blow. Armed with his own sword, he charged the brute, spinning Wickham away from Darcy's fallen frame before he could deliver another strike. Now, they faced each other, swords at the ready, and the match began in earnest. Surprisingly, Wickham adeptly fended off everything Damon threw at him as they zigzagged among headstones and mounted the banked earth indicating each of the graves. Sparks disappeared into the night as the blades crashed against each other and grazed markers, but for Damon, this was more than a simple fight. This was for Elizabeth, for what Wickham had done to her, and for the horror of seeing his cousin skewered by this animal.

Darcy's body pinned Elizabeth to the ground, but she managed to leverage herself away from him, scooting to the side until she freed her chest. Pulling her legs from his eased his weight from her badly bruised backside. Getting to her knees beside him, Elizabeth searched Darcy's body for the point of entry. Luckily, the blood flow slowed when she pressed her hand against it, so Elizabeth tore at the shirt she wore, ripping at it to make a bandage.

She could hear the battle going on behind her, but she needed to stop the life from being sapped from Darcy's body. It was too much like her dream, and she would not let him die. "Fitzwilliam!" She pressed against the wound, feeling the bandage go damp under her fingers. "Do not leave me!"

Miraculously, his chest heaved, and she heard him groan.

Elizabeth stretched out over his shoulders and kissed the side of his face. "Please stay with me," she whispered close to his ear.

"Help me up," he moaned, his mouth turned into the earth.

Elizabeth came as close as possible. "What?"

"Help me to my feet." In obvious pain, Darcy rolled to his uninjured side.

Elizabeth tried to turn him back. "You cannot!" she protested.

"Damn it, Wife. I need your help!"

Darcy pulled his knee up and prepared to stand. In opposition to what she knew he needed, Elizabeth braced his weight against her and helped him lift his frame to a standing position, although he hunched his shoulders forward in pain.

"Fitzwilliam, please," she begged as he took a deep breath and staggered in the direction of the foray. Ignoring her pleas, Darcy simply gritted his teeth and took a few more faltering steps before his momentum gave an appearance of strength. Elizabeth trailed along beside Darcy, preparing to help him maintain his balance.

The battle, once powerfully contested, now was one more of strike and retreat than of continuous blows. The colonel used both hands to steady his sword as he caught Wickham's downward thrust and deflected it. Spinning counterclockwise, Damon sliced into Wickham's side with a horizontal arc of the blade. As it was with Darcy's attack at the house, the blood ran in varying hues of red as it trickled down his side.

Now, hilts entangled, Wickham and the colonel struggled face-to-face, hellkite strength versus human resolve. Smelling of putrid decay, Wickham repulsed everything honorable in the colonel's body, and Damon momentarily retracted—a foolish mistake—giving Wickham the advantage he sought. He used his waning powers to send the colonel's body cannonading against the side of the church, fiercely knocking the breath from him.

Darcy and Elizabeth staggered into the midst of the horror, and now he stood between Wickham and his cousin. "Do what I ask when I ask it," he murmured softly as he shoved Elizabeth away from him.

Wickham sighed heavily. "I thought to have disposed of you." He pulled his shoulders back and prepared for another battle.

"I am not so easily discharged." In a like show of strength,

Darcy pulled himself up straight, allowing his height to speak for itself.

Wickham, a lover of all things pretentious, smiled. "How shall we settle it, Darcy? Are you prepared to die today?"

Blood running down his back, Darcy wanted to sink to his knees, but instead, he returned Wickham's jeer with one of his own. "Are you prepared to die *again?*"

"I do not believe that will happen, but I will accommodate you just the same." Wickham took a step back, preparing to attack. "How will you defeat me, Darcy?" Wickham arrogantly rolled his wrist, allowing the rapier to *whish* the air. "Everything you tried has failed."

Darcy feigned a shrug of his shoulders. "As you have a weapon, and I do not, I will have to rely on my wits, unless you choose to do the honorable thing and allow me to recover my cousin's armor." He shifted his weight as if to walk to where Damon lay unconscious against the building, but a countermove by Wickham cut that short, or so Darcy hoped it would appear. In reality, Darcy caught Elizabeth's eyes when he turned his head. She stood where he left her, but she did not cower from the danger. *His Elizabeth* would go down fighting. He willed her with a nod of his head and a lift of his chin to move closer to the nearest grave. Intuitively, as if he led her into the steps of a waltz, her body responded to his signal, and she knew he planned something and needed her help. A sign of recognition turned up the corners of his mouth, and Darcy winked before he returned his attention to Wickham.

"I seem to have left all my honor at Wickford Manor," Wickham taunted. "Hopefully, you will forgive me for taking the advantage." He pretended to bow to his opponent.

Darcy needed a few more moments for Elizabeth to be in place. He watched out of the corner of his eye as she moved closer to the nearest mound. He stalled Wickham. "You call what you did at Wickford honorable?" he challenged. "Sending a cauldron and the plates and the *antlers*…and even the snakes spinning around my head?"

Elizabeth heard the emphasis on the word and knew Darcy reminded her of her dream of driving the deer's rack into Wickham's body. Now, if she just knew exactly what else he wanted.

Wickham laughed lightly. "The snakes were a nice touch, do you not think, Darcy? And the cauldron nearly knocked you out of the picture."

"No more so than when I *speared* you with the horns. I have learned to control my *energy*." Darcy noted thankfully that she understood, because Elizabeth surreptitiously worked the stave from its place.

"Yet your powers are but half as strong as mine, for your weaker human half is a detriment." Wickham quit playing with the sword and set his chin with determination. "You, for example, have not mastered the power of the change, but I have."

A split second later, the sword lay idly on the ground, and Wickham was the vicious wolf advancing on Darcy again. However, Darcy did not balk, nor did he give any indication of what he planned. His eyes and facial expression betrayed nothing. Only Elizabeth observed the slight shift of his weight.

When Wickham sprang, she heard Darcy's "*Now!*" and she tossed the ash stave into the air.

Instantaneously, Darcy's arms rose and time slowed. Wickham, as a wolf, rather than a vampire, came under Darcy's control, and the animal pawed the air in slow motion, its unyielding jaw open in preparation for the attack. Slobber dripped from its gums, while the tongue lolled to the side. Coal black eyes widened as the energy sustained its flight. Sharp fangs lengthened in anticipation of finding its prey.

The wolf moved in a straight line towards the sharpened stave pointed at it, and nothing the animal did could change that fact. They were on a collision course, and, for a moment, Wickham fought the reality, and then he relaxed into the movement, accepting what Fate gave him.

Darcy watched with satisfaction as it all came together in a perfect crescendo. When the point of the pikestaff tipped for its descent, Darcy closed his eyes and brought everything together at faster-than-normal speed, envisioning the impact. *Twank!* The stave pierced the animal in the center of its chest, impaling it as if it were a butterfly specimen. And then Wickham abruptly fell upon the grave of what was once one of his followers—his twisted body broken and deformed.

"How did you learn to do that?" Damon's voice came from somewhere behind him. A heartbeat later, Elizabeth was in Darcy's arms, kissing along his chin line and sobbing his name. Recognizing the finality of the act, Darcy breathed out heavily and collapsed, sinking to his knees. Damon caught him on the way down, hoisting Darcy's arm over his shoulder and leading him to lie upon one of the benches lining the gravesites.

"I need to get some bandages," Elizabeth called over her shoulder as she ran in the direction of the church.

"It is finished, Darcy," Damon assured him as he unbuttoned Darcy's coat and waistcoat. "We will get you to a physician."

"Thank you, Damon." Darcy's words were breathy and a bit slurred. "For everything."

Damon ripped Darcy's shirt to see the wound better. "No thanks are necessary. We have always been more than cousins." The colonel touched Darcy's side. "This one seems to be a surface wound. Anyplace else?"

"Just my arm." He touched the colonel's shoulder. "And you, Damon?"

"More bruises and lacerations than I care to know about, but I will be well." Damon continued to check for other possible wounds.

Darcy's voice asked for the truth: "How did Elizabeth fare?"

"Mrs. Darcy did what was asked. There were a few close calls, but I tried to spare Elizabeth the enormity of what we did. I feared for how it might affect her disposition."

Darcy swallowed hard. He had never even considered how such destruction might affect his wife. Her personality always seemed larger than life; he had never thought that anything could put a dent in her armor.

"I could not have finished this without her." Darcy ran his hand in frustration across his face. "Elizabeth is everything right in my world, Damon."

"I know, Darcy."

Elizabeth's hurried footsteps ended the conversation. "I found some sashes in the priest's quarters," she said as she approached the bench, but then Elizabeth went rigid, staring off into the cemetery, and Darcy followed her gaze to see George Wickham standing ten feet away—a broken lance still embedded in his chest.

Realizing the contest still raged on, Darcy struggled to sit up, and as Damon supported his back, he whispered, "My right boot... gun...one shot...hit his heart." Damon helped Darcy swing his legs around to a seated position and then backed away.

"I will not make the mistake again, Darcy, of changing into something you can control," Wickham hissed. "Luckily, one of my powers is rejuvenation. A night's sleep will heal these wounds."

Darcy forced himself to his feet. "Your coffin is destroyed, Wickham. Where will you find such sleep?"

"I will sleep with Lady Ellender." Wickham took a menacing step towards Darcy, and, immediately, both Elizabeth and Damon stood between them. "We do not have to do this again, do we, Darcy?"

"You will need to go through me, Sir, to reach my husband." Elizabeth reached into her pocket for the small bottle of holy water the priest had left for Darcy in the back of the church. She had planned to use it to help clean his wounds. Now, she moved her thumb to uncork it.

"And through me, also," the colonel contended as he carefully cocked the gun he palmed in his hand.

"As you see, Wickham, even humans have loyal followers." Darcy smiled at the show of defiance.

Wickham bristled with anger. "I will not *have* this!" He strode forward, his right arm extended to bring forth his power, when, suddenly, in desperation, Elizabeth released the vial, showering Wickham with the blessed water.

A cry of alarm filled the air as the being now controlling Wickham's body covered his face with his hands. The smell of burning flesh filled the air as the colonel lunged to bring Wickham directly in front of him. The shrieks continued, but, undaunted, Damon placed the short muzzle of the gun to Wickham's chest and pulled the trigger.

The sound of the gun momentarily drowned out the shrieks, and then total silence reigned. Gunpowder mixed with the stench of death surrounded them, and this time when he fell, none doubted that Wickham would not stand again. His body shriveled to skin and bones. No one spoke. Darcy, Elizabeth, and the colonel stood transfixed by the sight of the rotted corpse of the creature who had plagued them and theirs for two hundred years.

"Mr. Darcy?" the softly accented speech of Ellender D'Arcy shocked them all. "Is he gone forever?"

Darcy found his voice first. "Seorais Winchcombe is no more, Lady Ellender."

"I am not sorry to hear it. It is time. I should never have traded Seorais's life for Arawn's, but I knew of no other way to save the man I loved. Yet nothing was the same after that. It affected my dear Arawn in ways to which I cannot put words." Pure sadness crossed her face.

Elizabeth edged forward and spoke to Ellender as though she were a troubled child. "Lady Ellender, it is nearly dawn; you should return to your bed."

Ellender looked about her, seeing the first streaks of light in the sky. "I wish to never spend another night without Arawn. You will see to that, Mr. Darcy?"

"I am your servant, Lady Benning." Darcy offered a pain-ridden bow.

Ellender D'Arcy pivoted to return to the open vault. "I will follow her," Elizabeth said as she handed Damon the bandages she held.

"Lady Ellender is still a vampire," Damon warned under his breath. "Take the sword."

Elizabeth nodded her head in understanding and then followed the apparition to the center of the cemetery, keeping a proper distance in case of a surprise attack.

At the crypt, Ellender D'Arcy turned to Elizabeth before entering. "Mrs. Darcy, what is your husband's relationship to my family?"

Caught unawares by the question, Elizabeth stammered, "I—I am unsure, Lady Benning. We have been married for so short a time. You are at least ten generations apart. Yet it is uncanny how much Mr. Darcy's sister looks like you."

"Does your husband suffer from the curse?" The lilting roll of her accent softened the evilness of the word.

"Mr. Darcy was told that he does. He exhibits some of the powers."

Ellender D'Arcy shook her head with concern. "He has not *infected* you?"

"My husband does the honorable thing and protects me."

"Once Seorais took his revenge, I refused Lord Benning. I would not take the chance that in a moment of passion that I would destroy the one thing I most cherished. I could not bring myself to hurt him any more than I already had." She straightened the bodice of her gown.

"Did you ever love Seorais, Lady Benning?"

Ellender looked off, as if remembering. "Seorais Winchcombe's father served as an overseer on the D'Arcy land. My father would never have tolerated such an alliance. I found him most pleasing in his demeanor, but from the first moment I saw Arawn Benning, I could consider no other. Surely you understand, Mrs. Darcy. Two men fight for your favor."

Elizabeth looked around to make sure no one would hear her respond. "I love the colonel, but I am *in love* with my husband. If I never knew Mr. Darcy, I could live a comfortable, loving life with the colonel, but I *do* know Mr. Darcy. Fitzwilliam is my reason to go on living; I cannot breathe without him."

Ellender smiled and looked lovingly at the Benning crypt. "It is as I suspected. Arawn will be pleased when I join him in heaven and when I convey how our families are joined again." Ellender turned and entered the vault. Elizabeth closed the inner door of the tomb and then closed the iron gate. The lock was not important. Lady Ellender would go nowhere; she was ready to know peace.

★ ★ ★

The three of them sat in the church, waiting for the first of the workers whom Gordy had promised to take to the graveyard. Damon and Elizabeth had concocted elaborate plans as to what would happen that day. By count, one and twenty graves needed to be addressed. From each, the coffin would be exhumed and opened; a coin would be placed under the deceased's tongue and a stake driven through the heart. Darcy and the colonel would see to that personally, trying to shield the town's folk from experiencing the mutilation of a loved one's corpse. And then the coffin would be replaced. Although highly unusual, the local priests agreed to last rites and to consecrating the land again, as those needing to be reburied were counterfeit in that manner.

They promised each of the twenty workers a month's pay if all the work was completed in one day. It would be hard, back-breaking work in the frozen soil of January, but the pay assured their diligence.

The physician arrived early. Each of the three of them antici-pated the need for one. Both Elizabeth and the colonel insisted he attend to Darcy first. The back wound, as they expected, was the worst; but miraculously, no internal damage seemed apparent. Bandaged and cleaned by the doctor and Elizabeth, Darcy looked very much the perfect country gentleman when they finished.

Elizabeth bathed in the small bowl provided by the priest and donned a simple day dress. She would not shock the locals by appearing in men's breeches. A bruise shadowed her cheek, and the dress covered more than one laceration. Yet Darcy thought her the most beautiful woman of his acquaintance.

The colonel, too, showed wear and tear. The concussion he had suffered was of most concern. Exhaustion—the natural letdown after such a battle—slowed his step, but his mind still raced. "Darcy, what do we do with Wickham's remains? Obviously, he cannot be buried anywhere around here."

"I think I have just the place."

Elizabeth joined the two of them in the front pews. "Of what do we discuss?"

Darcy took her hand; Elizabeth leaned over the back of the pew upon which he rested. The physician had ordered him not to move for fear of opening the back wound again. "What to do with Wickham."

"And?"

"There is an island less than two miles out called Lindisfarne. Have you heard of it?"

"The one from Scott's poem?" Damon seemed surprised by the reference. "It curled not Tweed alone, that breeze/ For, far upon Northumbrian seas/ It freshly blew, and strong/ Where from high Whitby's cloistered pile/ Bound to St. Cuthbert's holy isle/ It bore a barque along."[1] Elizabeth repeated the lines. "I never made the connection with how close we are to Berwick on Tweed."

Sitting up to address them, Darcy continued his reasoning. "The island is nearly deserted, and is called the Holy Isle as it was the base of Christian evangelizing in northern England and southern Scotland. About the time that this madness started, the parliamentarians took the castle on the island for the king during the Civil Wars. For me, though, the monastery and the holy relics associated with Lindisfarne will serve as a deterrent for this evil to ever resurface. Plus, an island serves another purpose. A vampire cannot cross running water. We can put Wickham by one of the springs or even by the lake."

"This is absolutely amazing," the colonel fumed as he paced across the front of the church. "You burn Wickham's house to the ground, impale him with an ash stake, wound him repeatedly with a silver sword, attack him with a symbol of his *god,* throw holy water on him, and shoot him through the heart with a silver bullet. How many ways will you protect yourself from this madness? Let us simply take him to the woods and burn what is left of Wickham's body!"

"Damon, you have not lived with this fear night and day for the past twelve years! I have! You will excuse me if I am *overcautious!*"

The two men stared at each other in a battle of wills. Finally, the colonel gave way. "Then I will do it. You cannot make a round trip by boat, trek across an island, and bury a corpse. Your injury will not allow it. Can you take care of this; I mean, get up and down in the graves and drive the stake through the heart of each of those Elizabeth and I vanquished?"

"I will help Fitzwilliam," Elizabeth added innocently.

"No!" Both men ordered in unison. Darcy continued while the colonel looked away. "You will *not* do this, Elizabeth. It is too gruesome."

"But, Fitzwilliam—" she began; however, when he raised his hand, she fell silent. Although she disagreed with his assessment of her "delicate nature," for once Elizabeth allowed Darcy his moment. She could only challenge his masculinity so many times without destroying it completely.

"If you must do something, take some of the village women who came out to help their husbands to the house. Gather the ashes from the fire and spread them about in the woods and on the hill. Wickham's coffin is buried among those ashes; we want no chance of his ever finding peace there again."

Elizabeth knew not to argue when her husband used that tone. "Yes, Fitzwilliam. May I, at least, join you when you address Lady Ellender?"

Darcy paused, considering her request. "If you wish."

"Gordy is here, Darcy. I just heard the wagon. I will take one of the horses into the village and make arrangements to take Wickham's remains to the coast. Possibly, someone in town knows of a boat we might use. Peter shall go with me. Could you get the workers started?" The colonel slipped on his coat and gloves. "I shall bring back food for all of us."

"Thank you, Damon." Darcy stood to put on his own coat. "Elizabeth, if you will assist me."

"I will return soon and help with the graves until the wagon is ready to take away the remains." With that, the colonel left the church and headed for Stanwick.

Darcy watched him go. "He does not understand how this haunts me." He turned to his wife. "Am I being unreasonable?"

Elizabeth helped him into the coat. His injuries made each of his movements stiff and restrained. "Probably. Yet if it gives you your own serenity, then celebrate it. Additional safeguards cannot be called foolish in that case."

Less than an hour later, Damon returned with the wagon and a makeshift coffin. He and Peter wrapped Wickham's remains in two blankets and loaded them into the box. Nailing it shut, they prepared to leave. "It is an hour to the shore and more than an hour to the island. I sent a man ahead to arrange for a boat of which he knew. I am afraid it will be near dark when I return." Damon pulled Darcy to the side, where they might speak privately. "I asked the innkeeper to provide meals for everyone throughout the day. He was happy for the extra business. That way, the men will not have to waste time returning to the village to eat. Will you be able to handle things here?"

Darcy glanced back at the men working diligently behind them. "Elizabeth and I decided I should stake the bodies when we sent the others in to meals. It is a ghastly business, Damon."

"Could you not use the coins?"

"As with Wickham's skeleton, I wish to safeguard against the possibility of this happening again. It is not of my nature to second guess if I did all I could to stop this madness."

Damon touched Darcy's shoulder. "Then see it through, Cousin. Are you in need of my services in dealing with Lady Ellender?"

"I am not sure I have the stomach." Darcy stared off into the cloudy sky. "I railed against the heavens because of her, and now I am asked to deliver her to a forgiving God. How may I mete out my own forgiveness?"

"Would you not, Darcy, make such a decision to save Elizabeth? I dare say she would for you. Anyone with half an eye could see that."

"Do you truly believe as such, Damon?"

It was now Damon's turn to look for something not there. "Darcy, you are the golden child—the heir to one of the most beautiful estates in all England, massive wealth, a handsome countenance, wit and intelligence, acceptance by society—however, I never was jealous of you in any matter until now. What man in England would not give up all his worldly goods for such a love? I cannot imagine such a one exists; and yet you continue to doubt, first, that you *deserve* it, and second, that Elizabeth can *give* it. Yours is a great love story, Cousin, if you would simply open your whole heart to it." Damon gave Darcy a level look. "Change your fate, Cousin. Conclude the story of Lady Ellender and Lord Thomas's love, and begin the one between you and Elizabeth."

Darcy's sky blue eyes softened. "How did you become so wise, Cousin?"

"I must excel over you in at least one way, Darcy." Damon smiled as the ease between them returned. "Now, if you will excuse me, I have a prior engagement with an island." Damon strode away to the waiting wagon.

Darcy blessed the heavens for placing his cousin on the London Road at the same time as Elizabeth left Pemberley. Without the colonel's help, this excursion would have had a disastrous conclusion; from delivering the final blow to Wickham to protecting Elizabeth, the results would have been quite different.

Reluctantly, Darcy returned to the task at hand. The men opened five graves. It was time for Darcy to go to work. "Gentlemen," he called out to the workers, "the colonel brought us breakfast. If you care to enter the church, my wife has everything laid out in the rectory."

The men immediately dropped the shovels and the pickaxes they had brought for the job. They good-naturedly made their way to the back of the church, thankful for the food and the break from such morbid work. None of them understood the logic of digging up a grave simply to fill it back in, but for a month's wages for a day's work, they would take orders from the Devil himself.

While the workers were busy sharing stories and food, Darcy took what he needed to address the bodies already exposed: six stakes, six coins, a bar to leverage each coffin lid, and a small hammer. Reaching the first of the exposed openings, he took off his coat and placed it on one of the nearby benches, and then he climbed down into the grave, the earth banked on either side of him. Finding a narrow foothold beside the wooden box, he wedged the lever between the sealed wood. Tapping with the hammer, he popped one of the nails, giving him the opening he needed. Then it was only a matter of moments before he lifted the lid on the resting place of the girl who had been the first to attack Damon during the early morning hours of the new day.

The girl in her white coming-out dress rested, as if in sleep. Her appearance shocked Darcy, for he had half expected a decomposed skeleton. Instead, before him lay a body in repose. Her full face appeared flushed, as if in permanent blush; her only apparent imperfection was badly scraped knuckles and fingernails. Automatically, Darcy looked at the inside of the coffin lid. Frighteningly, scratch marks, signs of the struggle to be set free, crisscrossed the closure.

Pulling back the supple lips, Darcy pried the girl's mouth open. The soft fullness of her mouth gave way to elongated teeth protruding from pink gums. He wedged a finger between the teeth and slipped the coin in. Then he readjusted the girl's mouth into a smile.

"You are a beautiful child," he mused. "You will forgive me, I pray." He placed the stake above her heart. "In the name of the Father, the Son, and the Holy Ghost." Then he struck the blunted end of the ashen wood with the hammer, driving in deep into her chest. A half-nasal, half-throaty grunt came from the body, and horrifyingly, blood oozed from the nose and mouth.

Unable to look upon the girl's face again, he repositioned the lid and nailed it closed. "At least, now I know what to expect. It will get easier with each one." He climbed onto the coffin and painfully pulled himself to the surface.

Learning from his mistakes, Darcy became quite adept at meting out eternity. He dispensed with four others before the men returned to work. "These may be filled in again," he instructed Gordy. "Keep digging until all of them have been opened."

"We be workin' in pairs, Sir. It not be long. The men thinkin' to leave before dark."

"As soon as the work is finished, Gordy, they are free to leave. The sooner, the better for all of us. But remind them that I am paying for the work to be complete." Darcy picked up his tools and moved to Lady Ellender's chambers.

A few minutes later, Elizabeth found him there. "You did not come to eat, my Husband."

Darcy sat in deep contemplation, perched on the ledge inside the iron gate. He looked up with Elizabeth's approach. "I seem to have lost my appetite." He reached for her and lifted Elizabeth to sit beside him.

Elizabeth took his hand and brought the palm to her mouth. The featherlike kiss placed the shadow of a smile on his lips. "We have lived a lifetime these past three months," she mused out loud.

"Only three months?" he chuckled. "I feel that I have known you all my life."

"Because we just began to live when we found each other." Still holding his hand in hers, she traced his lifeline with her index finger.

Darcy cupped her chin in his other hand. "Damon says we have a great love, one to surpass that of our famous relatives."

"One *equal* to the love of Arawn and Ellender would satisfy me. Even in death, she longed to sleep once more in his arms. Can you imagine such a love, Fitzwilliam?"

"Every time I look into your eyes, Elizabeth." For long moments they remained locked in total surrender to each other. Surrounded by death, they found life. "Let us give Lady Ellender the release for which she has longed for two centuries. Tonight, Her Ladyship will sleep with her Lord Thomas." Darcy climbed from the ledge and helped Elizabeth down to stand in front of him.

"These events were horrendous, but we must think of the good we leave behind: a community free to begin life again and an end to the unspeakable terror plaguing them."

Hand in hand, they entered Lady Ellender's spacious vault and made their farewells. As Gordy predicted, the men finished by midafternoon. All one and twenty graves turned, the Darcys left the priest to deliver his blessings. Returning to the inn, they waited patiently for the colonel's arrival.

★ ★ ★

Damon Fitzwilliam hated boats of any size, from rowboats to the largest warships. It was not that he held a fear of drowning; he actually swam very well. But the rolling of the ship upon the water affected his inner balance, and he always felt weak and not much of a man when his stomach pitched and heaved on its own.

With Wickham's coffin aboard, the small fishing boat cut through the rough waters of the North Sea. The rocking made Damon count to ten for the hundredth time as he took great gulps of air to settle the queasy feeling rumbling through him.

"Ye be lookin' for one of St. Cuthbert's miracles on the Holy Isle?" the ship's captain asked out of curiosity. For what the colonel was paying him, the captain did not care why the military officer wished to go to the island.

Damon looked confused, but then realized the fishing captain thought he wanted to take his *deceased passenger* to the monastery of St. Cuthbert, known to bring about inexplicable healing. "No…no, nothing of that sort. Just a dying wish that I intend to fulfill." He prayed that God would forgive the lie.

"I see," said the man, although he did not understand why it was so important to take the body to Lindisfarne that day. "We be in harbor in 'nother half hour."

"Thank you, Captain. I will be ready."

Landing in the harbor of a small fishing village on the southwestern tip of the island, the colonel, Peter, and two of the men from the ship—whom he had agreed to pay extra—took off for the interior, carrying the coffin and several shovels. Expecting sandy, barren beaches, the fertile rise of land surprised him. There were hundreds of birds, which did not shock him, but also rabbits and other small game, which did. In the distance, Damon saw the ruins of the old tumbledown monastery, and he chuckled at the irony of placing Wickham's bones within view of holy markers.

"This looks good," he said to the men as he prepared to lower the coffin to the ground. They had walked nearly a mile inland. "We were to choose a place close to running water." He offered no other explanation, and the locals asked for none from an outsider.

For nearly an hour, the four of them took turns digging a hole deep enough for a burial place. The process was slower than they had expected. Although the land was richly black and fertile, it was laced with rocks, and they good-naturedly stacked them in their own improvised altar.

"Here be 'nother one." Peter handed a heavy stone up to one of the fishermen. He and the colonel took their turns in the hole while the other two men rested.

"At this rate, we will never finish. If we had not wasted so much time digging this far, I would choose another spot."

Suddenly, the sound of running feet caught their attention, and Damon and Peter scrambled from the grave to find what caused such urgency. A boy from the ship scurried up the incline to meet them. Completely out of breath, the lad gulped for air, bent over at the waist, unable to deliver his message.

"What be it, Boy?" one of the fishermen demanded, impatient for the news.

The youth caught a few more deep breaths before he straightened. "Captain sent me," he began. "Bad storm comin'. We be weighin' anchor within the hour."

"It will take another hour to dig this grave," Damon reminded them.

"Captain say he wait no longer. He be 'fraid of losin' the boat. The sea be rough on the return as is."

"What do we do, Colonel?" Peter looked about. There was nothing in sight where they might find refuge.

Damon looked at the coffin and then back at the men. "Could we put the box in the ground as far as it will go and then cover it with these stones?"

"Makes sense to me, Colonel," one of the fishermen responded, and he picked up the shovels to move them out of the way. "Centuries ago, no one be put in the ground. Cold in the north and people used stones because the ground be frozen."

"Then let us make haste," Damon said, his military training taking over.

The coffin still needed about three inches to be fully flush with the surface, but they adjusted it as best they could. Then they began placing the bigger stones upon the lid. The youth brought handfuls of small ones to fill in the gaps. Soon the rocky mound was complete.

"Grab the shovels, Boy," the larger fisherman ordered. "The captain be a man of his word. He leave us if we be late."

They began their tramp back to the fishing village. Damon instantly regretted his choice: He had promised Darcy that he would see to the burial, but he had failed. He just could not face a storm at sea in such a small boat.

Reaching the harbor, they found the captain pacing the dock, looking for them. "It be past time," he called as they all clambered aboard. "Small boats already be in dock and tied down." He hurried in behind them and started barking out orders to set them in motion.

Damon retreated to one of the inner walls. He could not stand near the railing like his fellow officers. Seeing the swell of the sea caused his eyes to blur and his heart to pound unreasonably. When his father, the Earl, had bought him his commission, he had asked Damon to join the British navy instead, because there was less danger than in the army regiments; but Damon had insisted that the army was a better fit for his disposition. Even his father knew nothing of this uncontrollable fear.

"Be back on land shortly," the captain assured him as they got under way.

Damon nodded in agreement. *Shortly* would not be fast enough for him.

"It is fine, Damon." Darcy accepted his cousin's apology again for his inability to complete the task. "You did the right thing; I would not want to put others in danger."

"Besides," Elizabeth added, "placing stones on the grave is one of the suggested methods to retard a vampire's release."

Damon looked at her with thankfulness; she would not criticize him even if she knew the entire reason for his failure. "You are so kind, Mrs. Darcy. You take away the sting of my self-censure."

"I speak the truth, Colonel," she protested.

"So do I, Madam."

They took supper in Darcy's room, dressed casually for the evening and leisurely relaxing into the furniture. They would see no one regarding their recent activities, needing time to unwind naturally.

"I insist, Darcy, that we return in the spring and finish the task. I will not rest until it is so." Damon poured himself a cup of tea and then reached for another of the buttered rolls.

"Although in retrospect, it does seem foolish to go to such extremes, we will address it when the weather is more cooperative." Darcy reclined across the bed rather than sit at the table. His back wound needing attention after his task of staking the deceased today; he now allowed Elizabeth to nurse him properly.

Damon glanced at Elizabeth, fluffing the pillows behind Darcy's head. Feeling out of place in the domestic scene, he asked, "How long will you remain in Stanwick?"

"My husband is going nowhere until he begins to mend." She gave a level look to Darcy, daring him to dispute her.

Darcy chuckled before catching her hand in his and bringing it to his lips. "I bend to your wishes, my dear."

"Then may I take Trident? I left my horse in Derbyshire, and I am sure that my mother wonders what delays me."

"Must you, Colonel?" Elizabeth seemed troubled by his request.

Damon smiled to know his departure would affect her. "I must, Mrs. Darcy. I have responsibilities to my family and to my service."

Elizabeth blushed at making an issue of Damon's departure. She really had come to depend on him. "I just meant to say, you will be missed, Sir." She caught a glance of something in his eye, which told her that he did not want to leave.

"Are you to Longbourn, Darcy?" Damon needed to change the subject.

"I promised Elizabeth as such."

Damon looked back at Elizabeth; he worried about how all this might impinge on her. "What will you tell the Bennets of Wickham?"

"We told my parents we had a lead on Wickham. I instructed them to proceed with the service for Lydia without me, for the weather and circumstances might delay my following her return. I did not tell them any more than that."

"You should tell them of Wickham's demise. It would satisfy their sense of justice and give them a chance to grieve for their daughter rather than to seek revenge," the colonel said, reasoning out the situation. "In fact, tell them that Darcy took Wickham in an honorable fashion. It would explain his injury, and it is not an untruth."

"It is not the *truth* either," Darcy sardonically added.

Damon considered what he said. "No one would believe the truth. Besides, too many people know of what we did here. In my opinion, you should leave as soon as you can, before your identity becomes too well known."

Elizabeth looked concerned. "Maybe Damon is correct. The community knows us under the D'Arcy name, but the longer we are here, the greater the risk of someone recognizing the livery. Certainly, we want no one from society to come across rumors of our adventures."

"If we wish to present Georgiana this season, I would want no shadows darkening her prospects." Darcy began to examine the ramifications of their recent choices. "Should we not follow Damon, Elizabeth?"

She sipped her tea, taking her time to answer. "Although we should leave Stanwick, you are not well enough for such a tedious journey, Fitzwilliam, and even my body does not relish another week in your carriage."

"Do you have more extensive injuries than you led me to believe?" Darcy demanded.

Elizabeth blushed, as Damon remained in the room. "Just badly bruised."

Damon cleared his throat. "May I make a suggestion?"

Darcy disentangled himself from the bed covers. "Certainly."

"When Elizabeth and I registered, I told a tale of how the two of you planned to holiday in Edinburgh, and that I escorted her from London for that purpose. You could travel to Scotland and spend a few days recovering. It would only add a half day to your return journey. If word gets out of your being in the north of England, Edinburgh would be a good excuse for a newly married couple."

"I have always wanted to see the land of my ancestors," Elizabeth ventured.

Darcy actually liked the idea. "Are you up for another adventure, Elizabeth?"

She winked at him. "Absolutely, Sir."

Damon stood to leave. "I am weary and am in need of rest. I set out for Matlock early tomorrow. I shall see you in the morning before I depart."

"My wife would take me to task if I chose to do something as impulsive as stand up at the moment, but you, Cousin, know of my devotion and my gratitude for all that you did this past week. I owe you my life."

"It is not necessary to say so." Damon gave Darcy a quick bow, and then, taking Elizabeth's hand, he kissed the back of it. "Take care of that rascal, my dear, and of yourself. I never had a more capable partner or one quite so beautiful."

Elizabeth lightly touched the side of his face. "My house will always be your home, Sir."

EPILOGUE

The colonel rode off on Trident before the Darcys broke their fast. "It is time to let you and Elizabeth repair your marriage without a chaperone," Damon insisted when Darcy asked him to accompany them to Scotland.

"I do not know how I will ever repay you. You protected Elizabeth. I shall never forget that fact."

Damon looked away, still not comfortable with his *guilty* feelings. "You chose the perfect wife for you, Darcy. No other woman of our acquaintance would go through what Elizabeth did to save your life and to change your future."

"I see that my wife's natural charisma has won her another admirer." Darcy would play what he had earlier noted as being insignificant. "I have observed it so with everyone she meets, whether a lord of the realm or one of my servants. You just proved your fine taste, Cousin, and my exceptional good luck at discovering her for myself."

"Then you should address any misgivings the lady has." Damon embraced Darcy before turning to the mount. "I will send Trident on to Pemberley. Would you like me also to send some news of your success to Georgiana?"

"I will write to her later today, but you will arrive in Derbyshire long before the mail service. She shall be glad to hear the news from someone she trusts."

"Give my regards to Elizabeth." Damon strode to the horse and mounted. Reaching down, he patted the animal's neck. "He is an excellent example of horseflesh." With a salute, he sped away towards Matlock and family.

The Darcys neared the center of New Town in Edinburgh in the midafternoon. Throughout the trip, Elizabeth kept a running verbal journal of everything she observed out the coach's windows. Each prospect was more impressive than the one before, and Darcy simply sat back and enjoyed seeing the city through her eyes. "Did you ever see a building so tall?" Her mouth was agape as she moved closer to the window for a better view.

"That is St. Giles Cathedral," Darcy commented. "Although I have never seen it personally, Gladstone's Land is reportedly six stories."

"You practice a gammon, my Husband?" She eyed him to see if he manipulated his words as part of a tease.

"No, my love. I speak the truth." Darcy smiled, returning his gaze to hers. "It was not many years ago when one could smell what is known as Old Town from miles away, but in the latter years of the past century, the city made a concerted effort to change things. Renowned architects created a new look for Edinburgh by adding neoclassical elements and planning gardens as barriers to the filth of the walled palace and abbey."

"You know so many things, Fitzwilliam. I wish women had access to such an education."

"You would drive the professors at Oxford or Cambridge crazy—first, with your beauty, and then with how you hunger for new ideas—your insatiable need for knowledge." He laughed at his own assessment. "We shall see some of the city while we are here."

As if on cue, Peter pulled up on the reins of the horses in front of an upscale hotel. Scrambling down from the perch, he let down the steps before moving back. "We be here, Mr. Darcy."

"Thank you, Peter." Darcy dismounted from the coach and turned to help Elizabeth down. "I will send someone out to help you unload, Peter. Put the coach and team in the mews; Mrs. Darcy and I will stay for three days."

"Yes, Sir." Peter prepared to unload the luggage.

"Are you ready, Sweetling, for a new adventure?"

Elizabeth's eyes lit with excitement. "I am so glad we decided to follow your cousin's advice. I never imagined I would see any city besides London. Now I am in another country. My life has taken a turn I never expected."

Darcy tilted his head to speak only to her ears. "I would give you the world, Elizabeth, if you let me."

She wrapped her arm through his, snuggling into Darcy's shoulder. "I will allow you to love me. The world, for me, depends upon you, Fitzwilliam."

"Then you will forgive me for all the chaos I brought to your life?" he whispered.

Elizabeth laughed lightly. "Absolutely not." She paused to increase the drama. "It will take several hundred of your kisses to earn even an ounce of my forgiveness."

The hunger within him reawakened; he growled, "I begin earning that first ounce as soon as I have you behind closed doors, Vixen."

"I am your captive, Mr. Darcy."

They dressed for supper after spending several hours walking the intersecting streets surrounding their hotel and exploring gardens and visiting shops. Elizabeth served as his valet and he as her maid. They laughed, they teased, and they kissed. Everything seemed perfect; they did not mention anything about their night of terror.

Elizabeth sat at her dresser, trying to arrange her own hair, when Darcy came up behind her and kissed the nape of her neck. "You are beautiful," he whispered as he nibbled on her earlobe.

"Mmm." Elizabeth closed her eyes and enjoyed his closeness. "I never tire of your touch." Her breathing suddenly became shallow. That was all the encouragement he needed to continue his assault on her neck and shoulder. Instantly, as he always did— he wanted her.

Elizabeth watched the reflection of his head in the mirror as he moved lightly across her bodice, increasing her desires and feeling the blood pool in her stomach. Within moments, she moaned,

"Please, Fitzwilliam."

The need found in her voice shook him, and Darcy straight-ened and walked away. With his back to her, he willed his body to calm. "I am sorry, Elizabeth."

Still watching him in the mirror, Elizabeth counted to ten before she spoke.

"Fitzwilliam, we fought every apparition within a five-mile radius of Stanwick in order for us to have a normal life, but noth-ing has changed!" She laid the brush on the dresser and moved to the window.

Darcy wanted Elizabeth to be reasonable, but he did not know how to make her see his point of view. "Defeating Wickham did not change what I am."

"I do not care! Do you hear me, Fitzwilliam? I…do…not…care! I love you, and I want my husband to make love with me."

"We do not know whether we broke the curse."

Elizabeth began to pace in agitation. "How will we ever know? It is not as if the curse came with instructions! We can continue to deny ourselves, and *nothing* will change—or *everything* will change. But we will never know which it was. There is no guarantee. We eliminated the source of the vampirism, and all the books say to stop the line from continuing, one must go to the source. Wickham and Lady Ellender were the original victims for the D'Arcy family. What else can we do?"

"Think of our children," he pleaded.

"I am thinking of our children. Between your family and mine, girls outnumber boys six to one. We have better odds at having a daughter, and I want her, Fitzwilliam. I want to clothe her in ruf-fled dresses and see whether she has blue eyes like you or green ones as I do. I want to visit her in the nursery and read her stories."

"And what if the child is a boy?"

She came to stand in front of him. "We teach him to deal with what Fate gives him the same way we would teach him how to function in his world if he was born blind or with a deformed hand. In every generation the tendency would become weaker, because the human part would be more dominant."

Darcy moved a loose curl to behind her ear. "And what if I infect you?"

"I am not sure that I would mind. It is quite daunting to consider how I will grow older, and you will essentially stay the same. Every one of those we fought fundamentally never aged a day from the time he was infected. Did you never consider that?"

"Truthfully, I did not." Darcy tried to make sense of what she said. "Obviously, I aged," he thought aloud.

"Because you never used your abilities," she asserted. "What about now? Am I to watch you remain a virile man when I am turning grey?"

Again, she asked questions to which Darcy had no answers. "This is all new to me. I have no idea what the curse means to my private life. Now I regret not speaking to my father about his struggles. Although I respected him as the Master of Pemberley and as my father, I pretended, along with him, that I did not resent the infamy he practiced on my mother."

"But she loved him, Fitzwilliam. Think about it. Lady Anne bore him a second child—Georgiana. Do we have any way of knowing whether Lady Anne's demise was a result of your father infecting her? Could he not have just succumbed to the need to love his wife as a man, rather than as a dhampir? Can you honestly say your mother's passing came as a result of your father's lust for blood, or did she simply die from complications of childbirth as so many women do? It is not as if either subject would be discussed with a young boy of twelve, as you were when Georgiana was born, nor a young man of sixteen, as you were when Lady Anne passed."

Again, Darcy seemed surprised by her viewpoint. He knew of his parents' affection prior to their marriage; he heard it spoken of by all who knew them in those days, but after experiencing his own moments of lust as a young man, he imagined how his father had seduced the innocent Lady Anne, and he felt a certain repugnance for the man. "Do you believe it possible, Elizabeth?"

"I know nothing of the man other than his reputation as a kind and generous master, but I do know the man his son became, and I cannot imagine your father taught you the qualities of empathy, responsibility, benevolence, tenderness, and caring without possessing them himself. The Earl and Damon speak of the type of person your mother was. She loved you and Georgiana, and I am of the persuasion that she loved your father."

A bit discomfited by how her analysis contradicted everything he had believed about his parents' relationship, Darcy interrupted with his own angle. "With such logic, am I to believe that your mother's renowned silliness speaks of the type of person you will become?"

"You are to believe that my mother's hysterics are those of a woman doing all she can to ensure that her five daughters are well situated because society denies them what should be theirs. Will I move heaven and earth to protect my children in any way possible? I warrant it, Mr. Darcy. The basic premise is that Lady Anne could have left your father—and under the circumstance, he would have allowed it—but she chose to keep his secret and nurture the relationship. Can I envision a woman giving her body and soul to the man she loves? The answer is a resounding yes."

Darcy's gaze now rested purely on his wife. "Then you want this?" His voice told of shame and desire and hope.

"Yes, Fitzwilliam. With all my heart, I want whatever Fate brings us. I cannot imagine anything worse than what we have already faced." Elizabeth's chin rose in defiance. "I never agreed to be a part of your life because I desired your position in society or your wealth. I would love Fitzwilliam Darcy even if he were a simple cottager."

A curious spasm of guilt flexed his jaw line, and Elizabeth watched silently as he clenched and unclenched his right fist. "What if I do not agree, Elizabeth? What then? Will you leave me? You must know by now, I am not of the nature to be coerced into doing something I choose not to do."

"Neither am I, Fitzwilliam," she warned, "so please make no ultimatums we will both regret later."

"Then tell me what are my options, Elizabeth. I do not see where being married to one of the richest men in England can be such a deterrent; obviously, Pemberley is superior to your situation at Longbourn." Darcy offered more than any woman with similar connections could hope to achieve; he thought that should be worth something.

"Do—do not," she stammered, "do *not* twist this into a fight about position and social standing. I love *you*," she asserted. "I chose you over my family. Does that not prove my depth of affection? Yet it is not a competition to see who loves whom more. It is not a matter of sacrificing ourselves for our union."

Again a long silence wafted over them. "I will give up my powers and not practice them ever again."

"And that changes things how?" she demanded.

"If I do not use my powers, then we will not deal with age differences." He thought it a fair compromise.

Elizabeth's frustration exploded. She snatched up her reticule from the bed. "You may be only one of the richest men in England, Fitzwilliam, but you wear the *crown* as the most infuriating and stubborn one!" Darcy's heart clutched as she slammed the hotel door and stormed away.

Thirty minutes later, Darcy found her having tea in one of the corners of the hotel's sitting room. As the hours for supper service were well under way, Darcy was unsure how to approach her. "Elizabeth," he said as he came up behind her, "may I escort you to the dining room?"

She stood and took his proffered arm. "Thank you, Fitzwilliam."

The difference between the woman who had offered him strong condemnations less than an hour earlier and the amiable woman seated next to him now kept Darcy on edge. He expected that, at any moment, Elizabeth would return to the subject of their argument, but nothing happened. Instead, they talked of books they read and changes for Pemberley. It reminded Darcy of the late-night stolen hours at Netherfield.

"Thank you, Elizabeth," he leaned close to whisper.

Yet she did not respond with a retort or an acceptance. Again, Darcy felt fear in the pit of his stomach; it was not like Elizabeth to give up so easily. Did he not tell Wickham he did not have enough followers to stop her if she set her mind to a task? *She is more than either of us can handle.*

"Are you ready to return to our room?" he asked politely.

"I believe so. I find I am tired." Darcy remained wary. He thought they might revisit their earlier confrontation when they were once again behind closed doors.

Together they returned to the room. Darcy ordered a bath, and they sat in front of the fire while the hotel staff filled the copper tub with hot water. "If you do not mind, Fitzwilliam, I would like to go first."

"Of course not. Let me unlace you." Darcy stood to assist with the back of her dress. The nape of Elizabeth's neck tempted him again, but still unsure of what his wife would do, Darcy chose to ignore it this time. "I will enjoy a brandy while you relax in the warm water."

Once she was free of the clothing's fasteners, Elizabeth stepped behind a screen to undress. Darcy saw the silhouette: the roundness of her hips and the perfect symmetry of her figure, and he gulped his drink, pushing away his desire. He felt lecherous watching Elizabeth without her knowledge, but he was loath to look away. He listened as she hummed a ballad—the water faintly lapping against the tub in the background. He knew exactly what she looked like reclining in the tub, with the soapy water caressing her breasts, and he felt himself go hard with the memories.

The sound of her getting out of the water signaled his own ablutions, so he removed his jacket and boots while she toweled dry. He was unbuttoning his waistcoat when Elizabeth appeared from behind the screen. Darcy quit breathing. She wore nothing but a slight blush and a smile. Her damp hair cascaded down her back and across her shoulders. Darcy had no idea how long he watched her before Elizabeth gave him a renewed blush and moved away to the bed, slipping on a satin gown and wrapper.

So aroused that he did not believe he could take any more, Darcy swallowed the need bubbling in his chest and made himself walk away from her. Behind the screen, he unbuttoned the flap of his breeches. "Bloody hell," he murmured. Normally, he preferred his bath water hot, but tonight he prayed it was icy cold.

When he had finally regained his composure, Darcy climbed from the tub and dried off. He donned a nightshirt and put his toiletries away, stalling before he joined Elizabeth in bed. He hoped she had fallen asleep waiting for him. Finishing up a quick shave, he paused, thinking about what she had said. Was he right in denying Elizabeth a chance for children of her own? He had no doubt she would make an exemplary mother. Did his father have this same argument with himself? Had his mother made the same decision as Elizabeth, deciding she would take the good with the bad? *And is that not what every marriage is—the good mixed with the bad?* His mother had never seemed unhappy, except when she had begged his forgiveness for allowing the curse to continue. She had showered him and Georgiana with so much love: They were the center of her world.

The lamp barely lit the room when he reentered the bedchamber. Elizabeth lay curled on her side, her face turned away from him, the bed linens pulled up around her shoulders. Her even breathing made Darcy believe that his prayer had been answered. Sitting on the edge of the bed, he extinguished the light; and then he slid under the linens with her. As he always did, he rolled next to Elizabeth, to spoon her body with his.

He stilled immediately; completely naked, Elizabeth's body felt soft and inviting. Instantly, the arousal returned. They had never lain together without clothing between them. *What is she doing to me?*

Growling back profanity, he lifted his weight to move away from her, sliding as far to his side of the bed as possible. Elizabeth did not move; she remained facing away from him, so Darcy fluffed

the pillow behind his head and tried to put the image of his luscious wife out of his mind. He made himself take deep, steadying
breaths and jammed his eyes closed. Maybe it would be better if she
did leave him. At least, then his body and his mind could concentrate on something besides Elizabeth.

Twenty minutes later, feeling relaxed at last, Darcy let his eyes
close naturally, although he kept the distance between himself
and Elizabeth.

Elizabeth had waited quietly for Darcy's reaction when he
crawled into the bed. She had never done anything so bold in her
life. Turning down the lamp so Darcy could not see her embarrassment was the only way she could go through with her plan. Her
husband desired her; of that, she was absolutely certain. She had
simply decided to remind him of that desire on a regular basis. He
had controlled their relationship to this point, but now she would
take it over. That is, if she could overcome feeling like a complete
wanton. Thankfully, Aunt Merry had explained how some men
expected their wives to wear nothing when making love. Her aunt
feared the rich to be more "experimental" in their relationships,
and she offered Elizabeth a warning. It had seemed scandalous at
the time, but now it felt more like freedom.

Gauging the evenness of Darcy's breathing, Elizabeth smiled
confidently before she moved. Rolling casually over, as if in deep
sleep, she cuddled into Darcy's side and draped her left leg over his
body. Pretending to be in the nearly waking stage of sleep, she
lightly kissed the side of his cheek and muttered something unin-
telligible in a seductive breath. She briefly arched towards him and
then settled her head in the curvature of his shoulder.

Darcy stiffened, but, intuitively, his arm came around her, and
he held Elizabeth tightly to him. Eyes now wide open and heart
pounding, he oscillated between wanting to run far away from her
and desiring to lose himself in Elizabeth's body. His chest rose and
fell in shallow bursts as he closed his eyes and moaned her name.
Her hair draped across his arm and chest—the same chest where

Elizabeth's fingers now rested in the opening of his nightshirt. Suddenly, he felt very warm—almost unbearably so, but it had nothing to do with the room's temperature.

Elizabeth relished how Darcy's fingers began to trail fire down her spine and across the rise of her hips, but she did nothing more than snuggle closer and brush her lips across his chest. She played at being asleep and let her husband explore her body at his own pace.

Mystified by his inability to stop, Darcy saw himself as disengaged from his own body; his mind fought for control, but, unfortunately, his body overruled his mind's every objection. Elizabeth would not deny him his perverted pleasure. They had married a month earlier, and his resolve not to have her weakened by the moment. When he thought to die in Wickham's cellar, his one regret was that he would never know the pleasure of Elizabeth's love. Someone else would claim her after his death, and the thought nearly drove him insane. Now she lay in his arms, and all he had to do was commit himself to loving her completely.

Impulsively, Darcy rolled her to her back and hovered over her, burying his face in Elizabeth's hair. "God help me, Elizabeth. I surrender." His lips found hers in a deep, passionate kiss. "Tell me again. Is this what you really want? If you have any doubts, we should not go through with this."

"I have more love in my heart for you, Husband, than the dear Lord should allow a woman to feel. I want to be yours, Fitzwilliam, in every way possible—for a lifetime." Elizabeth did not breathe; she knew Darcy still wavered.

They remained staring into each other's eyes for several long moments. Then Darcy lowered his mouth to hers. This kiss spoke of hunger and need. "You know, Vixen, once I have you, I will want you again and again. I am a starving man. You will need to suffer my attentions for a lifetime."

Elizabeth stroked the side of his face with the back of her hand. "I want to feel your skin touching mine—to not know where either of us begins or ends," she whispered.

Two heartbeats later, Darcy stripped away the shirt, and then he draped himself over her. His lips found hers again in an open-mouth kiss, Darcy's tongue dueling with Elizabeth's before he licked the outline of her lips, coaxing a moan from her. "A marriage not in name only." His lips hovered above hers as he spoke the words aloud, giving them power—giving them life.

Passion flared between them as heat rushed to their every pore. Darcy drew Elizabeth closer to him, realizing she hungered for him as much as he did for her. The smell of the lavender oil she had used in the bath clung to her skin, along with some other undefined bouquet, one of wild desire and excitement, and it inflamed him as his fingertips traced a line from her temple across her jaw and down her neck.

His mouth followed his fingertips until Darcy sucked gently at the vein throbbing at the base of Elizabeth's neck. He nipped at her gently and then moved to the swell of her breasts.

He would make love to his wife—he would give himself completely to her—would forget his perverted sense of honor and responsibility and welcome hope, commitment, and love into his heart.

Elizabeth splayed a hand across his chest and pressed herself against him, robbing Darcy of breath and of any coherent thought. "I love you," she whispered close to his ear, "for an eternity. I am yours, Fitzwilliam." The ache of desire became a longing—a craving for what Elizabeth offered him, and intuitively his hands began to search her body, the need to know all of her overwhelming his senses.

"I will be gentle," he murmured.

"I do not fear you, Fitzwilliam. How could a person fear *love?*"

★ ★ ★

"Look, Mama," the girl called as she twirled in place.

"You are an excellent dancer, Lydia." Elizabeth sat on a blanket and watched the child playing barefoot on the bank of the lake. The day was sunny, and it called to them to be outside.

The girl stepped left and right and pretended to curtsy to an unknown partner. "Come dance with me, Mama."

Happily, Elizabeth rose to stand with the child in the clearing. Taking the girl's hands, she began to count, "One and two and three and four," as they sidestepped over the carefully manicured lawn.

The girl's curly auburn hair bounced in ringlets as they bobbed and twisted to the imaginary music, and soon they were in fits of laughter.

"Would you prefer to dance with me, Miss Lydia?" Darcy stepped from behind one of the nearby trees. He was covered in road dirt, but his appearance pleased both the ladies; he was pure masculinity.

"Papa!" the girl's arms came up in a hug as he scooped her into his embrace. "I am so glad you are home."

He planted a kiss on the side of the child's cheek. She might have her mother's hair and build, but Lydia Darcy was his child, right down to her icy blue eyes.

"Will you dance with me, Papa?"

"Allow me to greet your mother first, Child." He leaned to the right and placed a lingering kiss on Elizabeth's upturned mouth. "Did you miss me also, Mrs. Darcy?"

"From the moment you rode off to Matlock."

Darcy smiled that smile he always gave her right before he *seduced* her. "The Earl and Her Ladyship send their love. They plan to visit at Michaelmas."

"Excellent." Elizabeth moved away to the blanket. "Mr. Bingley and Jane will come next week. They are most eager to meet their nephew."

"How is James?" he asked as she picked up the squirming infant.

"Damon is perfect," she corrected as she brought the child for his father to admire.

Darcy rolled his eyes. "The child was named after my *father,* Elizabeth." He turned back the corner of the blanket to look at the screwed-up face of his son.

"After your father *and* your cousin. I just prefer to remember the living." She swayed to quiet the child's protests.

"Will I ever win another argument?" he asked good-heartedly.

Elizabeth laughed lightly. "Probably not, but I promise you will not suffer from the defeat."

Darcy bestowed another kiss on her lips. Then he turned to the child he still held in his arms. He placed her little feet on the tops of his boots. Lydia's head barely came to his knees. "Would you hum for us, Elizabeth?"

She began to sing "Lord Thomas and Fair Ellender." Darcy's head shot up in surprise, but his daughter sang the words, too, and so he, dutifully, stepped into a sweeping waltz. Lydia, happy to be the center of attention, laughed and sang until he lifted her to him, and she combed the air with her chubby legs.

"I love you, Papa," she proclaimed, her declaration of love mixed with wet kisses on his cheek and a giggling fit of joy.

★ ★ ★

"You were laughing, Sweetling." Holding her to him, Darcy kissed the end of her nose. They had made love twice, and now he wanted her again.

"Mmm." Her sleepy voice made him feel guilty about his hunger for her.

"You were laughing in your sleep. It was a good dream, then?" He kissed along her neck and shoulder.

Elizabeth rolled into his embrace and slipped her arms around his neck. The image of their children safe in their arms stayed with her, but Elizabeth did not share what she had seen. She just silently hoped that this dream came true, as had her others. "We were at Pemberley, and we were in love."

"We *are* in love," he corrected. "Now, in the present; and in the future. The past belongs to Ellender and Arawn. Ours will be the new legend."

"Then you are *happy,* my Husband?"

"Well, I would not mind being allowed to win an argument

occasionally," he mumbled as he nibbled on her neck.

"You never stood a chance, you know."

"I know," he said with some resignation.

"It was a glorious battle, though, do you not think?" Elizabeth wriggled her body against his.

Darcy's every sense was lost to her. "I succumbed too easily," he chastised himself. "However, I should make note that you do not play fair."

"It would bode well for you to remember that in the future, Mr. Darcy. I thought that you had learned your lesson long ago, during the snowstorm."

"In my defense, you distracted me both times." By now, his mouth had drifted down the front of her body. "You realize that you will pay for such treachery." He brushed his mouth over the swell of her breasts. Needing to mark her as his own, his mouth returned to hers, and he spoke only inches from her lips. "I never thought I could know contentment. You changed my life, Elizabeth. You made me whole." The kiss deepened, and the hunger of a lifetime settled between them.

References

Adams, Cecil. "What's the Best Way to Kill a Vampire?" *The Straight Dope.* 16 Jul 1982. Creative Loafing Media. 1996–2009. http://www.straightdope.com/columns/read/37/whats-the-best-way-to-kill-a-vampire.html.

"Baobhan Síth." *Mysterious Britain and Ireland.* http://www.mysteriousbritain.co.uk/Scotland/folklore/baobhan-sith.html.

Barber, Paul. *Vampires, Burial, and Death: Folklore and Reality.* New Haven, CT: Yale University Press, 1990.

"Cernunnos: The Horned One." *Hawthorne Grove, Inc.* 1994. http://hawthornegrove.Faithweb.com/writings/horndgod.htm.

Dundes, Alan, ed. *The Vampire: A Casebook.* Madison, WI: University of Wisconsin Press, 1998.

Evans, Dyfed Lloyd. "Iarlles y Ffynnon." *Celtnet.* 2005–2008. http://www.celtnet.org.uk/gods_i/iarlles.html.

Greenleaf, Elisabeth Bristol. "Lord Thomas and Fair Elender or the Brown Girl." *Folk and Traditional Lyrics.* Traditional Music Library. http://www.traditionalmusic. co.uk/folk-song-lyrics/Lord_Thomas_and_Fair_Elender_or_the_Brown_Girl.htm.

Heldreteth, Leonard G., and Mary Pharr, eds. *The Blood Is the Life: Vampires in Literature.* Bowling Green, Ohio: Bowling Green University Press, 1999.

"Holy Island, or Lindisfarne." *Encyclopedia Britannica,* 11th Edition. Online Encyclopedia. 2009. http://encyclopedia.jrank.org/HIG_HOR/HOLY_ISLAND_or_LINDISFARNE.html.

MacCulloch, J. A. *The Religion of the Ancient Celts.* Mineola: Dover Publications, Inc., 2003.

"Marmion: Canto the Second." *The Literature Network.* Jalic, Inc. 2000–2009. www.online-literature.com/walter_scott.

Matthews, Caitlín and John. *The Encyclopedia of Celtic Wisdom*. Shaftesbury, Dorset: Element Books Limited, 1991.

Nelson-Burns, Lesley. "Lord Thomas and Fair Ellinor." *Contemplator*. http:www.contemplator.com/child/Thomas.html.

Ogden, Daniel. *Magic, Witchcraft, and Ghosts in the Greek and Roman Worlds*. New Haven, CT: Yale University Press, 1990.

Perkowski, Jan L., ed. *Vampires of the Slavs*. Cambridge, MA: Slavica Publishers, 1976.

Preston, Cathy Lynn. "The English and Scottish Popular Ballads by Francis James Child." *The Internet Sacred Text Archive*. 2008. http://www.sacred-text.com/Neu/eng/child/ch073.htm.